HOOK ME

MEN OF INKED BOOK TWO

HOOK ME COPYRIGHT

Published by Chelle Bliss June 5th 2014
Editor Tee Tate
Proofreader Editing 720
Cover Design © Chelle Bliss
Formatting by Chelle Bliss
Cover Model Photographer © Mr. Big Photography

CHAPTER ONE

MICHAEL

Spring

WIPING the blood from my brow, I glared at Tito. The wound stung as sweat trickled into the open cut just above my swollen eye. He moved quickly, but I had more power. It felt like a game of cat and mouse. I let him feel confident in his abilities, before I made my move to take his ass down.

A sharp pain in my ribs stole my breath as I kicked him in the thigh before the bottom of my palm connected with his chin. As his head flew back, I grabbed him around the waist, lifted him off the ground, and threw him on his ass. When my body crashed on top of him, the dull pain in my ribs became excruciating. I couldn't relent, or release him. I fought through the discomfort and held him down as he kicked and flailed like a trapped bitch.

His grunts grew louder and I took the opportunity to hit him in the face as he was locked in my grip, turning red in the crook of my arm. The back of his heel connected with my calf and the muscle instantly tightened. My body may have been screaming for me to stop, but my determination to win the match had me push through the pain and not let go.

Blowing the whistle, the ref called the match to a close. Releasing Tito, I limped to my feet and held my ribs, trying to catch my breath. I smiled for the cheering crowd as Tito crawled toward his trainer. I wanted to fall down and sprawl out against the cool plastic material, but I couldn't, not yet at least.

"You won," Rob yelled in my ear as he smacked me on the back.

I winced, closing my eyes to block everything out. Through gritted teeth I said, "Fuck, don't do that shit." I exhaled slowly with shaky breath before opening my eyes to look at Rob.

His eyes grew wide as he searched my face, homing in on my hand. "What's wrong?" he asked.

"My fucking ribs. I think they're broken. I can't breathe," I huffed out, struggling to speak.

"Let's get you checked out. Make sure you didn't puncture a lung or some shit," he said as he wrapped his arms around my body and helped me out of the cage.

***

I closed my eyes and listened to the noise outside the room. Voices carried through the hallways—the cries, yelling, beeping, and telephones made it impossible to rest. I concentrated on my breathing, taking small, shallow breaths to stave off the stabbing pain.

"Mr. Gallo," a voice said from the doorway.

I jerked to sit up, but the pain sliced through my chest like a knife stabbing me. I collapsed against the mattress and raised my hand. "Here," I said, before resting my hand on my chest.

Placing her hand on my shoulder, she smiled at me. "I see you're here for your ribs."

"What gave that away?" I said, a little pissed off.

She pulled her lips in, hiding her smile. "On a scale of one to ten, how severe is the pain?"

"Seven when I breathe too deep, and about a two if I don't move and take short, shallow breaths."

"I need to remove your shirt," she said, touching the bottom of my tank top. "This is going to hurt."

"I can handle it, doc. Do your worst."

Her fingertips touched the flesh of my stomach, and I twitched as her nail grazed the spot just above my shorts. "Sorry," she said, blushing. "It may be easier if you sit up. Take my hand," she said, releasing my tank and holding out her hand to me.

Holding my breath, I used my free hand to pull myself up with her help. It wasn't as painful as when I tried it on my own, but it wasn't comfortable either. "Whew," I said as I inhaled and winced.

"Just sit there, sir, and I'll do the rest." Placing her body between my legs, she reached for my shirt again.

When a beautiful woman says she's going to undress me, then have at it—I'll just sit back and watch.

Her facial features were petite—small nose, high cheekbones, and large hazel eyes. She glanced up at me as she pulled the material up, exposing my stomach. The feel of her fingers moving up the side of my body sent a shiver down my spine.

"Can you raise your arms or shall I cut it off?"

"I can do it." I raised my arms, smiling through the pain, holding my breath.

"There," she said, pulling the shirt over my head. Moving to the side of me, she placed one hand on my back and the other on my chest.

Her touch seared my skin.

"Lie back," she said softly.

With a very serious look on her face, she tried to hold up my body weight as I reclined.

"Which rib is giving you the problem?" she asked, looking down at my chest. She tilted her head; her eyes raked across my skin as her tongue darted out, sweeping against her bottom lip.

I needed to think of something else beside her sexy-ass mouth.

Being in this position, a hard-on would be embarrassing.

"Left side." I tried to think of the fight, or my sister sitting in the waiting room, as the doc's fingertips glided across my skin. I felt her touch everywhere, moving down to my toes. I stared at the ceiling and tried to wipe out all thoughts of her, but it's pretty fucking impossible when a gorgeous woman is touching me.

"Right here?" she asked, pressing down.

My entire body jerked. My head flew off the tiny, crappy pillow and my muscles tensed. "Fuck, doc. Warn a person first, will ya?"

She bit her lip, her cheeks turning pink. "I'm sorry. Guess I did my worst." She chuckled. "I think you need an x-ray to be sure you haven't punctured your lung. How did you do this, anyway?"

"I had a fight and the guy kneed me in the ribcage."

She grimaced and sighed. "Men. I'll never understand them."

"Doc." I placed my hand over hers, stilling her movement before I pitched a tent. "It was a pro fight. I don't do street fights and I'm not into barroom brawls."

"Not much difference in my eyes when someone ends up here. Violence is violence."

I said with a grin, "Oh, come on. You've never hit someone?"

"Not unless I was defending myself." She pulled her hands back and picked up the chart from the table next to the gurney.

"Well, I was defending myself from his damn knee." I laughed. "Ouch, fuck."

"Did you win?" Raising her eyebrows and cocking her head, she stared at me with parted lips.

I wanted to grab her and sweep my tongue inside her mouth. Show her how a real man does it. My strength wasn't only good in the ring, but I could hold her against the wall and make her dirty with barely any effort. "I always win." I grinned, winking at her.

"Cocky bastard," she muttered under her breath.

"My ribs hurt, but my hearing is fantastic, doc."

She ran her hands down her face to hide her smile. "I'm sorry, that was rude of me."

"Make it up to me with dinner." I touched her hand and saw her body twitch from the contact.

She felt it too—the connection, the spark between us.

"I don't date men who use their fists, Mr. Gallo."

"My hands have many other uses that you'd quite enjoy."

She swallowed hard enough that I could hear it, before she looked down at the chart and back at me. "I don't date patients or cocky bastards." She chuckled.

"Don't know what you're missing."

"I have to go order your x-ray, Mr. Gallo, and I have other patients to see. I'll be back to see you as soon as I get the results."

"Just think about it, please? You've wounded my pride." Pretending to be hurt, I gripped my chest.

"Your pride is just fine, it's your lung I'm worried about. Stay put," she said as she started to walk away.

"Where would I go? I can't even sit up without your help."

"Good, then I'll know where to find you." She laughed and walked out the door.

Reaching down, I adjusted my dick in my shorts. Fuck, just talking to her made me semi-hard. The half-pitched tent vanished when a burly man walked through the door with an x-ray machine. Never thought I'd be happy to see a man.

His size made it easy for him to move me. After a few shots, he helped me sit up before he left.

I started thinking of all the lines I'd use on her. I wanted that date, but how could I get her to say yes?

My heart sank when I heard, "Well, Mr. Gallo, it looks like a clean fracture." It wasn't the sexy doctor, but a man that spoke.

"Where's the other doctor?" I asked, wanting to see her before I left.

"She's busy and asked me to give you the good news and get you checked out."

"Fuck," I mumbled. She'd foiled my plans. I sighed. "So I'm good to go?"

"It's going to take about four to six weeks to heal. You can tape them to relieve some of the pain if you'd like."

"I know. It's not the first time I've cracked a rib."

"Here's the paperwork with instructions, and make sure to follow up with your family doctor in a week or so."

"Got it," I said as I took the paperwork from his hand.

Grabbing my shirt, I stalked out of the room to find Izzy. The doctor had brushed me off, and I was pissed.

CHAPTER TWO

MIA

Summer

HUMAN LIFE SEEMED to be worthless to most people. That was what I'd learned during my time as an emergency room physician.

I'd wanted to help people for as long as I could remember. My mom said I raided the medicine cabinet to fix my Cabbage Patch Kids as a little girl.

Each day as I stood over my patients, trying to revive their lifeless bodies, my education and training felt meaningless. Medicine is still referred to as a *practice*. It hasn't been perfected, and even with today's advances in medicine, not everything can be fixed.

It's a hard fact that I don't always want to accept, but have no choice.

The hardest part of my job, the thing I dread most, is informing a family that we were unable to save their loved one, despite our best efforts.

Those words left my mouth twice today, and it had been soul crushing.

"Call it, Dr. Greco," Dr. Patel said as he stood next to the gurney.

I couldn't stop myself from pushing down again. Sweat trickled down my cheeks, as a lump had formed in my throat. Maybe if I pushed one more time, I could get his heart to beat again.

"I can't. Just give me a couple more minutes." I pushed with such force that I knew that a few ribs had cracked under my palm.

His life hadn't even begun and I would be the one that called his time of death.

"Mia." Dr. Patel placed his hands on mine, snapping my mental focus—to save the boy's life. "He's gone. You've been working on him for over thirty minutes. His injuries are too grave. Call it, or I will."

Dr. Patel had been by my side today, and knew the devastation that we were unable to repair—two car accidents, a gunshot victim, and the little blond-haired angel in front of me—a victim of a hit-and-run driver.

How could someone hit a child and leave him in the street to die?

A child…a goddamn innocent little boy.

I looked at Dr. Patel and was struck by the weariness on his face. His eyes were bloodshot; the tiny creases around them looked deeper with big, dark circles. I could see that the day had taken a toll on him too. I wasn't alone in my despair.

I rested my palms against the boy's chest and felt the silence within, there was no life left to save. "Time of death: seven twenty-one p.m." I closed my eyes and took a couple of slow, steady breaths before I removed my hands. I wanted to run to the bathroom and throw up.

A third life I couldn't save.

"I'll go tell his parents, Mia. You've done enough

today," Patel said, placing his hand on my shoulder, giving it a tiny squeeze.

"Thank you, Eric."

I usually argued with him. I wanted to be the one to talk with the families and help console them, but today, I had nothing. He patted my shoulder before leaving me with the boy that would never age or have the opportunity to experience all the joys in life.

I collapsed in the chair against the wall; pulling out my ponytail, I let my hair fall free. Placing my head in my hands, I ran my fingers through my hair as I tried to collect my thoughts.

More patients needed me, but I had to take a moment to myself. I couldn't take another loss; I didn't have anything left to give. Each time I lost someone, a small piece of my heart died.

Light footsteps broke my moment of serenity as I questioned my decision to work in an emergency room instead of an office practice, like most of my classmates.

"Sorry to interrupt, Dr. Greco. I need to prep the body for the family to say their goodbyes," the nurse said as she grabbed a damp cloth to wipe down his bloodied face.

"It's okay. I have patients to see. I just needed a moment to myself."

She gave me a weak smile before beginning to clean the body. I couldn't watch. I couldn't take the sounds of the cries and utter grief that would fill this room. It took everything I had to climb to my feet and pull myself together. The ER had an endless stream of people.

I had one hour left until I could go home and crawl in bed.

I had thought about moving back to Minnesota after I finished my internship, but Florida had become a part of me. I wanted to wear sandals year round, feel the sunshine on my face, and watch the sunset over the Gulf of Mexico from my beachfront home. I couldn't go back—snow and I never got along.

My work had become my life, especially in the summer months when my parents went back home. They were snowbirds, and came to Florida to enjoy the sunshine and warm weather when the deep freeze hit up north. They'd been gone a month, as spring had arrived back home. The quietness of my life had become almost deafening when I wasn't at the hospital. Today I was thankful I didn't have to go home and put on a cheery smile for them.

I felt needed here. I had something to contribute, something that many people didn't. The local population was poor and I wanted to help. It had become my calling. I spent my spare time helping at the free clinic in town and helped raise money for the homeless youth that plagued the county.

I stayed for the clinic, where I volunteered, and the chance to make a difference.

CHAPTER THREE

MICHAEL

MY MUSCLES REVOLTED with each kick; every single one screamed for me to stop, but I couldn't. I worked too damn hard to get to this point in my life to give up now. Sometimes I questioned my sanity for waking up at three in the morning to work out for hours at the gym, but my body had to be strong and I had to be ready to win my next fight.

"Pansy ass," Rob yelled. "Harder. Your ribs have been healed for weeks. Show me what you're made of already, Mike."

He egged me on and did everything in the world to piss me off. Rob had been my trainer for two years. Most days, like today, I wanted to knock his fucking lights out, but I knew his methods were right in the end.

"Your sister hits harder than you," he teased, a shit-eating grin on his face.

My sister, Izzy, was where the friend-trainer line crossed with Rob and me. They dated for a short time. When Izzy dumped him, I didn't think we'd continue working together. In typical Rob fashion, he brushed it off and moved on to the next notch in his bedpost.

"Cocksucker," I said, hitting the target in his hand hard enough to cause Rob to stagger backward.

"Better," he said as he regained his stance. "Ten more minutes and then we'll call it a day."

My drive to be the champion was so strong that I could almost taste the next victory. I wanted to show my family that I had talent and the ability, even though at times, at least in the beginning, their support had been questionable.

I won my first two matches, and with each victory, their support grew and my pop finally started to believe. When my ma said he was bragging to his friends, I knew I had him.

I grew up watching the fights with my pop and his buddies. They yelled at the television and made side bets. He liked to call my fighting career a hobby, but I needed to show him that it was more than that. I was meant to be the champion.

Wanting the gym all to myself when I trained, I paid the owner to wait until six in the morning to open the doors. He liked the idea of the publicity my victory and career would bring to his small-town gym in the middle of bum-fuck Florida, and it didn't hurt that he was Rob's brother, either.

"Bodies" by Drowning Pool pumped through the speakers, and it gave me the last push of motivation I needed. Sweat dripped from my brows and stung my eyes. Doing a roundhouse kick, I almost missed the target, nearly hitting Rob in the head.

"Maniac. I'll knock you on your ass if you do that again."

"In your fucking dreams, buddy." I laughed before landing a solid blow.

My forearms burned, my thighs trembled, but I wouldn't quit.

I had this shit.

"Time," Rob said, putting the targets down.

"I could go another hour," I said.

I knew that shit was a lie.

I ran for an hour before I walked in this morning, and my legs were shaking to the point of weakness.

"Sure you could, tiger." He laughed, holding his stomach. "Your muscles need to rest and recoup. We don't want to overdo it with the match coming up."

"Thank Christ," I mumbled under my breath.

"What did you say?" He cocked his eyebrow as he crossed his arms.

"Nothing."

"Why do you seem so fucking pissy today, Mike? Couldn't get it up last night?"

"That would seem like a fuckin' blessing right now." I sat on the bench to give my legs a break as I pulled the tape off my hands. "Tammy. What a fucking pain in my ass."

"I told you she's a crazy bitch. Stop thinking with your dick so much and use what brain is left in that thick head of yours."

I snorted. That had been the funniest damn thing to come out his mouth in a long time—he sure as fuck wasn't Dr. Ruth. "When did you become a relationship expert? Your shit isn't all together in the lady department, Rob."

"Maybe not, but I told you Tammy was a hot mess. She's got the cling thing going on and is crazy to fuckin' boot."

"Crazy is an understatement, man." I shook my head. I had a silent debate with myself on if I wanted to share the details of the entire fucked-up situation. "I went to her place last night to get a piece of ass."

"And?" He leaned against the wall and listened.

"And the crazy bitch had a scrapbook on her coffee table. Do you know what the cover was?"

He started to laugh as he pulled his lips in his mouth to stop from breaking out into hysterics.

"You do, don't you?" I glared at him.

"I've heard stories about her, but I thought they had to be made up."

"She had a picture of a bride and a groom. Somehow, she'd put our faces on their bodies. I opened it when she went to her room, and the book was filled with her version of *our* future. It was beyond fucked up. Gave me the fucking creeps."

Page after page contained images of our children with names and photos. Little hearts in all colors surrounded the pictures. She had our life planned out, and all I wanted was a little pussy.

She didn't have the brains to hold my attention, let alone make me want to spend an eternity listening to her chatter on about the Kardashians. Tammy wanted status and money, and they were two things I wasn't willing to share with a woman like her.

Tammy knew her role in my life—she was my late-night hookup. I never took her out, never led her on, and never promised her happily ever after.

She always replied, "You'll change your mind," but that never happened.

"Wow, I don't know what to say," Rob said as he walked toward the door to unlock it.

"I ended that shit right there. She cried like we'd been dating for years. What a fucking mess. I don't need the bullshit in my life, especially not now."

"Keep your eye on the goal—fighting, not bitches and pussy."

"Didn't you learn not to use that term when talking about women?" I laughed.

His cheeks turned pink as he looked away from me. "She's your sister, and I have nothing more to say about the experience." He drew the last word out. I knew he had a million things he wanted to say about her, but he kept his lips shut because he knew he'd get a beating.

Rob was crass. He referred to women as bitches once in front of Izzy, and she caught him off guard and knocked him on his ass. It was a proud brother moment. She took down a man double her size, and for one hell of a good cause. My baby sister has bigger balls than most men I knew. Growing up with four brothers made her rough around the edges and not willing to take shit from anyone.

"Good choice." I finished drying the sweat from my body. Grabbing my phone, I threw my bag over my shoulder. "Tomorrow, same time?" I asked.

"You got it." Rob reclined in the chair at the front desk, kicking his feet up and putting his arms behind his head. He looked like he was ready for a nap.

That shit wouldn't fly at Inked.

The screen on my phone lit up.

Tammy—there were at least a dozen text messages from her since I'd walked in.

Tammy: We were meant to be together.

Tammy: You'll come back to me.

Tammy: I miss you.

I told her last night we were through, even though we never really began.

I never asked her to be my girlfriend.

Fuck her and her insanity.

I turned the screen off as I reached for the door. The

top of my head hit the door before my chest connected with the glass. I saw stars from the impact. I blinked a couple of times before I noticed a woman on the ground. She was picking up the contents of her purse that had spilled.

"Fuck," I muttered, as I opened the door to a very pissed-off female. "I'm sorry; can I help you with that?" I asked, bending down in front of her.

"Why don't you fucking watch where you're walking?" she seethed, as she placed her wallet and other tiny items inside her black handbag.

"I didn't see you." I grabbed her lip-gloss that had rolled away, and held it out to her.

She grabbed the tube from my hand and glared at me with the most mesmerizing hazel eyes. "Obviously." She scanned the ground.

Instead of helping her, I stared at her like an idiot.

Her hair was an amazing shade of brown, with glints of red that sparkled in the light. The straight, smooth locks hung just past her shoulders. She had a small nose, full red lips, high cheekbones, and large hazel eyes with flecks of gold.

"Hey, I said I'm sorry and I am." Standing, I tried to be a gentleman and held my hand out to her.

Her eyes moved up my body, slowly at first, before she stopped on my face with scrunched eyebrows. Her skin felt like silk against my rough palm as she placed her hand in mine. In one quick motion, I pulled her to her feet. Her crinkled forehead and hardened expression disappeared and were replaced with softness. She pulled her hand away from mine with a weak smile and a reddened face.

"How can I make it up to you?" I asked, still staring. It wasn't her beauty that had my attention, but something about her eyes—a familiarity that I couldn't place.

She used the back of her hand to brush the dirt off her yoga pants. "I'm fine. No need to make it up to me. Just maybe watch where you're walking next time. You're kind of like getting hit by a Mack truck." She laughed. "Hey, I'm sorry I was such a bitch. Just a bad night and shitty morning and you're the icing on the cake."

Tilting my head, I gave her a small smile. "I understand. The last twelve hours haven't exactly been stellar for me either."

She fidgeted with her phone but kept her eyes locked on mine.

"Got everything?" I asked. I needed to leave. I didn't need to complicate my shit any further.

"Yeah, I think so. Thanks for stopping to help."

"I'm not a dick. Well, at least not all the time." I grinned. "How could I not stop and help the beautiful lady that I knocked over? I hope your day gets better from here." God, I sounded like a total moron, but I couldn't stop the verbal diarrhea that leaked from my mouth. "Let me get the door for you." I rushed and pushed it open.

"Thank you," she said, brushing against my body as she tried to fit through the doorway, my torso blocking the small entrance.

A hint of lilac or some flowery shit filled the air, disappearing with the distance between us.

"Maybe I'll see you again sometime," I said, not ready to walk away.

She smiled at me before turning around and walking away.

"Yeah, I'm here every day."

When did I turn into Mr. fucking Rogers? I couldn't stop myself.

"Maybe we can work out together or something," I yelled to her.

I'm officially a pussy.

"Sure." She didn't sound too eager, but then again, she didn't say no. She placed her bag next to the desk and signed in.

I watched her as I walked toward my truck.

My cock was hard last night when I went to Tammy's, and that turned in to a clusterfuck of epic proportions without me at least getting off for my troubles.

Seeing the girl that I crashed into wearing a tight, hot pink workout tank top and black yoga pants turned my dick into granite.

Obviously, I needed my fucking head examined.

***

I flipped on the lights at Inked as I walked through the door to peace and quiet. An ice-cold shower didn't do much to take my thoughts off the hot piece of ass I ran into at the gym.

As I sat down at the front desk, my phone danced across the appointment book. It hadn't stopped vibrating from the nonstop messages.

The girl was fucking clueless.

Last night my exact words to her were, "Don't ever call me again, you crazy bitch." I thought it was pretty cut and dry. My words were simple to understand, but apparently she didn't get the fucking message.

When I heard my sister's car beep in the parking lot, I braced myself for her bullshit. Izzy would have a fucking field day when she heard about Tammy. I held my breath, tapped the pencil next to my jiggling phone, and kept my head down as she breezed through the door, chattering on her phone to her asshole flavor of the month.

Izzy isn't an easy girl—she made the guys earn everything she gave.

Growing up with four brothers hadn't been easy for her

—we didn't leave her the opportunity to be easy. Most of her boyfriends got chased away when she was younger. It wasn't like she couldn't handle herself, but we made sure to keep her ass out of trouble.

She threw her bag on the floor next to her station before coming to a dead stop in front of me. I snuck a peek at her. She squinted at me, already reading me like an open book, shaking her head.

"I gotta go, John," she said into her phone, popping her gum and looking at the ceiling. Her hands opened and closed, with her fingertips touching, telling me that he was rambling. "Bye, John. I don't have time for this shit. I'll talk to you later." She pressed on the screen before blowing out a puff of air. She leaned over and spat her gum in the trashcan. Classic Izzy.

"Hey, sis."

"What's wrong?" Cocking her head, she waited, rubbing her finger across her lips.

"Nothing." I didn't want to tell her, but I knew it was inevitable.

"You boys are so bad at hiding shit. I've spent a lifetime studying you jackasses. I know you better than you know yourself. I'm guessing woman problems. Just tell me, because I won't stop asking until you do."

"Tammy."

"Ah, the fruitcake," she said as she giggled.

"What do you know about her?" My phone started to dance across the desk again, and I grabbed it to stop the jerky movement.

"I've heard stories. We've all heard *things.*" She made air quotes with her fingers.

My sister had been holding out on me. "What didn't you share with me, Isabella?"

"My formal name. Is someone feeling duped?"

"I swear to Christ, Izzy. Why didn't you warn me? I mean, I would've told you if you were going to date some crazy cocksucker."

"I tried to warn you, but you reminded me that you're a big boy."

If she used air quotes one more time during this conversation I was going to put her in a headlock and mess up her hair until she screamed uncle.

"You told me to mind my own business. So…I thought I'd let you learn the hard way, big brother." She couldn't stop laughing.

I sighed. "Next time slap me, will you?"

"Gladly." Her fingers tangled in my hair, ruffling it just the right way to make me cringe. "So tell me what happened, and why is your phone going crazy without you bothering to look?"

"I don't even know where to start. I ended shit with Tammy and she's been blowing it up for twelve hours."

"Why did you end it? Wait, were you guys really a *thing*?" She leaned over the desk and rested her chin in her hand.

"We weren't anything but fuck buddies, or at least that's what I thought. She, on the other hand, had our future planned out. She made a scrapbook, Izzy. A fucking scrapbook." I slammed my fist down on the desk and started to laugh. "Shit would be funny if it happened to someone else, but she's crazy."

"A scrapbook of what?" Her eyebrows drew together.

"The cover was a wedding photo with our faces glued on the bride and groom. I flipped through the book. It was our entire life planned out and in living color. That shit just isn't normal, Izzy."

She doubled over in laughter, smashing her fist against the desk. "No, wait." She couldn't catch her breath as tears began to stream down her cheeks. "Did you at least take the scrapbook with you? I mean, I need to see this shit."

"Fuck. I was so pissed I didn't even think about grabbing it." I rubbed my forehead, annoyed with myself for being such a dumbass. "She hasn't stopped calling and texting me since last night."

Hunched over, gasping for breath, she held her hand out. "Give it to me."

"What?"

"Gimme your phone, stunad."

She tapped a few buttons, the tip of her tongue sticking out.

"What are you doing? Please don't respond to her, Iz."

She gave me a sour look before turning her attention back to her task.

I sighed, leaning back in my chair, and waited.

"Here," she said, placing it in front of me.

"What did you do?"

"You really need to learn more about your phone, Michael. I blocked her." She rolled her eyes.

"You can really do that shit?" I was stunned; I didn't know it could be so easy.

I would've done it hours ago to avoid the barrage of bullshit.

Izzy just shook her head as she walked away.

Joe and Anthony walked in laughing. They said the usual "hey" when walking past me to put their stuff down and prep their areas for customers.

I checked over the schedule while I waited for everyone to finish. Anthony sat first and began to tap out a beat against the plastic chair. Leaning back, he put his head against the wall, and closed his eyes, looking lost in the rhythm.

By the time Izzy and Joe made their way to the front of

the shop, I wanted to rip Anthony's fingers off and shove them down his throat.

Izzy sat down next to Anthony, resting her head on his shoulder.

"Anything new since yesterday, Mike?" Joe asked, leaning against the desk. He cracked his neck with a quick push to his chin.

Izzy laughed as she whispered in Anthony's ear. They looked at me and smiled.

"Totally booked. No room for walk-ins unless anyone wants to work extra."

No one met my eyes.

"Didn't think so." I tapped the pen against the schedule and tried to avoid the looks from the two assholes against the wall.

Joe turned toward them. "What are you two giggling about over there?"

I waved my hands in the air and shook my head. I hoped Izzy would take pity on me. I knew the bullshit that was about to take place if she didn't.

"Talking about the nuptials between Tammy and Mike."

Fucking little sisters and their big mouths.

Joe's head turned quickly in my direction. "What the fuck are they talking about?"

"They're being jackasses."

"You didn't elope or anything stupid like that did you?" Joe asked.

"Fuck no! Give me an ounce of credit, will you please?"

We spent the next ten minutes laughing about Tammy and all the problems our dicks had caused through the years. It's strictly a male issue.

I had to own that shit.

When my first customer arrived five minutes early, I wanted to kiss her feet for saving me from my siblings' harassment.

CHAPTER FOUR

MIA

I GROANED, burying my face in the pillow and wanting to avoid facing the world. My body felt heavy and I didn't want to get out of bed, but the only thing that could help was working out. Even after a full night's sleep, I couldn't shake my sadness from work last night, and I figured, why the hell not? It was worth a shot.

The only thing that usually helped my mood was a good, ass-kicking workout at the gym.

Then I walked in the gym and the man knocked me on my ass. The impact scared the hell out of me as I fell on my ass, dropping my purse and spilling the contents everywhere.

He was the object of my anger. It wasn't from being knocked down; looking back, I was more mortified by it than pissed. I felt helpless over the lost lives that had piled up during my shift. The night before had been one of the lowest in my short career, but when I looked up into his rich caramel eyes, something inside me shifted.

My brain must have been rattled by the force of my fall.

I'd seen him before. I knew it.

I lost my breath as I stared into his eyes. I'd never had a reaction to someone like I had with him. Something unspoken passed between us as we looked into each other's eyes.

It took everything in me to not react when he helped me off the ground. The moment our skin connected, electricity passed between us. There was a snap, crackle, pop.

I couldn't get him out of my damn mind as I started to run on the treadmill. As my thighs burned and sweat trickled down my chest, I thought about only him.

How did I know him?

Tall with broad shoulders, muscular, tattooed-covered arms, and completely not my taste.

The track pants he wore hid his legs, but there was no doubt in my mind that they were as solid and powerful as his upper half.

When our bodies were inches apart in the doorway, my heart pounded in my chest—if he were any closer, he would've heard the frantic rhythm.

"Hey, Mia." A voice pulled me out of my haze.

Blinking, I looked over to see Rob leaning against the treadmill. "Oh. Hey, Rob."

"You're looking beautiful, as always." He stared at my chest as my body bounced.

"If you don't stop staring at my chest, I'll knock you on your ass," I warned.

He snickered, covering his mouth with his hand, but his eyes remained glued to my breasts. "Promises, promises. Why don't you let me take you to dinner?"

"Rob, I'm sure you're a nice guy." I coughed.

He was the farthest thing from nice. He wasn't an asshole, but he sure as hell wasn't boyfriend material.

"We wouldn't work. I'd spend too much time repairing the injuries I'd give you."

A giant smile crept across his face before he finally looked at my eyes. "You say the sexiest shit, Mia."

"Not happening. Who was that guy that left when I walked in?" I grabbed the towel and blotted the sweat from my chest.

Moving his eyes to follow the path of the towel, he asked, "You mean Mike?"

"I don't know his name. Tall, muscular, walked out right after you opened."

Brawn didn't equal brains when it came to Rob.

"Mike, yeah, he's a friend of mine." His eyes flickered between my breasts and eyes.

If they were friends, then in all probability he was an asshole too. I had attracted more of those in my time than I wanted to admit.

"Tell me about him. I think I know him from somewhere." I couldn't help myself; I had to figure out how I knew him.

"He's a fighter. He has a big fight coming up that I'm helping him train for." Rob flexed and punched the air.

"Is that all he does?" Fighter—code word for "unemployed and a workout junkie."

Rob shook his head and laughed. "Nah, he's part owner in a tattoo shop. He's a piercer there."

A busty blonde walked by and started to set up camp at a treadmill nearby. Rob's eyes wandered in her direction as he licked his lips.

"Thanks. You can go now," I said, wanting to be alone with my thoughts.

He put his hands over his heart and staggered backward as though he were in pain. "You just dismissed me like that? I'm wounded, Mia."

"Maybe the girl over there"—I moved my head in her direction—"will have the remedy."

"You may be right, beautiful. I'm off to find out." Winking, he tapped my treadmill with his palm before whistling as he walked away.

CNN played on the tiny screen in front of me, but I couldn't focus as my thoughts drifted back to Mike. The powerhouse that literally rocked my world this morning was a body mutilator. He pierced and punched his way through life while I patched up the damage caused by fists and dirty needles.

I grabbed my phone from the cup holder as it began to chirp.

Lori: Girls night out. Game?

I needed a night with my friends. I needed to laugh and hear the latest gossip. I had two days off, and an evening to let loose sounded like heaven and a great way to get my mind off work.

Me: I'm in. When and where?

I didn't give a shit if I had to drive to Orlando, I'd be there. My restless night would require a nap to keep up with the ladies, or I would do a face plant on the table after the first drink.

Lori: Ybor City. Be ready to party your ass off. I'll pick you up at 9.

Me: I can drive.

Lori: Fuck no, your ass is getting drunk. I got it all worked out.

She knew me so well. Lori and the girls went out all the time. They lived without their work to weigh them down emotionally. Unlike me, they didn't have to hold someone's heart in their hand and try to get it to beat again. Their pressures were different, but I could never stumble into work nursing a hangover.

Lori was a lawyer, Sarah a receptionist at an advertising agency, and Jamie was a bored housewife.

I wanted to buy a new outfit for tonight. I had a closet full of clothes, but screw it, I deserved something special. I worked my ass off and didn't feel ashamed to splurge on myself every once in a while. International Plaza called my name.

***

I straightened my hair—the humidity in Florida wreaked havoc on my long brown locks—before starting my makeup. I didn't wear much to work; the long hours typically had me questioning their claim that makeup was twenty-four-hour wear. It never stayed put, and caused my eyes to look more tired than they did naturally.

I took my time, giving my lids a smoky treatment to bring out their color before applying an obscene amount of Barely There mascara. It made my eyes look bright and my eyelashes long and lush. Lori texted me that she was almost at my house as I spritzed my body with Gucci Guilty and stared in the mirror—giving myself a once-over.

The short, tight black tube top showed off my stomach and hourglass figure perfectly. My tits didn't stick out too much, but would be noticed without flashing a sign that read "looky here." My form-fitting denim capris made my ass look perky. The leopard print stiletto heels caused my calves to tighten and pulled the entire outfit together.

I sat on the front step as I waited for Lori to pick me up. The neighborhood was bustling. People waved as they walked past with their dogs and sat on their front porches enjoying the warmth of the Florida air. Summer would soon be arriving in full force, and people would be scarce at this time of day. The summer sun felt like a flame against my skin, and even the mornings were stifling from the humidity.

I closed my eyes as Lori's headlight blinded me momentarily when she pulled in. The car shook from the loud bass of whatever hip-hop song she had blasting inside.

"Oh my God, I'm so excited. Fuck, you look amazing, girl." She bounced a little in her seat and held the steering wheel, a giant smile on her face, as I climbed in.

I leaned over and planted a giant kiss on her cheek. "I've missed you."

"Me too, Mia. Got everything?" She applied a layer of lip-gloss before smacking her lips together and checking her reflection in the rearview mirror.

I nodded at her with butterflies in my stomach. "Yep, let's hit it."

Lori and I met in college. I was pre-med and she was pre-law. We became thick as thieves sophomore year. Any free moment we had, and there weren't as many as we wished, we spent together at the beach or clubs. We danced our asses off and loved every minute of it.

When college ended and the real world sucked us in, we didn't have the time to hang out together and drink Coronas on the beach. We were lucky to see each other once a month, and to get everyone together had become virtually impossible.

We could go without speaking for weeks and pick up right where we left off. She was *that* kind of friend. I envied her beauty, though. Her blonde hair had a wave that I couldn't achieve, no matter how hard I tried. Her crystal-blue eyes sparkled in the light, and her teeth were so white they almost glowed in the dark.

"Did I tell you I started seeing someone?" she asked, as she turned the radio down when Justin Bieber started to sing. His high-pitched girl voice made me cringe.

"No. You've been holding out on me."

When most people were getting married and starting their families, we were still in school, finishing our degrees before starting our careers. Families and marriage were put on the back burner. Now that we hovered around the big three-zero, we both felt a pang of jealousy and remorse that we may have missed out on so much for our careers.

"His name is Sal and we work together. We'd been eye fucking for months before things got interesting one night when we both worked late."

"Dirty girl, doing it at work." I shook my head and laughed.

"Jesus, I can't even describe what it's like being with him. The first time I could barely think. We were going over a case. We argued about how to win and he went all cavemen and threw me on the table. It was fuckin' hot."

"Mm, that sounds nice. So are you guys casual or are you officially a couple?" I felt a bit jealous. Hospitals weren't sexy.

"We're not officially dating. We are seeing other people, but then again, who the fuck has the time with our schedule?"

"So, you picked a Guido. Hmm."

"What's your issue with Italian men?" She looked at me, wrinkling her nose, before returning her eyes to the road.

"I don't have a problem with them. They're typically bossy and believe a woman's place is in the kitchen."

"He's not like that." Her blonde hair swayed as she shook her head.

"Mm-hmm, not yet, maybe."

"Bitch, don't rain on my parade." She laughed.

I loved Lori. "Never, doll."

"You seeing anyone?" she asked, just like she did every time we spoke.

My answer was the same: "No."

I tried the online dating sites and they ended in disaster. I didn't want to date someone that lived with their parents or enjoyed sitting at home playing video games.

My world consisted of doctors and nurses, and I wanted to escape that at the end of the workday, not date someone that would want to talk medicine.

"Haven't found the right one." I stared out the side window, watching the palm trees sway in the breeze.

"It's not easy for girls like us." She threw the money in the toll box and waited for the green light. We were close to Tampa and Ybor City. Ybor is one of the oldest parts of the city, with a unique history. Cigar factories used to line the streets, but were replaced with nightclubs and bars.

"I don't want to be anyone's sugar mama. I worked hard for everything I have. I will not have someone leech off me. I want a man, not a child. You know what I mean?"

"Agreed." She nodded. "Text Sarah and let her know we're close."

Lori rambled on about Sal and his amazing cock until we pulled into the parking lot. I smiled and nodded, letting her talk. I applied a little more lipstick as she turned off the car.

"I'm so happy you could come tonight, Mia."

"Me too, Lori. I need a night of dancing with my girls."

"Fuck music, let's get inside and find you some dick." She giggled.

"I don't think my Romeo's inside. I just want to dance and get shitfaced."

"I said dick, not your one true love, silly woman. You

need a good fuck to remind you what life's all about," she said as we approached the long line filled with beautiful girls in skimpy outfits.

Lori pulled me forward, bypassing all the waiting people, straight to the bouncer. "Hey, Pete. This is my friend Mia." Lori kissed his cheek.

Pete's face softened with her kiss. His t-shirt looked painted on as it strained against his bulging biceps. His hair was cut in military fashion, flattop and perfect. Pete didn't look like someone you wanted to mess with.

He held out his hand to me. "Hi, Mia. It's nice to meet you," he said, bringing my hand to his lips and placing a gentle kiss on it.

There was no sizzle and pop. I wanted the spark, like Michael gave me, and although Pete had that sexy-as-fuck look, his lips did nothing for me.

"You too, Pete." I smiled, pulling my hand back.

"Your friends are inside waiting for you," Pete said, motioning toward the door.

"You're the best," Lori said, wrapping her arms around his waist.

"Only for you," he said, kissing her hair. "When are you going to go out with me, beautiful?"

"Pete," she said flatly.

"I don't give up easily. Can't blame a guy for trying." He shrugged and patted her ass. "Go on in before the line gets restless."

"Thanks again. Maybe we'll see you inside," she said as he opened the door for us.

The thump of the music made my chest rattle as we stood in the entrance, surveying the bar. People were everywhere, and the dance floor moved with the beat and didn't have a free spot on it.

We spotted Sarah and Jamie at the bar nursing their

martinis and checking out the men. Jamie's red hair bounced as she shrieked and clapped when she saw us. She was typically overdramatic, but fun to be around, especially when she had a few too many to drink. She had on a kickass black dress and red heels showing off her long legs. Her thin frame swayed as she grabbed the bar top.

Sarah wrapped her arms around me. "Been too long, girl," she said in my ear. Sarah's blue eyes were glassy.

"I know. We have to do this more often." I checked out her outfit. "Damn, you look good, Sarah."

She grinned and twirled. "I've been working my ass off in the gym. I'm wearing a bikini this year if it kills me." She snapped her fingers, catching the attention of the bartender, and signaled for two more drinks. "He's delicious, isn't he?" Sarah asked, watching him move in the tight space. "I'm taking him home as a treat." She laughed, as her eyes remained glued to his body.

"Always on the prowl," Lori said, before becoming enamored by his body too.

He placed our drinks on the bar and leaned over to whisper in Sarah's ear. Her lips turned up in an enormous smile, her eyes growing wide. He was definitely saying something X-rated. He backed away with a grin that could only be described as sinful. "Would you ladies like a shot?" he asked, never taking his eyes off Sarah.

"Hell yes," she said, still wearing the dopey smile he'd given her.

"A toast," Lori said as she raised her glass. "May your love last thousand years but come in six-inch increments."

We clinked our glasses together and laughed before taking a sip.

"Six seems a bit average, don't you think?" Jamie said as she wiped her lips with the back of her hand.

"Hey, when you're getting zero, six seems like fucking king dong."

"True, true." Jamie nodded and giggled.

"Drink those martinis, because the dance floor is calling my name," I said, grabbing the drink in front of me.

"I'd rather stand here and gawk at all the yummy hotness in this room," Lori replied.

"I know you would, Lori, but dance and gawk. Maybe you'll get felt up," I said around the rim of my martini glass.

"If I could be so lucky." She laughed as she finished the last of her drink. The others were ahead of us by a few sips and we had some catching up to do. "I'm usually the one doing the molesting, though." Lori sighed as she placed her glass on the bar.

Lori wasn't bashful, and made her intentions known to any man that caught her attention. We never judged her for going after what she wanted. Nine times out of ten, she hit a homerun, but I'd never been as forward as her.

"Fuck it," she said. "We're taking a taxi tonight, or sleeping at Sarah's place. I'm not going to be the sober one tonight."

When Prince's "Get Off" started to play, we ran screaming to the dance floor.

It reminded us of our college days, bringing us right back to where we all met at a frat party. The song was dirty as hell, and perfect. It wasn't the same song that we heard in the nineties—the DJ had spiced it up, making it techno—but the words were the same.

The mass of bodies moved to the rhythm, bumping and grinding with the music. I swayed, shaking my ass with the girls as we laughed. The colorful lights moved across the floor. I closed my eyes, getting lost in the beat. The alcohol made my legs feel weak as I continued to dance.

Running my fingers through my hair, I bumped into Sarah and leaned against her. We danced back to back, holding each other up. As I opened my eyes, I had the feeling that someone was staring at me.

I looked around and saw *him.* His eyes were focused on me.

My breathing stopped and my heart stuttered, as my body froze and I returned his stare.

I couldn't look away as he held my gaze. Leaning against the bar, he paid no attention to the man at his side. He raked his eyes up and down my body, and I felt flushed as heat crept up my chest to my neck.

"Why'd ya stop?" Sarah yelled from behind me.

All I could do was shake my head. My body felt frozen in place and my eyes were zeroed in on *him.*

Mike, the brick wall from the gym, stood there, watching me.

The dark pants and a crisp white dress shirt with the sleeves rolled up showed off the tattoos on his forearms. He looked calm and collected, but his eyes were fierce and pierced right through me.

The butterflies in my stomach from earlier came back with a vengeance.

What were the odds that I'd run into him again? Did he follow me or was it some cosmic force pushing us together?

"Mia, are you okay?" Sarah asked, as she stepped in front of me, breaking our eye contact.

My cheeks heated as I exhaled. "Yeah, I'm fine. Let's dance." I turned my back to where he stood, and focused on the music, trying to forget he was there.

Watching me.

CHAPTER FIVE

MICHAEL

"DUDE, YOU OKAY?" Anthony asked, nudging me in the shoulder.

I couldn't take my eyes off her. "Yeah."

"Who you looking at?"

I motioned toward her with my chin before taking a sip of my beer. "Her," I said.

"The blonde?"

"Fuck no, the brunette in the short jeans." She looked fucking edible.

"You gonna go talk to her?"

"Not yet." The connection was there—a strong enough one that she felt me staring and stopped dead in her tracks. I'd never had an issue with pursuing a woman, but based on her reaction to me at the gym, I'd wait before I approached her.

"Never took you for a pussy." Anthony laughed and slapped my shoulder.

She leaned into her blonde friend and turned.

Fucking women, I'd never figure them out.

The blonde looked over her shoulder at me. Her face

lit up before she spoke something into her friend's ear. They danced and laughed, and I became transfixed by the scene before me. Their bodies moved together, hips bumping, tits shaking, and I wanted to go on the dance floor and take her right there.

I swear to shit, God wanted to punish me, and used my cock to do it.

Her face shimmered, and her hair flew through the air haphazardly as they danced together. I envisioned her beneath me, on top of me, and against the wall, re-enacting her moves.

I sipped my beer, the bottle gripped tightly in my hand, as I felt the familiar throb in my dick.

When the song ended, they stood in the center of the dance floor and laughed. I didn't move. I called her over with my finger.

She shook her head, and started dancing when the next song started.

Fuck.

I thought I had the market cornered on cockiness, but she could be *stiff* competition.

Facing me, she put her hands above her head and shook her ass.

I caught a glimpse at her stomach muscles, and I wanted to run my tongue over the smooth skin. It met her hips to create a fuckin' knockout figure.

A man placed his hands on her hips, and she froze, holding my gaze. The cocky grin on her face disappeared, replaced with a pissed-off sneer. She slapped his hand away, but he didn't let go.

What the fuck?

I didn't want the sleazy bastard to have his hands all over her. I couldn't blame the guy, but you don't touch a woman unless she wants you to.

Clearly she didn't.

She turned to face him, her arms waving in the air as she laid into the guy.

His eyes grew large but he didn't back away.

I moved closer to them and waited for the moment to step in. I couldn't let her handle this guy alone.

He reached for her waist, but before he gripped her, her knee rose and met his balls in one quick thrust.

Ouch.

I winced, knowing the pain that just shot through his body. I smiled, knowing he deserved it, as he clutched himself, rolling back and forth on the dance floor.

"Fucker, when I say keep your hands to yourself, I fucking mean it!" she roared.

Clearing my throat, I drew her attention away from the asshole at her feet. I wanted to touch her, but thought better after what I just witnessed.

I liked my balls too damn much to let that shit happen.

She turned slowly, her eyes growing wide as they flickered to the floor. "Hey," she said as I caught a glimpse of her small smile.

"That was quite impressive. You took him down pretty hard."

"Thank you. I have bony knees," she said, laughing. She looked too sweet and angelic to have just taken down the overgrown asshole writhing on the tile floor.

"I don't think we were properly introduced earlier. I'm Michael, and you are?" I held my hand out, wanting to touch her skin again.

She placed her tiny fingers in my palm. "I'm Mia."

I closed my fingers around her small hand, lifting it to my mouth. "You smell different than this morning." I kissed the delicate flesh on the top of her hand gently.

Her scent was sweet and reminded me of fresh-baked

cookies. I couldn't forget her flowery scent from this morning.

She laughed, and her eyes twinkled. Honest to God, fucking twinkled.

"Not being a creep. Just making an observation." I'd never been such a dumbass with a woman before. She made me nervous and turned me into a horny teenaged boy.

"It's my lotion. Vanilla Bean Noel." Her cheeks turned pink as she looked behind her and waved to her friends.

"You smell like a cupcake." I licked my lips and now felt like the creep. "Can I buy you a drink, Mia?" I needed to do something to break the awkwardness and my inability to stop saying stupid shit in front of her.

Her eyes returned to mine, the corner of her mouth turned up before she answered, "Sure, Michael."

I held my hand out, letting her walk in front of me. Her hips swayed as she sauntered to the bar. I wanted to smack her ass for the wicked shit it did to my cock.

Leaning against the bar, shoulder to shoulder with her, I motioned for the bartender. "What'll it be? Pick your poison."

I expected her to say she wanted a girlie drink, something that required an umbrella, but I would've been dead fucking wrong.

"Dirty martini, please. Straight up, with extra olives."

The bartender approached, giving Mia the once-over.

It took everything in me not to punch his fucking lights out as he lingered a little too long on her chest.

"What can I get you?" he asked her without looking in my direction.

"Another beer, and a dirty martini straight up with extra olives for the lady," I said, without caring who he asked.

I wanted to take the rag he had in his hand and stuff it down his throat. He gave me a sour face before leaving us. I threw a twenty on the bar, trying to avoid as much contact between him and Mia as possible.

Mia began to laugh as he walked away. "Are you two going to have a pissing match next?"

Her laughter was infectious.

"I didn't like the way he looked at you."

"Used to being the center of attention?" she asked, with a cocked eyebrow and a grin.

"No. Are you clueless to the way he just eye raped you, woman?"

Her grin turned into a giant smile. "He's a man. It's what you *all* do."

"Glad you think so highly of us." I leveled my gaze and grabbed the beer that had been left for me.

"How would you describe how you were looking at me on the dance floor?" she challenged.

"I wasn't eye raping you, sweetheart."

"Call it what you want. Your eyes told a different story, Michael."

"What'd they say?"

"Something along the lines of, 'You and me and a *little* tryst in the bathroom stall.'"

She was a feisty little thing.

"You wouldn't go home with me if I asked?"

She coughed, almost spitting out her drink. "No, not even after five of these babies," she said as she held up her glass before taking another sip.

"I like a challenge. I don't like to lose, either."

She smiled over the rim of her glass. "I've never been called a quitter."

I never liked easy.

My life had been filled with hard choices and challenges that kept me moving to bigger and better things. Everything came easy to my family. We grew up with money, not the kind that Paris Hilton had that caused her to turn into a fucking train wreck, but my parents made sure we never wanted for anything.

"What do you do, Mia? What makes you tick, besides kneeing a man in the balls?"

She placed her glass on the bar and twirled it in her fingers. "I'm in medicine."

I couldn't take my eyes off her mouth. Her lips were full and red from the lip-gloss, or whatever shit she had coating them. I wanted to know if it tasted like strawberry.

"You're a nurse?" I felt like I had to pull information out of her.

She turned toward me with her mouth set in a firm line. "No. I'm a doctor."

I whistled, being thoroughly impressed by the statement.

Dr. Mia was sexy as hell, and had a brain to match. "Impressive. What kind?"

"I work in the emergency room at County."

"Wow, that's some hard shit. Wait, that's where I know you from." Her sassy mouth, beautiful looks, and sparkling hazel eyes made it all click when she said "County Hospital ER."

"You do?" Her brows shot up as her eyes grew wide. "I hope it wasn't for anything too horrible."

"Cracked ribs a couple months back. You called me a cocky bastard, I believe," I said, smiling as I remembered her playfulness.

The corner of her mouth twitched as she tilted her head. "Ah, it's all coming back to me now. I knew I met you before. Sorry I was mean to you." She blushed.

"Nah, I liked it when you called me that. You said you'd go to dinner with me, and I'm holding you to your word."

Her brows knitted together as her eyes moved around my face. "I don't remember it that way. If memory serves me right, I told you no."

"You were supposed to come back after the x-ray, but you sent in some schmuck instead. You blew me off."

She snickered as her eyes flickered to her drink. "Michael, I don't remember blowing you off. It gets hectic, and another patient probably needed my attention more than you."

"I don't envy you, doc. You work a stressful job. I couldn't do it."

"Some days are harder than others." A flash of sadness splashed across her face before quickly disappearing. "It has its rewards too."

"I give you a lot of credit. To hold someone's life in your hands is some heavy shit, and a lot of responsibility."

"Some days I question my sanity. I wonder why I didn't settle for a nice family practice with an office, treating the flu, but I'd probably grow bored quickly."

"Ah, you like the rush," I said, rubbing my chin and studying her body language.

"Yeah, I guess I do. What do you do, Michael, besides fighting?"

"Ah, you remember me now. I'm part-owner of a tattoo shop, where I pierce the willing, but my true love is fighting."

"I spend my nights repairing damage that people like you inflict."

I saw the flash of sadness again before it disappeared. That wasn't the reaction I expected. "I never do anything that isn't asked of me, whether it's in the shop or the cage. Which one are we talking about here?"

"The fighting." Her face hadn't changed.

Most women cooed when they found out, but Mia? Nothing.

"I don't street fight—cage matches, MMA style. They're professional. I have a big one coming up." I smiled and felt proud to be able to utter those words, but Mia still didn't seem impressed, with her lips set in a firm line as she brought the martini glass to her lips.

"Still, it's the opposite of my job. I help people and heal them and you injure them. Maybe they spend more time injuring you. I don't know." She cocked her eyebrow at me and took a sip.

"Don't be silly, woman. It's a job. We all go into the cage knowing someone isn't coming out looking as pretty as they did when they went in. All injuries heal. And wait a minute here…you just injured the hell out of that douchebag. He'll probably never be able to have children because of that wicked knee."

"Fighting for money is barbaric." She shook her head, but I didn't buy her distaste for the sport. "What I did was self-preservation. There's a difference." She looked me straight in the eye and didn't blink.

A bullshitter could smell another bullshitter a mile away.

"Liar." I brushed my fingers against her arm, and she shivered with the contact.

Maybe she didn't like what I did, but I could tell it turned her on.

She didn't smile, but there was a twinkle in her eyes. Her body responded to mine…no matter how hard she tried to deny it.

CHAPTER SIX

MIA

"I DON'T CONDONE VIOLENCE." The words fell from my lips in a flat tone, even as my body still vibrated from his touch.

Traitor.

My body betrayed me when Michael touched me. I tried to play it cool.

"Not buying it." He lifted the beer to his lips and took a sip.

I stared at them as they hugged the rim of the glass.

I wanted to smack the cocky grin off his face. His rich brown eyes sparkled, and were filled with mischief as he called me a liar. His words were true no matter how hard I wanted to deny them. Michael was pure man—strong, sexy, and self-confident.

"Can we agree to disagree?" I asked, pretending not to look at his mouth.

He licked the beer from his lips. I had the overwhelming urge to use my tongue to capture the few drops of liquid still left behind. "Want a taste?" he asked with a hearty laugh as he tipped the beer in my direction.

I could feel the blush as it crept up my neck. I wanted to avoid his eyes but couldn't give him the satisfaction. I always believed in fighting fire with fire.

"You missed a little," I said before I reached up and used my thumb to wipe the few drops on his lips.

His eyes stayed locked with mine as I touched his soft flesh, slowing dragging my fingers across his skin.

I placed my thumb in my mouth, closing my lips around it.

He leaned in close enough for me to smell the musky cologne on his neck. "You're wicked," he whispered, his lips brushing against my ear.

Pulling my thumb from my lips, I replied, "I'm just getting started, hot stuff."

He backed away and stared at me before giving me a giant smile. "I may have met my match with you, Mia."

"I'll drink to that." I couldn't help but smile. I forgot how much fun it could be to flirt with someone, especially when they were handsome and a smooth talker.

He made it easy and made me feel sexy.

At work, I never felt sexy wearing my drab scrubs and knee-length lab coat, and with my hair up in a ponytail. I looked half dead by the time my shift ended at the hospital.

"Shot?" he asked.

"I've given thousands," I replied, laughing at my hospital humor.

"You're difficult, Mia." He eyed me as he fiddled with the beer.

"You have no idea, Michael." I laughed, wanting to throw myself at him and give in to any wild sexual ideas he currently had, but I wouldn't allow myself to be so reckless. "What do you have in mind?"

He looked me straight in the eye and didn't crack a smile. "Blue balls."

"Seems like a personal problem. I could write you a prescription, if you'd like."

"Um, fuck no to a prescription, but I'm sure it's nothing you couldn't fix." He smirked. "Wanna help me out?"

I leaned forward, my lips almost touching his as I said, "Usually when someone walks in with an erection that won't subside, we drain the fluid with a very large needle. I'm a pro. Interested in seeing my skills firsthand?"

His mouth hung open as he gaped. "That's just inhumane. I mean, Jesus, Mia, how could you do that to another human being?" He stepped back, shaking his head.

"Better than it having to be amputated from lack of circulation. So, what did you want to drink, again?" I smiled until my cheek muscles ached. I couldn't remember the last time I had smiled or laughed as much as I had with him tonight.

"Lemon drop. Let's skip the blue balls," he said, swallowing hard, probably still reeling from the thought of the long needle in his dick.

"Good choice, and they're my favorite."

"I gotcha." He looked away and motioned to the bartender.

I studied him as he ordered our drinks. Without talking to him, I'd think he was just another meathead muscle guy without the ability to think quickly and hold a witty conversation, but I would've been dead wrong.

Michael was a conundrum to me—brains, brawn, and beauty. His eyes moved in my direction for a moment, but his attention was drawn away from me by the clinking of the glasses on the bar.

Grinning, he slid the clear liquid in front of me. "What shall we drink to?" he asked as he placed the sugar-soaked lemons in between us.

"To blue balls?" I asked, holding up the shot glass.

"Fuck that shit. Don't ever mention that to me again," he said, picking up his glass. "To new beginnings." He raised his glass and tapped it against mine.

Warmth cascaded throughout my body before the liquid ever touched my lips. I didn't want to read into his words and feel like a fool, but the thought of getting to know this sexy-as-hell man made my toes curl. "Cheers."

I watched him over the rim; he stared at me, never wavering, and I winked as the liquid slid down my throat. It burned for a moment, and I winced from the vodka before I slammed the glass down. I reached for the lemon, needing something to cover the taste of the vodka. He was one step ahead of me, and already had the lemon in his hand.

I blinked slowly. The martini and shot coursing through my system was already starting to cloud my vision. Opening my lips, I stuck out my tongue and waited for him to place the lemon on it.

I closed my lips around his fingers as the sugar made my mouth water. Running my tongue across the coarse pads of his fingers, I sucked the juice and swallowed. His eyes narrowed as he watched my mouth with parted lips.

I had him right where I wanted him. Two could play games.

"Fuck me," he muttered, and looked away as I opened my lips, allowing his fingers to slide out.

"You okay? You look a little off." I covered my mouth with my hand, trying to hide my laughter.

He leaned in, brushing the hair away from my

shoulder. "If you keep that shit up, I'm going to find another way to occupy your mouth."

I'd like to say it was the alcohol that caused him to have that effect on me, but I'd be lying. "I don't know what you mean."

He wrapped his fingers around the back of my neck, bringing his lips within centimeters of mine. "You know exactly what you're doing to me. Let's not play games here, Mia." He searched my eyes.

I could feel his warm breath against my lips, and my heart pounded in my chest faster than the rhythm of the music. Looking into his eyes without blinking, I melted against him. "Who said I'm playing, Michael."

I wanted him to kiss me.

He inched close, eyes locked with mine, as I placed my hand against his chest. The rapid tattoo of his heart thumped against my palm, matching the beat of mine.

Leaning forward, I closed my eyes and held my breath. Butterflies filled my stomach and my legs trembled. The warmth of his lips sent shivers down my body.

The noise around us disappeared as he kissed me. Nothing else seemed to exist except him and me.

As I tipped my head back, his grip on the back of my neck increased as he pulled me against his rock-hard chest. The feel of him against me was amazing as he kissed me perfectly. Not too much lip, a dash of tongue as he held me against him. I moaned into his mouth as he bit my bottom lip. I sighed against his mouth, melting into his touch—I wanted to be closer to him.

His tongue soothed the spot that he'd just sunk his teeth into, and my sex convulsed from the tenderness.

We became one, lost in each other.

Pulling away, he whispered, "Damn." He rubbed his

knuckles against my collarbone, before releasing his grip on my neck.

Instantly I missed the warmth of his palm. My body swayed, as I stood there in a daze, blinking as I tried to regain my ability to think. Dumbfounded and in a fog from his kiss, I stood there like an idiot, with a grin on my face.

CHAPTER SEVEN

MICHAEL

"SEE ME AGAIN." I wasn't asking.

It was a simple statement, and I thought I'd use the moment to my advantage.

"I know you're busy, but I'll make time for you," I said as I gripped her hand, squeezing it.

Her eyes closed and opened slowly before she peered into my eyes. "My life is hectic, Michael. I don't have a normal schedule." She frowned and looked at our hands as I stroked her fingers.

"Fuck normal, Mia. Do you want to see me again or not?" I cocked my head and stared into her shimmering hazel eyes.

"I do." Her face was soft as her frown melted away and her eyes flickered back to mine.

"Tomorrow," I said. "I want to take you to dinner."

"I'm off tomorrow; beyond that I can't make any promises, Michael."

"Give me your phone, doc."

She fumbled as she dug inside her purse, pulling out her phone.

I grabbed it, not letting her back out now, and dialed my number. Smiling, I snapped a quick photo and attached it to my number in her contacts. "I have your number and you have mine. What time do you want me to pick you up?"

She waved her hands in the air and scrunched her lips. "I can drive," she said, narrowing her eyes.

"I'm driving and paying. No arguments." I wanted to surprise her and hopefully make that sassy-ass mouth speechless. "What time, Mia?" I asked.

"Is six okay? I have to work the next—"

I rested my finger against her lips. "Six is perfect. Text me your address and wear something sexy."

"Yes, sir," she said, giggling before saluting me.

I liked her smartass attitude. She'd sure as hell keep me on my toes.

I grabbed her hand and brought the soft skin to my lips. Inhaling the vanilla scent, I peeked up at her face as I kissed it. She watched me with parted lips and wide eyes. "Until tomorrow, Mia. I don't want to keep you from your friends any longer."

"Tomorrow," she whispered.

I waited for her to disappear into the crowd before trying to find Anthony. He sat on a couch against the wall with a group of girls surrounding him. They were enthralled by the topic of conversation…him.

"Where ya playing next?" the blonde sitting to his right asked, as she stroked his leg.

"Yeah, we want to come see you in action." The brunette bounced in her seat.

I rolled my eyes as my brother looked at me and grinned. "Ladies, this is my brother Mike. He's a fighter."

Fucker.

The last thing I needed or fucking wanted was the attention of these "ladies," as Anthony so nicely put it.

"Oooh," cooed the blonde as she slithered away from him and turned toward me.

"Ready to hit it?" I asked, ignoring them. I didn't feel like making small talk.

"Sure, man." He pushed himself up and kissed their hands. "Next Saturday at the Ritz. I'm going to see each and every one of you, right?"

They replied "yes" and nodded with conviction.

I grabbed his shirt, pulling him away from his *fans*. "You're such a whore at times, Anth."

"I know. Whatever fills the seats, Mike. What girl doesn't like a rocker?" He shrugged and waved at them over his shoulder as we walked away. "Hey, can we stop by the Ritz? I want to ask the owner a quick question."

"Not a problem."

"Tell me about the girl you were talking to," he said as he slapped my shoulder.

I looked at him and laughed. "She's not who she seems to be." Sometimes there are things you keep close to the vest—especially in my big-mouth family.

"I saw her knee that guy in the balls. She seems pretty hardcore."

"She's something else. Impressed the hell out of me, really."

"Hmm," he said as we made our way toward the Ritz.

"What the fuck does 'hmm' mean?"

"Nothing. I think you need a ball buster in your life," he said through a laugh.

"Forget about it, brother."

"Did you make a plan to see her again?" He eyed me with one eyebrow cocked and a silly-ass grin on his face.

"Yes," I answered, as I stopped walking and looked at him.

"Maybe she'll break you."

"I don't need that shit in my life," I said, leaving him to catch up.

"You need to let loose a little, but in the right way. Maybe she's just what the doctor ordered."

"You have no idea, Anthony." I laughed as I grabbed the door handle, opening it to the most ear-shattering guitar riff known to man, and followed Anthony inside.

I leaned against the wall, watching the band as they played for their screaming fans. The looks on their faces reminded me of watching Anthony when he was entertaining the crowds.

His adrenaline rush came from the people that watched him like a rock god, and mine came from beating the piss out of someone.

When I fought, the blood pumped through my body so rapidly that I could almost feel it moving. It's hard to describe to another person. Every muscle in my body grows rigid and screams for release. My breathing increases to the point I feel like my lungs will burst if I suck in any more air. When I step into the ring, everything else fades away. I feel like a warrior, fighting for the thrill and challenge. There's so much adrenaline in my system that I barely feel the blows of my opponent as they land against my body, sometimes crushing my bones.

"I'm ready," Anthony said as he tapped me on the shoulder.

I'd been so lost in my thoughts I didn't notice his approach.

"Yeah. This place gives me a headache."

"Wait until we play here. We're going to blow the roof off this motherfucker."

His smile touched his eyes as he pumped his fists in the air. Anthony didn't care about playing music to make a living; he simply did it for the thrill and the pussy.

He loved tattooing too much to ever give it up, but since we owned the shop, we made our own hours. We worked out a schedule so that at least two of us were there in the evenings.

"You're driving," I said as I threw the keys to him.

"Fuck yeah, I love driving this truck. Bitch purrs when I got her in my clutches."

"Just get my ass home in one piece and stop talking nasty."

Sometimes I wanted to punch him, but I loved the big bastard too much to bloody his face.

"Just don't wreck her," I said as he pulled into traffic.

"I should've been an Indy driver. I feel the need, the need for speed," he hollered as he gunned it.

"Shut the fuck up and drive," I mumbled before closing my eyes, not really wanting to watch his idea of NASCAR.

CHAPTER EIGHT

MIA

THROWING DOWN MY BAG, I reached over the counter and grabbed the phone. Cammie was busy helping a patient book their next appointment.

"Hello?" I said as I surveyed the crowded waiting room.

"I need an appointment as soon as possible," the lady yelled in the phone, panic evident in her voice. "There's something wrong with my baby."

"Is the baby able to breath?"

"Yes," she cried. "She has a fever and is coughing, help me."

"How high is the fever?"

"103.1."

"Bring her in right away. I'll see you immediately. Hurry."

"Thank you," she said before the line went dead.

"Girl, you know we're booked. Whatcha doin'?" Cammie, the slightly round and always bubbly receptionist, asked.

"It's a mom, Cam. You know I can never say no when there's a kid involved."

"Oh Lord, child. Are you going to have time to see her with all this?" She waved her hand toward the waiting room and grimaced.

"Yes, Cammie, I'll make the time. Let me know as soon as she gets here. I'm going to put everything away and I'll come grab a chart."

"It's a full house today. I brewed a fresh pot of coffee—from the looks of you, you'll need it." Cammie felt like a fill-in for my mom when she wasn't around.

"Glad to know I look like shit, Cam," I said. "Thanks."

"Not shit, just tired, Mia. I know you don't sleep well; that's why I always have a fresh pot on hand when you're here. Now, get your butt to work, Mia." She swatted my ass. "We have souls to heal."

"Yes, ma'am."

I put away the free medication I was able to score courtesy of the pharmaceutical rep that visited the hospital this week, before grabbing a chart off the counter and diving right in.

"Mr. Needlemyer," I said from the doorway.

He looked up at me and a smile broke out across his face. "Ah, Dr. G," he said as he pushed himself off the chair, struggling with the simple task. "Looking beautiful as always."

"How are you feeling, Mr. N?" I asked, as he approached.

"Like an old fart." He snorted.

"I hope I look half as good as you when I'm your age." I smiled at him, patting him on the shoulder.

"Eh, looks are deceiving. My insides are worn out, but if I were just a few years younger…" He gave me a wink.

I slapped his knee as he sat down on the exam table. "Mr. N., come on now."

Since the first day I met him, he'd flirted with me… relentlessly.

"So tell me, how are you really feeling? Any problems like dizziness, fatigue, or any changes since last time I saw you?" I flipped through his chart, checking his vitals from his last visit.

"I feel about as good as I can for a man my age. Nothing new to report, doc. Right as rain."

I listened to his heart, checked his lungs, and felt his lymph glands before I wrote a refill for his blood pressure and cholesterol pills.

He sat on the exam table and watched me as he fidgeted with his hands.

"Something you want to ask me, Mr. N?"

"Well, um, kind of. I've been seeing this special lady. I wanted to talk to you about that little blue pill. Can I take it?"

"Do you need it? That's the more important question." I inched closer to him so we could talk a bit quieter. "Do you have a problem getting and maintaining an erection?"

His face turned pink as he looked away, momentarily avoiding my gaze. "I don't think so, but it's been so long since I've been with a woman. My wife died over five years ago. I don't know if the ol' pipes still work," he said, giving me a weak smile.

"Ever had any trouble in the past?"

"Never." He shook his head, looking down.

"With your medical history, I wouldn't feel comfortable prescribing it. If you have trouble with your lady, call me and I'll help you out."

"Doc, be still my beating heart."

"You know what I mean, Mr. Needlemyer." I blushed.

Did men ever lose their dirty minds?

"I do. If I have any problems with," he said, coughing, "I'll call you."

"Here are your refills, and I'll see you next month; just make an appointment with Cammie on your way out."

"Wishful thinking at my age."

"You'll be fine," I said as I laid my hand on his. A knock on the door made him jump. "Yes?" I called out.

"The mother is here with her child," Cammie yelled through the door.

"Coming," I said. "Mr. Needlemyer, I need to go, but remember to call me if you have any problems." I closed the chart and stood.

"Go ahead, doc. I'll be fine."

"Thanks, Mr. N." I waved to him as I shut the door and headed to the waiting room.

I knew there was joy in motherhood, but I'd always seen the other side, where children are sick or injured, and the panic in the mothers' eyes. I wasn't ready to become a mother, not yet. I had a career to focus on and a life to live before I invited a bundle of joy into my life.

After examining the baby and determining that she had a lung infection, I gave the mother antibiotics and directions to help her breathe easier. She left the clinic feeling relieved and looking calm.

The rest of the day was a blur—countless patients with various illnesses. At four o'clock the waiting room had finally emptied. I'd been so busy I didn't spend much time thinking about Michael.

I had a couple hours to get ready for him to pick me up. It'd been a long time since I'd been on a real date.

I wondered sometimes why men didn't ask me out, or never called me for a second date. I think I'm a good catch.

I have my shit together…maybe a little too together and independent for some guys.

"Where you rushing off to, doc?" Cammie asked as I tried to sneak out the door.

"I just have some things to do," I replied, stopping in the doorway.

I never was a good liar.

I could see the giant smile spread across her face. She slammed her hand on the desk and began to laugh. "You go, girl. I want all the details. Shoo now," she said, waving her hands at me.

I blew her a kiss, stepped out into the warm sunshine, and felt a sense of renewed hope.

The clinic didn't leave me zapped of energy and emotionally drained like the hospital.

***

I twirled the razor in my hand and debated with myself about shaving. If I shaved, I felt like I hoped the night would end with a roll in the hay. If I didn't shave, it guaranteed that I wouldn't commit a carnal sin.

Running my fingers over my shin, I could feel the prickle of hair. I sighed and caved, deciding to forgo the European look.

I carefully shaved, then rinsed out the heavy conditioner in my hair before climbing out of the shower. The mirror had fogged over, and I opened the door to let in some of the cool air. I had one hour to blow dry, do my makeup, and get dressed.

I towel dried my hair a little first before walking into my closet to pick out something sexy, as Michael had requested. I found the perfect little black dress that had a very low-cut back and stopped just below the knee. It showed just the right amount of cleavage, but it wasn't trampy. It made people stop and stare.

I wanted his eyes on me tonight, and no one else.

I did my best to do a smoky eye, as they call it in all the fashion magazines. I dried my hair before finishing the rest of my makeup.

As the minutes ticked away, my heart started to pound. I could feel my blood pressure rising. I felt flushed and clammy.

I blotted the thin layer of dampness from my skin just before six and then pulled the dress over my head carefully before strapping on my favorite black heels with the red bottoms.

The day I was able to afford to buy myself a pair was the day I knew I could take care of myself—I'd arrived and stood on my own two feet.

I looked in the mirror one last time and turned around, making sure my underwear didn't show and that everything was in the right place.

"It's just a date. I got this." My pep talk helped a little, until the doorbell rang. I'd never really felt nervous on a date before, but there was something different about him.

"Coming," I yelled, as I walked through the house, grabbing my purse and keys.

I opened it to the stunning man leaning against the doorframe, with the sexiest grin on his face.

He whistled, his eyes raking over my body before landing on my face. "Fucking beautiful. Turn around," he said, twirling his finger in the air. "Absolutely stunning." He held his hand out.

"Thank you. You're looking pretty damn good yourself."

He did, too. Wearing a sky-blue dress shirt, tucked into his black pants, the sleeves rolled halfway up his forearms. He looked like he just stepped out of *GQ* magazine.

His mouth enveloped mine as soon as I locked the door

and faced him. Pulling my body against him, claiming my lips with as much fervor as he had the night before, he stole my breath. His hand on the small of my back felt like a hot iron against my skin, searing into me.

"Ready?" he asked, as he released me.

"Yes," I said, a little too breathily.

He helped me into his pick-up truck before closing the door and jogging around to the driver side. The truck was modern and decked out. It wasn't a redneck truck but a total boy toy, black and trimmed in chrome.

"Where are we headed?" I asked, pulling my dress down to my knees.

"Sunset Beach for dinner." He adjusted and gripped the steering wheel tightly as he glanced at my legs.

"There isn't a restaurant there."

"I know." Resting his arm behind my head, he backed out of the drive.

I uncrossed my legs and shifted in my seat, and he glanced down before looking back toward the road.

"What did you do today?" he asked.

"Worked at the free clinic in town, and you?"

"I worked out and went to the shop for a couple hours. Tell me about the clinic."

I told him about the work we did, and the residents in the county that lacked simple things like medicine and insurance. He listened intently and asked questions throughout our conversation.

"Kids too?" he asked with a furrowed brow.

"They're the saddest to see." I frowned, looking out the window.

He rested his hand on my knee and squeezed, causing a wave of warmth to emanate through my body. "I never knew there was such a problem."

"Homelessness and poverty is pervasive in this area, Michael. Underemployment is almost an epidemic."

"Is there anything I can do to help?" His eyes were soft when he looked at me, waiting for the traffic light.

"Not unless you have a medical degree." I laughed.

"Don't have that, but there has to be another way I can help. My family does a lot of charity work. My parents are huge in helping people in the area."

"Maybe. We do have a small fundraiser coming up. Last year we raised ten thousand dollars, which helped us update some of the equipment in the clinic, but there's so much more that's needed."

I didn't really want to ask for his help, but if his family already helped organizations in the area, I couldn't turn it down.

"I honestly have never heard of it. I'm sure my family would love to help."

"It's very kind of you, Michael." I smiled at him. His kindness made me feel giddy.

"I've always had a soft spot for kids."

"Do you have any of your own?" I didn't want to pry, but I wanted to know his situation.

Did he have a crazy-ass ex or a gaggle of kids running around all over town that I needed to be aware of before we went any further?

"No kids, you?"

"No, I barely have time to date with work, let alone have a child."

"You shouldn't work so much, Mia. Life's too short not to enjoy it."

Staring out the window, I thought about his words. I did enjoy my life, didn't I? "I do enjoy my life," I said without conviction.

"Are you telling me or trying to convince yourself?" he asked, as we pulled into the deserted parking lot.

"Where's everyone? I've never seen the parking lot empty before."

"It's closed for a private event."

Giving him a confused look, I asked, 'Then why are we here?"

He turned off the engine and turned toward me. "I rented the beach for tonight. It's all ours."

"I don't know what to say," I said as he climbed out of the truck. "Does this man know how to do anything small?" I mumbled, as I reached down and removed my heels before he opened the door.

"Great idea," he said as he looked at my feet. He kicked off his dress shoes and threw them on the driver's-side floor before helping me down.

A small white canopy sat in the distance, near the edge of the crashing waves. The sand felt hot on my soles, the sun still beating against the small glass crystals. It was like walking on warm pillows as it squished between my toes.

"Thank you," I said as I stared at the waves crashing against the shore.

"For what?" he asked, sliding his hand into mine.

"The beach at sunset. It's one of my favorite places and I rarely get to come here." I squeezed his hand, feeling completely at peace.

"It's one of my favorites, too. Great for thinking and getting away from it all," he said as we approached the canopy.

A small, round table was in the middle, decorated with a white linen tablecloth, fine white china, wine glasses, and candles. The floor was the warm sand, and a chandelier hung from the beams. Soft music filled the air, along with the warm breeze flowing off the ocean waves.

It may have been the single most romantic date I'd ever had.

"You did all this in a couple hours?" I asked, in shock.

"I have mad skills, and connections don't hurt either." He laughed.

"I may have underestimated you, Michael," I said as I kissed his cheek and inhaled his musky scent, mixed with the salty ocean air.

"Most people do," he said as he pulled out my chair.

Leaning over, I brushed my fingers against his cheek. "You're sweet," I said, wanting to kiss him.

Grabbing my hand, he planted a sensual kiss on the inside of my wrist, making my knees feel weak. If he kept this up, my panties would be wetter than the sand after high tide.

"Thanks," I said, sitting as I brushed the bottom of my dress against my legs.

Michael lifted my chair off the ground, tucking my legs under the table before taking a seat across from me.

A man dressed in a tuxedo poured champagne and smiled at us both.

Michael looked at me, raising his glass. "A toast," he said, tilting his head.

I grabbed my glass, holding it up to his.

"To new beginnings." He clinked his glass against mine.

That was the second time he'd used that phrase. A warm, gooey feeling oozed through my body as I sipped the champagne, letting the tiny bubbles pop on my tongue. We had run into each other less than forty-eight hours ago, but I felt comfortable with him—content.

I placed the glass on the table. "Tell me more about you," I said, rubbing my fingertips across the crystal stem.

"What would you like to know?" he asked, as he motioned to the gentleman.

"Are you a piercer or a fighter?"

Two dishes were placed in front of us. Each contained a mouth-watering steak with asparagus and a baked potato. The man grabbed my napkin off the table and placed it on my lap.

Looking at him, I smiled. "Thank you, sir."

"My pleasure," he said, before walking away and making himself busy.

"I'm part-owner in the tattoo shop. I don't have the artistic ability that the rest of my siblings have, so I learned everything I could about piercing. I've been doing it for years. I couldn't tattoo even if I wanted to. My hands get pretty messed up sometimes after a fight."

"I still can't wrap my head around the fact that you let someone hit you."

"Only if they're fast enough," he said as he laughed.

"Why?" I cut into my steak, avoiding his gaze.

"It's a rush, Mia. I can't explain it, but it's the greatest high ever."

"I still think it's barbaric."

"Street fighting is barbaric, not MMA matches. We both know what's going to happen. It's sport."

"Softball is a sport and much safer," I said, placing the steak on my tongue.

He laughed, and it was so genuine that it warmed my body from the inside out. "It's a sport for girls. No offense to you."

"None taken," I said as I waved my fork in the air. "Sexist, but I wouldn't expect anything less." I laughed, covering my mouth with the back of my hand.

"Hey, now. My sister would kick my ass if she thought I was sexist."

"Oh? Tell me about her. She sounds like my type of girl." I giggled.

"Yeah, you and Izzy would get along very well. She's the baby in the family, but we're all scared of her. She's an *in your face* kind of girl. She takes no shit, but I guess that happens when you grow up with four brothers."

"She's lucky. Sounds like a great way to grow up."

"She'd see it differently."

"Why?" I asked with a frown. "I'm an only child, and I always wanted someone to play with as a kid."

"She didn't get many dates as a teenager." He laughed. "We scared most of them away."

"I could only imagine, but she was lucky to have brothers that cared."

"You'll have to tell her that."

"So, there are three more of you walking around?"

"Yeah. We're all very different. My brother Thomas is an undercover cop, Anthony likes to call himself a musician, and Joseph is just a tattooist."

"Your poor mother." I shook my head and sipped the champagne.

"She kept trying for a girl, which she got after four boys. Now she wants grandchildren." He smirked at me.

"Oh." My stomach flipped from the look on his face.

He was so drop-dead gorgeous, I'd almost be willing to drop my panties and start working on making her dream a reality.

"Enough about kids. Tell me about your family, Mia." He wiped his mouth and set his napkin on the table.

"My parents are snowbirds, and right now they're back in Minnesota. It's just me here, but I would never move back to the freezing cold."

"Cold has some good points." He rested his head on

his hands and watched me as I cut the last piece of steak on my plate.

"Like what?"

"Lying by a fire and being snowed in together."

"Those are the only positives. I think more of scraping my car windows, shoveling snow, frostbite, and other crappy things that go with Minnesota life."

We stared at each other as I chewed the last morsel and finished off the champagne in the glass. The sun hovered over the ocean, and the sky blazed with the most beautiful shades of red and orange.

He stood, holding out his hand. "Come on, Mia, let's go watch the sunset."

"I thought we were," I said, placing my hand in his, feeling the electricity that sizzled between us.

"I want to be a little more comfortable for the show. I have a blanket that's calling our name."

Walking hand in hand, we snuck glances at each other as we approached the blanket. Suddenly I felt shy, and my stomach flipped as I sat down and he moved behind me.

"Come here," he said, placing his legs on either side of me and grabbing my hips.

I closed my eyes, inhaling sharply from the feel of his fingers digging into my flesh. I shimmied my body backward until our upper bodies connected. The warmth that permeated off him felt hotter than the setting sun hanging just above the horizon.

"Lean back, Mia," he whispered in my ear, sending a chill across my skin.

Placing my hands against his knees, I rested my head on his shoulder and stared at the sky. Peace overcame me as I sat straddled between his legs; our bodies connected, and we watched the changing colors over the water. His fingers traced a path around my ear to my neck and brushed the hair off my shoulder.

"It's so beautiful," I said as tears formed in my eyes.

"Not as beautiful as you. Are you crying?" he asked with knitted brows.

"I don't know," I said, laughing and wiping at the corners.

"Do you want me to take you home?" His lips brushed against my temple as he watched me.

"No," I said quickly.

"Then what's wrong, doc?" He wrapped his arm around my chest and gripped my shoulder.

"I'm going to sound crazy."

Damn it. How could I explain the peace and happiness I felt without sounding like a total wack job?

"I'd rather know than sit here and wonder why I've made you cry," he said, stroking my collarbone with his thumb.

I shook my head and sighed, relaxing against his body. "I'm stressed out after work, and sometimes it takes me days to shake off what I've seen at the hospital. It's been a long time since I felt truly at peace, but being here, in your arms and watching the sunset with the sound of the waves, I feel it—serenity that I haven't been able to find in so long."

"I can't imagine the things you've seen." He pulled my body closer, wrapping his arms around me, making me feel safe and secure, enveloped by his warmth and muscle.

"You don't want to, Michael. The people I've lost haunt me at night. I can't remember the last time I slept without a nightmare or sleeping pills." I placed my hand on his arm and squeezed. "So to have this brief moment where I'm reminded of the world's beauty and feel like only the two of us exist brings tears to my eyes. You chased away the demons, if only for a little while." I stared across the water, watching the sky turn purple as the sun kissed the edge of the world.

"Stay in the here and now. Nothing else matters but the two of us, on this beach, in each other's arms. I'm not going anywhere, are you?"

"We can't stay like this forever," I said, turning my face toward him.

"I'll stay as long as you need to help chase away your nightmares, Mia." Grabbing my chin, he pulled my mouth to his.

We stared at each other, and I searched his eyes. They were soft and kind and made my heart feel funny. Michael Gallo did not fit the mold of fighter bad boy. He was a romantic, and made me feel like the only person that mattered in the world.

My body ignited as his lips pressed against mine. He glided his hands across my shoulder until they rested against my throat. My heart danced under his fingertips as he kissed me softly.

Our eyes remained open as I turned in his arms and straddled him. Our breathy moans and the lapping of the waves on the shore were the only sounds, as his kiss became more demanding and I opened to him.

I never wanted to kiss someone as much as I wanted Michael to ravage my mouth and put his hands all over my body. The power of his grip on my back as I kissed him had me wanting more. Pushing him back against the blanket, I sat up and stared down at him, as his hands slid up my legs and caressed my hips.

As I leaned forward, my hair sheltered us from the world as it cascaded around his head. "Make me forget, Michael," I whispered.

His hand stilled. Squeezing my thighs, he leaned

forward and nipped at my lips. I collapsed against his chest, my nipples hardening with the contact. His cock grew hard and I gasped in his mouth.

"Sorry, doc. Some things I can't control," he mumbled against my lips.

His hands roamed my body as our lips and tongues stayed entwined. Fisting his hair in my hands, I demanded to be kissed harder. My body ached for his touch. I wanted to be filled and feel alive, as I ground myself against him to relieve the throb I hadn't felt in so long.

A small moan escaped his lips, as he grabbed my hips, his fingers digging into my flesh.

"Not here, Michael. Not like this," I whispered, leaning over him.

"I wasn't even thinking about it, Mia." He looked in my eyes as he pulled my face closer to his. "You want to stay or do you want me to take you home?"

I wanted to stay on the beach in his arms all night, but I couldn't. I wasn't ready to give myself to him, and I knew the longer I kissed him the more I'd want to.

"Take me home," I whispered against his lips, still feeling his hardness against me. A lump formed in my throat as I questioned my decision.

Sitting up, he adjusted my body, breaking the contact that had almost driven us over the edge. "Just promise me that you'll see me again."

The lump that had formed in my throat disappeared, and was replaced by warmth that flowed throughout my body. Leaning forward, I rested my forehead against his and listened to his breathing—rapid and jagged. "I'd love to, Michael. Thank you."

"What are you thanking me for?" he asked, backing away.

"For not pressuring me and still wanting to see me after I turned you down."

"Mia," he said as he grabbed my face, "if anything, it made me want to see you more. I didn't think that was even possible. I like you a lot, and we'll do things at your pace and when you feel comfortable. I didn't do all this just to get in your panties."

"But you were hoping to," I said as I smiled, my face growing flushed.

"I won't lie. I can't wait to rip those off of you and feel your body against mine. It's worth the wait. You're worth the wait," he said, holding my cheek in his hand.

I smiled, resting my hand against his chest. "Want me to take care of that with my needle?" I asked with a smirk, and pointed to his crotch.

His grip on my arms grew tight. "Don't ever, and I mean ever, talk about my cock and your needle again, doc. It was funny at the bar, but right now, not as much." He laughed, his body shaking under mine. "Come on, let's go before you get any more crazy ideas."

I kissed him tenderly, still laughing, as he picked me up and carried me from the beach. Michael wasn't the cocky bastard I thought when I first met him—well, not entirely.

I looked at him in a new light after our first date. There was more to the man, and I wanted to know every inch of him.

CHAPTER NINE

MICHAEL

IT HAD BEEN a week since I'd seen Mia, and I was at my breaking point. I needed to touch her again. We spent the time apart talking on the phone, texting, and learning a lot about each other.

I found out silly things, like her favorite color, which was purple, and that she loved listening to music and dancing around her house.

When she talked about her work, her mood usually changed. "Happiness" wasn't a word I'd use to describe her feelings about her job. The ER seemed to suck the life out of her. When she lost a patient, she'd share her feelings of despair with me.

It was like a punch to my gut, more damaging than any blow I'd ever felt. I couldn't imagine working in a place that was filled with sorrow.

But when she talked about the clinic, the entire conversation oozed happiness. I heard the change in her voice as she told me about the people and how she felt like she made a difference.

Me: Why don't you just work there full-time? It seems to make you happy.

Sitting on my parents' couch, I tried to pay attention to the conversations around me as I texted Mia. Football season had ended, the basketball playoffs were wrapping up, and baseball season became the main after-dinner attraction at the Gallo Sunday dinners.

"Fuckin' Cubs," my pop yelled at the television.

They were his favorite team, and hadn't won a damn thing since before he was born. Think he'd be used to it by now, but not my pop—he was a die-hard believer, and no Gallo would ever be called a quitter.

Mia: It's all donations with little government funding. No money for that.

"Hey, Ma," I said as she sat across from me, rolling her eyes at her still-cursing husband.

"Yeah, baby." She turned to me and smiled.

"Ever hear of the clinic in town that offers free medical care to the poor?"

Her smiled faded as she shook her head. "No, I don't think I have. Why are you asking?"

I shrugged and turned the phone over in my hand. "Just curious. It's all donation based, and I know how the two of you are about helping local charities."

"What do you know about it? If it's worthy, your father and I would be more than happy to help." She leaned back in the chair, picking up her yarn to work on a baby blanket.

"A group of doctors volunteer their time, but I don't know much else. I'll find out about it and let you know." I glanced down at my phone, on silent around my family to avoid the questions.

Mia: Hey, what time are you picking me up?

"Okay, baby." She placed the blanket over her lap before starting to work on it.

Me: At five, and wear a swimsuit under your outfit.

"Who you making that for?" I asked.

"My grandbaby," she said in a flat, even tone.

"Is someone having a baby I don't know about?" I asked as I looked around the room, but everyone ignored us.

"Not yet." She frowned and said, "Soon, though, I hope."

I looked at Suzy, who was staring at the television, a little too engrossed in the game. She hated sports, but at the moment she was totally enthralled. My brother, Joe, and Suzy could never tell Ma no. It had become the giant elephant in the room, as both of them always pretended not to hear her when she talked about babies.

"I'm not ready for a kid," Joe leaned over and whispered in my ear. "I'm too busy enjoying Suzy and I'm way too greedy to share my time with her."

"She's not going to stop," I said softly.

"I may be old, boys, but I'm not deaf," Ma said with a laugh.

"Busted," I said.

"I'm watching your face as you type feverishly on that phone, Mike. I hope it isn't the crazy lady," Joe said as he leaned back and turned his attention toward the game.

"Hell no. I've been knocked in the head a couple times, but I'm not stupid."

He hit me on the knee with a smile. "Stupidity isn't the issue—our dicks are the problem."

"Amen to that, brother." I laughed. "Nah, this one isn't like that."

Raising an eyebrow, he said, "They're all like that."

"I haven't even slept with her, Joe."

He looked at me in horror. "When did you meet her?"

"That's a complicated answer."

"I'll take your complicated over the Cubs any day."

"We met at a bar over a week ago, and I took her on a date last week, but she treated me in the ER when I broke my ribs."

"Wait. You went on a real date?" He eyed me suspiciously.

"I did."

"And you didn't sleep with her after?"

I shook my head and smiled. "Nope."

"Well fuck me, never thought that was possible," Joe said, hitting my leg and laughing loudly.

There was no way in hell would I share that I rented the beach, and all the sappy-ass shit I did for Mia.

No fucking way.

That was for her and I, and Joe sure as shit didn't need to know. He'd laugh at me and probably call me Romeo for weeks, but I knew the truth about my brother. He was just as big of a softy as me. He swept Suzy off her feet, and she described him as a Casanova.

"I'm not a walking hard-on. I can date someone without fucking them." I looked at my ma, surprised she hadn't yelled at us for our language, but she was wrapped up in grandbaby world.

The couch shook with his laughter. "We're all walking hard-ons, but I'm proud of you, brother. When are you seeing her again?"

Before I could answer, Izzy walked in and stretched out on the floor with her head perched in her hands as she stared at the television.

"Today." Looking at my watch, I said, "One hour, in fact."

"What's today?" Izzy asked, turning around.

"Nothing, Iz. Why do you always have to be so damn nosy?" I sounded like a dick, and I might as well have put a billboard above my head with my response.

She giggled like she did when she was a little girl watching her favorite television show, *Fraggle Rock*. "God, you boys are so easy to read. Don't come crying to me when this one wants your name tattooed on her body. You sure know how to pick 'em, Mikey."

I swiped my hands across my face, shaking my head. "Where's your man, Iz? We've been dying to meet him," I said, looking down at her.

"Hell no, I'm not bringing him around you baboons for a long time. When I do, you'll know he's the one—until then, he's only for me. Learned my lesson long ago with you boys."

"We're not the same. We've grown up," Joe said, before grabbing Suzy's hand and kissing it.

"In some ways," she said over her shoulder, turning her attention back to the game.

"Anyway," I murmured, changing the subject and looking at my ma. "Hey, Ma, can we have dessert now? I have an appointment."

"On a Sunday?" she asked, putting down the needles.

"He has a date, Mom. A hot one, I'd say, for him to be rushing out of here on a Sunday." Izzy smiled at my mom before looking at me with a shitty smirk.

I grabbed the pillow from the side of the couch and threw it at her. "I have a date, Ma. I have to leave in thirty minutes. Forgive me?"

One thing you didn't mess with was the Sunday Gallo dinner. Days like today, they seemed like torture.

"Anything for love, Michael." She smiled.

She didn't have to say it, but I knew my mother well

enough that she'd do anything for love, even hand out dessert a little early. The visions of babies danced around in her head too much for her to deny any of us a pass on family time, for the chance of love and that elusive grandchild.

CHAPTER TEN

MIA

MY PALMS WERE slick and my heart felt like it would burst as I put on the harness. "I can't believe you talked me into this shit," I said, my hands shaking so badly I couldn't snap the latch between my legs.

"I thought you liked an adrenaline rush, and I know you love the ocean. Couldn't think of a better thing to do. Two-for-one deal." He smiled at me, fastening his harness without a problem.

"Just my fucking luck. Yay," I said, and clapped. "But you forgot one thing." I held up my finger and waved it in the air.

"What?" he asked as he stepped closer, grabbing my finger.

"I'm afraid of heights."

"Shit, I didn't know. Probably the one thing we didn't talk about this week. It's safe, and I'll be with you. It's the most amazing view from up there. We have to do it. I promise, you'll love it."

"And if I don't?" I asked, as I tilted my head and smirked.

"Then I'll do anything you want, but I know you will. Plus, you can just hold on to me and scream. I won't think any less of you—well, not much, at least."

I couldn't believe I was going to follow through and let myself be pulled over the ocean by a thin rope. "Fine, but I can't get this damn thing on," I said, frustrated and scared as I threw up my hands in defeat.

"Let me. It would be my pleasure." He kneeled before me, brushing his hand against my inner thigh as he grabbed one end of the strap.

I sucked in a breath, shuddering, as I grabbed his shoulder to steady myself. If it wasn't bad enough that I was petrified to the point of almost hyperventilating, the feel of his skin against mine took my breath away.

He looked up at me, smirking as he brought the latch forward, rubbing his hand against my other inner thigh. I closed my eyes and ignored how close he was to me, how near his hands were to the ache between my legs.

No matter what I did all week, I couldn't get the throbbing I felt from being on top of him at the beach to go away.

The latch snapped. I could do this. The nearness of him dulled my fear.

His fingers brushed against my mound, sending an electric current through my body, as he grabbed the latch. "Safe and secure," he said, pulling on the latch with a chuckle.

I opened my eyes and looked down at him. "I wouldn't use either of those words right now," I said as I smacked his shoulder.

I wasn't talking about parasailing, either.

"Come on, beautiful. There's no turning back now. Up ya go," he said, grabbing my legs and throwing me over his shoulder.

I squealed as I flopped against his body, my chest colliding with his shoulder. I smacked his back, bouncing as I kicked trying to break free. "Put me down!" I yelled through a laugh.

"My view is too damn good to do that, doc," he said, and swatted my ass.

"Pig." I reached down and tried to pinch his ass.

Fucker was rock solid, and I could barely get enough between my fingers.

"Nice try," he said, unaffected by my effort and swatting me on the ass again.

I yelped, the sting from his palm making me wish I could reach back and rub the tender spot. "Ugh," I said as I bounced and grew slack in his arms, finally defeated.

The beach disappeared as he stepped on the boat. "Will you put me down now, please?" I asked, trying to sound sweet as sugar.

"If I must," he said, before placing a light kiss against my hip.

I closed my eyes and tried not to think about it, about him. The feel of his mouth against skin that hadn't been touched in so long had me at my breaking point.

He wrapped his arms around my legs, pushing the harness into me, before pulling my body down against him. He controlled the speed, making the journey to my feet as drawn out as possible.

By the time my feet touched the boat, I forgot how scared I had been. The sexual frustration I felt trumped everything. "You're not safe," I whispered as I looked up at him with one eye, the sun behind his head almost blinding me.

He laughed, pulling me against his shaking body. "Doc, I'll make sure you survive the trip up there." He bent down, rubbing his nose against mine.

"It's not the ride I'm talking about, Michael."

"I know." He smiled and kissed me, his lips shaking under mine from the laughter still rumbling through his chest.

"You two ready?" the attendant asked as he approached with the hook, ready to attach us to the boat. My whole life rested in the hands of a guy in flip-flops and a baseball hat with a pair of Tom Cruise Ray-Bans. Fucking marvelous.

I shook my head against Michael's forehead before he pulled away.

"Yeah, we're ready," he said to the man, with a nod. "You'll thank me, Mia. It's spectacular."

I smiled and kept my mouth shut. Right now, being in the air felt a whole lot safer than standing here touching and kissing Michael. My resolve was wearing thin.

The man attached us to the parasail and the boat. There were so many cords and ropes it made my head spin.

Butterflies filled my stomach as the boat started to skip across the water, and I reached for Michael's hand and squeezed. I could already feel the scream inside me building in my belly.

He turned and smiled, returning my squeeze, before leaning over and kissing my temple.

With the whoosh of the air in my ears, the sunshine on my face, and Michael by my side, I felt a combination of excitement and fear. The driver motioned thumbs up to us. Michael nodded before the man released the lever.

We glided backward and anxiety gripped me as the boat disappeared, turning to a sea of blue. "Fuck," I said, clinging to Michael's arm as I stared at the water passing below my feet.

"Nails," he said, as his arm grew tense under my grip.

I looked at him and yelled, "What?"

His eyes shot to my hand currently in a death grip as he yelled, "Your nails, Mia."

"Whoopsie," I said with a smile, and removed my fingernails from his skin. Blood dotted the surface where my fingers had been. "I'm sorry," I mouthed, the wind making it impossible to hear. "Oh shit," I screamed, as my stomach plummeted and the parasail rose in the air. The rope was rigid and we were the highest we could go. I sealed my eyes shut, scared to look. Gripping Michael with one hand and with the other holding the rope next to my head, I concentrated on my breathing and repeated "I will survive" over and over again in my head.

Michael patted my hand, and I peeked at him through one eye. "Look, Mia, there are dolphins," he yelled, pointing to the water.

I tried to swallow, but my mouth felt like sandpaper. I followed his finger with my eyes. Below us were three dolphins jumping in and out of the wake as they kept up with the boat.

Even though I spent a lot of time at the beach in college, I rarely saw much of anything in the water besides the tiny fish near the shore.

I became lost in their play, taking in the moment and forgetting my fear. Michael stroked my fingers as I watched with a giant smile on my face. It was breathtaking, and reminded me that we were just a small part of this planet.

The parasail jolted, and I almost lost the contents in my stomach out of fear as the driver started to reel us in. Michael squeezed my hand and laughed from the obvious look of fright on my face.

A small pang of sadness hit me as we descended toward the water. The dolphins disappeared below the surface as we hovered over the boat.

"It's all over, Mia. You did it," he said as our feet touched the boat deck.

"I did," I muttered as I grabbed his arms and tried to gain my balance. My legs felt shaky as I wobbled from the sway of the waves against the small boat. "I n*ever* want to do that again."

"Don't you feel alive, though?" He looked pretty damned pleased with himself.

I couldn't be shitty with him. He looked too sexy with his brown hair tousled and windblown, his cheeks sun-kissed, and his body glistening from the heat.

I smiled, but couldn't lie about the sheer panic I had experienced. "I always knew I was alive, Michael. You almost killed me with fear alone."

"Mia, I thought you'd love it. You said you loved the beach and I thought I'd give you a whole new view." His thumbs rubbed my arms, calming me. "I won't make you go again. I'm sorry."

I shook my head and smiled. "I'm just being an asshole. It's okay, really. It's something I would've never done, and I liked it once I saw the dolphins, but I don't think I could do it again."

"It's off limits." He grabbed my face, kissing me passionately, making my tension melt away. "It won't happen again," he murmured against my lips.

"It's okay," I replied, my mind mush and the fear forgotten.

"Want me to carry you?" he asked, as the boat docked. "I liked helping you when we boarded." He smirked.

"I can do it," I said as I pushed him away and stepped on the wooden dock.

"You ruin all the fun."

"My ass in your face is not *fun*, Michael." I fiddled with

the latch between my legs and couldn't get the bastard unclipped.

"It's the best kind of fun there is, Mia." He watched me, rubbing his chin. "You want help with that?"

"No, no. I got it." I still felt buzzed from the rush and fear that had coursed through my system during the parasailing ride. I certainly didn't need his fingers brushing between my legs again.

His laughter filled the air as I yanked and pulled to no avail, trying to break free from the harness. Luck wasn't on my side today. I hung my head and whispered, "Can you help me, please?"

Without a word, he bent down and ran his hands up my legs slowly before grabbing the harness and giving it a quick jerk. "I'm more than happy to help you down here."

"Just unhook me, please," I said, closing my eyes, trying to block out the feel of him against my skin. "You're torturing me on purpose."

"It doesn't have to be torture, doc. I don't have a needle, but I can find a way to ease your suffering." He winked as I looked down at him.

"I'm thirsty," I squeaked out, wanting to avoid thinking about the ways he could help me. If I thought about it too long, I'd give in and throw myself at him.

"Avoiding the offer," he said, with a hint of laughter. "Let's grab a drink and watch the sunset again."

Thank God he let me off the hook. Another stroke of his hand would've sent me over the edge and begging for his cock. He stood and grabbed my hand, leading me to a tiny beach bar with colorful umbrellas.

A reggae band played while we sipped on ice-cold beer and waited for the sun to set. His free hand stroked mine, toying with my fingers, never breaking contact.

Just as the sky started to change to a vibrant shade of red, a crack of thunder caused everyone to jump and scream.

"Come on, Mia," Michael said, pushing out his chair as he stood.

Large droplets of water splashed down on the metal table as I reached for his hand. Thunder rumbled as we ran from the patio toward his car.

My swimsuit and cover-up were drenched as we made our way through the parking lot. My hair slapped against my skin, lashing my face with each bounce. The sky lit up, the lightning in the distance causing the ground to shake as we climbed in the cab, slamming the doors to the truck.

We wiped our faces as small drops fell from our hair. I flipped back my hair, pushing it out of my eyes, and ran my hands down my arms, watching the water splash to the floor. "Jesus, that scared the crap out of me," I said, shaking from the excitement.

"Just when you were relaxing, God finds a way to give your ass a jolt." He laughed, grabbing his chest.

"You're a funny man, Michael. I don't think my heart can take much more today."

He leaned over, pulling me into his arms as he grabbed my chin and tipped it back. "I have something that'll take your mind off of it while we wait for the storm to pass."

His brown eyes held my gaze before he crushed his lips against mine. If the interior of the truck hadn't been hot and steamy enough, being close to Michael, wrapped in his arms and smothered by his kiss, made it close to impossible to breathe.

His hand rested against my back, pulling me closer, and I became lost in his kiss. The feel of his rough thumb pad as he stroked my face made my body feel on fire. The sound of the rain beating against the truck, the thunder rumbling outside, and our breath, frantic and quick, filled the cab.

I climbed in his lap as he gripped my ass and pulled my bottom to him. I could feel his hardness against me, and I ached to feel him inside.

I couldn't deny myself any longer.

"Take me home, Michael. Stay with me tonight." I didn't even have to think about it.

I wanted him.

The light touches, commanding kisses, and feel of his hardness had me wanting more, needing it.

"Mia, I don't know if that's a good idea," he whispered against my lips.

"I want to feel your skin against me. Remind me what it feels like to be loved, Michael. Show me the beauty and make me forget." I held myself up and stared in his eyes. "Please."

His fingers swept against my cheek and I leaned into his touch, closing my eyes. "I'll do anything you ask," he said.

I smiled at him before climbing off his lap. "I don't want to be alone tonight," I said as I put on my seatbelt.

He started the truck and grabbed my hand, stroking it, with a smile on his face. We sat in silence as I stared out the window during the drive.

I wasn't alone in life, but I did feel lonely.

Being with Michael reminded me how much I missed that connection to another person. I wanted someone to hold me until I fell asleep and comfort me when the nightmares came.

Our bodies stayed connected as he drove; the energy never waned.

"Mia, are you sure about this?" he asked as he pulled in my driveway.

Turning toward him, I smiled. "Never been more sure about anything in a long time, Michael."

CHAPTER ELEVEN

MICHAEL

"YOU WANT to just go to sleep?" I asked, giving her one final out. "I don't know if I can do gentle, Mia. I'm giving you fair warning." I held her face in my hands as I pushed my hardness against her.

"Don't be gentle with me, Michael. I'm not going to break." She pushed against my chest, breaking the kiss. "Shower first," she said, pushing me toward the shower. "We're covered in sand."

"Only if you're coming in with me." I smirked and reached in the shower to turn on the water before pulling off my rain-soaked shirt.

As she ran her soft fingers across the tattoo on my chest that spelled *Gallo*, my dick ached and strained in my pants. I wanted to be inside her. Her touch felt like torture.

"Verita?" she asked, running her nail down the letters on my ribs.

Goose bumps dotted my flesh. "It means 'truth' in Italian," I said, trying to keep my voice even.

Walking behind me, she kissed my shoulder before sinking her teeth into my flesh.

Inhaling sharply, I tensed. "If you do that again, we won't make it to the shower," I said, on shaky breath. I wanted to feel her nails rake across my balls as she sucked me off. "My turn." I turned around to face her.

I slowly lowered the straps of her swim dress, holding it between my fingers, as the material clung to her skin. As her dress slid from her body, it cascaded to the floor. She stood before me in nothing but her black bikini. Her breasts made my mouth water, as her nipples grew hard with the cool air. She stood stock-still and looked at the floor with her cheeks turning a light shade of pink, as I took in her beauty.

I placed my fingers under her chin, forcing her eyes to mine. "You're breathtaking." A small grin spread across her face, but there was uncertainty in her eyes. "Stunning, actually. You still want this, Mia?" I had to know for certain that she wanted to be with me.

She nodded and palmed my dick through my swim trunks. I shuddered, the ache turning into a throb with the warmth of her hand. Reaching down with a smirk, she pushed from the sides of my trunks, but it caught on my stiffness.

I chuckled when her eyes grew wide, and I heard her swallow.

She yanked harder, before they slid down my hips and fell to the floor with a thump.

As I stepped forward, my cock brushed against her soft, wet skin. Closing my eyes, I inhaled, needing a moment to get my hunger under control.

I wanted to slam her body against the wall and take her, but I wasn't here to hit it and quit it.

Leaning into me, she grabbed my sides and squeezed, her breath catching as my cock bobbed against her stomach.

I ran my mouth along her cheek, relishing the softness of her skin. There was a connection there, something greater than us, and out of our control. We both needed this.

The running water and the sound of our breath filled the room as our lips smacked against each other. I kicked the trunks free from my feet, hissing into her mouth, as her fingers grazed the tender, aching flesh of my dick.

I craved her touch more than I thought possible.

She lightly touched the top of my shaft before running her nails across the head, moving underneath. Her hand stilled as she felt the first piercing and she froze.

I'd failed to mention my hardware.

I grinned, opening my eyes to see her expression.

Her eyes grew wide as she peered down before continuing to feel the underside of my cock.

"Never felt a Jacob's Ladder before?" I asked with a smirk.

"No, I've seen them, but never felt one." She palmed my cock and pulled it up, getting a better view. Biting down on her bottom lip, she gawked at it like it was going to bite her.

"Wait until you feel it inside, sweetheart," I whispered in her ear, as I slid her thong down her legs, waiting for her to step out.

I picked her up and she wrapped her legs around me. It took everything in me not to sink my dick into her as I reached in the shower to check the temperature.

With one foot in the shower, she stopped me, digging her feet in my ass. "Wait."

Fucking hell. My cock was going to explode at any moment. Just carrying her was enough friction to set me off.

"What's wrong?" I asked, resting my forehead against hers.

"We need a condom. Do you have one?" she asked, biting down on her lip.

"Fuck, I don't. Didn't plan on sinking my cock balls deep in ya, doc." I laughed. "Do you?"

"I have one. It's in the top drawer on my nightstand. Put me down and I'll go grab it." She started to pull away.

I shook my head, pulling her tighter against my body. "Hell no, we're not leaving this position. You feel too fucking good to put you down now."

She giggled as I carried her to the bedroom. Leaning over, I held her ass, keeping her in my arms, as she reached into her nightstand.

"Don't look!" She tried to cover my eyes with her hand as she opened the small drawer.

"Whatcha got in there?" I asked, even though I could see through her fingers.

The drawer overflowed with lace panties, and my eyes zeroed in on a sex toy. I liked a girl that didn't have a problem with masturbation. I'd give my left nut to watch her use it on herself.

"Nothing. Stop peeking." She dug her heels in harder, rubbing my cock against the warmth of her pussy.

I was about to explode if she wiggled any more against me.

Her hand moved through the drawer as she put on an acrobatic act to stop me from seeing the contents. "Got it," she said as her hand emerged with a condom before she pushed the drawer closed.

I captured her fingers in my mouth as they fell from my eyes. Sucking the soft digits, I ran my tongue along her succulent flesh.

She held the condom up to my eyes as her eyes rolled back in her head. "You play dirty," she whispered.

I released her fingers as I squeezed her ass roughly in my palms. "You have no idea, Mia." I kissed her, not wanting a reply.

She fisted my hair, sucking on my bottom lip as I carried her into the shower. As her back collided with the cold tile, she gasped in my mouth.

I rubbed my throbbing cock against her pussy, loving the sounds of her moans. She felt velvety soft, and I didn't know how much longer I could wait to be inside.

I wanted to touch her; holding her body up in my arms just wasn't doing *it* for me. Moving to the small corner bench, I placed her body on it and stood.

"Condom?" I asked, stroking my shaft.

She watched with wide eyes, and placed the condom in my palm softly.

I tore open the wrapper with my teeth, as she stared, mesmerized by my movement. I rolled it down, paying careful attention to each piercing, not wanting to tear the thin latex.

I picked her up and placed her in my lap as I sat down, my ass hanging over the edge slightly. I licked a trail to her collarbone, the saltiness filling my tongue as I continued my descent to her breast. I leaned her body back, holding her in my grip as I tried to get a better angle. I captured her nipple in my mouth, and her head fell back, a moan escaping her lips. I ran my tongue over the hardness and bit down.

"Jesus," she said as she rubbed against my cock, writhing in my arms.

Reaching between us, I ran my fingers through her wetness before I found her clit. As I rubbed, making tiny circles, her movement became more demanding, and she pressed herself against my hand. "Not yet. I want to feel your pussy squeeze the life out of my cock when you come."

"I make no promises if you don't do it soon." She took control of the situation as she pushed harder, rocking her hips. Her moans grew louder.

I moved my hand, denying her what she had been so close to accomplishing.

She glared at me, stilling her body against me.

Leaning back, I stroked my cock against her body before I pushed…slowly. I had to go slow; I felt like I'd come at any moment if I didn't move at the torturous pace.

I held her by the hips as I gripped her roughly. I didn't want her to slam down on my shaft and take it deep, at least not yet. I pulled her body down, impaling her with my cock as I sucked her nipple.

When her pussy was an inch from having my entire shaft buried inside her, I thrust my hips upward, burying my dick inside her.

She let out a gasp as the tip hit her cervix. "Oh," she said as her eyes closed partially, and I pulled out just as slowly as I went in, not releasing her hips or giving her the ability to fuck me.

"Feel them?" I asked, studying her face.

"Yes, oh. My. God. I. Do," she said, stumbling on each word as I moved in and out of her.

I couldn't control myself anymore. Fuck this. I never liked slow. I wasn't built for it.

Her feet were barely touching the floor as I pulled her down my length. I controlled her like a rag doll in my arms as I fucked her.

God, she felt fanfuckingtastic.

My thighs burned as I plunged inside of her, pulling her against me with each thrust.

The impact was volcanic.

The sound of our skin slapping and the water sloshing in the shower filled the small space, echoing. Her moans grew louder with each collision until she trembled in my arms.

I couldn't hold out any longer. I picked up the speed, using my dick as a battering ram and her pussy as the object of its blow.

Her body bounced in my arms, her limbs moving on their own as her head fell back, exposing her neck.

"Eyes on me, Mia. I own this orgasm. I earned it."

Her head snapped forward and she stared at me with glassy eyes. Her tits bounced with each blow—a spectacular fucking sight.

My brute force drove her over the edge as she screamed, her pussy milking my cock. I rammed into her as my balls grew tight and my dick began to jerk. My entire body tingled as all my muscles grew stiff.

I began to shake.

Fuck.

I couldn't remember the last time I came with such intensity. It was better than any high I ever chased in my life. Mia had become my new addiction.

CHAPTER TWELVE

MIA

WRAPPING A TOWEL AROUND MY BODY, I looked at him with a small grin. "Michael, will you stay tonight? I'm not looking for anything more from you, but I'd—"

He put his finger against my lips. "I'll stay, Mia. I want to." He pulled his finger away, smiling.

He looked beautiful with a towel around his waist and tiny droplets of water sliding down his muscular torso.

"I mean, I don't want—"

He shook his head, wrapping me in his arms. "Woman, I said I want to. No one makes me do anything I don't want to. There's nowhere I'd rather be than with you. Can you stop talkin' and get that fine ass in bed?"

Biting my lip, wanting to laugh, I nodded and broke free from his embrace.

"Which side?" I asked, as I walked in the bedroom. "I tend to sleep in the middle."

"The middle it is, then—get in and scoot over and I'll work around you," he said, following me.

I nodded, looking down at my towel. "Let me grab some pajamas first."

I took one step away from the bed before he grabbed the towel and pulled, stripping me bare. "Seen it all, doc. Felt it too. No clothes, just us and the bed."

Shrugging, I said, "Okay," with a soft voice.

In the center of the bed, I watched as he folded my towel and disappeared into the bathroom. A moment later, he emerged stark naked, in all his glory. The phrase fit him perfectly. It was a damn glorious sight.

I stared, licking my lips as he walked toward the bed. It's not often a person can actually see the flex and release of a muscle with such definition.

The man didn't have an ounce of body fat anywhere that I could see. Even his ass had felt rock hard underneath my heels earlier.

His cock twitched, and I quickly looked up at his face. My sex ached from the battering it took earlier. I missed that feeling, the one that reminded me of being pleasured.

"Like what you see?" he asked, winking at me as he lifted the sheet.

"Not bad," I said, trying to seem indifferent.

He slid across the material and pressed his body to mine.

His hard to my soft felt amazing.

Brushing the hair off my forehead, he asked, "You sleep on your back or your side?"

"I toss and turn mostly." I stared into his soft brown eyes.

He smiled as his hand stilled against my hair. "Good, I sleep on my back," he said, rolling over. "Come here."

I scooted across the bed as he lifted his arm. I put my head on his chest, sighing, and smiled against his skin. The hardness under my cheek softened as he wrapped his arm around me and started to stroke my arm.

I moved my legs a couple times, trying to get comfortable.

"Put your leg over me. Make yourself comfortable."

I adjusted my body, placing my hand that had been smashed between us on my leg, and wrapped it around his bottom half.

Placing his arm back on my shoulder, he whispered, "Good now?"

"Perfect," I said as I placed my hand against his hard pec.

I stroked the spot between his two pecs, watching the path of my fingers until my eyes felt heavy. Mindlessly running my finger back and forth, I didn't feel the need to toss and turn like normal.

I felt at peace.

"Just close your eyes, Mia." He stroked my forearm and dug his fingers in my hair, massaging my scalp.

I mumbled against his skin, unable to speak, lost in the feel of him all over me.

***

Stirring my cup of coffee, as I watched the cream swirl in the cup, I felt more rested than I had in years.

Michael did this.

I felt so safe in his arms that I didn't wake up once last night with a nightmare. I didn't think I'd had a dream at all, as a matter of fact.

Michael kissed me goodbye early in the morning after we talked about seeing each other again soon.

The relationship wasn't going to be easy, but he promised he wasn't kissing me goodbye.

"You must have had a real good time this weekend, doctor." The voice pulled me out of my happy thoughts. A nurse leaning against the counter studied me with a shitty-ass grin.

"Yeah, it was decent." I didn't feel like talking to her. It was none of her damn business.

Pointing at my neck, she laughed. "From the love bite on your neck, I'd say it was a little more than decent."

I dropped the spoon and my hand flew to the spot that he'd bitten the night before. "Shit," I muttered, covering the spot.

"Happens to the best of us." She giggled and shrugged.

"I have to go cover this up before I see patients. Nice seeing you."

I didn't know her name and felt kind of shitty about not addressing her properly, but there were too many damn people that worked in the hospital to memorize them all.

I started to walk away, but she called out to me, "You're not even going to give me any details? I did help you out."

I called out over my shoulder to her, "I'm in a rush, but maybe another time."

I heard her mumbling nasty words as I closed the door to the bathroom.

"Fuck," I said as I leaned closer to the mirror, inspecting the red mark on my neck.

We were both too caught up to put much thought into anything, especially a hickey.

I pulled a tube of cover-up from my purse and dabbed the cream over the spot on my neck and sighed. It screamed "love bite." I pulled my ponytail to the side as I tried to hide it.

It shouted "hey, I'm hiding something."

I walked down the hall and nodded at the few people who walked by before making it to the heart of the ER.

"Who needs to be seen?" I asked Constance, the station supervisor, as I leaned over the counter, staring at her mountain of paperwork.

"Room seven needs assistance, I think. Check the board." She didn't look up at me as she shuffled the papers.

My eyes looked over each row and stopped dead on one name.

Gallo.

Unable to move, I stared at the board, and heaviness settled over my body. My heart ached as it hammered inside my chest, wanting to burst.

"What's wrong, doc?" Her warm hands touched my fingers, breaking my trance.

"Gallo in room seven," I said, swallowing the lump that had formed in my throat.

"Motorcycle accident, serious injuries. Is there a problem, Dr. Greco? You're white as a ghost."

I shook my head without looking at her. I needed to know if Michael lay in that room. "No, I'm okay. Let me get in there and help."

As I walked down the hallway, I felt like my shoes were filled with cement. I stood outside the room, gathering my thoughts before I walked in.

Even if it were Michael on that table, I had to help save his life.

I needed to separate myself from our…whatever we were.

Holding my breath, I approached the gurney slowly.

A dark-haired man lay motionless on the table covered in blood and dirt. Dr. Patel stood over him, shining a light in his eyes, as nurses hung IVs.

"What do we have, doctor?" My voice cracked.

The heaviness in my chest eased when my eyes flickered on the man's face again.

It wasn't Michael.

"Mr. Gallo, can you hear me?" Patel shouted to him, but he was unconscious. Looking up at me as he placed the light in his pocket, Patel spoke quickly, "Dr. Greco, we have an adult male thrown from a bike but wearing a helmet. His leg is mangled and we've controlled the bleeding. We're still assessing the damage before sending him to surgery. We need to cut his clothing off and check for other injuries."

Grabbing a pair of scissors, I looked at his face before I started to cut the material around his injured leg. "Head trauma?" I asked, looking at the dried blood on his face and neck.

"The helmet took the brunt of it, but he's been in and out of consciousness. We've started him on pain meds for his leg and hand. He came in conscious, but the pain meds knocked him out. We need an x-ray on that leg for the surgeons." His hands never stopped moving as he checked the patient's body for visible damage.

"X-ray, please," I yelled to the nurse near the doorway before she scurried away.

His blood pressure was elevated and needed to be brought under control before surgery.

"Have you started him on anything for his BP?" I asked.

Patel squinted at the monitor and grabbed a small vial from the cart, filling the needle before pushing the liquid into the line.

"Clear the room, please," the technician said, standing in the doorway with the portable x-ray machine.

"After the films are taken, he can be prepped for surgery," Dr. Patel said as we walked into the hall.

I felt useless.

I hated coming into a room late and feeling left out of the diagnosis, which usually happened at the start of the shift.

"He'll need surgery to repair his leg and most likely his hand." Dr. Patel rubbed the back of his neck and sighed.

"I can go talk to the family while you handle the transfer papers if you'd like," I offered.

I needed to see Michael if he was in the waiting room.

Patel nodded, giving me a small smile before going back into the room when the technician called out, "All clear."

My stomach started to cramp as I walked toward the waiting room. I knew the other Gallos would be there.

This wasn't the way I wanted to meet them.

When I pushed opened the door, the first person I saw was Michael. My heart raced and I wanted to jump into his arms. I had the urge to kiss him and tell him how worried I was when I saw his name, but I couldn't.

I needed to remain calm and do my job.

His pained eyes met mine, and the cocky grin he wore so well was missing.

"Gallo family?" I said, staring in his eyes.

"Yes," an older woman said, standing as she wiped her tear-stained face.

I moved toward her, grabbing a chair, and positioned myself close to Michael.

"I wanted to let you know he's being prepped for surgery. Although we don't know the full extent of his injuries yet, we know his leg needs surgery, being badly damaged in the wreck." I looked at Michael, and swallowed as my nose tingled. "His hand is broken and may also need to be repaired. We won't know more until he's in the operating room."

"Was he awake, doctor? Can I see him?" the older woman asked, as she leaned forward, choking on her words.

"He's been in and out of consciousness, ma'am. You can see him when he's in the recovery room."

"Will he live?" the blonde at her side asked, clutching the woman's hand.

"All I can say is that he's currently stable, but his injuries are serious."

I could feel Michael's eyes on me, almost boring a hole in my skin, as I talked with the two women.

Tears began to stream down the younger woman's face as she choked out, "Just make my Joey all right."

I patted her knee, trying to reassure her. "We'll do everything in our power to help him." I stood, looking at the entire family. "You can move to the surgery waiting room when you feel ready. Don't hesitate to ask for updates and watch the monitor on the wall. It'll indicate when the surgery begins and finishes."

Reaching out, the older woman touched my hand. "Thank you, dear."

I nodded before I looked at Michael, giving him a weak smile.

"Come on, Mother, let's go wait where the nice doctor told us for our boy," the older gentleman that sat next to Michael said. Grabbing her by the waist, he helped her walk, allowing her to lean on him for support.

I envied them. They loved each other. I smiled at them until screaming drew my attention toward the hall.

"Outta my fucking way," a woman yelled as she walked into the room.

"Isabella, watch your mouth," the mother said, her voice stern.

Frowning, the woman looked at the floor, not making

eye contact. "Sorry, Ma. What happened to Joe? Is he okay?" Her eyes glistened as a tear slid down her cheek.

The mother touched her face, wiping away the tear. "He's going to surgery. We'll know more soon, baby girl. I know you adore your brother. He's strong and a fighter. He'll be okay," she said, wrapping the girl in a loving embrace.

"He has to be, Ma," Isabella said, crying on her mother's shoulder.

"There, there, baby. Come on, let's go." She rubbed her back to soothe Isabella's sobs.

The older man motioned for everyone to follow him as he walked toward the door.

I turned and looked at Michael, pleading for him to stay with my eyes.

"I'll meet you guys in a second. I need to talk to the doctor," Michael said to his father after everyone else cleared the room.

CHAPTER THIRTEEN

MICHAEL

"DON'T BE TOO LONG," Pop said, watching us with his head tilted, rubbing his lip.

Holding up my hand to him, I said, "Five minutes, tops."

Nodding, he walked out, leaving us alone.

Mia threw herself in my arms with such force that she almost knocked the wind out of me.

Wrapping her legs around my waist and her arms around my neck, she said, "Oh my God, Michael. I was so scared it was you in that room." Her voice broke as the words came out quick. "I wasn't happy it was your brother, but I was relieved it wasn't you."

Leaning back, I put my finger against her lips, stopping her from going any further. She blinked, the corners of her mouth turning up.

"I'm fine, doc. How's my brother, really? Not the bullshit stuff you tell all the families. Lay it on me."

"Sorry," she said, wiping her eyes and swallowing. "It's hard to say right now. He's unconscious, so it's hard to determine the extent of his injuries until he's been fully evaluated, Michael. Thank God he wore a helmet." She slid down my body, resting her hands on my chest.

Holding her cheek in my palm, I caressed the soft skin. "Is he going to live?"

She leaned into my touch, closing her eyes. "I can't answer that with certainty." She didn't open them as she spoke. "I know they will do everything they can, Michael."

I inhaled and held my breath, trying to not break down into tears.

Joe and I had a bond. He was my rock and my best friend. We'd busted each other's balls for as long as I could remember. I couldn't even begin to think about a day without him in my life.

I *wouldn't* think about it.

I rested my forehead against hers. "Just keep me posted, Mia. If you hear anything or if you get any information before us, please don't keep it from me. The waiting is driving me fucking crazy."

She cupped my cheeks and whispered against my lips, "I will, Michael. I'm so sorry."

We stood there for a moment, not moving, touching each other before I kissed her and let her go. "I better go before someone comes looking for me. I need to be there with them."

"I wish I had met them under different circumstances." She frowned, wiping the corner of her eye.

Tipping back her chin, I kissed her lips softly and smiled. "They won't remember. It'll be a blur after all is said and done." I rubbed my nose against hers. "Message me when you get any information."

"I will," she said, before we walked in opposite directions.

***

After I'd been pacing for an hour and staring at the

monitor that stated *Joseph Gallo—Surgery in Progress*, my phone vibrated in my pocket.

Mia: They're starting now. No internal injuries and he woke up before surgery.

I exhaled the breath I'd held in as I pulled out my phone. The sick feeling in my stomach and the lump in my throat subsided as I read her message.

I hated hospitals and wouldn't feel at ease until he walked out of the front door.

Me: That's good news, no?

I looked around the room at my family—I couldn't keep the news to myself. They looked as shitty as I felt.

"I have news," I said as I stopped in the middle of the room.

Everyone looked in my direction with hope in their eyes.

"How?" Isabella asked, scooting forward in her seat. "Doesn't matter," she said, shaking her head. "What is it?"

"My friend who works here said Joe has no internal injuries and that he woke up before surgery. They're working on his leg and hand now."

"Oh, thank God," my ma said as her body visibly relaxed in my father's arms.

"He's going to be okay?" Suzy asked, as she jumped from her seat and approached me.

"Yes, Suzy, babe. He's going to be okay," I said, wrapping her in my arms. I rubbed her back until my phone started to vibrate. I looked over her shoulder to read the message.

Mia: It's great news. Still going to be a long recovery, but he'll survive.

Suzy clung to me, her silent sobs of joy dampening my shirt. Needing the comfort as much as she did, I rested my head against her hair and held her.

"I was so damn scared, Mike," she said, fisting my shirt in her hands.

"I know, Suzy. We all were. You know Joe. He's not going out that easy. He loves you too much to go out that way."

Instead of that consoling her, she cried harder into my chest, breaking out into a sob.

"He's never going back on that goddamn bike. Over my dead body," she muttered into my shirt.

I bit my lip, trying to hold in my laughter. "Good luck with that, Suz. But if anyone can keep him off that bike, it's you."

She patted my stomach as she backed away.

He was so head over heels in love with her that he'd do just about anything to make her happy, but his bike might be a bone of contention.

I knew why my brother loved her so much. Suzy was a special kind of girl—the needle in the haystack. Why he hadn't married the girl was one thing I didn't understand.

They had recently begun building a home on his property in the middle of nowhere. They called it a "love shack," but it was more like a grand palace. My mother was giddy when she learned they would have five bedrooms. She started planning for her future grandchildren immediately like a woman possessed, hence the baby blankets.

I tossed my phone on the side table as I collapsed in the chair and rested my head against the wall. I couldn't relax, even though my eyes burned and my body felt heavy.

Out of the corner of my eye, I noticed the phone dancing across the *Time* magazine, and I scooped it up. I rubbed my eyes as I looked at the screen.

Mia: I'm in the hallway, come out.

Looking around, I saw her standing in the corner as

she motioned for me. My heart sank until I noticed the smile on her face, but I couldn't shake my paranoia about the entire situation.

"I'll be right back," I said as I stood and walked out.

"Hey," she said, walking to me.

"Everything all right? Something wrong with Joe?" Reaching out, I grabbed her hand and squeezed.

"Nah, he's doing great and your family will be able to see him soon." Peeking over my shoulder, she looked in the waiting room. "I wanted to make sure you're okay. I needed to check on you."

I smiled, brushing my thumb across the back of her hand. "Aw, you got a soft spot for me, doc?"

She punched me in the shoulder. "You ass. I was being nice and thoughtful, but you're smug as always, I see." She laughed, the joy touching her eyes.

"I'm doing okay. Everyone is relieved and waiting to see him."

"His surgeon will be in soon to talk and give you the details." She smiled and closed her eyes, exhaling. "I'm glad he made it, Michael." She blinked slowly as her face softened, the smile gone.

"Me too, Mia." I slid my hand up and down her arm before grasping her hand again. "When's your shift end?"

"I don't get off work until tomorrow," she said, moving closer.

"I'm sure I'll see you around tonight and in the morning. I'll be in and out, but can I see you after work tomorrow? Away from all this." I waved my hand in the air.

"I'll be exhausted and useless, but if you want to…I'm yours." Her large hazel eyes sparkled as she smiled.

Warmth spread through my body; from my core it radiated outward to my limbs. "Text me when you're done if I don't see you before then." I touched her cheek. I wanted to lean forward and kiss her, but I stopped myself.

It took everything in me not to give in to my craving.

"I have to go," she said, touching my hand.

The electricity between us felt as strong as the first time we touched.

"I'll text you when I'm done," she said, and pecked me on the lips.

"Don't forget me," I whispered, swiping my finger against her soft cheek.

"One thing you aren't is forgettable, Michael."

She smiled before walking away, and glanced back before turning the corner, disappearing.

Looking at the floor with a stupid grin on my face, I walked toward the waiting room and was met with a pair of black leather boots.

"Who's the girl?" Izzy asked, with a shitty grin and her arms across her chest.

My big-mouth sister should be the undercover cop. She never let anything get past her.

Looking at her with my mouth set in a straight line, I responded, "My friend."

Grinning at me, she turned her head to the side, essentially calling bullshit. "Uh huh," she muttered before moving to the side, letting me pass.

Her stiletto boots click-clacked against the floor as she followed me. She stopped in front of our ma as my ass hit the chair.

"Ma, Michael's friend is a female doctor at the hospital. They looked to be a little more than friends, too." Izzy smirked as my mother looked at me and then back to her.

"Isabella, leave your brother alone," my ma said in a

stern voice, as Izzy sat next to my father and rested her head on his shoulder, glaring at me.

Patting the chair, my ma called to me, "Come sit with me, Michael."

I moved to the seat next to her and winked at Izzy.

My ma squeezed my leg before turning to me. "Did she say anything about your brother?"

I told her everything Mia had shared with me about Joe.

I could see my ma's entire body relax with each word. "Is she your girl, son?" she asked, with a small smile on her face when I finished.

Laughing, I shook my head. "I don't know what we are, Ma. We just met a bit ago."

"It was nice of her to give you information about Joseph. She a good girl, baby?"

I didn't want to get into a debate on her meaning of good. To me, she was that and more. "Yes, Ma. I think she actually is." I grinned, thinking about her tiny snores as she slept.

"Don't let that one go, you hear me?" She arched her eyebrow as she stared at me.

"We just met, Ma."

"A mother knows, son." She winked.

"You just want grandbabies. Let me get to know her first, but I'll hold on tight if she's the one for me, Ma."

"Good, Michael. Now go grab me a cup of coffee, please?"

"Light and sweet?" I asked as I stood.

I'd do anything she asked me to do. I loved my ma.

She was my first love.

"No other way," she said, laughing.

"Anyone want anything? I'm headed to the cafeteria," I

asked, happy to be leaving the room for a bit. I needed to stretch my legs and get some fresh air.

Standing up, Anthony replied, "I'm coming with you. I need to get out of this room for a while."

"We're good," my pop said, placing a hand on Izzy's shoulder as she tried to stand, forcing her back in her seat.

My sister's face turned red and I expected to see fire come out of her nose, but she remained quiet, for once.

***

I stirred the sixth packet of sugar in my ma's coffee as Anthony paid for his drink.

Someone poked me in the shoulder. "Mikey," a female voice purred in my ear.

Fucking shit. I knew that voice.

Tammy.

Psycho Tammy.

Scrapbook Tammy.

Closing my eyes, I felt the need to slap my ear like a gnat buzzed around it, annoying me.

"Where ya been, baby?" she said, grabbing my ass.

I jumped, and the coffee spilled, scalding my hand. "Fuck," I said, gritting my teeth.

I crumpled the packets in my hand and turned around. I didn't really need her fucking bullshit right now.

"Sorry." She smiled as I glared at her. Her smile fell. "I've missed you." She reached out, trying to touch me.

"Tammy." I backed away, my ass bumping into the counter.

"Mikey, I've been thinking about you for days." She wrapped her arms around me. "Why haven't you texted me back?" She stared in my eyes, pouting.

Anthony made faces at me as I looked to him for help. He knew all about her kind of crazy, and loved to see me miserable whenever possible.

Dickhead.

Grabbing her arms, I peeled her off me. "Tammy, we're nothing. You need to get some help."

Her mouth gaped open as she gasped for air.

Holding her firmly, I quietly said, "I don't want to see you or get another text from you. Forget I ever existed." I pushed her body away from mine.

She glared at me. "How could you say that, Michael? We're engaged." Holding her hand in front of my face, she wiggled her finger. A very large diamond ring sparkled on her finger.

She was fucking crazier than I thought.

Shaking my head, I tried to remain calm. "I don't know who gave that to you, but it wasn't me. We. Are. Not. Engaged."

Anthony doubled over in a fit of silent laughter, his body shaking as he grabbed his chest.

Her eyes grew wide, and she covered her mouth with her hand as she shook her head.

"Seriously, Tammy, get some fucking help. I didn't give that ring to you. Don't ever say those words to anyone. We. Are. Nothing. You hear me? Nothing." I gritted my teeth; my jaw ached as I tried to keep myself from screaming.

She shook her head vigorously. "Don't say such hurtful, mean things, Michael."

When she reached out to touch me, I grabbed her wrist and stopped her. "I got too much shit going on right now to deal with your crazy bullshit." Releasing her wrist, I stepped back and glared at her. "Stay the hell away from me."

I smacked my brother on the back of the head as I walked by him and away from Tammy. I needed to get the fuck out of here.

"But I'm having your baby!" she yelled, her voice echoing through the cafeteria.

I stopped dead, my body stiffening as my blood turned cold.

What the fuck did she just say?

Bitch just played her last damn hand, and I sure as fuck wasn't going all in.

I turned around, pointing at her. "I have to go, Tammy. I'll deal with your ass later. Don't call me. I'll call you when I'm ready." I dropped my hand to my side. I squeezed my hands into hard fists before leaving her in the dust.

CHAPTER FOURTEEN

MIA

WALKING INTO THE BATHROOM, I saw the nosy nurse who'd pointed out my hickey in tears. It was too late to turn around without looking like a total asshole.

Just my fuckin' luck.

She leaned on her hands, bending over the sink, her tears plopping into the bowl.

I sighed, wanting to walk away.

I really didn't give a shit what made her sad, but my humanity won.

Asshole conscience.

"Are you okay?" I asked as I approached.

"No," she said, sliding the back of her hand across her face, wiping the tears.

"Sorry, I'll leave you be." I stepped back and reached for the door handle.

"No, don't go," she said, turning toward me. "Everyone leaves me," she wailed, her body almost collapsing against the counter.

"Fuck," I muttered under my breath as I rushed to her side.

How in the hell do I get involved in these situations?

"I'm here. What can I do?" I asked, sounding thoughtful, surprising myself.

"There's nothing anyone can do." She hiccupped as she cried.

"Everything is fixable." I patted her back and stared at the ceiling. "I only have another moment between patients. I'm sorry."

"My fiancé left me and I'm pregnant." She choked on her words, starting to fall forward again.

I held her, pulling her upright. "That's terrible," I said, trying to be horrified.

"How could he be so mean? He acted like we never meant anything to each other."

I had the words on the tip of my tongue, but I bit it instead. "Maybe he'll change his mind."

If the man had any sense, he'd run for the hills or go into witness protection.

"I have to win him back." Standing up, she looked into my eyes. "He needs to understand all he's giving up by walking out on *us*."

"Oh, I'm sure he has no idea." I knew I sounded snarky, but whatever.

"I can do it, you're right." She blotted her cheeks with her fingers and smiled. "Thank you so much." Her tears vanished.

Cuckoo.

Wrapping her arms around me, she squeezed so hard I thought my ribs were going to crack.

"I have to go," I said, pulling away.

"Oh, sorry," she said with a half-smile. Mascara had smeared down her cheeks and her eyes were red and swollen. "You helped me more than you'll ever know." Her smile grew wider.

"Don't give up the fight," I said, walking out the door.

"I won't," she yelled, as the door swung shut.

I shook my head and wondered what the hell happened to my *normal* stressful day at the hospital. Today had been one for the record books.

***

The night had been relatively calm compared to the nutty nurse and thinking Michael had been seriously hurt.

His brother was in ICU for the night post-surgery. When I'd looked at his chart earlier, it stated that he would be moved to a regular room tomorrow if he did well through the night.

The ICU was quiet and the lights were dim as the sounds of the ventilators, heart monitors, and other machines filled the hallway. I wanted to check in on him and see if he needed anything.

Michael's brother crouched in the hall outside his room, leaning against the wall, typing on his phone. Looking up at me, he smiled. "Hey," he said, trying to stand, but he fell over, catching himself on the wall. "Fuck," he mumbled.

Rushing to his side, I reached for him. "Hey, are you all right?" I asked.

Waving me off, he said, "Yeah, just exhausted. This has been a day from hell." His shoulders slumped as he sighed.

"Why don't you try and catch a couple hours sleep in the visitor's lounge? He wouldn't want you to make yourself sick."

"I will soon. You looking for Mikey?" He grinned, making the bags under his eyes more pronounced.

Laughing at the nickname, I replied, "Yeah, is he still here?" I looked around.

"He's inside, but he was asleep when I came out here," he said, pointing to the room behind him.

"I'll just text him. Everyone may be sleeping and I don't want to disturb anyone."

He laughed. "My family *is* the disturbance. They're loud and obnoxious in the most loving way, but I don't blame you for not wanting to go into the lion's den." He shook his head. "At least not armed."

I barely knew any of them, but I wanted to. They seemed loving and playful, just my kind of people. The funny smartass personality must be hereditary.

"You make them sound horrible." I said, shaking my head, laughing.

"Nah, just Italian."

"Don't wake him. Just tell him I stopped by and have him text me in the morning. I'm going to try and get some rest while the ER is slow."

"Okay, doc. I hope to see you again soon." The sides of his eyes crinkled as he smiled at me.

I nodded and walked away, leaving Michael to sleep. I wanted to catch a few minutes' rest in the doctor's lounge while I still could. I thought about the Gallo boys as I made my way down the corridors. They were all handsome, but Michael was heart-stopping.

I flipped off the light in the lounge before I collapsed on the couch. My head began to spin from exhaustion when I closed my eyes. Lying on the lumpy couch, I covered my face with my arm and thought about Michael.

"What?" I asked as someone touched my shoulder. "My eyes were closed for only two seconds. Jesus," I mumbled.

"It's been an hour, doctor, and someone is at the desk asking for you."

"I'm coming," I said, rubbing my eyes, waiting for them to adjust to the harsh fluorescent lighting. I grabbed the Visine from my pocket, dropping the liquid in the hope of alleviate the stinging.

I prayed I didn't look like the walking dead. I sure as hell felt like it.

Walking like a zombie, my mind clouded, eyes blurry, I made my way to the reception area. Michael stood there looking exactly how I felt. Fidgeting with his hands, he leaned against the desk and looked around.

I touched his back lightly, trying not to startle him. "Michael, everything all right?"

He rubbed his hands across his face as he turned to me. "Yeah, Anth told me you came by while I was asleep. Thought I'd find you down here."

"I decided to sleep a bit too," I said, a yawn breaking free as I quickly covered it.

"Shit, I'm sorry I woke you." He frowned. The lack of sleep and stress had dulled his eyes' luster.

"I'm fine. I needed to wake up anyway," I said, wiping my eyes. "How's your brother?"

The huge smile on his face said it all. "He woke up for a bit and mumbled some nonsense," he said, laughing.

"Anesthesia can do funny things to a person's brain."

"I thought about messing with his head, but my ma would've beat me. He seems okay, but he's pretty fucked up. The surgeon said it's going to be a long recovery. They had to put a metal rod in his leg and there's pins sticking out and shit. His hand is in a cast and his fingers are swollen. Yeah, he's fucked for now." He shrugged. "At least he's alive."

Touching his hand, I caressed the rough skin on his palm near his fingers. "It's going to be tough on him, but your family will help him through it. How are your parents holding up?" Stepping closer, I leaned against him.

He stared at my fingers as I stroked them. "They're

doing okay. Worried, naturally, but better now that he's out of the woods. They need sleep. I keep telling them to go home and rest, but they're hard-headed."

He wrapped his arm around me and feathered a kiss against my forehead.

"Seems to be a family trait," I said, laughing and gripping his shirt. I closed my eyes, inhaling his musky cologne.

"Code blue, room two," a voice blared through the hallway.

Damn. I wanted more than a minute against his warm, hard body.

"I have to go." I frowned, resting my head against his chest. "Go home and rest, Mikey, and I'll see you tomorrow or today…whatever it is," I said, pushing off him and starting to walk away.

Grabbing me around the waist, he brought his lips to my ear and whispered, "It's Michael, doc. I don't remember hearing you moan Mikey as you came on my cock."

The vibration of his voice and his breath in my ear made me shiver.

"I have to go. You're a naughty boy, Mikey," I said as I pushed away from his body, freeing myself from his grip.

I could hear his deep laughter as I ran toward room two and the patient in cardiac arrest.

CHAPTER FIFTEEN

MICHAEL

I KEPT a vigil at my brother's bedside with the rest of my family throughout the night. On the verge of collapse, I found a quiet spot to close my eyes. Pulling up a chair, I stretched my legs out, and rested my head against the wall. I wanted to wait for Mia to finish her shift.

I tried to quiet my mind, but all I could think about was Tammy. I didn't believe for a moment that she was pregnant, let alone with my child.

I knew sure as shit we weren't engaged, so why would I even remotely believe her bullshit? The woman was clearly delusional, and I needed to find a way to set her ass straight, and quick, before it blew up in my face.

Using the front of one shoe, I pried the other one off my foot before repeating the process with my toes. I grabbed my shirt, brought it to my nose, and sniffed. Didn't smell as bad as I thought it would after being at the hospital so long.

Rubbing my face, I yawned and crossed my arms, resting them on my chest.

What the fuck was I going to do about Tammy?

Batshit crazy Tammy.

A pregnancy test would show her for the bullshitter she was and put her lies to rest in a hurry, but how?

We didn't have sex more than a couple times in the last six weeks, and I always wore a condom.

I didn't want a baby—at least not yet, and certainly not with a woman like her.

Could someone even know that they were pregnant in that time? I had a dick, and the female reproductive system mystified me.

I tried to force Tammy out of my mind. Just the thought of her pissed me off, making my blood pressure rise.

I thought of Mia, trying to calm my nerves. There was something different about her, but I couldn't put my finger on it. There was a natural ease I felt when she was at my side.

What if they knew each other? Fuck, I never thought of that.

My heart pounded as my eyes flew open. My palms grew sweaty as I thought about the possibility of my worlds colliding in one giant clusterfuck.

I couldn't make myself crazy.

I pushed the thought of Tammy out of my mind and thought of Mia—the feel of her skin, her brilliant smile, and her infectious laugh.

My head fell to the side, scaring the living shit out of myself. I needed my bed, solid sleep, and a good ass-kicking in the gym to set my body and mind right. I felt stiff after sleeping for three hours in an unnatural position.

I cracked my neck, gaining my bearings as I walked back to Joe's room. I needed to check on him.

My parents, Izzy, and Anthony had disappeared while I was gone. Suzy had crawled in bed and carefully placed her body around him. He watched her as she slept in his arms.

I cleared my throat to get his attention.

Holding his finger to his lips, he motioned for me to sit.

"You scared the shit out of us, Joe." I grabbed the chair, setting it down on the opposite side of the bed that Suzy lay on.

"I wouldn't go out like that, brother. I have too much to live for to leave this world," he whispered, looking down at Suzy. "I feel like shit, though."

"You look like shit too." I smiled.

I would've never been the same without him in my life.

He laughed, wincing as his body shook. "Everything fucking hurts. I'm going to be out of commission for a while—a long while."

"Doesn't matter. Just get better, man."

"At least I didn't fuck up my tattooing hand, but I'm not going to be walking anytime soon." He flexed his good hand, balling it into a fist.

"I'll wheel your ass in every day if I have to. Maybe you can get one of those scooters all the old bastards use." I smirked.

Fucking old people drove him nuts.

"Shut the fuck up, asshole," he whispered, glaring at me.

"Well, at least the accident didn't ruin your ability to use such eloquent language." I laughed. The joy I felt with the simple conversation was unexplainable.

"Since when does your ass say eloquent?"

"You aren't the only one with a college education, Joe. Listen, man, some shit went down in the last twelve hours—more shit than just your accident. I need your advice, but I'll wait until your mind is clear."

"My mind's clear as a whistle."

I shook my head. "Nah, your shit got scrambled, and I need it at its best to help me figure out the shit storm that's about to rain down on me." I rubbed my eyes and raked my hands down my face.

"No, fuck? I gotta know now."

"Why me?" I laid my head on his bed, wishing it all away.

The bed moved slightly as the sound of his laughter rang in my ears.

It was the best damn sound in the world.

"You're going to laugh your ass off when you hear about the clusterfuck," I said, sitting up to face him.

Suzy stirred as her eyes opened, a small smile on her lips. "Mikey," she said, her voice sounding sleepy.

"Hey, Suz. I didn't mean to wake you. Sorry, sweetheart," I said, watching her body melt against him.

"Don't worry. I want to be up. You need anything, babe?" she asked, staring up at Joe.

She looked relieved. Yesterday I thought she was going to have a meltdown and lose it completely.

They had a love that I hoped to find someday. I wanted someone to be my world.

Fuck, I sounded like a pussy.

I needed to sleep and get my head right.

"Nah, sugar. I'm fine just how we are right now." He pulled her tighter against his body and kissed her head.

I watched them with a dumb, jealous grin on my face. I touched my dick to make sure it was still there.

"Did the doctor come in while I slept?" she asked, nuzzling her face into his chest.

"Not yet. The nurse said he'd be in this morning before they move me to a regular room."

"I can't wait to get you home, baby," she said, closing her eyes.

"You just want me in bed and immobile," he teased as he smelled her hair.

"I'd prefer you unable to talk, but being stuck in bed won't be the worst thing in the world." She giggled softly, trying not to jostle him.

Holding my hands up in mock surrender, I said, "All right, love birds. This is my cue to get out of here. Call me if you need anything." I stood and touched my brother's uninjured arm. "I'm happy you're all right, brother. I love you even though you're an asshole sometimes." I squeezed his forearm, looking at the both of them with their mushy grins.

"Love ya too, man." He smiled.

"Bye, Mikey," Suzy said, without moving.

As I walked out of Joe's room, I sent Mia a text.

Me: You done yet with work?

I'd had as much hospital as I could take. The smell of antiseptic and pine made my stomach turn. I worried it would be permanently part of my sense of smell if I stayed any longer.

Mia: I'll be done in thirty.

Me: I'll be in my car waiting or do you want to meet at my place?

Mia: Meet you at your place.

Me: Hungry?

Mia: Famished.

Me: I'll have food, cock, and a comfy bed waiting for you.

Mia: What if I don't want it in that order?

Me: I offer—you choose.

I laughed, shaking my head. I really liked her.

Mia: I'll be there in one hour.

Me: Don't keep me waiting.

I approached my car with a giant smile on my face,

and tucked the phone in my pocket. A white piece of paper flapped under my wiper, catching my eye. I ripped it off the windshield and glanced at it before crumpling it in my fist. Slowly, I peeled the crushed paper apart and stared at it.

Mikey,

You can't just leave us like this. How can you deny your own son? I'll never let you go. You're mine and we're yours.

I'll fight for you until my last breath.

I sighed, wanting to vomit, and crumpled the paper before throwing it on the ground. I'd deal with her shit soon and end her games.

Crazy and me did not fucking mix.

CHAPTER SIXTEEN

MIA

I SNUGGLED against Michael and relished the stark contrast of his warm skin and the cool sheets against my body.

The soothing of his hand as he rubbed the back of my arm made me melt into him. I slowly moved my fingers over the scruff lining his jawbone; each hair tickled my fingertips. The coarseness on my skin felt like tiny shock waves moving through my hand. Listening to the beat of his heart, I drifted to sleep.

"Mia," Michael whispered in my ear, waking me.

"Mm." I was too tired to speak.

"I need you." His lips brushed against my ear as his hand caressed the skin just above my underwear.

"Yeah," I whispered, pushing my ass against his hardness, still feeling half asleep.

He wrapped his arm around me and pulled me closer, and his fingers dipped inside my panties. His breath felt hot and sounded heavy against my ear. Raking his fingers through my wetness, he moaned as he found my clit.

His damp fingers moved rhythmically against my

tender flesh. I squirmed, a small moan escaping my lips. Arching my back, I pushed my ass against his erection. Moisture pooled between my legs; I needed more than his hand to dull the ache.

Moving away from my body, he placed me on my back without speaking. I didn't have to wait as I heard the crinkle of the wrapping before the bed dipped as he crawled between my legs.

I blinked through blurry eyes and watched his dark figure kneeling before me as he slid on the condom.

Leaning over my body, he whispered against my lips, "You okay, Mia?"

"Yes," I said in a sleepy voice, still not fully awake.

When he stroked the head of his cock against my opening, my eyes flew open. He thrust himself inside, waking me.

Warm hands pressed against my ribs before holding my arms above my head.

I relaxed my arms under his grip, enjoying the small grunts that filled the room and the feel of him inside me.

He pumped into me slowly, caressing my insides. Moaning, I felt the orgasm hovering just out of reach. I need more friction, more power to push me over the edge. I wrapped my ankles around his legs, as the pressure from the piercings hit me deep and in just the right way, sending a shock wave through my system.

The force of his thrust increased as he fucked me relentlessly. My fingers curled around his as he held my arms against the pillow. Wet warmth against my nipple made my body jerk. The sensations were overwhelming in my sleepy state.

As he bit down, I cried out, pleasure radiating throughout my body.

I pushed my head against the pillow; my arms grew

rigid under his hold and my breathing halted. In the darkness, my eyes filled with vivid colors as the orgasm tore through me. Feeling like someone had knocked the wind out of me, I grew limp under him as he chased his release. Ramming his cock inside me over and over again, Michael cried out, body shaking until he collapsed on top of me.

Rolling away, he snapped the condom, pulling it off. The bed moved as he rolled over, wrapping his arms around me. Michael Gallo spooned.

"Sleep, Mia," he whispered in my ear, planting a soft kiss against my hair.

I closed my eyes, shuffling my ass back, leaving no space between us.

The peace I knew only when in his arms returned as I drifted back to sleep.

Michael seemed on edge when we woke. We both needed the gym to relax and unwind.

I touched his arm as he drove, seemingly lost in his thoughts. "He's going to be okay, you know that, right?" I asked, hoping to make him feel better.

He nodded his head. "Yeah, I know."

I studied his profile. His forehead was crinkled and his eyes seemed vacant. His sparkle and dirty humor had evaporated somewhere between falling asleep and our drive to the gym.

"What's wrong, then?"

"Just some stuff on my mind. It has nothing to do with us, Mia. Just some bullshit going on."

"I'm a good listener, Michael." I rubbed his arm, wanting him to share his worries with me.

Looking over at me, he exhaled and frowned. "I imagine you are, but some things are for me to deal with."

I pulled my hand back, placing it in my lap. "Okay," I

said, looking out the window. I didn't have anything else to say.

We pulled into the gym parking lot after riding in silence. He could say whatever was on his mind had nothing to do with us, but I knew bullshit when I heard it.

He reached for my hand, giving it a small squeeze, as we walked into the gym.

"I'm going to run on the treadmill, want to come?" I asked.

"Nah, I need to lift some weights." Bending down, he kissed my cheek. "I'll catch you in a bit."

It felt platonic and impersonal, unlike the sex we'd had during the night.

"Don't forget me, handsome." I started to walk away and looked back at him with a smile. That just sounded needy and totally not me.

He had scrambled my brains.

He grabbed my arm, drawing me to his body. "I could never forget about you, Mia. You need to stop that thought right there. There's no other woman I think about." He swatted my ass and whispered, "Off you go. No checking out anyone but me. Got it?"

Yes, the playful Michael was back!

As I walked away, I looked over my shoulder. "I can't help if someone is in my line of vision. What are you going to do about it, big boy?" I smirked.

His mouth broke out in a drop-dead sinful grin. "I have my ways of making you pay." He winked, and I wanted to jump in his arms and capture his mouth in a kiss.

Whatever had been on his mind in the truck had vanished.

Butterflies filled my stomach as I walked a little bit faster before he sidetracked us both.

"You know where to find me." Using my thumb, I

pointed to the treadmills over my shoulder. I turned around, relieved to have a few minutes to myself.

The man had seemed simple to read until today.

I jogged on the treadmill, catching up with my emails. I'd been trying to finish reading a book for a week with no luck, and I used the time to read while I ran. After each page, I watched Michael for a moment before continuing to read.

He started with free weights for his arms. He looked in a mirror, studying his movement, and our eyes met from time to time.

He was stunningly handsome, with rippling muscles and not a lick of fat on him. I knew he worked out like a beast, but for God's sake, couldn't the man have a pinch of something somewhere? I loved the feel of his rock-hard body against mine.

He put the bar behind his head, squatting slowly before standing with a grunt. His face turned red and a vein protruded from his forehead with each lift.

I licked my lips, my book no longer interesting, as I kept my eyes glued to him. That was how he kept that rock-hard ass and the tree-trunk thighs.

I stared, mesmerized by his ass, watching it move up and down. Every muscle in his body rippled as he removed his shirt before lifting the weight again.

Holy fuck, he was hot.

He grunted with each squat. It was different than the one I heard during sex. This was a grunt of exertion and strain, not of pleasure. The effect it had on me was the same. My face grew flushed, as my core convulsed and my heart pounded against my chest. I grabbed the towel off the bar and blotted the skin around my neck.

Our eyes were glued to each other as we moved around the gym. The air between us was thick, the lust evident to anyone paying attention. He placed the weights on the floor and dried off his damp flesh.

I wanted to lick the sweat off his body, and I wasn't a girl that usually enjoyed a sweaty man.

His smile grew larger the closer he came to me before stopping between my legs.

He stood between my legs, staring down at me as I lifted the weight. "Need some help?"

"Nope, I got this. Twenty-four," I said as I pushed the bar up, trying to ignore his eyes raking over my body. "Twenty-five," I grunted, latching it in place, trying to catch my breath. "You shouldn't gawk, Michael." I smiled up at him, breathing heavily.

"I'm not gawking, Mia. I'm just undressing you in my mind and fantasizing about all the dirty shit I'm going to do to you when I get you back to my place."

My mouth gaped open as I sat up and stared. My attempt to slow my breathing was crushed by his words. The dull ache between my legs turned into a throb.

He touched my sternum, following the path the beads of sweat had traveled into my cleavage. "I want you this sweaty when you're under me, coming on my dick, screaming for me to stop." He kissed me whisper light, before backing away with a grin.

Smug bastard.

CHAPTER SEVENTEEN

MICHAEL

POINTING to the erection about to burst through my sweatpants, I said, "I can't believe you're going to leave me like this, doc."

"Yep." She nodded. "You'll survive; it's not a life-threatening affliction," she said, laughing as she adjusted her shirt. "You have to go see your brother, and I need to go home for a while."

"I can't call my mother or Suzy for help. This can only be fixed by you." I grabbed myself, adjusting my dick.

"Absence makes the heart grow fonder," she said, pulling up her pants.

Standing, I walked toward her, and she backed away. "Fuck my heart. It's my dick that's aching." I smiled and tried to touch her, but she moved out of reach.

"Call me when you're done at the hospital, and I'll see what I can do to help you out with that situation." Grabbing her keys off my kitchen table, she moved quicker than I thought possible.

"Come here, woman." I darted to the left, using the edge of the table for traction.

Squealing, she ran the opposite direction. "You may be big, but I'm quicker, Mikey."

I moved to the left and then quickly to the right, trying to throw her off kilter. "Woman, what did I tell you about callin' me Mikey?"

Stopping on the opposite side, she placed her hands on the table and leaned over with a huge smile. "I must have forgotten, but I remember there was talk of punishment, Mikey."

Moving again, I reached for her arm, but she slipped from my grasp. "Fuck, this goddamn hard-on is slowing me down. Rub it for me, please?"

"You're a pig," she said, laughing before sticking out her tongue and closing her eyes.

I moved as fast as I could to grab her. "Got ya. Come on, Mia. I can be quick." Dragging my tongue across her neck, I nipped her earlobe. Her laughter grew quiet as her breasts pressed against me. "Please?" I whispered, sucking on her ear.

She moaned, squeezing my arm. "No," she said in a breathy tone.

I palmed her breast, stroking her hard nipple with my thumb. "I'll make it worth your while." I pushed her backward toward the table.

"I don't want quick. I want long and hard." She bit my lip. "Call me when you're done seeing Joe, and if you're good, I'll make it worth your while," she said against my lips, causing my dick to twitch.

"Cock block." I released her from my grip and adjusted myself.

"I'd classify myself as more of a pussy hoarder than a cock block," she said before kissing my cheek.

It took everything in me not to slam her to the table and rip her pants off her. "You're maddening."

Her laughter filled the room as she walked to the door. Following close on her heels, I turned her and pushed her back against the door. I placed my hands on either side of her. "Are you sure I can't convince you to stay?"

She grinned before rubbing her nose against mine. "No. Go be a good brother. I'll be home later. Hit me up then." She kissed my lips and as she drew away; I pushed my body into hers and captured her mouth. "Still no," she mumbled against my lips.

"I'll call you. I'm going to need some serious help if I walk around with this hard-on all day."

"Probably won't be the first time in your life or the last." She giggled.

We both jumped as my phone vibrated in my pocket. Sighing, I pulled it out and glanced at the screen.

"It's my ma. I better get this."

Nodding, she opened the door. "Talk to your mom. I'll talk to you later," she said as she waved and closed the door behind her.

"Hey, Ma."

"Where have you been all day, Michael?"

"I'm coming, Ma. I had to work out."

"We have to be here for your brother while he's in the hospital. No one likes to be alone."

That was the problem with an overbearing Italian family. Mine had a tendency to be up each other's ass all day, every day.

Joe probably wanted some time alone with Suzy, but knowing my parents, his room had more people in and out all day than the Bunny Ranch in Vegas.

"Ma, you know my fight is coming up soon. I have to make sure I work out every day. I've slacked a bit and needed to blow off some steam. I'm jumping in the shower and I'll be there. How is he, by the way?"

"He's looking better and they moved him to a regular room. He's out of the woods, thank God."

"I'm glad to hear it. Anyone call Tommy yet?"

"No, I don't think he needs to know about it. Joseph will be fine. No need to worry him, Michael."

"Ma, he deserves to know."

My parents aggravated me with the bullshit. Thomas would want to know if something happened to any of us. He was going to be pissed when he found out he was kept out of the loop.

"We'll see. That's for your father and me to decide. Get your butt up here."

Thomas had been able to use his job to avoid Sunday dinners and family events that would bore any breathing human. My parents never harped on him.

Lucky bastard.

"Let me get off the phone and I can get there quicker, Ma."

Her soft laughter filled my ear. I loved the woman, but at times she drove me berserk. "Very true. See you soon, baby."

She called all of us baby. Guess it was better than "jackass."

My parents smothered us with love at times. Suffocated us, but at least we knew where they stood. We loved them unconditionally and wholeheartedly.

"Bye, Ma," I said as I tapped end before she could get another word out.

I walked in the bathroom, thinking about Tommy as I turned the phone over in my palm. I couldn't keep this from him. It just wasn't right.

I sent him a message before climbing in the shower.

Me: Call when you have time, got news.

I showered quickly, wanting to get to the hospital

before my ma called again to chew my ass out.

As I grabbed my keys to walk out the door, my phone began to ring.

"Hey."

"Hi, Mike. What's going on? I don't have much time, but I wanted to check in," Tommy said quietly.

"It's Joe. He's all right now, but he got into a bike accident on Sunday."

He sucked in a breath before replying, "How bad?"

"Fucked-up leg and a broken hand. He was thrown, but he had on a helmet, or else we'd be planning a funeral right now."

"Fuck, I'm going crazy not being able to see everyone and know what the fuck is going on." He sucked in another breath before exhaling.

"You smoking again?" I asked.

"Yeah, when in Rome, brother."

I shook my head. I couldn't imagine the life he led or what he had to do to blend in with MC that he'd been assigned to.

"Should I come home?"

"Nah, I just wanted you to know."

"What the fuck took so long to get me the word?" he bit out.

"Ma and Pop didn't want to bother you and make you worry," I said as I climbed in my truck.

"Mike, text me anytime to tell me when bad shit's going down. I'll always call as soon as I can. Don't let them hide shit from me, ya hear me, brother?"

"Yeah. Are you okay, Tommy?"

I felt relieved talking to him. Every day I wondered if he was okay or even if he was alive. Being cut off from him was scary as fuck.

"I'm okay, just some crazy shit going down. I got it,

though. Don't worry about me, Mike. Give my love to everyone. I gotta run."

"Take care of yourself, man. Watch your back."

"Tell everyone I love them, Mike. Please give Ma a kiss for me." His breathing had grown a little more uneven.

"Love ya too, Thomas," I said, tearing up as the line went dead.

I hadn't cried since I was a kid and got hurt on the school playground, but hearing Thomas' voice made it hard to keep my composure. It had been over a year since I'd seen him, and I felt relieved knowing he was okay and ready to fight another day.

Wiping the mist from my eyes, I threw the phone on the passenger seat and headed toward the hospital.

***

Walking down the halls of the hospital, I kept my guard up, expecting psycho Tammy to pop out of nowhere. I was sure she was stalking the halls looking for me.

Walking into Joe's room, I said, "I've arrived."

Izzy looked at me and rolled her eyes. "About time, you ass."

"Love you too, sis." I blew her a kiss and smiled. "Thank God for a private room." I laughed as I looked at them all.

Poor Joe. They were here staring at him all day.

"Joe, how ya feelin,' man?" I approached his bed and kissed him on the cheek.

He puffed out a breath, adjusting his body. "Bored to death and ready to get the hell out of here."

"I can only imagine, but I think you're going to be here a while. Sorry I wasn't here sooner."

"Don't worry about it. You have shit to do. When's the fight?"

Sitting on the edge of his bed, I replied, "Couple weeks."

"I want a front-row seat. I'm so pumped for you. Going to win this one?" He raised an eyebrow.

"Hell yeah. I got this shit in the bag if I stay on track. Have you ever seen me lose a fight?"

He shook his head. "Never, and you never answered about the front row."

"I have tickets for everyone. I grabbed a couple extra too." I bent my knee, putting it on the bed.

The room was filled with chatter. Izzy and Suzy were talking about clothes or some girl shit. My parents talked to Anthony in a whispered tone that I couldn't make out. I never knew my family could talk this quietly.

There was a brief lull in the conversations around us as Joe said, "What did you want to talk to me about?"

I hung my head and rubbed my eyes with my thumb and index finger. Fuck, bring on the Gallo Inquisition.

"What's he talking about?" Izzy asked behind me. Naturally she'd be the one person to pipe up after hearing that statement.

Turning around, I looked her straight in the eye and showed no fear. "Male shit, Iz. Don't concern yourself with it."

Her eyes became slits as she glared at me. Izzy knew me as well as anyone sitting in this room, and I prayed she knew when to drop the subject. "Always playing the penis card. Such bullshit."

"Isabella," my ma chimed in. "Did I raise you to speak that way?"

"I'm a grown woman, Ma, and yes you did. You had four boys and a girl. How else would I talk?"

My ma and Izzy broke into a fit of laughter.

I looked at Joe and I mouthed "later" to him.

He tipped his chin, not making any other movements. He knew as well as I did how nosy this group was, and I needed to deal with Tammy on the down-low.

"Why don't we all go to the cafeteria and let the boys have their talk?" My ma always tried to be diplomatic.

"Great idea, my legs could use a stretch," Pop said. "Come on, baby girl." Standing, my pop held his hand out to Izzy.

She sighed and put her fingers in his palm. "For you, Dad, anything you ask." She had him wrapped around her little finger.

They worked each other well and knew how to get their way. Izzy gave in on the small things because she knew my pop would always have her back; she'd always be his little girl.

"I'm going to stay here," Anthony said as he looked at my parents. "I'm playing my penis card." He smirked at Izzy.

I swear to shit I could see a vein pop out of her forehead.

"We'll be back in ten minutes," Pop said, yanking Izzy out by the arm.

We sat in silence as we waited for them to walk far enough away that we wouldn't be overhead. Anthony poked his head out of the doorway. "All clear," he said.

"What the fuck is up, man?" Joe asked.

"Tammy has gone off the rails." I shook my head, still not believing her bullshit.

His eyebrows scrunched as he looked at me. "Tammy?"

"Scrapbook crazy girl? Did you hit your head harder than we thought?"

He laughed and grabbed his side. "Fuck, I remember her now. I've had other things on my mind than your women."

"She isn't one of my women. She saw me in the cafeteria here and she claimed we were engaged, dude."

"No fucking way." His mouth hung open as he looked at me.

"Yes, I told her to leave me the hell alone and she said how could I just leave her since we were engaged. When I denied her and I went to walk away…" I didn't want to finish the sentence. The mere thought of her words made my stomach churn. "She yelled out that she was pregnant."

His body stilled as his eyebrows drew together. "With whose kid?" Joe asked.

"Mine, dumbass." I shrugged.

"Is that even possible?" Joe asked, trying to sit up.

"Fuck no. I don't think so. I mean, I'm not a doctor, but if I remember my human bio class, there's zero chance."

"Were you careful?" Joe asked, as he rubbed his forehead.

Anthony just sat there, shaking his head as he played on his phone.

"Yes, and we only did it a couple of times. She couldn't possibly know if she was. Could she?"

"Shit, I don't know, but you need to find out, Mike."

I rested my head in my hand, running my finger through my hair. I had to find the craziest bitch in the county and stick my dick in her.

"I got to work this shit out and shut her ass down." God was getting the last laugh.

"I'd say you better do something before that shit blows up in your face." Joe pointed at me and shook his head. "Fight crazy by facing her head-on and putting her down."

"I'll figure it out. You have your own shit to deal with." I motioned to his fucked-up leg.

"Eh, a mere flesh wound," Joe said with a straight face.

We all started to laugh as we got the reference to Monty Python. The best movie scene ever made. When the guy loses limbs but still states it's just a mere flesh wound, until he's jumping on one leg without arms and spewing blood everywhere…epic. I think we drove my mother crazy for months re-enacting it as kids.

"You need my help, Mike?" Anthony asked.

"Nah, it's my mess to deal with, Anth. I just don't want it ruining whatever Mia and I have going on."

"Who's Mia?" Joe asked.

"Girl I met at the gym. She's a doctor here and we've been spending time together." I rubbed my eyes and raked my hands through my hair. "I really like her and don't want Tammy fucking it up."

"A doctor? I'm impressed, Mike. Wait, why was Tammy here?"

"She works here too. I'm so screwed if she runs into Mia."

Anthony looked up from his phone. "Oh, fuck. You better get it handled quickly before the shit hits the fan."

"Just once I'd like my dick not to cause problems," I said, looking up at the ceiling.

"Keep sticking that shit in any pussy around town and your problems will never go away."

"Just because you found Suzy doesn't mean you're the authority on relationships, Joe."

"No, but I knew when I found something so damn good that I'd do anything in the world to make her mine."

"Pussy whipped," Anthony muttered under his breath before laughing.

I had to get control of the situation.

Why did her ass have to go off the hook as Mia came into my life?

CHAPTER EIGHTEEN

MIA

MICHAEL HADN'T SEEMED himself all week, distant and preoccupied. I asked him repeatedly to share whatever bothered him, but he said no and I stopped trying to pry. Sometimes, there are things I don't feel like sharing as I deal with the situation. I gave him his space and hoped he'd tell me in his own time.

My week had been busy, almost to the point of hectic. I worked at the hospital and the clinic every day. Michael trained, spent time with his family at the hospital, and kept the tattoo shop running.

His life was just as full as mine. We had to be creative when it came to seeing each other while his brother was at County. I met him early one morning to watch him train with Rob. There was a small ring that had been set up in the gym just for Michael and Rob to practice.

I was tempted to jump in the ring and take out some of my stress on the target or Rob, but I didn't want to make a fool out of myself. I used the time to run on the treadmill as I watched Mike kick Rob's ass. It brought a smile to my face.

Saturday night, Michael brought the DVD of his fight in New York to my house. He fought Victor "The Mauler" Torrez.

Sliding the disc into the DVD player, he explained that the match wouldn't be fought in a boxing ring and that he didn't box. I was clueless to MMA rules. To me it was just a fancy name given to a sport where two men beat the shit out of each other.

As soon as the match started to play, I knew I was right with my first assumption about what he called a sport—it was barbaric.

There was something about watching Michael that had me shifting in my seat and made me feel flushed.

Fuck, he looked sexy and powerful as he jostled from leg to leg on the video.

"Look at this next hit," he said, sitting next to me on the couch, punching the air.

His foot swept the other man's legs out from underneath him. Michael struck him in the face. Sweat and blood flew through the air as he connected with his jaw. High-definition television showed a little too much detail for me.

"That's called a ground-and-pound move." Staring at the television, he was transfixed, with a smile on his face.

"Did you win?" I asked, covering my eyes to avoid seeing the man struggle.

He turned to me with a look of shock on his face. "You'll have to watch to find out, but what do you think?" He said, laughing.

"You won or you wouldn't be showing this to me," I said with a smile before turning back to the television.

Although I knew the outcome, it made my stomach hurt to watch the footage. My heart beat in my throat as I sat on the edge of the couch, watching the recording through my fingers.

Michael squeezed my knee, patting it gently. "I can't wait to get back in the cage."

"How long did you say until the next match?" I looked at his face.

"Just a couple of weeks. I'll be cutting way back on my schedule at the shop for final preparations."

"Where is it?" I asked, praying it was far away.

How would I feel seeing him fighting with another man in the flesh instead of on a recording? The roar of the crowd with each blow was shocking, and in person had to be almost deafening.

"Right here in Tampa. I wanted in because it's close to home. You're gonna come, right?"

"Um, yeah, I guess I'll be there." I turned my attention back to the television as his fist made contact with the opponent's jaw again. His head flew back and I could see the satisfaction on Michael's face. "What made you travel to New York for this fight?"

"I want you there, Mia," he said, ignoring my question. "You have to watch at least one in person. That was a huge fight. It was on pay-per-view and helped get my name out there. I want to make a name for myself in this industry."

"Why would you do this when you're a successful business owner?" I looked at him, totally confused by the man I knew and the one I saw on the screen. The fighter scared the hell out of me, but the man to my side made me feel safe and comfortable. I thought of him as a softy, although I'd never tell him that.

"I do MMA for the thrill and the challenge. I'd give up working in the tattoo shop to fight full-time. Wait, here's the end, you have to watch." Touching my chin, he pushed my eyes back toward the television.

Michael had "The Mauler" on the ground in a chokehold. Their legs were twisted together, their bodies entwined as he squeezed the man's neck, cutting off his airway. I couldn't look away no matter how much I wanted to—I was transfixed—and then they released each other.

"What just happened?" I asked, confused why it ended suddenly.

"I won. The ref ended it because the guy was losing consciousness. Stupid rule, but…" He shrugged with a tiny grin.

"Oh," I said as I turned my attention back to the screen. His chest heaved from exertion; his eyes looked fierce, as tiny droplets of sweat slid down his body. Maybe high-def was a good thing after all.

"I could watch this recording a million times," he said, switching off the television, turning toward me.

"You probably have," I said, smirking.

"Smartass woman." He started to tickle me on my ribs.

I squirmed, trying to break free. "Stop!" I yelped as he pushed me back into the couch.

His fingers moved across my ribs as I tried to find my breath. "I have to teach you a lesson." The weight of his body made it harder to breathe.

I laughed and tried to pry his hands from my side. "Michael, stop. I can't breathe," I huffed out through the laughter, pushing at his fingers.

His hands stilled as he hovered over my body, face to face. "You're so fucking beautiful when you have a smile on your face." His eyes roamed my face as his erection pushed against my leg.

He was hard as a rock.

"Is it me or did the fight turn you on?" I asked.

I would never admit it, but my body ached for him. God, I was such a hypocrite.

"Your laughter did this to me, not the fight."

"I highly—"

He covered my mouth with his hand and placed a kiss on my neck. "No more talking for you."

I giggled behind his hand and my tongue darted out to taste him. "I thought you loved my voice," I mumbled behind his fingers.

"Shh," he whispered, running his nose down my cheek before he licked a path down my neck. The warmth of his tongue sent tiny sparks straight to my core.

My fingers dug into his back as I held him to me, enjoying the feel of his tongue. I wanted more. I craved him.

When his lips met my collarbone, my body flinched as my sex convulsed. I could feel the wetness between my legs. My body was a traitor, but at this point, relieving the throb was all that mattered.

My head fell to the side and I opened my eyes. The clock read six—I would be late to work. I pushed Michael off in a panic.

"What's wrong?" he asked, frowning.

"I'm going to be late to work. You have to go and I have to get ready." I jumped from the couch, pulling down my shirt.

"Your fucking job is getting in the way," he said, sitting up.

I hushed him with my finger. "We both have a lot of shit to do. I'll be off tomorrow if you can find the time to squeeze me into your busy schedule."

He smiled behind my finger. "I'll make the time. I'll do everything early so I can spend time with you."

"Michael, I'd say you're smitten if I didn't know you any better. Are you always this easy?"

"Smitten doesn't even begin to explain what I am at

the moment, doc." He grabbed my hand and placed it on his cock. "Rock hard is more like it. You're always leaving me fucking hanging."

I chuckled as I stared into his eyes.

The man probably never had to wait for sex. Woman probably hung on him and begged for it.

"If you can't get it to subside, you know where to find me and my needle, handsome." I kissed his lips before moving out of reach, trying to avoid being pulled down on top of him.

"I've always had a fantasy of doing it in a storage closet where we could get caught." He smiled as he adjusted himself in his pants before standing.

Crossing my arms, I stared at him and shook my head. "I could be fired for that, Michael."

"Not if we're quick and quiet. It's the thrill of getting caught that makes it so fucking great." He winked as he looked down at me.

I swallowed hard, my mouth feeling dry suddenly. "I'll take your word for it."

"You'll see," he said as he brushed his finger across my lip.

I sighed. The man liked to live life on the edge, and so did I. I fully expected a visit to the hospital in the coming days.

"Okay. Now scoot. I have to get ready. People's lives depend on me." I pushed him toward the door.

He pouted and grabbed his chest, pretending to be wounded. "I'll show myself out."

He pulled me into a kiss. I wrapped my arms around his shoulders as he held my head in his hand. The velvety texture of his tongue and the hint of mint left me wanting more.

I moaned, my lips following his mouth as he pulled away.

"A little something to remember me." He released me and made his way to the door.

"Hey, what's your MMA nickname?" I called out to him.

"Why do ya ask?" he asked with one hand on the doorknob.

"Curiosity."

"Michael 'The Iceman' Gallo." He smiled and left.

I stood there and tried to think of him as "The Iceman," but he should be called the "The Raging Inferno."

CHAPTER NINETEEN

MICHAEL

WALKING THROUGH THE HOSPITAL, I looked over my shoulder, paranoid that I'd run into Tammy. I still hadn't done a damn thing to deal with her the last week.

I'd been too fucking busy with the shop, family shit, and Mia.

With a smile, I pushed open the door to Joe's room, and found it empty. The bed was neatly made and everything was back in its rightful place, but no Joe. My smile evaporated.

"Can I help you?" a nurse asked behind me.

Walking out of the room, I approached her. "That's my brother's room. I was coming to visit."

"Ah, they released him a couple hours ago. He went home, darlin'." She smiled.

"Thanks, ma'am," I said before walking away.

Pulling out my phone to text my ma, I headed to the elevators.

Me: Mom, why didn't anyone bother to tell me they released Joe?

I loved that my ma had finally decided to join this century and learn how to text. It was easier to keep the conversations shorter, because she always found something else to say when we actually spoke. If I ignored her texts, she'd call anyway, but for the most part it was the best way to communicate with her—at least for me.

Mom: We weren't there when it happened. We're not going to see him until tomorrow. Let him rest and enjoy your night.

My night would be spent without Mia. I had plenty to do. The shop needed to be organized and cleaned, and I could use an extra workout. The match would be here before I knew it.

The elevator arrived, and I pushed the button for the first floor. I leaned against the wall and thought about what to do first. When the doors opened, I saw a sign for the emergency room and the decision was made for me.

I sweet-talked the receptionist. I explained that I was Mia's boyfriend and I was here to see her, but only if she wasn't busy.

"Let me go see if she is. Take a seat and I'll be right back." She smiled as she stood from her desk, smoothing her skirt with her palms. She swiped her badge and disappeared behind the door.

I cracked my neck, rolling it on my shoulders, as I sat in the chair and stared at the door. The people sitting in the chairs around me looked miserable. They were coughing, moaning and grimacing. I knew the people beyond the doors were worse than those sitting here.

The door opened; the receptionist stuck her head out and motioned for me to come.

"She's in between patients right now. Come on." She opened the door, and I stepped into the noisy corridor.

"She's grabbing a cup of coffee down the hall on the right, last door." She pointed, smiled.

I nodded and smiled. "Thanks."

"Mm hmm," she said, eyeing me up and down, before leaving me to find Mia.

I debated if I should walk in and surprise her or wait in the hallway. I didn't want to scare the shit out of her. The hall was empty as I approached the door marked "Staff Only."

I leaned against the wall, crossing my arms as I waited patiently for her.

A few people gave me dirty looks as they walked by at the other end of the hall, and I smiled and waved. Fuck them. I couldn't wait any longer. I knocked on the door to get her attention. "Mia, are you in there?"

The door cracked open and she smiled at me. "Hey, what are you doing here?" she asked, stepping out into the hall.

"I've come to live out my fantasy." I smirked, resting my shoulder against the doorframe.

Her hazel eyes grew wide as a smile spread across her face. "Why are you really here?" She crossed her arms and laughed.

"Came to see my brother, but my family forgot to mention that he was released."

"Good for him."

"Now I'm the only one in need of attention." I stepped closer to her. "Can you spare a moment to take a look?" I looked down and back at her.

"Is stamina your problem?" Her eyes twinkled.

She was a total fucking ball buster.

"Why don't you tell me, doc?" I whispered against her lips. Her hair was perfectly slicked back into a tight bun, with her lab coat over her scrubs. The scrubs I could've done without—not sexy at all.

The corner of her lips twitched as she grabbed me by the shirt, pulling me down the hall. "I don't have long," she said, looking around to see if the coast was clear before pushing me inside the storage closet.

Fuck yes. Finally.

I locked the door and turned my attention on her.

Kneading her ass in my hands, I ravaged her mouth. Hard breaths and small moans fell from our lips. Finding her breast, I squeezed gently, caressing the hard nipple under my fingertips. Her body quaked at the contact. My dick ached to be inside her, not content with rubbing against her leg through my pants.

"Fuck, Mia. I want you," I growled, my erection straining to break free.

We nipped each other's lips.

She smirked, reaching in her pocket. She laughed, pulling a condom out.

"Did you know I was coming?" I unfastened my pants without hesitation. My cock sprang free and bounced off her stomach.

"I knew it was a possibility," she said against my lips.

"Better not be for anyone else, Mia." I grabbed the wrapper from her hand and tore it open with my teeth.

"There's no one else," she said with a straight face.

"Turn around, hands on the wall."

As she placed her hands on the wall, I pulled her scrubs and underwear down to her knees. The lab coat covered her ass, but I'd handle it.

Pushing down on the small of her back, I tapped her feet apart, giving myself a better angle. I placed the condom over my rock-hard dick carefully in the dim light.

It glided easily against the silky wetness as I rubbed the tip against her.

She wanted it.

Grabbing her hips, I thrust myself inside in one quick move.

She cried out when I was fully seated, and my piercings stroked her depths.

"Shh. You're going to get us in trouble," I whispered in her ear, placing my hand over her mouth.

I pumped into her, searching for my release as I held up her lab coat. My body slammed against her ass, moving her with each thrust.

There was nothing tender about this type of fucking.

For the first time in a long while, I didn't care about my partner getting off before me. Mia always left me with a hard-on, and for once, I'd leave her wanting more.

Releasing her mouth from my grasp, I used both hands to steady her hips, and pulled her against me. She fucked me back, moving in my hands, as my cock disappeared inside of her.

Watching my dick move in and out was better than any porn movie I'd ever seen.

She whimpered as I pounded into her flesh. God, she felt fucking amazing—tight and wet as her pussy pulsated against my shaft.

She'd be sore and hopefully walking a little differently for the rest of her shift.

Biting down on her neck to stifle my moan, I gripped her tighter and pumped into her one last time.

"Fuck," I said against her neck, my teeth still biting down as my body twitched and shook. Dizziness and exhaustion overcame me as I rested my face in her back, trying to catch my breath.

"Hey, that's not fair," she said, wiggling her ass with my cock still inside her.

"All is fair in love and war. I'll make it worth your while, Mia…tomorrow." I grinned against her coat before I felt her body stiffen.

I pulled out, grabbing a piece of crappy brown paper from a roll on the shelf. I folded the condom inside before stuffing it in my pocket. She bent down to grab her pants, and I could see the redness my body had caused when it slammed into her.

I smiled, knowing she'd feel me on her for a while.

"You're an asshole," she said, glaring at me as she smoothed out her scrubs and coat.

"I'll own that." I smirked, stuffing my dick inside my pants and zipping them.

I kissed her on the lips, rubbing my nose against hers. "You made my fantasy come true, and we didn't even get caught."

"Yeah, but I would have at least liked to get off too." She glared.

"Tomorrow," I said as I tapped her on the nose. "Lemme make sure your clothes are right before we walk out." She turned around slowly, and I checked her out from head to toe. "You look like nothing happened."

"Good." She smiled.

"Shit, I didn't do it right."

Her laughter filled the small space as she opened the door. We walked into the hallway and she closed the door behind us. "Where are you headed now?" she asked.

"I'm going to head to the gym. Enjoy your night, doc. Think of me." I winked at her.

"I'm sure I will. That was so unfair, Michael. It's going to be the longest shift of my life," she said, frowning.

"Gives you something to look forward to." I reached out to grab her hand.

"You!" someone yelled from down the hall.

We both turned toward the voice as I pulled my hand back to my side.

At the end of the corridor was my worst nightmare.

Tammy.

Motherfucker.

I closed my eyes and held my breath as I waited for my fucking world to fall apart.

I went from ecstasy to agony in under one minute.

CHAPTER TWENTY

MIA

MICHAEL LOOKED like a trapped animal as a nurse walked toward him screaming. Not just any nurse, but the one I had soothed in the bathroom days ago.

Her hands were balled into fists at her sides as she approached with a red face, sneering.

I looked at her and back to him.

Fuck me, it couldn't be possible. Was he?

No, no.

Son of a bitch!

"Where the hell have you been?" She placed her hands on her hips, standing toe to toe with him.

"Do you know her?" I asked, hoping I was wrong.

She turned her glare toward me. "This is the asshole I was telling you about."

"Wait a minute," Michael said. "Let me explain." His face turned white as he reached for my hand.

Suddenly, my mouth felt dry as her words hit me full force. "He's your fiancé?" I asked, still in shock. I stared at them, blinking as my mouth hung open.

"Yes *and* the father of my baby." She smiled as she

stood there with her hands on her hips. Her right eye ticked at the corner.

My heart sank as a wave of nausea hit. "Is this true, Michael?" I asked, turning to him, needing to hear his answer.

I looked at him and could see sheer terror.

He shook his head with wide eyes. "No, it's not true at all. Please, let me explain, Mia." He tried to touch me again, but I backed away.

I felt like a fool.

How did I honestly think I was the only woman in his life?

I knew better than to believe the bullshit of a smooth-talking, beautiful man, but I listened to my heart instead of my head.

I looked at the floor, shaking my head as I tried to decide if I should stay or go.

"Tammy, you're a crazy bitch. I'm not your fiancé. For fuck's sake, don't do this to me," he pleaded with her, as the veins on the side of his neck protruded and visibly pulsed.

"What's this, then?" she asked, thrusting her hand in his face.

He gawked, his mouth moving but nothing coming out.

"You asked me weeks ago before I even told you about the baby," she said, pushing her hand closer to his face.

She shoved the large princess-cut diamond ring in my face and wiggled her fingers, with a wide grin. My chest ached as my heart thundered against my insides.

I felt sick. I wanted to curl into a ball and cry.

"You knew about the baby?" I asked in horror.

His nostrils flared as he blinked slowly. "She's not having my baby, Mia," he said through gritted teeth.

Tammy pushed on his chest. "How can you deny your own child?" she screeched.

"Shut the hell up, Tammy," he roared as a crowd began to form in the hall.

I had never been so embarrassed in my life. I hung my head, gathering my thoughts.

I needed to get the fuck out of here.

"Mia, you've got to believe me. She's crazy and making it up," he begged, holding out his hand to me.

Looking at his hand, I took a step back. "She has a ring, Michael. I don't know what to think. I need time." Wiping the tear with the back of my hand as it slid down my cheek, I said, "Don't call me anymore."

"But Mia." His eyes were large and sad.

"No," I replied quickly. "Don't touch or talk to me. You need to work things out with your fiancée and future mother of your child. There's no room for me in your life. I don't date cheaters, and I certainly don't fall in love with men that run out on their responsibilities."

His hand dropped to his side as he stared at me. "Mia, you know she's crazy, right?"

"I'm right here, dickhead," Tammy yelled, punching him in the arm.

His arms flexed and his hand twitched. "Don't fucking touch me, you insane bitch. I know where the fuck you are; you're like a crazy nightmare that won't go the fuck away."

"I don't have time for this bullshit." I shook my head, tears threatening to turn into sobs. "You two deserve each other," I said before turning my back to them.

"Mia," Michael yelled as I walked away.

Hanging my head, I hid my eyes from the onlookers that had gathered in the hallway. I could hear their voices as I disappeared in the bathroom.

Finding an open stall, I closed myself in and shut the

outside world out. I sat on the toilet and rocked. Silent tears racked my body. I realized the only person that had made me feel safe had turned into my biggest fear, heartache, and devastation.

Michael Gallo crashed into my world and turned it upside down.

I couldn't sit here and cry over a man that I'd only known a couple of weeks, even though I wanted to. Patients waited for me. I couldn't spend another moment wallowing in what could've been and will never be.

Fuck Michael Gallo and that crazy whore too.

Anger bubbled inside as I stood and walked out of the stall to dry my face.

My phone started beeping, text messages coming in rapidly from Michael. I turned the ringer off and stuffed it in my pocket before reaching for the door.

It was going to be a miserable shift at the ER.

CHAPTER TWENTY-ONE

MICHAEL

"SIT DOWN, baby. Tell me what's wrong," my ma said, pulling out a chair for me.

She really was sweet, and I felt shitty to throw this on her, but I needed her.

"I didn't know who else to come to, Ma." Sitting down, I rested my hands in my lap. I stared her straight in the eye as I leaned back and figured out how to break this to her.

"I'm always here for you. You look like shit, Michael." She reached out and caressed my cheek, with a small smile.

I smiled and leaned into her touch as she soothed me. "I don't even know where to begin with this clusterfuck," I said, scrubbing my hands across my face.

"Only because you're so upset will I let that word slide in this house today."

"Sorry, Ma." I shrugged. "All right, here it is." I let out a breath before speaking. "About six weeks ago I started seeing this woman, Tammy."

"Seeing as in dating or…" She looked at me with one eyebrow higher than the other.

I sighed, wishing I could avoid the entire conversation. "We weren't dating. We hooked up a couple of times."

"God, I hope you used protection." She shook her head. "All these horrible diseases out there today."

"Ma, can I tell you the story or are you going to interrupt me?"

She laughed, patting my hand. "You go ahead, son. Sorry. I'll sit here and listen." Resting her head in her hand, she stared at me.

Her facial expression changed as I told her the story. Her eyes were as big as saucers and her mouth hung open by the time I finished. "Can I ask some questions now?" she asked.

Nodding, I motioned for her to ask.

"So you didn't ask her to marry you?"

"Nope."

"And she's not pregnant either?"

"Nope."

"Are you sure she's not pregnant?" she asked, tilting her head as she rubbed her chin.

"Fuck if I know, Ma. I wore a condom the couple of times we did it. Not one busted and all came from my pocket."

"You said she's crazy, how crazy we talkin'—Kathy Bates *Misery* crazy or what?"

"She could be Kathy Bates' daughter." I laughed.

"Jesus Christ, son. Didn't we raise you boys right?" She rubbed the back of her neck. She shook her head, leaning back in her chair, and stared at me.

"You did, Ma. Sometimes we just kinda let our other head do the thinking." I looked down at the table, flicking a crumb near my arm.

"We're going to have to talk with your father about this. We may need to call George and get a restraining order against her. Maybe you can get a pregnancy test done, and if necessary, an ultrasound to determine the date of conception." Her cheeks puffed out before letting the air escape slowly.

"I hoped she would just forget about me and move on. She ruined everything with Mia."

I was miserable without Mia. I never felt lonely, ever, but I felt the emptiness when she had walked away from me, from us, in the hospital a couple days ago. The longest two days of my fucking life.

"Is Mia the doctor from the hospital?"

"Yeah, you know about her?"

"Your siblings can't keep a secret worth shit, son, except for Joe. He's like a rock, and it makes me nuts." She laughed, her smile almost kissing her eyes.

"Well, Tammy confronted me when I was with Mia. Mia's confused and doesn't know what to believe. She hasn't returned my phone calls or replied to a text in days, Ma. I have to fix this."

Her smile fell. "Have to be crafty, son. Outthink her. Fight fire with fire." She paused and scrunched her lips. "Maybe you can get Tammy to go see a doctor and let you come." She patted my hand. "You can verify the pregnancy or lack thereof, and we'll proceed from there. It would give you tangible proof sooner than waiting for the court system, but if she's dangerous, then you need to stay the hell away from her."

"I got it, Ma. I can handle her. I'm not worried about her hurting me. She's already done enough damage. I'll do it. I'll call her. I think she'll go for it if she thinks there's any chance of us getting back together."

"It's playing in dangerous territory, but I leave the decision up to you. Just be careful, Michael."

I didn't have a choice.

I had to risk it all to win back Mia.

I needed to show Tammy for who she really was—a liar.

"I don't need this bullshit right now, Ma. My fight is in a week and I have too much going on to deal with this. I need it to end now."

"You'll do it, son. I'll talk to your dad tonight and he can call George. He'll get the paperwork ready to put the restraining order into action. You can call him and find out what to do next."

As I stood from my chair, I bent over and kissed the top of her head. "Thanks, Ma. You always have great advice." I inhaled the strawberry scent of her shampoo and was instantly brought back to my childhood.

Reaching up, she stroked my cheek as she said, "That's what I'm here for."

As I started walking to the door, her voice stopped me.

"Michael," she yelled.

"Yeah, Ma?" I paused, not wanting to miss her parting advice.

"Keep it in your pants, son. Got me?"

"Hear ya loud and clear, Ma." Shaking my head, I opened the door and left to set the plan in motion.

Searching through my phone contacts, I couldn't find her number.

Damn it.

Izzy had blocked her. I headed to the shop to find my sweet little sister and see if she'd be willing to help me smash Tammy once and for all.

Leading up to my match, my schedule at the shop had almost been nonexistent. I tried to work out and practice as much as possible without having to worry about the day-to-day operations.

Piercings were by special appointment. I'd only had to

go in twice in the last ten days. Joe wouldn't be back for weeks. That left Anthony and Izzy to deal with running the business and tattooing.

Everything seemed to be in order as I walked through the front door of Inked. The waiting area looked tidy, just as I had left it, and the familiar buzz filled the shop. Soft voices came from the tattooing area. Death metal—Izzy's choice, I'm sure—played quietly so it blended in as background noise.

"Honey, I'm home," I yelled, walking toward the work area.

"Michael?" Izzy's voice echoed. "Get your ass back here, man."

Her face lit up as soon as she saw me. She snapped off her gloves and kissed me on the cheek. "Hasn't been the same without you here, driving us crazy and keeping our asses organized." She squeezed me, smashing her face in my chest.

I loved my little sister. Why? Because of moments like these, but definitely not her mouth.

"Thanks, Izzy. Sometimes you can be sweet…sometimes."

"Don't get too used to it," she said, sitting back down and putting on a new pair of gloves.

"Hey, how are ya?" I said to her client, whom I'd seen before. Couldn't remember his name for shit.

"Trying to survive your sister here. She's not as smooth as Joe with the needle." He winced, closing one eye.

"No one's as smooth as he is. He'll be back soon, though. You should've waited."

"I can hear you both," she said as she rubbed salve into his skin. "I can do this dry if you'd prefer." She snickered.

"No, no," he replied. "Please, you're doing beautiful work."

I laughed and turned my attention toward Anthony. "How you holding up being here with her by yourself, Anth?"

He smiled as he leaned back in his chair and stretched. "She's been pretty good without you and Joe here." His back cracked, and he sighed.

I could never tattoo and sit in the same crippling position for hours. I didn't have the patience to deal with customers for extended periods of time, and I certainly couldn't handle working on the same design for six hours like they sometimes did.

Piercing was quick, with little time for chatting.

"They're the ones that make me the way I am." She shrugged, talking to the man in her chair. "Anthony is my partner in crime. Isn't that right, Anth?" She laughed.

"Oh, how I know that shit. You two give me a headache most days," I said, shaking my head.

"You speak the truth, Izzy." Anthony laughed as he worked on the design. "What brings you by to visit us working people?" Anthony asked as he shaded in a rose.

I cringed because I knew her ass would be so ecstatic to hear the words. "Well, I need Izzy."

Her eyebrows shot up. "What? Are you feeling okay?" she asked as she looked up.

I rolled my eyes, sitting down in Joe's chair. "Yes, I need you to unblock that number you got rid of for me the other day."

"That girl with the damn scrapbook?" Her eyebrows drew together and a small crease formed between them.

"Yes, Tammy. I need you to unblock her number."

She sat back, tilting her head, and leveled me with her stare. "Why in the fuck would I do that?"

"Please, I just need you to. For me, Izzy, please," I said, pulling the phone from my pocket.

"You need to explain it to me first. I'm thinking you're the one that bumped your head, not Joe. I can't believe you're asking me to do this shit."

"Everything has turned into a mess. Mia won't see me or talk to me and it's all Tammy's fault."

"Still not giving me enough detail here, Mikey." She went back to working, not finding my request important enough to stop. "If she fucked everything up, why in the hell do you want to talk to her?"

"She's claiming I asked her to marry me and that she's pregnant with my baby." There it was, out in the open. I might as well have put that shit on a billboard now. Izzy never kept a secret.

"Wait, what?" She stood suddenly. "You drop that shit on me like it's nothing while I have a needle in someone's skin?"

"You asked for details, and those are *the* details."

"Give me fifteen minutes to finish this and we're going to have a talk before I do what you're asking me to. I want to know what the fuck happened with the doctor, too."

"Fine, I'll wait." I sighed and kicked my feet up on the customer chair. "How's Joe?" I asked. "Anyone see him lately?"

"He's well. You should go see him. He's been home for two days," Anthony said.

"Kind of had other things on my mind," I muttered.

"I know, but I'm sure Suzy is smothering him to death at this point," Izzy said, laughing.

"Joe loves that shit. He's probably milking it for all it's worth." Anthony mimicked a blowjob.

I missed being here every day. I missed the four of us as it had been weeks ago.

Everything had changed in my life in the last week—the highest high to the lowest low.

I wanted so badly to talk to Mia. I wondered if she knew how to block someone like Izzy had done on my phone. I hoped she hadn't blocked me. She hadn't read a damn message I sent her. I couldn't help myself. I had to keep trying.

Me: Mia, please talk to me. Tammy's lying and insane. You have to believe me! I miss you, doc.

I stared at the screen, hoping my message would show *read,* but nothing. It just sat there delivered and unread.

I opened Facebook and searched for her page. She'd posted something yesterday. I shouldn't have looked, because it made me feel more rejected than I already did.

She'd posted a quote from Cicero; "Nothing is more noble, nothing more venerable than fidelity. Faithfulness and truth are the most sacred excellences and endowments of the human mind."

I sat there, stunned into silence by her words, as I waited for Izzy to finish.

I still caught myself thinking of Izzy as a little girl. I pictured her with her pigtails flopping, playing hopscotch in the front yard, or begging us to play football. She always felt left out because we worried she'd get hurt. She turned into a tomboy in her teenage years before she realized the power of being a female.

Izzy was a tagalong, and we hated it when she was a little girl, but as she grew older, we'd used it to our advantage. We scared away more men than she'd ever know.

She was ours to protect…no matter the cost.

I had been lost in thought when she walked back into the work area after her client left. "All right, let's go outside and you can tell me what happened."

"Thanks, Izzy," I said, following her out back.

We walked into the Florida evening sun, and my skin

felt like it was being burned. There wasn't a cloud in the sky, just a brilliant blue color and the sun shining brightly.

"Why do you want to talk to that psycho?" She crossed her arms over her chest, leaning against the building in the shade.

"I want to catch her in her lies," I said as I ran my fingers through my hair. "It's the only way I can do it quick."

"Why not just go to the police? I'm sure they can speed shit along if you tell them you're Thomas' brother."

"I will if I have to, but I need to prove to Mia that she's full of shit, Izzy. I can't have this hanging over my head with the fight coming up, either." I moved my neck from side to side, trying to crack it. I gave it a push before hearing the bones crack.

"What's your plan?"

"I'm going to pretend I give a flying fuck and ask her to take me to the doctor with her. I want to be the proud daddy. I'm hoping they can confirm that she isn't pregnant, and that it will at least win some favor with Mia. Hopefully it will get Tammy out of my life once and for all." I kicked a stone, watching it skip across the back parking lot.

"Could backfire in your face, brother."

"It's not my kid even if she is pregnant."

"It only takes once." She rolled her eyes like I was a fucking idiot.

"No shit, Sherlock. I used protection every time. She's grasping at straws."

"Fine, but when this shit blows up in your face, just remember I told you so."

"Oh, I'm sure you'll remind me every day, baby sister." I laughed.

"Give it to me," she said, holding out her hand.

Giving her my phone, I watched as she tapped the screen, and within seconds handed it back.

"You really have to show me how to do that," I said, scrolling through my contacts and stopping on Tammy's name.

"Nope. I'd miss out on all the good shit if I taught you boys everything."

"You're right. I'd give my left nut not to have to deal with your ass sometimes. Thanks, though, for this." I wrapped her in my arms, kissing the top of her head.

"Just let me know if you need reinforcements. I know Ma told you you're not allowed to hit girls, but that rule doesn't apply to me." Her smile grew so large it almost touched her eyes. "That's the bonus of not having a dick and being part of the pussy party." She laughed, slapping me on the chest.

"You're my go-to chick for an ass beating, Izzy." I smiled at her. She really could be adorable.

"Go get your shit straightened out. You have a fight to win, and I may or may not have something very important bet on the outcome."

My smiled faded. "You didn't bet on my fight, did you? Please tell me you at least picked me to win."

She nodded. "Fuck yeah. Who else would I pick? You're going to break that dude's neck."

"Only if I can get my mind in the game before that day. My life needs to even out so I can concentrate on one thing at a time."

"Well, what the hell are you still standing here for? Get." She shooed me.

"Yes, ma'am." I saluted her as I walked away.

I reminded myself I had a mission as I sat in the hot car, waiting for the air conditioning to kick in. I had a mission. I gave myself a pep talk, psyching myself up. "You can do this. You have to do this. " I held my breath and hit the call button. My stomach flipped with each ring.

"Michael?" she asked in almost a whisper.

I heard her voice, and I had to choke down the bile rising in my throat. "Hey, Tammy." I almost convinced myself that the hello was sincere.

"Oh my God. I'm so happy to hear your voice, baby. I've been waiting for your call."

I closed my eyes and gripped the steering wheel. "I'm sorry I've been a dick. Think you could forgive me?" I asked through gritted teeth.

"You know I love you, Michael. I could never stay mad at you."

Her voice made my skin crawl. "How's the baby?" I asked, rolling my eyes.

"Safe and sound. Growing bigger every day," she replied in a cheery voice. Clearly she had an entire jar of screws lose in her head.

"I was thinking…" I stopped and gave myself a moment to carefully form my next words. "I was wondering if we could go to the doctor so I can see the baby on the monitor, like an ultrasound. I told my mother and she said it's the most amazing experience to see the baby in the womb."

She gasped. "You told your mother?"

"I did. She's so excited to finally have a grandbaby. I want to show her a picture of *our* baby. What do you think?" I held my breath. *Please be crazy enough not to question my lie.*

She sucked in a breath. "Okay, I know a doctor at the hospital that I can call, I guess. Maybe she can get us in," she said with a shaky voice.

"Tell her it needs to be as soon as possible. I can't wait any longer, and it would make my mom really happy."

"I'll try and track her down at the hospital tonight. She may be there when I go into work."

"Perfect," I said, feeling relieved. "Listen, I gotta run. I'm supposed to be at my brother's. Text me when you have the details."

"I will, Michael. I love you." She drew out the words.

Cue the creepy music from *Psycho*.

"Back at ya." I tapped the end button, unable to spend another second on the phone listening to her and lying through my teeth.

She deserved the deception.

CHAPTER TWENTY-TWO

MIA

I IGNORED MICHAEL, his calls, and his text messages. The anger inside me hadn't waned since I found out about Tammy.

He was the first guy in a long time that I'd let into my life. We weren't on the fast track down the aisle, but I had spent more time with him in the last couple of weeks than I had with any other man in the last few years.

I didn't drown my sorrows in ice cream and cry myself to sleep. I may have shed a tear or two after the shock wore off, but that was all Michael Gallo had been worth. I had too much on my plate to walk around all day upset about the shitty end to our relationship.

I did my shifts at the hospital and volunteered more than usual at the clinic. I filled my free time with work and kept my mind off *him*.

I hadn't been to the gym to work out since it all exploded in my face. I couldn't see him. Not yet. I didn't have anything to say to him.

I stood on throbbing feet, filling out my last chart, about a child that had arrived via life-flight, before I could head home. She had drowned in the family pool and was found by her mother. The little girl had been revived to the point that she was breathing upon arriving in the ER. Brain damage was almost a certainty with the lack of oxygen for an extended period. Talking to the parents was bittersweet. They were happy that their baby had survived, but mortified about the possibility of complications and the possibility they'd never have their little girl back.

Every day the hospital chipped out another piece of my heart. Between losing patients, talking with families, and a general feeling of helplessness—I felt broken. I was a shell of the person I used to be before I started med school with big dreams and foolish hopes.

"Guess what?" a woman asked in a giddy tone, distracting me from the chart.

I ignored the voice, signing my name and flipping the chart closed. The outline of a person standing a little too close caught my attention, but I still I ignored her.

"Hey, I'm talking to you," she said again, not moving.

Hell. I sighed before turning. "What?" I took in the sight of her—Tammy.

My blood turned ice cold as I stared at her smile. An overwhelming urge to claw her eyes out hit me, the fantasy in my mind bringing me a moment of joy.

"Michael and I are back together." She smirked.

Well, isn't he quick? She's as big of an asshole as he is. He'd been texting me since the day I left him in the hall with her and they were already back together.

"That's great news. I'm very happy for you." I gave her my best fake smile. "I'm kind of in a rush. My shift ended and I need to go."

The smile on her face faded. "I wanted you to know since you were so supportive, but I know there was something going on between you two. When I found you in the hallway it was obvious." She crossed her arms.

"Nah, we're just friends. You two are back together and you have a bundle of joy on the way. I'm truly happy for you both." My cheeks hurt from the smile; I still needed to make the bullshit happiness I pretended to feel be a little more believable.

She squinted at me, her mouth set in a firm line. "You slept with him, didn't you?"

I looked her in the eyes as I spoke very slowly. I wasn't about to jump on the crazy train. "Michael and I are and *were* nothing. He's yours."

"Oh my God, you did. You're a fucking whore. You're the reason he broke up with me in the first place, aren't you?" She bit her lip, gnawing on it, glaring at me.

I could almost see the wheels in her head spinning. Fucking great.

"I'm out. You can talk to Michael about me, but I don't have time for your bullshit, sweetie." I knew I sounded patronizing, but I couldn't get in a fight with a pregnant woman.

"I'll have a *long* conversation with him when we go to the doctor tomorrow for our first visit. He can't wait to see his baby and show it to his mother." Her phone rang, distracting her before she could continue.

I took the opportunity to get the hell away from her. "Good luck and congrats," I said, walking away before she could catch up to me.

"Wait, wait!" she screamed only a few footsteps behind me, her heels clicking on the tile floor.

I stopped in my tracks, closing my eyes. "What?" I asked in a clipped tone.

"I wanted to show you our engagement photo." She thrust her phone in front of my eyes.

If she had a knife in my chest, she'd turn it, just to make the pain that much worse.

I glanced at the photo and looked away quickly, not wanting it to be thrown in my face more than it already has. Something about the photo was off. "Wait, let me see that again." I grabbed the phone.

"Look all you want, sweetheart. He's mine, and this time, I'm not letting him go." She released the phone with a giant-ass smile on her face.

Touching the screen, I enlarged the picture. The faces weren't right. They didn't match the bodies. I stood there gawking at it until Tammy grabbed it from my fingers.

"He's so romantic. He proposed at the beach," she said, staring at the picture.

It was creepy, and her mind must be totally twisted. I hadn't realized until then how entirely off she was, and the depths of her craziness.

"It's a fairytale," I said. *This bitch lives in La La Land.*

"More than I could've ever dreamed of, really. He's mine, all mine." She hugged the phone, moving her body side to side.

"Yep, all yours." I smiled. "I really have to go." I needed to get away from her. "Good luck with your ultrasound," I called out as I walked away.

I snuck a glance over my shoulder. She stood in the middle of the hall with her hands on her hips, glaring at me. Her very presence put me on edge, but her delusions told me she was far more dangerous than I had imagined. I was the enemy to her.

I wondered if Michael knew about the type of over-the-top nutty that was his fiancée. I asked the security guard to walk me to my car. I didn't explain, but I never needed to. I felt a little more at ease as I drove home, but I looked in my rearview mirror every few seconds to make sure she wasn't following me.

Sitting in my driveway, I opened my text messages, my finger hovered over Michael's name and his last message.

Michael: Goddamn it, Mia. I need you.

My resolve wavered until I thought about Tammy. I wanted no part in their crazy bullshit. I would've described him as romantic and an amazing lover, but fuck, there wasn't a cock in the world worth this hassle.

I wasn't going to come between them.

My body felt heavy from a long shift on my feet, my mind was in a fog, and my heart ached. A small part of me wanted to see why he needed me, but I convinced myself it was a ploy.

The day had been emotionally draining already without opening my heart to him again and rubbing salt in the wound.

I pulled down the room-darkening shades and closed the drapes. I tossed my clothes to the floor before I grabbed a glass of water and my sleeping pills. I needed for this day to be over.

I climbed into bed and closed my eyes, wishing the day away. Sleep didn't come easy. Every time I drifted off, a different nightmare would wake me up. Images of patients and their horrific injuries and the screams of the injured, faceless people startled me awake. The last one dealt with Tammy waiting to slice my throat open in my car after work.

The sleeping pills were supposed to help knock my ass out, but tonight, they sure as hell weren't doing the trick.

I turned on the television, giving up on sleep, and looked through the guide. There had to be something happy to watch to help replace my nightmares. *Sleepless in Seattle* had an hour left, and I'd seen it a dozen times. I flipped to the channel and watched with stinging eyes. I needed the happily ever after.

I could recite the lines in the movie verbatim. When they meet on top of the Empire State Building at the end, it always brought me to tears.

I drifted off to thoughts of Sam and Annie.

CHAPTER TWENTY-THREE

MICHAEL

"I HOPE your ass has been working out, man. Countdown is in single digits. What the fuck have you been doing?" Rob said as I landed another blow.

"I got this, Rob. Shit's been going on in my personal life that I've had to deal with, and I'm still dealing with it." I stretched my shoulders, cracking my neck, readying myself for the next round. My heart hurt more than my muscles ached, but I couldn't stop.

"You need to get everything worked out before the fight. You need your head in the game. An hour here and there will not make you a champion."

"Oh ye of little faith. I took down 'The Mauler' and I sure as fuck can handle 'The Heat.' One problem will be taken care of today, and then I just have to win Mia back," I said as I grabbed a bottle of water, downing it before crushing the plastic.

Mia walking away and shutting me out hurt more than any injury I'd ever suffered in the cage. She gave me something good and pure to look forward to each day, but it was ripped from me by the devil.

His eyebrows shot up in surprise. "You hooked up with Mia, huh? You're a lucky son of a bitch." He shook his head but smiled. "She did ask me about you."

"When?" I asked, feeling hopeful.

"Weeks ago. Wanted to know who you were." He shrugged.

"Oh. I'd say we more than hooked up. I really like her, man."

"Before you grow a pussy, can you at least train while you pour your heart out?"

"I'm done talking, dick. I'm going to make you pay for the pussy comment."

I spent the next hour doing just that. Cocky bastard talked a good game, but he wasn't as fast as me. Rob knew the moves; his technical skills couldn't be beat. He used to be part of the circuit, but a nasty injury ended his fighting career.

I took my anger out on him. My jabs, kicks, and takedowns were aimed at him, but in my mind, Tammy received each piercing blow. The bitch had crossed the line, making me miserable, and today I would call foul.

"Jesus, that's the hardest you've hit me in a long time, man," Rob huffed, grabbing his shoulder.

"I don't have another outlet for my anger. You're my personal punching bag," I said, wiping the sweat from my eyes.

"Save some of it for the cage. He won't know what hit 'em. Maybe you shouldn't straighten the shit out first." He smirked.

"Fuck you, Rob."

"Kidding, Mike." He laughed. "Let's call it a day. Be here tomorrow morning at five. We don't have a moment to waste."

I collapsed on the bench, every muscle screaming as I

rubbed my thighs. "I'll be here. Be ready for another ass kicking." I smirked. I never hit him hard enough to hurt him. I had more power in me than I ever took out on him. "Today I get everything ironed out and I'll be back on track. My mind will be focused."

"I hope so. If you want to get another big match like New York, you can't lose the next one."

"Shut the fuck up. I got this. I'm not losing. He won't be an issue." I pulled the tape off my hands, squeezing them to get the blood to flow to my fingers.

"That's the type of thinking that'll get your ass knocked out."

"Aren't you supposed to be in my corner?" I looked at Rob as he stood in front of me.

He had a cocky grin on his face; the bastard was trying to get me riled up more than I already was with the Tammy bullshit. "I am. Just reminding you to get your shit straight."

"Okay, Mom. I gotta go do just that. Now shut the fuck up and get outta my face."

Putting his hands up, Rob said, "I'm out. I expect a full report tomorrow. Bring some of that piss and vinegar with you for training. We're sparring for real, and I better not be able to take you down or you're in real trouble."

Pointing at him, I smiled. "Keep spouting your shit and I'll make sure you walk into the match with a limp."

He laughed as he walked away and unlocked the doors. I looked through the glass, trying to will Mia to walk through the door.

"She hasn't been here in a week. You can stop looking, pussy."

I didn't reply. She was avoiding me, and it stung more than his words.

***

I stared at Tammy as she looked around the exam room. She had a triumphant smile on her face and excitement oozed off her.

The thought crossed my mind that this could be a huge mistake. What if she really was pregnant? I shook my head, removing the thought, as someone knocked on the door.

"Come in," Tammy said, looking at the door with her hands clasped in her lap and moving her dangling feet.

A heavyset woman with gray hair entered the room. "Good morning, Tammy. How are you feeling today?" she asked as she sat down on the stool next to the exam table.

"I'm doing really great, Dr. Singh."

Kicking back, I put my hands behind my head to watch it unravel. I wanted to speak, but I figured that if the doctor had a brain she'd figure out Tammy's scam quickly.

"That's always nice to hear. How far along do you think you are?" The doctor asked, looking down, flipping through the file.

"I'm not sure. Not too far." Tammy fidgeted with her hands, looking down.

"You said the pregnancy was confirmed, though, right?"

"Yes, my family doctor confirmed it, but Michael"—she looked to me and back to Dr. Singh—"he's the dad and wanted to get an ultrasound picture as soon as possible."

"It's nice to meet you, Michael." Dr. Singh nodded at me and smiled.

"You too, doc. I want to know when the bundle of joy will be entering our lives." I couldn't just come right out and say I didn't believe a word that came out of Tammy's mouth—at least not in front of her, anyway.

"Well, let's see if we can get you a photo and determine a due date for you."

"Is it too early for that?" Tammy looked worried, but I honestly thought she was too nuts to really grasp the enormity of what was about to happen.

"No, I can see the stage of development and can give you an educated guess. Depends how far along you are, sweetie." Dr. Singh patted Tammy's leg.

"I can't thank you enough for doing this so quickly. I know how busy you are," Tammy said with a smile.

"I always try and help out the hospital staff the best I can. You're lucky I had a cancellation."

I was bored with their chitchat to the point where I had started to become annoyed. "Ladies, I don't mean to be a jerk, but I'm on pins and needles here." I rubbed my neck and tried to calm myself down.

"I know you're both excited. Lean back, Tammy, and lift your shirt," Dr. Singh said, pulling over the ultrasound equipment. She grabbed a paper cover-up, tucking it in Tammy's pants, pulling them down to expose her belly. She squirted blue liquid on her stomach as Tammy began to laugh.

"I know it feels funny, but at least it's warm. Now, let's see what we have here."

Swallowing hard, I moved to the edge of the seat. My legs began to shake as my stomach felt like someone was inside beating the fuck out of it.

The wand glided across her stomach as the doctor stared at the screen. She leaned forward and stared before moving the wand a bit.

I had no idea what the hell I was looking for, but it didn't stop me from trying.

"That's strange," Dr. Singh said, her face almost pressed against the black-and-white screen.

"What's wrong?" Tammy looked panicked as she bit her lip, sitting up on her elbows.

"I don't see anything." Dr. Singh moved the wand again and squinted at the monitor.

The angels began to sing in my head, and I felt vindicated as relief flooded my body.

"Wait," Dr. Singh said.

Fuck, no way did something magically appear.

My heart stopped and every ounce of air left my lungs.

"False alarm," she said, frowning.

Jesus fucking Christ, she almost gave me a heart attack. I started to breathe again, almost dizzy, on the verge of a panic attack.

"Tammy, I don't see an embryo, sweetie. Are you sure you were pregnant?"

"What do you mean 'were'?" Tammy's mouth hung open.

"I don't see anything at all." The doctor shook her head and looked at me with sad eyes.

I wanted to fist bump her, not cry.

"I lost the baby?" Tammy's lips began to quiver and her eyes glistened.

The crazy bitch actually was an amazing actress. I'd give her a fucking Oscar.

"I can't say that you were ever pregnant, but if you were, then yes, I'm sorry," Dr. Singh said as she put the wand in the holder.

Every muscle in my body relaxed, and I felt exhausted as I watched the doctor wipe Tammy's abdomen.

"I can't believe it," Tammy whispered as she wiped away tears.

"You can try again. This is common in the first trimester." Dr. Singh was trying to be supportive, but I'd bet money based on her facial expression that she didn't think there ever was a baby. "Sometimes tests can be wrong, sweetie."

"Stop calling me that!" Tammy yelled, covering her ears.

Enter psycho Tammy.

"You're lying about my baby." Her hands fell to her stomach as she cradled herself. "He's in there." She caressed her stomach.

Dr. Singh looked stupefied. I was sure she was used to a bit of crazy dealing with hormonal pregnant women all the time, but Tammy was her own special brand.

"You can always get a second opinion." The doctor rubbed her head before she started to scribble in the file.

I sat there, not wanting to cause a scene in the doctor's office by confronting Tammy with her lie.

"I will. You obviously don't know what you're talking about."

The doctor's eyebrows shot up. She saw the crazy. Recognized Tammy for who she really was—cuckoo.

"It's your right as a patient," the doctor said.

Tammy jumped off the table, adjusting her pants as tears streamed down her cheeks. "Let's get the fuck out of here, Michael. I need to find a real doctor." She glared at Dr. Singh.

The doctor looked at me, dumbfounded. "I'm sorry," she said with a halfhearted smile.

I shrugged and tried to hide my smile. "Don't worry about it, doctor. It's not your fault."

"What the fuck? Yes, it is. She's lying to us, Michael." All the tears on her face had disappeared, replaced by coldblooded hatred.

"Let's go, Tammy. Let's get you out of here." I held my hand out to her as I bit my lip.

No one spoke as we walked out of the room. Tammy walked right by the checkout desk before bursting into the waiting room. "She's a fraud," she yelled at the room full of women with swollen bellies.

"Shh," I said as I clamped my hand around her mouth from behind. "Save it for outside," I whispered in her ear.

I kept my hand on her mouth as we left the doctor's office.

As soon as we made it outside, she yelled, "I can't believe her. There's a baby in my belly." She rubbed her stomach and stared at her hands.

"Let's just get you home." I wanted to drop her off and immediately file for a restraining order. My suspicions were correct, and it was time to put Tammy in the past.

"Will you stay and hold me?" She looked at me with wide eyes, clinging to my shirt.

"I will." I hated lying, but with Tammy it was easy. I didn't flinch with my words. "Come on, get in. I'll stay as long as you need," I said as I held the door open.

She gave me a weak smile as I closed the door and fought every instinct I had to run. After I climbed in, she curled up to me. She held my arm as I drove, and I didn't look at her or return her touch. We drove in silence.

"You're coming in, right?" She looked up from my shoulder with a meek smile on her face as I pulled in her driveway.

"Yes." I wasn't going to fucking cuddle, either. This time I wouldn't leave her house without the scrapbook safely in my possession. "Let's get you into bed so you can rest."

Her smile grew wide as she looked into my eyes. "I can't think of anything that would make me happier, Michael." She climbed out of the car and waited for me.

Holding my arm, she opened the front door.

"Go get ready and I'll be right in. I'm going to make us some tea," I said, wanting her to go away.

"Oh, okay," she said as she stood on her tiptoes, kissing my cheek.

"Take your time, put something comfy on, and I'll meet you in bed."

She walked away with a giant smile on her face, looking back at me before disappearing inside her bedroom.

I turned on the water, to hide any noise, before I looked through the living room.

Where the fuck was the scrapbook? It wasn't on the coffee table, like it had been the last time I was here. I started to panic, my heart pounded, and sweat beaded on my brow. I needed to find it and get the fuck out of here.

As I walked by her television, I spotted it. Victory was mine. I grabbed it and tucked it under my arm.

Turning off the water, I stood in the kitchen, out of her line of sight from the hallway. "You okay in there?" I called out to her.

"Yeah, I'm going to jump in the shower to freshen up. Okay, baby?" she replied from the bedroom.

"Go ahead. I'm just finishing up with the tea. I'll be waiting for you."

"I'm hurrying," she yelled.

As the shower turned on, I waited, listening for her to climb inside. I left the house as quietly as humanly possible before jumping in my truck and breathing a sigh of relief.

I could only imagine the scene when she walked out and didn't see me there. She wasn't my issue to deal with anymore; it was for the law to handle.

First stop would be Izzy to put the block back on my

phone, and then to George. I needed to sign the restraining order and have it executed.

Mia was the next thing to resolve.

I had to get her back.

She was the one prize I couldn't lose.

CHAPTER TWENTY-FOUR

MIA

I STARED out of the sliding glass doors that led out to my lanai, sipping a cup of coffee. I inhaled the sweet scent as I watched the palm trees sway in the summer breeze. I needed to blow off some steam. Running was the best option, but out of the question in the blazing sun and humid air. Even early in the morning, the humidity outside was enough to make your hair instantly frizz and your skin damp within seconds.

I tapped my coffee cup with my finger and weighed my options. Pass out from running outside or head to the gym and possibly run into Michael. Why couldn't my life be simple anymore?

A pounding on the door made me jump and spill my coffee.

"Fuck," I muttered, wiping my hands on a napkin. Nothing like a peaceful morning ruined by a Mormon searching for a new convert.

I trudged to the door, annoyed with the interruption. Instead of a gaggle of religious people, Michael stood there with a package tucked under his arm, looking really pissed off.

My heart hammered, wanting to burst through my chest.

"Mia," he said, holding the doorframe.

"What do you want, Michael? Haven't I made it clear that I don't want to see you?"

He closed his eyes, letting go of the doorframe and taking a step forward. "I can't let you shut me out." He shook his head as he opened his eyes.

"It's not your decision to make." Crossing my arms, I didn't let a bit of weakness show through. That's the problem with men—they want control, and I wasn't used to giving it up.

"Fucking hell," he muttered as the hardness in his face melted away. "I *need* to talk to you."

I didn't move. "We're talking. Say what you need to say and go."

I had to stay strong, when all I wanted to do was jump in his arms and make up. I wanted to erase the last week. I needed to be strong. I'd never play second fiddle to anyone.

"Can't I come in?" He straightened, taking another step forward.

I held out my arm, stopping him. "Here will do."

He balled his hands into fists as he stared at his feet. "First, Tammy is *not* pregnant. I had that confirmed yesterday by a doctor." He paused.

I took that opportunity to jump in. "That's lucky for you. I ran into Tammy yesterday and she told me you two were going to get an ultrasound." His eyes widened as I spoke. "I was also told that you're very much back together and happier than ever."

"We are not back together. I spent yesterday afternoon filing a restraining order against her."

My stomach filled with butterflies as he reached to touch my arm, but he pulled away at the last second.

"I needed her to trust me to prove she wasn't carrying my baby. She's nothing to me," he pleaded.

"Are you so careless with women, Michael? We're here to be used?"

He stiffened and glared at me. "Are you fucking kidding me right now? I've never used you. I did nothing to make you feel that way, Mia."

"I felt dirty in the hallway of the hospital when Tammy flashed her ring in my face. I felt used and worthless. No one has ever made me feel that way." I choked back the tears that wanted to escape. "I've never allowed anyone to make me feel that way until you came into my life." I shook my head, and my shoulders fell.

"Mia, sweetheart," he said tenderly. He touched my arm, and the electricity passed between us. The snap, crackle, pop. The spark hadn't died, no matter how hard I tried to smother it.

"Tammy's not in my life. I never promised her a relationship or a forever, and I never asked the crazy woman to marry me. You have to believe me." He rested his hand against my cheek, and I wanted to melt into his touch, but I didn't.

"I want to, Michael. I really do." I looked into his soft caramel eyes and felt his sorrow. It was like a punch to the gut. "How do I know it's really over between the two of you?"

"My lawyer is taking care of it."

"Sometimes the law can't stop someone like her. It's a can of worms I'm not sure I can handle right now. I have enough shit happening in my life without looking over my shoulder all the time."

"I'll protect you." He smiled.

It was megawatt strength, and amazing. It sent a thrill through me that he wanted me so badly, but could I willingly lay myself out for this man?

He grabbed my chin, bringing my eyes to his. "Don't throw what we have away, Mia. There's something that brought us together. I feel like I've known you forever, and I don't want to be without that feeling. I can't lose you."

I felt at home in his arms, and truly at peace when he entered my life. I closed my eyes to break the connection. The enormity of the moment sank in as I opened them. "I don't know," I said, staring at his chest. He'd be able to see my vulnerability if I looked at him.

"How can you deny what's between us, Mia?" His soft lips touched mine, and I couldn't pull away. I leaned into him, inhaling the soft, musky scent that was purely Michael. "We have something here that can't be denied," he said against my lips.

"Michael—" Before I could finish the statement, his mouth enveloped mine, effectively shutting me up.

He wrapped his arms around me. The touch that I had missed for days almost brought me to my knees. Pushing me into the house, he kicked the door closed behind us. I couldn't deny him any longer. I couldn't lie to myself and say what we had wasn't magical in some way.

I pulled away and stared into his eyes. "Only me?" I asked. I needed the affirmation that I was it for him. I wouldn't be in competition with anyone else for his love and affection. I'd never let myself be *that* girl.

"No one else," he said before capturing my mouth.

The sound of his breath as he devoured my lips sent an electric pulse through my body. I loved everything about this man, down to the small noises he made when we kissed.

"I'm scared, Michael," I whispered as he broke the kiss.

"Of what?"

"You." I sucked in a breath.

He held me at arm's length. "Mia," he said, lifting my chin. "I won't break your heart. For the first time in my life, I've found something worth fighting for, someone more important than me." His eyes searched mine. "Give me a chance to prove it. I'll do everything in my power to make you happy."

"How do I know I can trust you? I want to believe you, but what if I was the other woman, Michael? I can't just pretend like nothing happened without knowing for sure." I stared into his eyes.

"I have proof. I brought this to show you." He held out the large brown envelope.

"What is it?" I asked, not sure I wanted to open it.

"Just look. I want you to see Tammy for who she really is. My statement to the police is in there, along with evidence and screen shots of her text messages. She never mentioned a baby, Mia. She lied and tried to trap me." He pushed the envelope forward into my hands.

I walked to the couch and set it on the coffee table. Michael sat next to me, not speaking, as he watched me. I removed the contents one by one. A book and a couple of sheets of paper were inside. Setting the book on the table, I grabbed the papers and flipped through them.

I read the text messages first, paying close attention to the timestamp. Not one said anything about a baby, just Tammy begging him to come back to her. The messages went from pleading to downright mean and threatening. The conversation was entirely one-sided. They were all from before we met. He had ended it with her. I wasn't the other woman.

"What's this?" I asked, holding the black book in my hand.

"Take a look. It's an eye-opener for sure. Tammy made it."

I nodded, opening the cover to reveal the first page. It read "Michael & Tammy Gallo," with a picture of them on their wedding day. Only it wasn't them. I started laughing.

"I told ya," he said, running his fingers across my hand.

"No, it's just…" I tried to stop laughing. "She showed me a picture like this, but an engagement photo."

"Just great." He reached for the book.

I batted his hand away. "I'm not done," I said as I turned the page.

"Knock yourself out. It gets more bizarre the deeper you go." He leaned back and relaxed.

The engagement photo she had showed me was next, followed by a series of wedding shots. When I came to a page filled with children, I stopped and the laughter I had fought so hard to stop bubbled to the surface.

"Madelyn Gallo," I said, still laughing as tears formed in my eyes.

"Don't forget about Mason," he said, sitting up. "She picked out all the names." He smiled.

"She's seriously a wack job." I shook my head, still stunned by her audacity. "Didn't you know she was this nuts before you slept with her?"

"We were never a couple. I didn't figure it out until I found the book. I walked out of her house that day and never looked back." He rubbed my arm and grabbed my chin. "Mia, I never lied to you. Not about Tammy or anything."

I searched his eyes. With all the information and the sincerity on his face, I knew he spoke the truth. "I believe you, Michael."

"About damn time," he said, moving to kiss me.

"I'm still mad at you," I mumbled against his lips.

Pulling away, he rested his forehead against mine. "Take it out on me in the bed, Mia. I can't wait another minute to feel you under me."

"Wait," I said, pushing him away.

His smile evaporated. "What?"

"I said I believed you, not that I'd have sex with you." I shook my head and tried to make the statement believable. All I wanted to do was make love to the man and fall asleep in his arms. I missed his body against mine as I slept.

He gave me a cocky grin, the one that I loved. "Are you mine, Mia?" he asked, the corner of his mouth twitching.

"I haven't decided," I lied. There was nothing that I wanted more than to be his.

"Let me help you with that decision," he laughed, as he picked me up and hoisted me over his shoulder.

I laughed, swatting his ass so hard my hand stung.

"That's it baby, I like it rough," he said, chuckling, as he walked toward my bedroom.

I bounced on his back, biting his shoulder blade, smacking him again.

"Damn," he said as he spanked my ass twice, making me yelp. "I'd say we both have some emotions that need to come out. I'm going to fuck every bit of pissed-off out of you and show you who you belong to."

"I wanna see you try," I said, giggling.

He threw me on the bed, and all the air left my lungs as I hit the firm mattress with a bounce. He looked large and imposing standing at the foot of my bed. His shoulders were broad and the muscles in his neck were corded tightly. The t-shirt stretched across his torso looked like it would rip with the slightest movement. His brown hair lay across his forehead in a mess. He looked delicious and more handsome than ever.

"I'm up for a challenge," he said with a smile, as he removed his t-shirt.

Fuck, he really was beautiful. I sat up on my elbows and watched him undress. Every movement made his muscles stretched and contracted. He wasn't wasting a moment or doing a seductive striptease. I needed to feel him.

This wouldn't be lovemaking or rekindling—this was anger banging.

He pushed me back against the bed, opening the tie of my robe. He pushed it open, exposing my nightie. "Still mad?" he asked, his hands gliding across the cool silk on my abdomen.

"Yes." Damn, my voice wasn't strong. I knew he didn't hear the conviction behind my words.

He sat on his knees, grabbing the material with both hands. His palms slid effortlessly against the smooth nightie. His hands stopped just under my breasts before making the journey back down to my bare thighs. He grabbed the bottom of the nightie, pulling it from the middle, and tore it in half.

"Michael," I yelled. The air conditioning caressed my skin and goose bumps covered my flesh.

He laughed. "Quicker this way."

"I could've just taken it off, for fuck's sake."

"That *was* for fuck's sake, Mia. I'm sick of waiting. It's been days since I've been inside you."

I hit him square in the chest as he leaned over my body. Why did men have to destroy shit in the name of passion?

"Oh, yeah. Just like that. I like a little fight in you." His eyes turned dark.

"I hate you." I glared at him.

"No you don't," he said as his mouth clamped down on my nipple.

I arched my back, crying out in ecstasy.

He moaned against my trapped breast, causing a vibration to skate across my skin and my core to pulsate as I pushed him. "Don't fight it; you know you want it, doc."

I sighed, lying back to enjoy the feel of his lips on my skin, because I did want it. I ran my fingers through his hair before gripping it tightly in my fists. I held his mouth in place as tiny shocks shot through my body. The familiar ache between my legs became almost unbearable. I dug my heels into his ass and ground myself against him.

He tried to lift his head, but I pushed it harder against my chest, almost smothering him. I could feel his laughter against my torso as his body shook in my grasp.

"Put your cock in me," I said, releasing my heels, to give him the ability to move his lower half. I felt powerful, even if it was a lie. He could overpower me in a minute, but he let me play the game.

His lips popped off my skin and he looked into my eyes. "Don't you want to kiss a little first?"

"This isn't lovemaking, Michael. You're fucking me. Put it in or get the fuck out." I sounded harsh and strong, and it sent a thrill through me.

His eyebrows shot up, a small smirk on his lips. "That's fuckin' hot, doc."

"Shut the fuck up and do it." I kicked him in the ass.

"I love when you talk dirty to me. It makes me rock fuckin' hard," he said as he reached down and fisted his cock before rubbing it against me.

"Stop!" I yelled, frozen in place. "Get a condom from my nightstand."

"'Put it in. Stop. Any other commands?" he asked, as he reached for the drawer.

"You forgot, 'shut the fuck up.'" I laughed. I didn't know what had gotten into me, but I liked it.

"Kinda rough on me, aren't you?" he asked, as he unrolled the condom, paying careful attention to his piercings.

"I'm just getting started, big boy."

"You just made my balls tingle," he said as he nestled between my legs. Hooking his arms under my thighs, he pulled my body to his. "Let's get one thing straight, doc, I'm in charge here," he said as he stroked the tip of his shaft against me. "This is my pussy." He smacked my clit with the head.

"I don't see your name on it," I said, winded from the sting.

"It will be, but for now, possession is nine-tenths of the law," he said as he rammed his cock into me in one quick thrust.

My back arched as he pulled out and pushed back in with greater force. I wouldn't have described him as gentle the other times we'd been together, but this was rough and raw.

With the next thrust, I smacked him in the face. He flinched, stopping to stare at me through slitted eyes. "What the fuck was that for?"

"What you put me through."

His eyes searched mine for a moment before he pounded into me again.

I smacked him harder, but this time he didn't flinch. "For not being straight with me," I said quickly, before he could ask.

His eyes grew dark as his mouth set in a firm line. He pummeled me and I swung again, but he captured my hand. "You got two free shots, no more." Leaning forward with my wrists in his grasp, he held them above my head.

I fought to free myself, bucking against him. His muscles contracted with each thrust, and the sight of him alone could have me on edge. I bit my lip to quiet the moans that I wasn't ready to give to him.

Beads of sweat formed across his skin as he pounded into me.

He released my hands and I grabbed his biceps, curling my fingers around the thick muscles. Using my grip to push myself against him, I met his thrusts, our bodies slamming against each other. My body bounced off him, and the pressure of his cock hitting my depths drove me closer to the brink.

Our bodies collided, the impact hard enough to cause the headboard to hit the wall with a loud thud. I planted my feet into the mattress, using them to steady myself as I continued to push into him. It only took a few more thrusts before my body tightened and I spiraled into the most glorious orgasm of my life.

It wasn't the body-tingling orgasm that I'd experienced before. This was earth shattering—life changing, no one else would ever compare. Colors burst behind my eyelids as I rode the wave of ecstasy until I gasped for air through blurry eyes.

Michael wrapped his arms around me, cradling me against his chest as he cried out in his own rapture. He twitched, and his body shook in waves.

Releasing my body from his arms, he held himself above me. "Jesus Christ," he huffed out before shaking his head. "That was amazing. Fuck, I've never felt anything like that before."

I didn't reply. My mind was muddled from the bliss it had just experienced. He rested his forehead against mine; his harsh breath skidded across my skin. "Getting you pissed off has its advantages."

Not in a million years did I think we'd be in this situation when I sat there staring out the window sipping my coffee. I figured I was through with Michael Gallo, but after a kiss and mind-blowing sex, the craving was back worse than ever.

My vision blurred as I thought about all we'd been through the last couple of days. I didn't think the Tammy situation was over, but Michael said he'd handle her. I had no doubt in his abilities, but her craziness couldn't be planned for. She was the most dangerous form of opponent.

"What are you thinking?" he asked as he turned over, stretching out across the bed. He slid his hand under my body, pulling me to him.

"I don't know what to think." I snuggled into him and let the tears flow.

"Hey, hey. Don't cry. I know it was good, but I've never brought a girl to tears before."

"You ass," I said, smacking his chest. "I'm scared, Michael."

"Of what?"

"You, Tammy, this," I said, waving my hand over his body.

"Don't worry about Tammy. She's being dealt with. Don't be scared of me or us. We got off track, thrown off by a person nuttier than a Snickers bar."

I bit my lip to stifle a laugh. "You have such a way with words." I couldn't hold it in any longer. I laughed and buried my face in his side.

"Well, how would you describe her?"

I looked up at him, and the tears of worry turned to those of uncontrollable laughter. "You hit the nail right on the head."

"That's enough about her. Let me just enjoy the feel of you in my arms. No more talking, doc."

I snuggled into his side and closed my eyes. I'd never slept so contently as I had when I was in his arms. Closing my eyes, I let his warmth and steady breathing lull me to sleep.

CHAPTER TWENTY-FIVE

MICHAEL

I STROKED her arm until her breathing deepened and soft snores fell from her lips. I didn't know if I should be proud or a little disturbed at how easily she slept in my arms. I'd do anything to keep Mia in my life and make her happy. I wasn't anywhere near ready to get down on one knee and propose, or to whisper the words "I love you" in her ear, but I cared for Mia and didn't want to be without her.

I slept for a short time and watched her sleep after I woke. She had small, faint freckles on her sun-kissed cheeks. Her eyebrows were thick and dark, but neatly groomed. Her nose fit her face and had a delicate, narrow shape. Her lips were luscious and thick and were made for kissing. The filthy things she said to me this morning had almost made my heart stop. All blood in my body went to my dick as she smacked me around a little.

"Hey," she said in a drowsy voice.

"Sleep well?"

"Like a rock." She yawned and nuzzled her cheek against my pec.

"What do you want to do today, Mia? I want to spend the day with you." I brushed the hair from her eyes.

"I'm going to the clinic for a couple hours this afternoon."

"Can I come?"

She looked at me and smiled. "Yes, but it won't be a happy day. Have you ever noticed the real poor people in this area?"

"I have seen the homeless people on the corners."

"They're the tip of the iceberg, Michael. It's the ones that you don't see that are the most heartbreaking. The little kids that come in dirty and in need of basic medical care."

"If it's that sad, why do you do it? Why not just stick to the ER?"

"It's rewarding, and I feel I'm making a difference. The ER has its own type of rewards, but mostly it's filled with sadness." She sighed as she rolled out of my arms. She sat up, pulling her knees against her chest.

I sat up, running my fingers across her damp cheeks. "Why don't you find a way to work at the clinic, then?"

"There's no money; it's all volunteers. We get some money from the state and county, but it's minimal, laughable actually."

"Maybe my family could help. What would you guys need to fund the clinic?" I pulled her in my lap and wrapped my arms around her.

"I don't even know. I haven't looked at the books." She sagged against me, resting her head on my shoulder.

I kissed her shoulder. "You give me a figure and I'll see what I can do to make it happen."

"What is it exactly that your family does to have all this money, Michael? I'm all for charity, but if it came by criminal means then I'd have to decline."

"You mean like the mob?" I laughed. Stereotyping at its finest.

She turned her head, looking me in the eyes without smiling. "Ah, yeah. I couldn't take dirty money." She shook her head.

"You just made my day." I laughed, squeezing her tightly. "Totally stereotyping, but funny as hell, Mia." I held her chin in my grasp and kissed her on the lips. "We own a vineyard in Italy. It's been in our family for generations."

"Why do you work at the tattoo shop and fight, then? You could just sit at home all day."

"My parents didn't raise us to be lazy. We were taught to work and be appreciative of what we have. I fight for the fun and challenge. The shop feels more like a hobby than a real job."

"I get it. I couldn't sit on my ass all day either."

She turned in my lap and the friction against my dick made it start to harden. She held my cheeks in her small hands and stared in my eyes. All the craziness of the past week had vanished.

All that mattered in this moment was us.

"You have a big heart under that Superman exterior, Michael. You're a big softy." Her fingertips rubbed against the five o'clock shadow on my face, and I could feel every hair move under her touch.

"Don't tell anyone. You'll ruin my reputation." I laughed. "What's pressing against your ass isn't soft."

She giggled as she rested her forehead against mine. "It'll have to wait until we get done at the clinic. There are needy people waiting for me."

"I'm needy," I said as my dick twitched against her ass. "Real needy."

"You're horny, there's a difference." She smacked my shoulder.

Her smile made my heart ache. I'd do whatever I could to help her make her dream of working at the clinic full-time a reality. She deserved to have that smile every day.

"Tell that to my cock." I took the opportunity to kiss her neck as she tipped it back, laughing. Her heartbeat thundered against my lips as I inhaled the sweet vanilla scent.

God, I wanted to eat her.

"Remember, I have a needle for that problem."

"You and the fuckin' needle, woman." I pushed her off me. "Get up, let's go, or I'm not letting you out of this bed all day."

She snickered as she climbed off the bed and walked into the bathroom.

It felt like we hadn't missed a day together. The air between us had been cleared, and Tammy was an inconsequential part of the past. I climbed off the bed and threw on my t-shirt and shorts, and went into the kitchen to wait for her.

I helped myself to a cup of coffee, since I knew she'd take more than a few minutes to get ready. Her cheeks had been tear-stained and her hair had that "I just got fucked" look. I called the one person I knew who would be interested in helping me make Mia's dream a reality.

"Hey, Ma," I said, and sipped the black, velvety liquid.

"Hey, baby. How are you?"

"I'm great, actually. I'm over at Mia's and I think we patched things up."

"Hmm," she said with a small laugh. "You're a big boy."

"That's what she said, Ma." I chuckled at my wittiness.

Her laughter grew loud until there was silence and

static. She must have covered the phone so I wouldn't hear her giggling. "Son, there are things a mother doesn't need to hear, and I changed your diapers so, I know. That poor girl."

"All right, enough about that. I know we're pals, Ma, but I called you for a reason." I sat down, placing my cup on the table, and stared at Mia's neatly manicured yard.

"What is it, baby?"

I explained to my mother the work that Mia did at the clinic. I shared all the information I knew and told her about Mia's dream to work there full-time and help the people in the area.

"What do they need?" she asked without hesitation.

"Money."

"I know that." She laughed. "How much?"

"I don't know. They get some funding from the government, but not enough. The doctors that volunteer help pay the rent, and they get some medicines for free."

"Find out all the details and come see your father and me. I'm sure we can work something out. I'd love to help any way I can."

"Thanks, Ma. I'm going to spend the day there snooping around, and I'll stop over when I get a chance."

"Hey, how's the training coming? Your fight is soon." She sighed into the phone. I knew she hated the violence and could never understand why I chose to enter the cage.

"Really good, and now that Mia and I patched things up, I can finally focus on kicking that guy's ass."

"Make sure you stay focused. I don't want to see my baby hurt."

"I'm like a brick wall, Ma."

"Don't be too cocky, son. Your father is calling me. He wants a cup of coffee. He's lucky I love him."

I wanted a love like theirs—long-lasting and unbreakable.

"You'd go pick the beans if he asked just to make that man happy."

"Let's not give him any ideas, Michael. Call me later, okay?"

"Love ya. I'll talk to you tonight."

"Love you too."

Mia wrapped her arms around my neck, kissing my cheek. "That better have been your mother or I'm getting that needle ready as soon as we get there."

I grabbed her hands and leaned into her kiss. "It was. You're dying to stick a needle in my dick, aren't you?" I laughed.

"Just remember that it's always an option." She laughed against my ear, and I closed my eyes and let the happiness sink in.

I stood, grabbing my keys off the counter. "Let's go, Dr. Jekyll. I'm driving."

"We can take my car." She stayed by the table.

"Nope, I'm the man, so I drive." I opened the door and waited for her.

As she walked by me, she said, "Let's not start the macho bullshit."

"My dad drives my mom around all the time. I just grew up with some beliefs. Let's not kill them yet. You relax and talk and I'll be your chauffeur."

She sighed but nodded. I opened the truck door for her and waited for her to get situated before I closed her in and jogged around to my side. Her eyes were glued to me as I made my way around the truck.

"You really have the chivalry thing down," she said as I sat.

"It's one thing my ma always taught me. How to be a gentleman when necessary."

We held hands and listened to music, stopping on the song "Happy" by Pharrell to sing along. How could I not shout the words at the top of my lungs?

"Is this it?" I asked, as I pulled into the parking lot.

"Yep. I know it's not pretty, but it gets the job done." She shrugged.

"Yeah. This place doesn't look like much, doc."

"I know. The people that come here deserve better."

"I hope you don't pay a lot in rent." I stared at the old brick façade. A tiny sign that read *GS Health Clinic* hung above the door, but the average person driving by would miss it entirely.

"No, we rent the space for pretty cheap. The owner gives us a deal because he likes what we do."

"Does the inside look any better?"

"It's old but clean. We spend the money we have on rent and supplies."

"Let's get inside. I want to check it out." There wasn't an open spot in the parking lot, and that told me that there was a need for this clinic.

"How do you know the people really can't afford medical care?"

"They have to bring in their government assistance paperwork and proof that they've been denied Medicaid."

"Seems fair, and keeps it legit." I followed Mia into the building and a bustling waiting room. People of all ages and races sat patiently in the space.

Mia stopped and smiled at the woman behind the desk. "Cammie, this is Michael. He's going to hang out here today."

Cammie looked at me with the warmest smile on her face as she held out her hand. "It's always nice to have an extra set of hands around. Especially ones as big and strong as yours." She laughed as she stroked my fingers.

"I'm all yours," I said as I looked at Mia.

The stress that was evident on her face at the hospital was gone. Her demeanor at the clinic was different…she was radiant.

"You just offered yourself up to the devil," Mia said, laughing.

"I can handle her," I said, winking at Cammie.

Her face flushed before she cleared her throat. "We have a full house today. Lots to do, Mia. You leave this hunk in my hands, child."

Mia picked up the schedule and studied it before she replied, "He's all yours. I know you'll take good care of him."

"Mm hmm," Cammie said.

Mia kissed my cheek and started to walk away. "You're just going to leave me here?" I asked.

"You'll be just fine. Cammie knows the most about the clinic. Pick her brain if you want to know about the finances."

"Okay, I'll be waiting for you, doc." I patted her ass before she stepped out of reach.

"One second," Cammie said as she held her finger up. "Mr. Johnson," she called into the waiting room.

Leaning against the desk, I watched Cammie interact with the patients. She had a way with people, making them feel important. She was the beating heart of the clinic. She'd be my link to getting this place on track and keeping it running like a well-oiled machine.

"So, what can I help you with, Michael?" Cammie asked as she swiveled her chair in my direction.

"I want to talk about funding, Cammie. I want to help

the clinic financially and see about having Mia here full-time. She loves this place."

She clapped her hands. "Wow, I think I just fell in love with you. If Mia wasn't my girl, I'd snatch you from her."

I laughed at the ease with which she spoke to me.

"You know anything about accounting, handsome?" She winked.

"I do. I have a business and I do the books."

"Perfect. I'll let you in the office and you can take a look. It may be easier and quicker than if I told you everything. We're so busy today that I couldn't give you my full attention, no matter how badly I wanted to."

"That would be fine, Cammie. I can see what's going on and how I can help."

She showed me to a tiny office in the back. I could hear Mia speaking with a patient in the next room. The words were muffled, but it was her voice. Cammie had the office organized and the files up to date, which made the task of determining their financial need easier.

They had a couple thousand dollars in the bank, and Cammie said that rent was the biggest expense. The place needed to be rehabbed from the inside out.

I searched the filing cabinet for the rental agreement. They paid a thousand a month, which was cheap for commercial space. I made a list of needs with an estimated cost to keep the place in check, with some extra financial padding. The first step would be purchasing the building and the land it sat on, then giving the place a facelift.

It certainly was doable, and it wouldn't take much financially to make this a stable non-profit that wouldn't have to scrape by to make ends meet.

As I was rubbing my eyes, the door opened and Mia walked in. "How's it going in here?" she asked, wrapping her arms around my neck and settling in my lap.

"Good. I have a plan and just spoke to my ma and the landlord."

"Oh?"

"We're going to make it happen, Mia. I already have the wheels in motion." I leaned back in the chair, lifting her to move with me.

"You don't waste any time, do you?" She rubbed her nose against the tender skin of my neck and inhaled.

I cupped her ass and squeezed. "You're going to owe me something big for all this."

"What do you want?" She smirked.

"I'm going to think *long* and *hard* about that before giving you a definitive answer."

"You do that. I just wanted to say hi. I have to go. There are a bunch of people out there waiting to be seen." She patted my shoulder before trying to climb off my lap.

I pulled her back down, running my lips down her jaw. "I want some sugar first."

She laughed and rolled her eyes. "Only a kiss."

"What else would I mean?"

The kiss was soft and sweet. I smiled as she winked at me before walking out the door.

I spent the afternoon jotting down notes, making lists, and calling everyone I knew to help make this place the best it could be. It would be Mia's dream and her little bit of serenity.

CHAPTER TWENTY-SIX

MIA

IT WAS FINALLY THE NIGHT—MICHAEL'S MMA match.

I wanted to look stunning.

Picking through my closet, I found my favorite black pencil skirt, a white cami, and my kickass Jessica Simpson peep-toe heels. I spent extra time on my makeup, and straightened my hair.

I felt tense as I drove to the arena to see him before his fight. I sat in the car for a few minutes to calm my nerves before I made my way to the doors. My stomach gurgled as I followed the extra-tall security guard through the backstage area to a door that read "Michael 'The Iceman' Gallo."

After knocking on the door, I smoothed my skirt, wiping my hands against the soft material. My legs were wobbly as I waited for someone to open the door.

Why in the hell was I so nervous? I didn't like the thought of Michael fighting another man, but my stress level was high enough that someone would think that it would be me stepping in the cage.

The door cracked opened and Rob smiled. "Hey, Mia," he said, opening the door.

"Hey, Rob," I said as I entered the dimly lit room.

"Yo, dude, Mia's here," Rob yelled, causing me to jump. "Sorry, didn't mean to yell in your ear."

"Oh, it's okay. I'm just jumpy." I saw Michael sitting in a chair, looking more stiff than normal, and turned to Rob. "Is he okay?"

"Yeah, he's doing great. He gets moody before a fight."

Nodding to Rob, I moved toward Michael, stopping in front of him. I placed my hand on his head, running my fingers through his hair as he kept his eyes pointed at the floor. "Michael," I said as I stroked his hair.

He didn't say a word, but reached out and wrapped his hand around my calf. He slid his fingers up my leg and under my skirt, gripping my thigh roughly.

"No sex before the match," Rob said before walking out.

Michael's eyes slowly moved up my body, stopping at my breasts before settling on my face. His grip tightened as he pulled me closer, resting his head against my abdomen.

"You okay, Michael?" My hand stilled in his hair.

"I can smell you," he said hoarsely.

"Dick," I said as I swatted his back. "You had me freaked out, and you're being a pig."

His body shook as his laughter grew and filled the room. "I'd rather pound your tight, wet pussy than beat this guy's face to a pulp right now." His fingers slid against the edge of my panties and stopped.

"You can have me all night long after you win your match. The quicker you end it, the sooner you'll have me in your bed," I said with a shaky breath.

His finger glided across the satin material of my

underwear and rubbed against my clit. My breath caught in my throat as I stood before him, lost in his touch.

"We have a few minutes, and I know just how I want to spend them," he said, wrapping his other arm around my waist.

His fingers dipped inside my panties as I fisted his hair and closed my eyes. My head tipped back as he brought me to the brink of orgasm. My body swayed as his grip increased, steadying me.

My calves stung from the tension and the orgasm that was just out of reach. I opened my legs as far as possible in the restrictive skirt and leaned into his touch.

"You want to come?" he asked roughly.

"Yes," I pleaded.

"After I kick some ass." He smirked, removing his hand from my panties and dragging the wetness down my leg.

"Fuck," I muttered.

"Doesn't feel so good, does it, doc?" He laughed before sticking his fingers in his mouth, licking them clean.

I glared at him. It was funny when I did it to him. To leave me like this now felt downright cruel.

"You're a bastard."

My entire body had been tense, and he had made it so much worse. I was wound so tight at this point I worried walking would cause me to orgasm. I ached that badly.

He patted my ass as he stood and wrapped me in his arms. The warmth of his naked flesh seared through my thin silk camisole. "We'll finish after I win. I want to take my time with you tonight."

I rubbed my cheek against the smooth skin of his pec. "I should hate you right now, but I can't."

"You two done in there?" Rob yelled, knocking on the door.

"He's a pain in the ass," I said, sighing against his chest.

"I know." He kissed the top of my head, burying his nose in my hair. "Yeah, come in."

Rob plopped down on the couch across the room and watched us.

"I better go, Michael. You have to get ready and I need to find my seat." I peered up at him, getting a last look of his beautiful face. I worried it would be bloody and bruised the next time I touched it.

"I'll text Izzy to meet you in the corridor." His kiss burned my lips as he crushed his mouth against mine. "Thanks, Mia, for coming." The smug asshole winked. "I know you hate the very idea, but you being here means a lot to me."

"No other place I'd rather be." I slid my hand down his arm, moving away from him. "Oh, and Michael?"

"Yes."

"Kick his ass, handsome," I said, trying to help him relax.

He winked, and his smile made my heart melt.

Fuck, I hated the thought of that beautiful face being hit. I hated everything about what was about to unfold before my eyes.

I waved to him with a faint smile as I left. I could hear the cheers of the crowd echo through the corridor backstage. I followed the noise, finding Izzy waiting for me near the arena entrance.

Her mouth moved as she waved for me to follow her, but it was so loud I couldn't hear her words. I smiled and nodded before following her to the seating area.

"Down front," Izzy yelled in my ear, as I looked around the arena.

The crowd was larger than I would have expected for a

MMA match. Not everyone had such great disdain for the sport as I did. I hated the idea of two men beating the crap out of each other for a title, but I promised Michael I'd be here.

The entire Gallo family, with the exception of Mrs. Gallo, sat in the front row, looking as anxious as I felt.

"I found her," Izzy said as we sat down.

They were a stunning family. The men were all cut from the same cloth. Handsome, rugged, and muscular, and the sister was a spitfire. Even Mr. Gallo was classically handsome and didn't show his age.

"It's nice to see you again, doc," Joe said, a couple of seats away.

"Call me Mia, please. I see you're getting around better these days."

"Physical therapy works wonders. I wouldn't miss this fight for the world. Suzy would have had my balls if I didn't bring her tonight." He turned and kissed her cheek as she kept her eyes glued to the cage.

"Hello, my dear," Mr. Gallo said, taking my hand, planting a soft kiss on it. "You've missed some matches already."

I winced as I watched them clean the floor. There was blood and sweat everywhere. "This isn't my idea of entertainment, Mr. Gallo. I'm only here for Michael," I said, trying to stop my stomach from spilling its contents. "Where's Mrs. Gallo?"

"Oh, she hates the very idea of him fighting. She stayed home tonight to read. So, how's he doing? Is he ready?" he asked.

I shrugged as butterflies filled my stomach. I hoped he was ready, because I really couldn't take watching him being beaten. "He seemed pretty calm when I left him to finish preparing."

Our conversation was interrupted as the announcer spoke: “Ladies and gentleman, the main event you’ve all been waiting for is about to begin.”

The crowd stood, and the screaming made my eardrums throb. Loud music began to play, and I knew it was Michael’s song, “Bodies” by Drowning Pool. It had been playing in his dressing room before I left. I covered my ears as I stood, facing the back of the arena.

“Weighing in at 260 pounds, I give you the one, the only, Michael ‘The Iceman’ Gallo.”

The crowd screamed before chanting, “Ice Man, Ice Man.”

Michael wore a black silk robe as he entered through the dark curtain and started to walk down the aisle. The crowd went crazy, and people tried to grab him on his way down the ramp into the arena. Bloodcurdling screams from female fans professing their love to him made me laugh. I could see how this could be an adrenaline rush.

I had the perfect vantage point to watch him. I stood with one leg in the aisle and leaned over to watch him. He stared straight ahead, as he walked with his shoulders pushed back, looking bigger than ever. His lips were set in firm line, and there was no happiness in his eyes. The sparkle had been replaced with fierceness. He looked mean as hell, but I knew the real man underneath.

Michael held his fists up to the crowd as he stopped in front of me, turning to face them. He glanced at me from the corner of his eye as a small smirk danced on his lips, but quickly vanished.

The excitement of the moment wasn’t lost on me.

He walked into the cage, stopping dead in the center. He shrugged off the robe, exposing his beautiful physique and breathtaking face. The cheers grew louder, mainly from the females, as he stood there bouncing up and down, moving his neck from side to side.

I wanted to run into the cage and jump in his arms and beg him not to fight.

"And now we bring you his opponent. Weighing in at 257 pounds, we give you Tommy 'The Heat' Ramirez."

All eyes in the arena turned as a man in a red robe emerged. He looked almost as big as Michael, but scarier, maybe because I didn't know him like I did Michael.

I swallowed the lump that formed in my throat, and my chest began to ache.

Both of these men would leave bloody and bruised before this was all said and done. I worried about Michael getting hurt, and his male ego if he lost.

"Isn't this exciting?" Izzy said, pulling on my arm.

"Captivating and scary as hell," I responded before turning back to watch "The Heat" enter the cage and mimic Michael's previous movements.

"He's going to kick Tommy's ass," Izzy said as she stared at the fighter.

"I hope so." I gnawed on my lip as I watched Michael size up the competition.

He was ready, and chomping at the bit to get his hands on the guy.

People jumped up and down as the men readied themselves for the fight. I sat there almost breathless and scared for what would unfold before my eyes.

Both men stood in the middle of the cage, staring each other down. It would be comical if I didn't understand the brutality that was about to happen.

I was transfixed as I studied Michael's every movement.

The men touched hands before the referee screamed, "Let's get it on." Before he moved out of the way quickly.

Ramirez lunged at Michael and kicked him in the

thigh. I could hear the snap of the skin from the impact. I closed my eyes, cringing, before peeking to see what happened next.

Michael seemed unfazed by the strike, hitting him back with an elbow to the face. Ramirez' face lurched back before he shook it off and steadied himself. The men moved around the cage exchanging kicks and jabs, and I could feel the lump inside my throat growing larger. I touched my throat, resting my hand there as I stared at Michael.

Michael looked magnificent as he moved around the cage and kept pace with Ramirez. He backed Ramirez against the fencing, holding him in place, striking him with the meaty part of his palm square in the chin. I grimaced when I saw blood drip from the corner of his mouth.

Michael wrapped his arms around the man's lower half and picked him up, tossing him to the mat.

I stood, my heart hammering in my chest, praying it would end.

"Hey, lady, you're blocking my view," a man behind me yelled.

I turned around and glared at him before taking my seat. "The Heat" kicked Michael right in the balls. Fuck. Holding himself, Michael backed away, trying to regain his composure.

I had no idea what that felt like, but shit, it had to hurt.

Michael came back at Ramirez a moment later, with more anger than I had seen before. Ducking down, he swept his leg across the mat, knocking Ramirez on his ass.

I gnawed on my lip, but I couldn't look away. Seeing Michael in action, I knew he was made for this. He was a fighter.

Snaking his legs around the man, he held him in place. Ramirez beat on Michael's back, wiggling like a worm, but he couldn't get out of the hold. Michael slammed his fist into the man's face, and I watched in horror as it bounced off the mat.

Blood trickled down his chin as Michael held him in his grip.

"He's winning," Izzy said as she stood, screaming, "Kill 'em Michael!"

I held my breath and prayed it was over.

"Ice Man, Ice Man," the crowd chanted as they rose to their feet.

Ramirez kicked free, both men jumping to their feet.

Fuck, it wasn't over. I exhaled, feeling lightheaded, as Ramirez struck Michael in the ribs. He winced, leaning forward and running his fingers across the spot.

I shook my head, scared that it could be the end for Michael. He had fractured those ribs months ago. They were vulnerable.

Michael straightened and bounced, shaking off the pain before spinning and kicking Ramirez right in the face. His head snapped back as blood flew from his mouth before he fell backward onto the mat.

The crowd stood and began to cheer again as Michael moved around the unconscious Ramirez and yelled something at him.

I stood, gripping my neck, and waited for it to be over.

Grabbing Michael's arm, the referee held it up as Michael pumped his fist in the air with a giant smile on his face.

"It's over?" I asked, as I grabbed Izzy's hand.

"It is. He won! That guy never stood a chance against him." She smiled.

Michael looked like a champion. He was one. I closed my eyes and let out the breath I'd been holding in.

A small cut had formed on the side of his left eyebrow

and blood oozed down his face, but he looked relatively unharmed. His body glistened under the bright lights, showing off each ridge and valley.

A giant grin crept across Michael's face as he walked toward us. He looked at his family and then to me as he approached. Wrapping his arm around my waist, he smashed me into his sweaty torso and kissed me.

I collapsed against his body, exhausted from the nervous tension.

Pulling away, he stared into my eyes and said, "That wasn't so bad was it, doc?"

"I fucking hated every minute of it, Michael."

"Liar." He smirked and turned toward his father.

The simple statement and the cocky smirk reminded me of the bar where we had officially met each other. Same statement, same smirk, and totally Michael.

His dad held out his hand and grabbed Michael's shoulder with the other. "Good job, son."

"Thanks, Pop," Michael said as he pulled his dad toward him, kissing his cheek.

The tenderness Michael showed his father was a strange juxtaposition to the cruelty he'd displayed in the ring.

"Couldn't be prouder." His dad slapped him on the back and released him.

Joe and Anthony hugged him as I stayed at his side. Suzy kissed him on the cheek. I watched in awe at the amount of love and support that his family gave him.

After he hugged his family, he turned to me, pulling me tightly against him. The dampness of his skin soaked through my clothes, but I didn't care. He was safe and the fight was over.

"I have to go clean up. You want to come with"—he cocked an eyebrow—"or wait here with my family?"

I touched the open cut near his eye, causing him to jerk away. "You go get patched up and I'll sit with them until you're done."

"I'll be right back, beautiful. You'll come to the next one, right? I know you secretly loved it."

"It's still barbaric," I said against his lips.

"I bet if I touched your panties right now they're as wet as my skin," he whispered in my ear, causing me to squeeze my legs together.

I shook my head and laughed. "You'll have to take me home to find out, won't you?" I smirked.

"You just gave me the perfect reason to make this quick." He kissed me tenderly and walked away. "I'm keeping them as a souvenir too," he yelled over his shoulder.

I collapsed in my seat, exhausted. I couldn't imagine how he felt.

Mr. Gallo took the seat next to me and smiled. "How are you doing, my dear?"

I gave him a small smile. "It's a lot to take in, but I'm doing okay, considering."

"Ah, it's thrilling and scary. I get it. Seems like yesterday Michael was just a little boy. He was always a scrapper." He punched the air. "I always had to pull him off his brothers. He was a rough one, a born fighter."

"I can't imagine him as a little boy, but I'm sure he was handful, Mr. Gallo." I laughed.

He looked so proud as he sat there staring at the cage. "He was never a small boy, but he's grown up into a fine young man. Anyway, Michael told me he's already hired a crew to start the renovations at the clinic. When do you start there full-time?"

"He has, and I'm so excited. I start next week after my

time is over at the hospital. I can't thank you and your family enough for everything."

"You need to thank Michael. It was all his doing. My wife and I always like to help out community organizations. What good is having money if you can't help those that need it most?" He smiled, genuine and sweet.

I held his hand. "Thank you, Mr. Gallo. I'll make you proud."

He patted my leg and stood. "I have no doubts, my dear. I'll be right back," he said, smiling, and walked away.

A hand gently touched my shoulder, and I turned expecting to see Michael, but it wasn't him. I swatted the hand away and stood to escape his reach.

"Excuse me," I said, crossing my arms across my chest.

"Sorry, a pretty lady sitting here all by yourself made me curious." His eyes moved over my body.

"Um," I said as I looked around for someone to rescue me, but no one was looking in my direction. "I'm not here alone."

"Oh," he said as he looked around the arena.

"I'm here with Michael."

"Really?" he asked, scratching his goatee.

"Really," I said, tilting my head.

A hand landed on the man's shoulder as he turned quickly to come eye to eye with Michael.

"You bothering my girl, Torrez?" Michael crossed his arms over his chest, giving the man a cold, hard stare.

"Maybe I was—whatcha gonna do about it, Gallo?" Torrez stood, placing his hands on his hips.

"Kick your ass like last time." Michael broke out into laughter.

Torrez punched him in the shoulder. "I let your sorry ass win that match."

"Fucking liar."

"Wanna go for another round?"

"You're more worthy of my time than the pissant I fought today. Mia, this is 'The Mauler,'" Michael said, using air quotes and rolling his eyes.

Now it kind of made sense to me. I had seen him before—he was the guy Michael fought in NYC.

"Don't you two hate each other?" I asked.

"Nah, we went for beers after the match in NYC," Torrez said as he shook Michael's hand. "It's good to see you, man."

"Just remember Mia's mine, Torrez. I'd hate to embarrass you by kicking your ass in public *again*." Michael grinned, holding back a laugh.

"Wait, I don't think I ever said I was yours," I said.

"Possession, remember," he said as he wrapped his arms around me. "You're mine."

I bit my lip. I was proud to be called his…he was a man with the iron fists and a warm heart. Michael Gallo could call me anything he wanted, as long as he spent his nights in my bed.

CHAPTER TWENTY-SEVEN

MIA

LIBERATING. That was how it felt knowing I didn't have to work in the ER anymore. I walked in and quit, not wanting to spend another day working there. Michael's family had found donors and used their own money to have me be the clinic physician on a full-time basis.

I could finally do what I loved. Help people without the nightmares and sleepless nights.

Michael spent his mornings working out and then coming into the clinic before heading to Inked. He gave himself wholeheartedly to making the clinic a success. They were officially starting the remodel next week and, Michael would oversee the project first hand.

Taking a sip of coffee, I looked over the chart for my first patient of the day. Female, unemployed, general check-up—an easy way to start. Grabbing the chart and tucking it under my arm, I walked toward the room. I felt stress free for the first time in a long time.

Closing the door, I set the chart on the counter and turned toward the exam table. My heart stopped and I froze in my tracks.

"Hey, Mia," Tammy sneered.

"How in the hell did you get in here?" I said loud enough that I hoped someone would hear, especially Michael. Fuck, I really didn't need her crazy ass here. "What do you want, Tammy?" I asked, glaring at her.

"I came to make peace with you. I wanted to apologize for my behavior," she said, hopping off the exam table.

I held my hand up, stopping her. "It's in the past, Tammy. Whatever happened is between you and Michael. Leave me out of it."

"You two aren't together, then?" She cocked her eyebrow and grinned.

"We are together. We're happy. I think you should go before he finds you here and calls the police."

"He's here?" she asked, and looked at the door with excitement in her eyes.

Fuck. That wasn't the response I'd hoped for when I told her that Michael was here. "He's going to be really pissed if he sees you, Tammy. You better go, for all of our sakes."

"Maybe I can apologize to him too." She smiled.

Clearly she was still delusional.

"Tammy, you need to leave," I spoke louder than before, hoping to draw the attention of Michael or Cammie.

I was getting pissed. My hands were balled at my side. I never wanted to hit a person as much as I wanted to smack the shit out of her.

"Not until I can see Michael." Sitting back down, she crossed her legs with that Snickers bar smile she wore so well.

"Fine," I said. Turning my head toward the door and keeping my eyes on her, I yelled, "Michael!" I turned back toward her and we waited, staring at each other.

The door opened and I heard Michael say, "What's up?"

"We have a visitor." I pointed to Tammy without look at him, and held my hands up.

"What the fuck are you doing here?" he said, stepping in front of me, cutting off my view.

"I…I," she stuttered. "I wanted to see you."

"You've seen me and you're violating the restraining order, Tammy. I will have you arrested for coming here." Every muscle in his body tensed as he stood between us.

He trusted her less than I did, but then again, he knew her better.

She slithered off the table and touched his cheek.

He recoiled, taking a step back, almost knocking me over. "Get out," he said, pointing at the door.

"Come on, Michael. We were so good together." She slid her arm around his neck.

She was totally insane. Was I invisible to her?

I bit my lip, trying not to say something to aggravate the situation.

Peeling her off him, he said through gritted teeth, "Are you shitting me right now with this shit?"

"No, I'm just stating the truth." She looked at him with a frown, and hurt in her eyes.

I'm not an angry person, but this bitch needed to be taught a lesson. Tammy wasn't and never would be a threat to our happiness, but to throw shit in my face was too much for me to take.

"You wouldn't know the truth if it slapped you in the face. Go, Tammy. I don't hit women, never have and always said I never would, but you're getting real close to getting knocked on your ass," Michael said calmly.

"You know I like it when you're rough with me,

Michael," she said, moving closer to him with a sly smile. "The harder, the better, like old times."

"Okay, I've had enough," I interrupted. I placed myself between her and Michael. He. Was. Mine. If anyone were to knock her on her ass, it would be me.

"I wasn't talking to you, whore. I sucked his cock way before you came along. Sloppy seconds aren't fun, are they?" She smirked.

"Calm down, Mia," Michael whispered in my ear, grabbing my arm.

Motherfucker. My body shook from anger.

"Yeah, Mia. Know your place. I'm sure you don't bring him to his knees like I did. You don't have him smacking your ass as you come on his cock. His body was made for me, and I gave him everything he ever wanted," she said, stepping closer to me.

"You need to shut your damn mouth," I seethed, with clenched hands, wanting to punch her in the face.

"Ladies," Michael said, pushing us apart.

"What's going on in here?" Cammie asked as she looked in the room.

"Call the cops, Cammie. Tammy is violating a court order," Michael replied as he held us apart.

Tammy stood there with her hands on her hips, like she was proving her point. Did she not hear a word he'd spoken?

"I'm fine, Michael. You can let me go," I said.

Michael nodded, releasing his hold on me.

On the inside, my belly was burning and my hands were itching to smack her. I judged Michael and called him a barbarian for fighting, but in this moment, it clicked.

"You listen like a good bitch, don't you?" she asked.

I looked at Michael, and he winced. "He. Is. Mine,

Tammy," I said, separating each word to drive the point home.

"He may marry a girl like you, but he'll always come to me for all the dirty things you don't give him. You're plain and boring and probably a rotten lay. He'll always be mine."

I closed my eyes, trying to control my rage. My heart pounded feverishly in my chest, my skin grew hot, and I could hear the blood flowing through my ears.

Michael turned to her, crossing his arms in front of his chest, as he squared his shoulder. "Shut the fuck up, Tammy. Mia's my girl, not you."

"She stole you from me," Tammy said, sounding wounded.

"I did not," I said, stepping around him as he gripped my arm.

"You fucking did," she yelled before smacking me in the face.

Everything else in the room disappeared except her and me. I lunged at her, my palm connecting to her face with a crack. "He's mine," I said as I landed a smack with my other hand. My hands throbbed as we tumbled backward, her body slamming against the tile floor.

"Fuck," Michael yelled as his strong arms gripped my torso, trying to pull me off, but I had my legs wrapped around her body. "Stop, Mia," Michael roared, trying to untangle me.

Blood trickled from her mouth as she lay there crying.

I blinked. I did this to her. I went apeshit and hit her…twice.

I released my legs and leaned over her body, resting my weight on my arms. "I'm sorry," I whispered. "I don't know what happened."

"It's okay, baby girl," he said, lifting me up and cradling me in his arms.

"No, it's not. I just snapped." I didn't know I had that in me. I'd never been pushed to that point in my life.

"She deserved it, Mia," he said, kissing my forehead as he walked out of the room, leaving Tammy on the floor in tears.

"She just wouldn't shut her damn mouth." I looked at her face through the open door; bloodied and tear filled. A wave of guilt rolled over me.

"You hit pretty fucking good for a girl," Michael said, chuckling.

"Shut up, before I pop you one too," I said, reaching for his lips.

I felt the smirk on his face as he laughed. "My, my, how you've changed since that night in the bar. What did you call me? Barbaric?"

"Yeah, well. She clearly didn't understand the English language. I didn't have any other choice, and she hit me first so I'm claiming self-preservation and defense." He was right, but there was no way in hell I'd admit it.

"So, I'm yours, if I heard you right?" he asked.

I sighed and cradled his face in my hands. "Possession, remember?"

"I could never forget. I love you, Mia." His eyes grew wide. He was shocked at his own words.

My heart stopped. I didn't know how badly I wanted to hear that phrase until it slipped from his lips. My insides warmed and felt gooey. I loved Michael, but I would have never been the first to say it. Tears filled my eyes as I looked at him.

"Gonna leave me hanging here, doc?"

I smiled against his mouth. "Just this once…I won't. I love you too, Michael."

He crushed his mouth to mine, and we claimed each other, branding one another with a passionate kiss.

CHAPTER TWENTY-EIGHT

MICHAEL

Two months later

MIA WRAPPED her arms around me as I looked around the room, admiring the remodeled clinic. "You did an amazing thing here, Michael," she said, resting her head on my back, smashing her breasts into me. Damn, she felt good.

"*We*, Mia. We did an amazing job." I rubbed her arm and thought about how much life had changed in three months.

I couldn't imagine a day without her. She made me happier than anything else in my life. I quit fighting and trying to climb the ranks. For her, I'd do anything.

My time was spent between the shop, the clinic, and Mia. There wasn't time to fight without sacrificing my time with Mia.

Did I turn into a pussy? Not a bit. I could kick any motherfucker's ass if given the chance.

I had a greater purpose in life—one that mattered and made a difference. I loved seeing the sparkle in Mia's eyes every day. She wasn't stressed and no longer had nightmares as often as she did before quitting her job. She made a difference to the people in the community, and I felt like I played a role in making her dream become a reality.

"Is everyone here?" I asked, turning around.

"If you mean your family, yeah, they're all here. There's a big crowd outside waiting for us to cut the ribbon and open up this bad boy." She laughed. It was infectious.

"I have something for you first," I said, reaching for an envelope I'd left on a waiting room chair.

She grabbed it. Looking up at me she asked, "What is it?" as she tore it open.

"Read it," I said, tapping the folded paper.

She slowly opened the paper; her eyes flickered to me and back to the paper. "Michael," she said, covering her mouth.

"I couldn't think of a better owner than you, Mia." I brushed the small tear that trickled down her cheek.

Tears of joy had never made me feel so kickass. Some of the money came from donations and the rest from my family, and I filled the gap personally. We knew that Mia was the perfect person to be the rightful owner of the building, giving her security that the clinic would always be there.

"I can't believe this, but how?" she said, her eyes moving across the paper as she gripped it with two hands.

"Doesn't matter, Mia. It's yours now." I grabbed her chin and kissed her.

She jumped in my arms, kissing my lips before kissing my face. I laughed, letting her plant soft kisses on my skin.

"I'm speechless. I don't know how to repay you for all this," she said, waving her hands toward the room.

"I can think of a few ways," I said, squeezing her ass as I laughed.

"I'm sure you will." She rubbed her nose against mine, giggling.

"Let's do this, then. No reason to wait any longer." I released her, letting her body slide down mine until her feet hit the floor.

"Ready," she said, wiping her lips and eyes.

We opened the door, stepping outside to a group of about thirty people, including patients, local media, and my family. Mia's smile was radiant as she waved to the patients that she recognized in the crowd.

"This is so exciting," Ma said, grabbing my face and planting a sloppy kiss on my cheek. "And you, my sweet girl," she said, turning to Mia, "thank you for allowing me to be a part of this."

My ma loved Mia as much as I did.

Mia's cheeks flushed. "Thanks, Mrs. G. I couldn't have done it without you." Mia hugged my ma, giving her a kiss on the cheek.

"Come on, ladies. Let's cut this ribbon and get the party started," I said, ready to let everyone in to see the amazing work we'd done in the last two months.

My parents, Mia, and I all stood in front of the red ribbon, with the largest pair of scissors I'd ever seen in my life being held up by Anthony and Izzy. Suzy stood next to Joseph, holding him by the arm as he leaned on his cane. The only person missing was my brother, Thomas.

Flashes from the crowd blinded me as Mia fidgeted at my side. I squeezed her hand, hoping to calm her.

My father held his hands up, motioning for quiet. He turned to Mia and nodded.

"I'd like to thank you all for coming," she said. "The Gallo family has been kind enough to help give the clinic a new life. They helped raise funds to renovate and bring the facility up to date. We're proud to offer the community the best medical care possible." Her voice was strong as she spoke.

She was meant for this, meant to be in the spotlight.

"Without their generosity, none of this would be possible. We will have a full-time on-staff doctor, a nurse, and a receptionist, along with the volunteer physicians that will work in the clinic to meet the needs of all patients. Thank you for coming today and making this moment even more special." With a beaming smile, she looked at me and winked.

Fuck, I loved her.

The crowd clapped and cheered as we held up the scissors before cutting the ribbon. Flashes illuminated around us as I grabbed her, kissing her as the people in the crowd cheered louder.

"Come on, doc. Show the people around," I said.

She smiled at me before turning her attention back to the people. "Come on, everybody, I can't wait to show you all the changes."

The people entered the clinic with the same shocked expression. Their mouths hung open; their eyes looked around as they turned their head, taking in every inch.

Mia showed people round the new exam rooms as I stayed in the waiting room. I watched her walk in and out of the rooms with small groups of people that hung on her every word.

"Is my baby in love?" my mother asked, standing at my side.

I jumped, grabbing my chest. "Ma, you about gave me a heart attack."

She laughed before resting her head on my bicep. "I

see the way you look at her, Michael. You wouldn't do all this if you weren't in love with Mia."

Heat crept up my chest to my face. "I do love her, Ma."

"Well then," she said, clearing her throat, "someone better give me a damn grandchild already. I know I taught you boys about birth control, but for the love of God, you or Joseph better make it happen, and I mean quick."

"I've been practicing." I smirked as I looked down at her beautiful smile.

"You've had enough time for that—you're getting older. Don't wait too long, Michael."

"Ma, Joe and Suzy have been together longer, and they live together. Put a little pressure on them first, will ya?" I turned, getting a glimpse of Mia before looking back to my mother.

"Oh, don't worry about that, I am." She laughed. "They're *practicing* too—plenty, from what I hear from your sister. Is Mia coming to the party at the house after this?"

My family was filled with gossips. Nothing stayed a secret for very long.

I swear, sometimes my ma used any excuse to have a party. She loved to cook and have everyone over to talk. She hated how quiet the house had become since we moved out. "Yeah, she's coming. You didn't invite too many people, did you?"

"Baby, do I ever invite too many people?" She smiled at me, but it was a bullshit smile.

Sighing, I said, "Always." I kissed the top of her head.

Her body shook against my arm with her silent laughter. "Never you mind that. I'm going to head home and start getting things ready with your father. Gather the troops when everyone is gone and come over. Don't dilly-dally."

She patted my stomach and walked toward my father. He nodded at her and shook the hand of the man he'd been talking with, before they walked to the door hand in hand.

"You did real well, Mikey," Izzy said as she crept up next to me.

"Does everyone feel the need to sneak up on me today?" I crossed my arms over my chest, but didn't turn to face her.

"Cranky ass, aren't ya? I didn't sneak up anywhere. If you weren't so hypnotized by Mia you would've heard me."

I was that obvious. I thought I hung out and blended in with the crowd, but I guess I didn't. "Am I staring at her like a creep?"

Izzy smacked my arm. "Nah, like a love-sick puppy is all."

"Great," I muttered, scrubbing my hands across my face.

"I'm going to go. I have to make a stop before I head to the party," Izzy said, and stood on her tiptoes, grabbed my arm, and kissed my cheek.

"Don't be long, Izzy. Ma will have a cow."

"No worries. I'll be there in plenty of time." She winked and waved as I turned my attention back to Mia.

I shook hands with the people as they left. They thanked me for my family's generous gift to the clinic. I told them that none of it would be possible without Dr. Greco, and they'd nod and smiled.

When the crowd thinned, I sat down, resting my head against the wall. I could hear Mia talking in the back as she continued to walk room to room with the few people left. I closed my eyes and listened to her voice.

Soft, warm lips pressed against mine. As I opened my

eyes, I hoped they were Mia's. "Everyone's gone. Are you ready?" she asked as she pulled away.

"Yeah, we better go before Mama Gallo puts out an APB."

She giggled, climbing in my lap. "You make her sound so horrible, but your mom is a sweetheart," she said, resting her forehead against mine.

"You've never seen her other side, Mia. She's Italian and has a temper. No mild-mannered woman can raise four boys."

"I'll remember that," she said, caressing my cheek.

"If we sit here any longer, I'm going to christen the waiting room and maybe one of the exam rooms. How do those stirrup things work again?" I smirked against her lips.

Mia smacked me, shaking her head. "Oh, no you don't. Not today, at least." She jumped off my lap and held her hand out.

"You're lucky my ma is waiting, or else I'd say fuck it, and take you right here, right now." I grabbed her hand.

"Yeah, just my luck." She rolled her eyes and giggled.

To see Mia so happy and full of laughter made everything worth it. The long hours at the clinic and shop, busting my ass to get it done right.

She completed me.

Jesus, now I'm quoting *Jerry Maguire.*

Dick check. Still there. Whew.

I may not be a pussy, but although I'd never admit it, I was pussy whipped.

Mia did that to me, and I couldn't be fucking happier.

***

"All women are crazy," I said as we walked to my parents' front door.

"Let's qualify crazy." Mia coughed.

I called Tammy crazy, but my ma wasn't. Ma was more

excessive than crazy. There wasn't an open spot in the driveway, or on their block for that matter.

"What's wrong?" Mia asked, tilting her head.

"I told my ma to have a small get-together. There has to be at least fifty people in that house, based on all these cars."

"Leave her alone. It makes her happy, right?" Mia asked, rubbing my arm.

"Yeah," I said, grabbing her hand and placing a kiss in her palm.

"Everyone is waiting to see you."

"To see us, Mia, not just me." I pushed open the door and shook my head.

"Hey," a few voices sounded as we walked inside.

I couldn't see an open space from the foyer, through the great room, and out to the pool. Wall-to-wall people holding drinks filled my parents' home. I held Mia's hand as we made our way through the house.

"Wait," she said, stopping to grab a photo from a side table near the couch.

"What?"

Holding it close to her face, she asked, "Is this you?" She looked at me and back to the photo.

"Yep, that's me." I forgot my mother had the photo sitting out for the world to see.

"You look so…so…" She swiped her fingers across the glass with a smile.

"Handsome? Buff? Sexy?" I asked with a grin.

"I was going to say young, but we can go with your descriptions if you prefer," she said, and giggled.

"I was a whole lot of trouble back then," I said as I grabbed my freshman year wrestling photo.

Too much of my manhood showed through the tiny

maroon singlet, but when I had it on back in the day, I wore it like a proud son of a bitch.

"You haven't changed much since then," she said as I put the photo back exactly where my mother had it.

"Checking out my cock?" I whispered in her ear.

"Shh." She turned, hitting me. "Someone might hear you."

"They're loud and Italian—trust me, they didn't hear a thing."

"I did," Joe said as he smacked my ass with his cane.

"Lucky I don't hit the handicapped, brother." I gave him a giant bear hug. "Where's Suzy?" I asked, looking around.

"Girl talking. It makes me batshit crazy. I love the woman, but being with her twenty-four-seven can be a test to any relationship." He shook his head and laughed. "Thank God I can walk now and go to the shop for a couple hours."

"I haven't talked to the girls lately. Maybe I'll go join them and let you two chat." Mia kissed my cheek.

"Go ahead, love. I'll find Ma and let her know we're here." I patted her ass and watched her walk away.

"You got it bad, bro. It's nice to see I'm not the only one around here being led around by my balls." Joe slapped me on the back.

I sighed. This family—I loved them, but they were all a pain in the ass.

Mia

I felt like I weighed two hundred pounds as I grabbed the open spot next to Suzy on the couch. "My God, do they always eat like this?" I asked.

"Always," Suzy said with a sigh, leaning back as she rubbed her stomach. "I swear I've gained ten pounds since I started hanging out with this family. Everything revolves around food. Doesn't matter the occasion, food is always on hand."

"At least it's good food," I said, happy to be off my feet. The couch felt like lying on a cloud of feathers. The soft cotton material would make it hard to stay awake.

"She's the best cook ever. I look forward to coming here on Sunday. Don't get me wrong, Joey is an amazing cook, but nothing beats his mother's home cooking."

"I wish Michael could cook."

"Whatcha girls talking about?" Izzy said as she plopped her skinny ass between us.

"Talking about your brothers," Suzy said.

"I have all the dirt, ladies. I can tell you some stories that would make you fall off the couch in a fit of giggles," Izzy replied.

"Why isn't Anthony taken?" I asked.

"He likes to play the field. Someday a lady will bring him to his knees and have him begging to be hers. Until then, he prefers the manwhore status. He's gets a little carried away with his *groupies*," Izzy said sarcastically. "Men, total pigs. It's bullshit that he's sowing his wild oats and playing the field, and if a girl did that shit she's easy and a slut."

"Sexism will never die," Suzy replied, patting Izzy on the leg.

"Not in this damn family—too many cocks for it to be equal. Having you ladies around helps, though. My ma and I have always been outnumbered."

She made me feel like I was part of the family. I wanted to fit in and be a member of this tight-knit group. Holidays, including Christmas, had consisted of my parents and me for the last couple of years.

"If you two bitches have kids, they better have

vaginas." Izzy laughed. "The world isn't big enough for any more Gallo men."

"I don't think you have to worry about that for a while," I said quickly.

"Yeah, not an issue," Suzy said, sitting up.

"Suzy, come on. Joey has your ass on your back more than a two-bit whore looking for her next fix. Your ass is going to get knocked up sooner or later."

"We're careful, Izzy."

"Whatever. Someone better give my mother a damn grandchild. She's already crocheting blankets, and she's going to get desperate and start bothering me if you ladies don't come through. I'm entirely too young to ruin this body."

"Oh, shut the hell up, Izzy," Suzy said as she slapped Izzy's hand down.

"I'm just saying, Suzy. It's your duty to carry on the Gallo Legacy."

"Fucking great. Don't let Joey hear you say that," Suzy muttered, closing her eyes and pinching her nose between her fingers.

A shadow fell over us, and I peered up to see Joe looking at us with curiosity.

"Let me hear Izzy say what?" Joe asked with a crooked smile.

Suzy looked up, a giant smile painted on her face. "Nothing, sweetie," she said without flinching.

"Babies, Joe. Get on that shit," Izzy said, smacking his good leg.

"I'm on that shit all time, aren't I, sugar?

Suzy's cheeks turned pink as she looked at him "There's always room for improvement," she said with a smirk.

I loved this family as much as I loved Michael. They

had become my home away from home, with my parents back in Minnesota. Suzy and Izzy were the sisters I never had and always wanted.

Michael was my savior.

Saving me from my nightmares, from the heart-crushing sadness of the ER, and giving me the greatest gift of all—happiness.

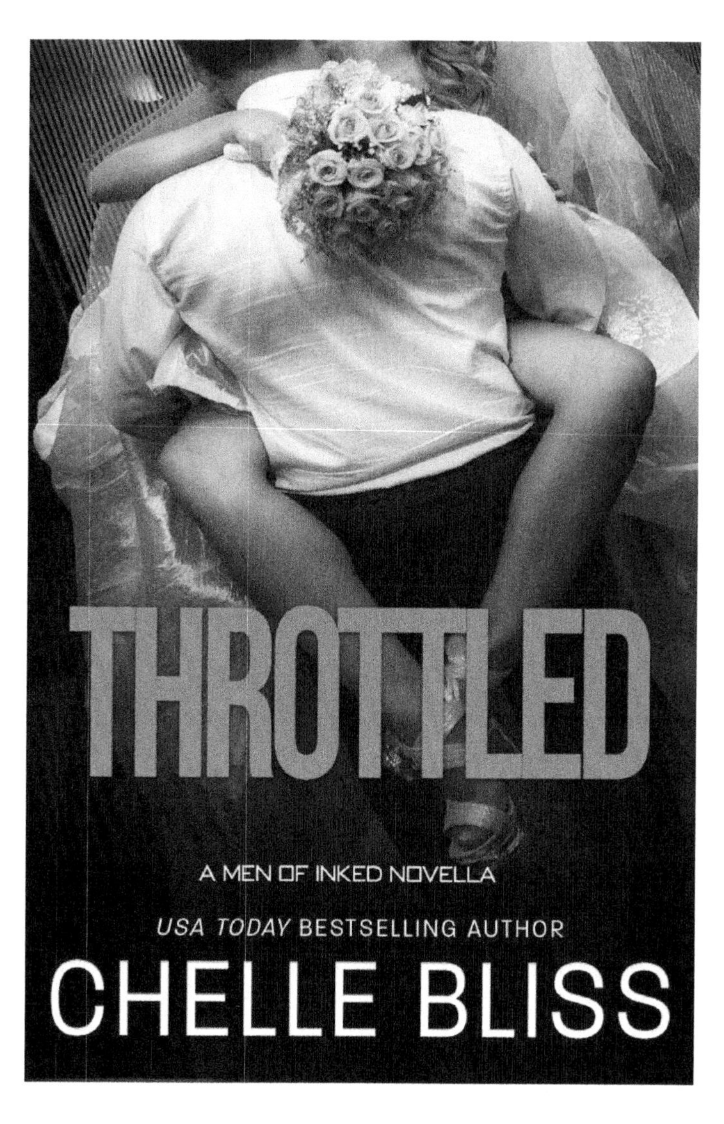

City & Suzy's wedding

CHAPTER 1
SUZY

THANKSGIVING

"Push," City barked as his face turned red.

"I am pushing, damn it." I could barely breathe.

"More, just a little bit more," he said through gritted teeth. "One more push, sugar."

I bore down and used my legs as leverage. My face felt prickly and I wanted to give up. It was too much for me to handle. I couldn't do this. Why did I ever think I could? City always made my mind crazy and had me agreeing to do things I didn't want. I knew I didn't have the physical strength to handle this.

I grunted, exhausted. "Fuck, I give up," I said, gasping for air but not letting go.

"You know your filthy mouth does wicked shit to me," he said, winking at me.

"I'm in no mood to talk about your dick right now, Joseph." I glared at him. Sweat broke out near my hairline as my legs began to tremble.

"As soon as we're done, I'm going to show you exactly how hard that mouth makes me."

I glared daggers at him. I didn't want to think about his beautiful cock. "Not happening," I said as I pushed with all my strength. "Are you even helping?" I bit out.

"What the fuck does it look like?"

"Looks like you're standing there getting a kick out of watching me push this damn thing by myself." I grunted, my knuckles turning white.

"If I could push and get this shit done, I sure as fuck would, sugar. You can do this."

I shook my head just as the bed slid into place. "I'm never helping you move furniture again. Shit's for the birds," I said as I collapsed on the bed.

The light streaming through the windows threw a shadow on the bed as City stood between my legs. "You were the one that said I shouldn't do it alone. Who am I to stop you when you put your foot down?"

He looked like an angel with the glowing sunlight behind him. His body was just as divine as it was the night I met him over a year ago. He had a chiseled jaw covered in short, dark hair, his fierce blue eyes shining as bright as the sun, his dark brown hair a mess. I wanted him just as much as I did the first time we touched.

I smiled at him as I admired his ruggedness. "You're still recovering, City. I didn't want you to get hurt. We didn't have to do it right this second, I just made a suggestion."

"Sugar, I know how you are. You don't do suggestions. You wanted it moved and now it is." He leaned forward, hovering over my lips. "I'm not breakable. I'm healed and got the okay to go back to full activity." He wiggled his eyebrows.

I giggled; the man made my heart skip a beat because I loved him so much. "I didn't know you were holding out on me." I wrapped my arms around his neck and kissed him. "You couldn't have moved the bed by yourself anyway. It's too heavy."

"I could've, but it was more fun to watch you struggle." The deep vibrations of his laughter shook the bed.

I smacked his shoulder. "Could not." I grinned.

"Could too. Where was I?" He stared into my eyes. "Ah," he said, grinding his dick into my leg. "That filthy mouth of yours."

"You made me this way. I used to be sweet and pure. Now look at me," I said, digging my fingers into his thick hair.

"I'm looking, Suz, and I'm loving everything about you. I fell in love with the girl I found on the side of the road. You're mine forever now," he said as he pulled my arm down and placed a kiss on the diamond ring he gave me after his accident.

The happiness I felt was mixed with sorrow at the bitter memory of almost losing him. I would've been lost if he died that day. I never realized how full my life was and how much he meant to me until he was almost ripped from my grasp. "Always yours, City. Make love to me," I whispered against his lips.

"There's my cock-loving girl." He crushed his mouth to mine, his hands sliding up the side of my tank top. His touch gave me the shivers; the depth of his voice stole my breath even after a year. I couldn't get enough. I was his cock-loving whore, but only his. He had that effect on me.

Just as the rough tip of his finger touched my nipple, an alarm sounded from downstairs. "Fuck," he muttered, pulling back.

"Ugh, really?" I whined. "Can't we just let it go for a little while longer? Please?" I begged, grinding my panties against him, feeling the hard piercing press against my clit.

He leaned his forehead against mine, drawing in a

shaky breath. "We can't. You know how my family is. I can't ruin the turkey. I'll never hear the end of that shit, and neither will you."

I pouted, running my fingernails up and down the back of his neck. "Five more minutes won't matter."

"When have we ever taken five minutes?" he asked, sitting up. "Up ya go. We have cooking to do, woman. Everyone will be here in two hours." He grabbed my arms and pulled me forward.

"I don't know why we couldn't just get everything precooked. I survived Thanksgiving without having made everything from scratch." I collided with his chest, peering into his baby blues with a smile.

"Gallos do not do already prepared. You watch and I'll cook." He kissed the top of my head, reaching under my ass and pulling me into his lap.

"How about," I whispered against his lips, rubbing the rough stubble on his face, "if I help and I get a little City appetizer before they get here."

He smirked, a small laugh escaping his lips. "You want to cook?" He raised an eyebrow.

"I want cock and for that I'll cook." I smiled, nipping his lips.

"You got yourself a deal, sugar," he said as he grabbed my sides and tossed me on the bed and ran. I giggled and kicked, hopping off to run after him.

CHAPTER 2
CITY

"YOU LOOK FLUSHED, DEAR," Ma said to Suzy as she hugged her. "Are you feeling well?"

I covered my mouth, hiding the smile while Suzy blushed an even deeper shade of red.

"I'm just fine, Mrs. G." Suzy glared at me as she patted my ma's back.

"Are you sure?" Ma rested her hand on Suzy's stomach. "No bun in the oven yet?"

Oh, fuck. Suzy was about to pop her lid. I looked down, holding my face in my hand, unable to look Suzy in the eyes.

"Sorry to disappoint you, but no. No bun, Mrs. G."

"It's okay, love, and stop with the Mrs. G. Call me Ma. Soon it will be official."

"Yes, Ma."

I couldn't look up. Pissed-off Suzy was too damn cute and I knew I wouldn't be able to stop my laughter.

"Son." My ma rested her hand on my shoulder.

"Hey, Mama." I wrapped my arms around her and

snuck a glance at my bride-to-be. She had my pop's full attention.

"Happy Thanksgiving, baby." She kissed my cheek, standing on her tiptoes.

"You too, Ma. Thanks for pissing Suzy off for me." I laughed.

"Just don't want anyone to forget about a grandbaby." She smiled innocently.

"We wouldn't forget, Ma. We watch you knit every Sunday."

"Crochet," she corrected me. "Is she really okay? I haven't seen her so red in a while."

I couldn't stop the laughter bubbling out. "She's just fine, Ma. She had her hands full before you got here." I looked over my ma's shoulder, winking at Suzy.

Her mouth dropped open as she realized what I said. Before my parents walked in the door, she was on her knees sucking me off. Her hand cupped my balls while the other stroked my shaft. Pure motherfucking heaven.

"I know Thanksgiving is a lot of work, Joseph. We appreciate all your hard efforts." She wrapped her hands around my back and turned toward Suzy. "It means a lot to us."

"It was *hard*"—I coughed—"work, Ma, but Suzy took it like a champion." My body shook against my mother as I placed a kiss on her hair.

Suzy's eyes almost bugged out of her head. "Just a little thing, Ma," Suzy said, and then laughed.

I nodded to Suzy, impressed with her quickness. I'd get her later for that comment. "Hey, Pops." I couldn't take the double meaning anymore. I needed to change the direction of this conversation.

"The house looks amazing, son." He wrapped his arms

around me, giving me a giant bear hug. I loved that my father wasn't afraid to show us how much he cared.

"We just finished everything last week. I don't ever want to build another house again. What a pain in the ass!" I said as I smacked him on the back.

"The fireplace framed by the ceiling-to-floor windows is breathtaking," Ma said, as she walked to look out at the windows. There was a large pool with a waterfall on the lanai.

"I always thought you'd go with more of a classic Florida style of architecture, but I must say, I love the log cabin look. Reminds me of when your ma and I would take trips to the mountains before we had you kids." He walked next to Ma and placed his arm around her. He rubbed her shoulder, slowly stroking her skin while they rested their heads together.

Ma patted his hands and then turned. "Where's the nursery?" she asked with a large smile on her face.

"It's a spare bedroom, Ma," I said, trying not to laugh. The woman was relentless.

"Someday there will be a baby in there," she said, pointing at Suzy.

A change of subject was needed quickly. "Want a drink, Pop?" I asked, wrapping my arm around him, leading him into the kitchen.

"I'd love a stiff one," he replied, looking around the finished living room.

"Yeah, Suzy had one before you got here." I smiled, looking back at her over my shoulder.

"I'll get it for you, Mr. G," Suzy said as she walked by and elbowed me in the ribs. "Why don't you show your parents all the hard work we've done?"

I hunched over, feeling the sting of her bony elbow as I pretended to catch my breath. "Sure." I smiled at her.

Suzy was a vision. Skin slightly pink and pale, blonde hair flowing down her back with her knee-length white sundress. She looked like an angel, but I knew the truth. The girl came off as sweet and innocent, but she was a tiger and had developed quite a liking for curse words. I rubbed off on her. To say I was proud to call her mine was a complete understatement.

"The house is beautiful," Ma said as she grabbed my arm. "You trying to kill her?" she whispered as we walked into the great room.

"Ma, she gives as good as she gets."

"I'm sure, baby," she said as she patted my stomach. "Wow, the fireplace really turned out better than I thought."

I looked at it with pride. It took me days to get it just right, laying each stone one at a time. "Thanks, it was worth all the hours." The rounded river rock made it a challenge, but I sure as fuck wasn't going to let it beat me.

Ma touched the stones and ran her hand across the large wooden mantel. "I'm speechless. The entire place is…" She smiled, looking around.

"I know, Ma. It's perfect. Turned out better than I could've dreamed."

"Here's your drink Mr. G," Suzy said as she handed him a glass of whiskey on the rocks.

A loud pounding on the door made my mother jump. "I'll get it," I said.

Suzy nodded. "I'll show them around."

The banging continued. "Jesus," I yelled as I opened the door.

Mike's fist stopped in midair, as he was about to land another blow. "Sorry, didn't think you heard me."

"I think the dead heard you, brother." I opened the door, letting him inside. His large body hid Mia. "Hey,

Doc. How the hell are ya?" I asked Mia as Michael walked inside.

She smiled, holding out her hand to me. I shook my head, grabbing her, and pulled her to my chest. "I want a hug. We're beyond handshakes, Doc. You've seen me naked, for shit's sake." I laughed, feeling her tense in my arms.

She blushed, her cheeks turning red as she pulled away. "Well, um…"

"It's okay, Mia. I was dying and you saved me. I'm just harassing you."

She swallowed, looking at Mike before turning back to me. "You know how your brother gets." She chewed her lip as she looked around my body to Mike.

"Don't worry. He doesn't give a shit about me. He knows I have my girl. Come on in." I stepped aside, letting her pass. "How's the clinic?" I asked as I followed her toward the sound of Mike's voice.

"I promise I didn't look, by the way." She winked, with a small smile on her face. "It's so great, Joe. Your family has done so much." She smiled, stopping at the counter to watch everyone else in the great room.

"Mia," Ma said, holding out her arms.

I smiled as Suzy wrapped her arms around me, placing her head on my chest. Life couldn't get much better than this. Mike and Pop sat on the couch talking, Ma and Mia greeted each other, and Suzy was at my side.

The front door opened and I turned to see who it was. We were only missing Izzy and Anthony. "Smells damn good in here," Izzy said as she walked into the kitchen.

"Hey, sis," I said, walking over to hug her.

"I brought someone, I hope you don't mind." She smiled, looking up into my eyes. Izzy was never this sweet.

"Who?" I asked, looking up.

Anthony waved and stepped aside. Fuck. “Really?” I whispered in her ear, grabbing her by the shoulder.

“Come on, Joey. He didn’t have anywhere else to be. He was in town and I told him he could spend the day with us. I know you made enough food for an entire army.” She batted her eyelashes at me.

“He’s here now.” I shook my head, looking down at her. “Next time ask, Izzy.”

“Okay,” she whispered in my chest, squeezing me before ducking under my arms.

I held out my hand to Sam as Anthony walked by and grimaced. He felt the same way I did about this fucker. “Nice to see you again, Sam.”

He placed his hand in mine, gripping it roughly. “I go by Flash now.”

“Whatever,” I said, rolling my eyes. “Welcome to my home,” I said, pulling him close as I crushed his fingers in my grip. “If you hurt my sister, I’ll fucking bury you. Got me?”

“Easy now, City. I wouldn’t dream of it. We’re just friends.” He stood toe to toe with me, gripping my shoulder.

“I don’t care who the fuck you think you are or what MC you’re in. You’re still Sam to me and I can still whip your ass. Just so we’re clear.” I glared at him. Who the fuck did this punk think he was?

Suzy’s arms slid around me as her tits crushed against my back. “Everything okay, baby?” she asked.

“Just perfect, sugar. This is Sam, Izzy’s friend.”

She released me and held out her hand to him. “Hi, Sam, I’m Suzy. Nice to meet you,” she said, smiling, unaffected by his inability to dress up. He had on his MC cut and jeans—classy for the holidays.

"It's my pleasure, Suzy." He pulled her hand to his lips and kissed it gently. "You have a beautiful home."

"Thank you, Sam."

I growled, wanting to punch him in the face. His eyes flickered to me, his lips turning up in a half-smirk before he looked back to Suzy.

"Joe's a very lucky man. I hope you don't mind me crashing the party." Sam's eyes flickered to me with a shitty grin before looking at Suzy. I wanted to rip his head off, the fucking weasel.

"Not at all. Come on in and make yourself at home," Suzy said with a smile.

As Sam walked past me, I glared at him but I knew I should be nice. Suzy stood on her tiptoes, rubbing my cheek and staring at me with her head tilted. "What's wrong, City?"

I looked down at her, giving her a half-smile. Her kind eyes and big heart always did a number on me. "Nothing, sugar. I just don't like him."

"I'm sure he's harmless. Let's enjoy our first Thanksgiving in our new home."

I kissed her hair, taking in the coconut sweetness on the silk strands. "Harmless isn't a word I'd use to describe Sam, but you're right, let's enjoy it."

"No more sex references either," she said as she pinched my ass.

"Sugar, I make no promises when it comes to you and that sweet pussy," I said as I crushed my lips to hers, stealing her breath.

CHAPTER 3
SUZY

"WHAT STILL NEEDS to be done, dear?" Mrs. G asked as I sipped my white wine. "We're just over a week away." She smiled, her eyes soft. I knew she was happy and excited. The wedding was all we talked about anymore.

"I think everything is ready. I have a couple to-do lists, but it's last-minute stuff." I set my fork down, unable to take another bite. "Maybe you can look over the seating chart with me one more time while the boys watch football after dinner."

Her teeth sparkled as her smile grew wide. "I'd love to help."

"Me too," Izzy said from across the table. "Maybe we can have the boys do the dishes for once." She grinned, looking around the table.

"Oh, hell no," Anthony said. "That's women's work." He shook his head, shoveling another forkful of stuffing in his mouth.

Clinking from all the ladies dropping their forks on the table made me laugh. That wasn't the thing to say at this table.

"No shock why your ass is still single," Michael said, slapping Anthony on the back of the head.

"When have we ever done dishes on Thanksgiving? I'm just saying. It's our job to eat and watch football, and the ladies cook and clean. It's the Italian way." He smirked and his body jerked. "What the hell was that for?" He looked at Izzy.

"Being a dumbass," Izzy said as she rolled her eyes.

"Anthony, you boys can handle it this year. The ladies have wedding plans to finalize," Mrs. G said.

"But Ma," Anthony replied with wide eyes.

"No buts, mister. There are enough of you that you'll get it done quickly. Joseph and Suzy's wedding is more important than football this week." Her mouth was set in a firm line. Mrs. G was sweet as apple pie, but no one, and I mean no one, challenged her.

"Fine, Ma." He covered his mouth with his napkin and mumbled.

I bit my lips, stifling my giggle. "We never went around the room sharing what we're most thankful for."

"You're right, Suzy. The boys were so hungry, I didn't even think about it. Forks down," Mrs. G said, placing her fork and knife next to her plate.

A collective groan filled the room. The boys didn't like anyone getting between them and their food, or their women, for that matter. The two things were non-negotiable.

"I'll start," she said. "I'm thankful for my children and loving husband. I'm thankful for the new additions to the table and new members of the family, Suzy and Mia. I'm thankful that Thomas is safe even though he's missed another holiday. I've been blessed with each and every one of you being a part of my life." She smiled, wiping her eyes.

Mr. Gallo stood and cleared his throat. "I'm thankful to live another year to hopefully see the Cubs win the World Series." He laughed. "I'm thankful that I can be proud of each of my children, Mia and Suzy included. When I met and married your mother, I never dreamed that she would give me such wonderful children and a life filled with such joy. I can honestly say I have no regrets, and for that I thank my lucky stars each day." He tipped his head and winked at Mrs. G before sitting.

She blushed and blew him a kiss. I wanted that life. I wanted that love. The lifetime-enduring happiness that seemed out of reach for most.

"I'm thankful for my uncomplicated single life. No offense." Anthony looked at his mother. "I'm thankful for this meal and having you all part of my life. That's enough sappy shit for me to say in one day." He blew out a breath and smiled.

"Aw, you're so sweet, Anthony, you almost made my teeth hurt," Izzy said. "I'm thankful for having two wonderful parents. I'm thankful for having more women around the table. Being outnumbered sucks." She looked at Flash, and he shook his head before he turned to Michael.

Michael glared at him. "Fine, I'll go, you pansy ass." He cracked his knuckles and put his arm around Mia. "I'm thankful for all of you, but most of all for the woman at my side. I haven't been the same since the day I knocked her on her ass. I love ya, Mia, baby." He leaned forward, holding her chin, and kissed her gently.

All the love around the table made my eyes water. This family had become everything to me. City was the icing on the cake, but they were the silky-smooth filling.

"Pussy whipped," Anthony choked out.

"Shut the fuck up." Michael slapped Anthony on the

head without looking, as his lips lingered over Mia's mouth.

City stood, looking down at me with a smile that made my stomach flutter. "On that note, I'll get the mushy shit out of the way. I'm thankful that Suzy has agreed to be my wife. I couldn't ask for a better person to share the rest of my life with. We had a rough beginning, but I knew I had her the moment I kissed her. I'm thankful to Mia for helping save my life after the accident." He smiled at Mia, and she blushed. "I'm thankful for my family…well, maybe not Anthony, but everyone else."

He wrapped his arm around my shoulder, pulling me forward before he kissed me. His lips were warm and sweet from the wine. My nose tickled from the facial hair he'd become so fond of. As he pulled away, I moved with him, wanting more of his mouth. He winked, giving me the cocky grin that always set my body on fire.

I swallowed, trying to regain my composure. "I'm thankful that City is still with me after all we've been through. I'm thankful that he survived and is healthier than ever. I'm thankful for each and every one of you for being around this table, even Anthony." I laughed as Anthony smiled, winking.

All the Gallo men were to die for—they were the panty-dropping variety. Women couldn't say no to them; that was how City stole my heart. Everyone dug back into their meal, scooping up the stuffing and dreaded green bean casserole, and chatter filled the large dining room. I set my napkin down, sat back in my chair, and let the joy I felt seep inside me.

There was something about a man that could cook. I hadn't gone hungry or worried about which brand of Ragu jarred sauce to use since I met City. He had so many skills, and every first impression I had about him was wrong. He was cocky, I hadn't been wrong about that, but City wasn't the overbearing brute I thought he was when we first met.

City was an artist, a romantic, a loving partner, a cook, and an amazing person. The most diverse and well-rounded person I knew. His artistry when it came to tattooing was beyond amazing, colorful and intricate; he spent hours in his studio upstairs creating designs for clients.

He wasn't easy or simple, but he was mine.

"Sugar, you okay?" City brushed the back of his knuckles against my cheek.

I turned to him, smiling, tears welling in my eyes. "Yeah, babe. I'm great." I wiped the corner of my eye, turning to him and taking in his rugged beauty.

"Why the tears?" he whispered in my ear, rubbing my cheek with the rough pad of his thumb.

"I'm just happy." I touched his hand, moving into his touch, and leaned to the side to kiss him.

He smiled, moving toward me and enveloping my lips in a loving kiss. "I can't wait to call you my wife." He searched my eyes, a small smile on his face. "You'll be mine legally."

"I've always been yours, City." I smiled, warmth flowing through my body. He'd never let me think otherwise. He'd laid claim to me early in the relationship and never let me too far out of reach. No matter how scared I was or how hard I tried to fight him, the pull he had over me was too great.

The cocky grin I could no longer live without spread across his face as he grunted. "There's no going back now, sugar." He crushed his lips to mine, stealing my breath, the familiar dull ache returning between my legs.

"You two are kinda nauseating," Anthony said, pretending to gag.

We both turned to glare at Anthony. City cleared his throat. "Someday you'll understand, brother."

"Not going to happen," Anthony said, grimacing before stuffing a piece of bread in his mouth. "I have too much to offer to be tied to just one woman," he said with a muffled voice and small pieces of bread falling from his mouth.

"Yeah, I can see that. Who couldn't resist such a specimen of a man?" I said, breaking out into laughter.

Mrs. G pushed back her chair to stand; the sound of the wooden chair scraping against the slate flooring sent a chill through my body, reminding me of fingernails on a chalkboard. "All right, boys, the ladies are done and we're going to work on the wedding plans. Get this place cleaned up." She raised an eyebrow and looked around the table. The boys, including Mr. G, nodded at her but grumbled under their breath. "Come on, ladies, we have work to do. We have eight days to make it perfect."

Mia, Izzy, and I rose from our chairs and followed Mrs. G out of the dining room. "I can't believe I'm going to have a sister," Izzy said, throwing her arms around me. "Finally, the tables are turning. We're so close to equalizing the cock in this family," she whispered in my ear, a small giggle escaping her lips.

"That's not possible," Mia said as she walked behind us. "All the vaginas in the world couldn't outnumber those boys. They're too…"

"Full of themselves," Mrs. G chimed in, turning to face us. All of us laughed as we walked up the stairs. Gallo men were unique, and we knew it. "It's my fault. I made them who they are, but never fear, ladies—we control everything, even though they think otherwise."

We sobered, hanging on her every word. “You control them, Ma. We sure as hell don’t.” Izzy rested her body against the wall outside the wedding war room I’d created.

“I’ll share my secrets when we’re inside and out of the boys’ earshot. They don’t need to know who really holds the power. It may bruise their male egos,” Mrs. G said, her body shaking with laughter.

“Come on, ladies. Be prepared, it’s organized chaos inside.” I smiled as I opened the door, standing back to let them walk in first.

“Wow,” Mia said as she stepped inside and looked around with her mouth agape.

“Holy shit,” Izzy said, stepping into the room with wide eyes as she spun around.

“I wouldn’t expect anything less from you, dear,” Mrs. G said as she put her arm around me and gave me a tight squeeze as we entered the bedroom.

I smiled at her, blushing. “We haven’t made it into a bedroom yet. We’re using it for the wedding only right now. It is pretty damn cool, isn’t it?”

“Will it be a nursery?” Mrs. G looked at me with hopeful eyes.

“Maybe someday.” I smiled, my stomach in knots.

We weren’t ready for a baby, not just yet. I had too much City left to enjoy.

“No worries. I have all the faith in you, my sweet Suzy.” She released me and walked toward the gown.

My body warmed from her sincerity and love as I took in the most important women in my life, all in one spot and without our testosterone-laden other halves.

“This is stunning,” Mrs. G said, running her fingers across the lace skirt of my wedding gown.

“Joey is not allowed in this room anymore. I can’t risk him seeing my dress.” I shook my head. He begged me to wear it for him, he wanted to dirty it—his words, not mine—before I walked down the aisle. That wasn't going to happen.

"Good idea," Mrs. G said, smiling at me.

I watched them as they looked at every detail I'd laid out across the expansive space. I had a seating chart that looked more like an invasion plan for a war, tables and sticky notes everywhere in different colors to represent our two sides. Izzy eyed the party favors while Mia grabbed my wedding shoes and studied them.

"These shoes are amazing. Everything is going to be beautiful, almost magical." Mia placed the shoe back in the box. "You're so organized. I thought I was anal, but babe, you have me beat by a mile," she said with a small laugh.

"What needs to be done?" Mrs. G asked, staring at the seating chart.

I stood next to her, looking over my work. "I just need to make sure I have everyone seated correctly. I don't know most of the people on here. Joey said this person couldn't sit near that person. I'm so confused and don't want to mess it up."

She touched my hand, looking at me with a smile. "I'll inspect it, but from what I see so far, it's perfect."

"Thanks, Mrs. G."

She looked at me, her mouth set in a firm line.

I gulped, realizing my mistake. "*Mom.* Thanks, Mom," I quickly corrected.

She smiled, her face growing soft as she turned back to the poster board.

"Let's talk about the bachelorette party while Ma is busy." Izzy grabbed my arm, pulling me toward the small table on the other side of the room.

"Maybe she wants to come," I said, looking at Mrs. G.

"Nope, she's staying home with Daddy. I have everything planned out."

"Izzy," I warned, my eyes snapping to her face.

She smiled, looking overly pleased with herself. "Don't worry. I have it all under control," she said, winking at me.

"That's what I'm worried about." I said, leveling her with my stare.

"As a bridesmaid it's my duty to give you a kickass bachelorette party. Whatever happens, just blame it on me. I can take care of those boys."

"Give us the rundown," Mia said, not letting me respond to Izzy.

"Okay, well, we have a party bus picking up all the girls here on Friday night and the boys will have their own," Izzy said. "We'll be spending the evening at Shepard's Beach Resort. I reserved the top floor, where the suites are located, and we'll party our asses off. They have a dance club set up at night and we can drink till we puke and crawl to our rooms." She bounced up and down in her chair. "This shit is going to be so kickass."

I looked down, twisting my fingers in my hands. "No stripper, Izzy." I wasn't asking. I wanted to make it clear that I didn't want any half-naked men touching me.

"Don't worry," she said, her smile growing wider as my stomach turned over.

"Izzy, I'm serious." I stared at her, holding her with my gaze.

"Relax, Suz."

"I'm looking forward to a girls' night out," Mia said, squeezing my arm. "Michael doesn't let me out of his sight much. Well, really he doesn't let me out of his bed." She laughed, her face turning red.

Izzy winced. "My ears are going to bleed or my brain will explode with that image. Do not mention my brothers and sex. Ever. Ick," she said, sticking out her tongue like she was going to throw up.

"What about Flash?" Mia asked, smirking.

"He's just a friend." Izzy frowned, looking to her mother.

"He looks like he wants to be more than friends," I added. "You've never brought anyone around for family dinners, let alone a holiday, Izzy."

"Eh, he was in town and he doesn't have any family in the area. We hang out sometimes but it's nothing more than that." She drew in a breath. "He's not right for me, and the guys, well, they'd never allow him to be part of this family."

"What are you girls talking about?" Mrs. G asked as she sat down with us.

"The monsters that you've created," Izzy said quickly, changing the subject.

"Ah," Mrs. G said, turning to me. "Suzy, everything looks perfect. I wouldn't change a thing on that seating chart."

I smiled, happy that I hadn't messed it up. "So Ma," I said, the words still foreign on my tongue. "You were going to share your pearls of wisdom with us about how to handle our boys."

She laughed, her eyes twinkling. "Well, it's taken me many years to hone my skills and learn how to get what I want. It's a fine line, though, ladies. You can't let them know you're the one silently controlling the strings from the background. They like to think they're the puppet master, when in reality we hold all the strings."

"Still not giving me details," Mia said, shaking her head.

"Michael and Joseph are tough boys, and Izzy, any man that steals your heart will be just as tough as your brothers, if not more. This information will be for all of you to file away and use when necessary."

We leaned forward, waiting to hear her next words.

"Always remember to make them think they're in charge." She smiled and laughed. "That's the key. Don't ever make them think otherwise. Love them hard, ladies. Smother them with your love. Be fierce when necessary and never back down. Once you give in, they'll expect it always. When they won't give you what you want, well, that's when you deny them the thing they want most." She paused, wiggling her eyebrows.

"Oh my God, Ma. I don't even want to think about you and Pop having sex." Izzy stuck her finger in her mouth, pretending to gag.

Mia and I broke into a fit of laughter.

Mrs. G shook her head. "Deny them food, Izzy." She laughed. "Your mind is always in the gutter, child."

I couldn't control myself. I sagged into the chair, hysterical, with tears streaming down my face. Izzy glared at her mother, unconvinced by her pearls of wisdom. Mia put her head down on the table, her body shaking from the giggles we'd all developed.

I sobered, sitting up in my chair and leaning my elbows on the table. "That won't work for me, Ma. I don't do the cooking. It's hard to deny a man food when he does all the cooking."

"Well then, you only have one other weapon." She smiled, patting Izzy on the leg.

"For the love of God, Ma. Really. My ears are going to explode and I'll never be able to have sex again if you keep talking." Izzy closed her eyes, rubbing her fingers roughly against her skin. "No more. I can't listen."

"Izzy, dear. I was going to say that Suzy shouldn't snuggle with Joey. Snuggle, Izzy."

"Snuggle?" Izzy looked at her ma with wide eyes. "Really? Who the hell snuggles?"

My laughter returned, worse than before. Izzy and Mrs. G were the cutest two people I knew. I could listen to them talk all day.

"All Gallo men snuggle, Izzy," Mrs. G stated calmly and matter-of-factly.

"Bullshit," Izzy coughed. "Suzy?" She looked at me for confirmation.

"I'm sorry to blow the image you have of your brother, but he loves to snuggle. He'll never use those words, but there's not a night that goes by that I'm not required to fall asleep in his arms."

"You've ruined the image I have of my brother being the big bad wolf." She shook her head, turning her attention to Mia. "Michael too?"

Mia nodded. "Yep, but there's no place I'd rather be. I feel so safe in his arms. He's like an overgrown security blanket. I don't think we've ever fallen asleep without our bodies being entangled."

Izzy rubbed her forehead, looking to the floor. "My mind is blown. Jesus. I know there's no way in hell Anthony is a snuggler. No goddamn way." She shook her head and looked at her ma. "You did this to these men, Ma."

"I snuggled them since the moment they were born, just like I did you. Even as little babies, their fingers would tangle in my hair, playing with the strands."

"I'm not a snuggler," Izzy interrupted, holding up her hand. "Never have been and never will be."

"You will, my dear. When you find the right man." Mrs. G swept her fingers across Izzy's cheek, tilting her head and smiling. There was so much love between the two women, it radiated off of them.

"Nope. I like my space. I'll never give in. Who knew I was really the one with the penis after all these years?" Izzy laughed, hitting the table.

"Don't let the boys hear you say that," I said, grinning at her.

"What are they going to do? Cuddle me to death?" she asked through her laughter, her body slipping from the chair in hysterics.

CHAPTER 4
CITY

"GET your ass up and help, Sam. We aren't done. You may think you're a guest, but you help like the rest of us. Earn your meal, *friend*," I bit out, trying to hide my obvious dislike of the man.

He sat at the table like a king, watching us as we cleared the table and started to clean up dinner. "Really? Izzy said I was a guest."

I walked over and leaned over the table so only he could hear. "I don't give a fuck what Izzy said. This is my house and you ate my food. Get your fuckin' ass up and help."

"I knew you were a prick," Sam said as he stood, grinning. "I don't remember your mother treating a guest like this in her home."

"I'm not my mother and I don't like you. Never have and sure as fuck never will." I leaned farther across the table, coming eye to eye with him.

"What the fuck did I ever do to you?" Sam glared, not breaking eye contact.

"I don't like you being with my sister. It's that simple."

"Izzy and I aren't together." He crossed his arms.

"I don't give a shit what you say. I don't like her even being near you. You're trouble, Sam."

"I'm not trouble, Joe. You know me. I've never done shit wrong." He walked around the table, coming to face me without a barrier.

"I know you're prospecting with the Sun Devils. They don't play games, Sam. They're the real deal. I don't want my sister involved in their bullshit." I snarled, fisting my hands at my side.

"They're good guys, Joe. I never take your sister around them. She and I spend time together when I come to town to see my parents or go on a run. Nothing more than that." His eyes softened as he stared at me; the glare had vanished. "I'd never hurt your sister. We've been friends since we were little kids. She'd kick my ass anyway. I mean, seriously, Joe, your sister doesn't take anyone's shit."

I shook my head as I laughed. "Good, Sam. Remember that. If she doesn't get ya, I sure as fuck will." I placed my hand on his shoulder, giving it a firm squeeze. "There's a whole line of Gallo men that have my back. Don't get her involved in that MC, you hear me?" I raised an eyebrow as my laughter vanished.

"I got ya, man. Your sister is the only girl that has ever earned my respect. I would never do anything to endanger her," he said as he held out his hand to me.

I stared at him, trying to judge his sincerity. "I'm going to hold you to your word, Sam." I gripped his hand, squeezing it between my fingers, letting him know that I could easily overpower him.

A hand landed on my shoulder as Michael said, "What's going on over here? While you two ladies chitchat, the real men are doing all the work." He looked at Sam before turning to me.

I smiled, increasing my grip on Sam's hand. "We're done, Mike. Just having a little heart-to-heart about Izzy."

Sam gritted his teeth and tried to pull his hand away. "I got it, guys. I'll treat your sister right."

"Damn right you will," Michael said, taking a step forward.

"What the fuck? I've never done anything to her."

"Keep it that way, Sam, and we won't have an issue," Michael said.

"Boys, get your asses over here and clean some shit. Football's on and I'm not going to miss the game. Move it," Pop yelled, causing us all to turn.

"Coming, Pop," Michael said over his shoulder. "Let's go. I think Sam has a clear enough picture of what's at stake."

"I do." He nodded, shaking out his hand after I released it.

I grabbed the remote, turning up the volume on the football game that was just about to kick off. We finished clearing the table, loaded the dishwasher, and polished off the pots and pans while we listened to the game.

Just as I put the last pot away, the girls walked back down the stairs. Their laughter filled the space, overpowering the sports announcer on the television. The guys had piled into the living room, making themselves at home on the couch.

I captured Suzy's wrist, pulling her against my chest. "What's so funny, sugar?" I asked, rubbing my nose against her temple.

"Just girl stuff. Did you boys have fun?" she asked, staring up at me, tears hanging in her eyes.

"You okay? You look like you've been crying." I swept my fingers underneath her eyes, catching a single tear.

"We were laughing so hard, City. I love them so much." She beamed.

"I don't think I want to know what you girls were talking about. They love you just as much, Suzy. You're family now." I pulled her chin up, brushing my lips against her tender skin.

She closed her eyes, parting her mouth for me. My dick twitched, wanting to be inside of that pretty little mouth again. Grabbing the nape of her neck, I held her in place, claiming her mouth. The feel of her soft lips on mine drove me closer to the edge. I wanted to throw her over my shoulder and run upstairs for a quickie. She acquiesced, giving herself to me with her mouth as she snaked her arms around my body. My dick throbbed in my pants; the blowjob earlier wasn't enough to dull the constant ache I felt when near her.

Placing her hand on my chest, she pushed gently. "City," she said breathily against my lips. Her eyes opened slowly, blinking back the haze. "Later. Your family is here."

"I don't give a fuck. They won't notice if we disappear for a few minutes. I need to taste you, sugar. I need to sink my cock in you so deep that my balls slap against your clit until you scream." I held her in place, staring in her eyes, watching them dilate.

"Okay," she whispered, scrubbing her hands across my chest.

I looked over her head at my family sitting in front of the television. "Come on, let's sneak upstairs." I released her neck, putting her hand in mine, and pulled her toward the stairs.

"Shouldn't we say something?" she asked, looking back at them.

"No, they won't notice, I'll be fast." I winked at her as we walked up the stairs.

"We've gone over this. You're never fast."

I reached down, picking her up from under her arms and tossing her over my shoulder. She squealed and giggled.

"Everything okay in there?" Ma yelled.

"Perfect, Ma. Be right back," I yelled down the stairs.

"You've given us away."

I swatted Suzy's ass. "Now I *have* to be quick. Fuck."

She wiggled and laughed, grabbing my ass as I rounded the corner to our bedroom. Kicking the door closed, I released my grip, letting her body slide down mine. Her soft to my hard. I wasn't in the mood to take her gently. She wasn't my bride-to-be in this moment. She was mine, and mine to use.

"I don't think—" she started to say as I placed my finger against her lips.

"No talking." I shook my head, claiming her lips as I unzipped my jeans. As she walked backward, her hands found the top of my jeans. She pulled them down at the sides; my dick sprang free, slapping against her arm.

She moaned in my mouth. "Jesus, babe. You're so hard."

"You did this to me walking around in that hot-ass sundress shaking your ass." I reached under her dress, my eyes growing wide when I didn't feel any panties. "What the fuck, sugar? No panties? You never go without," I murmured against her lips, running my fingers through her wetness.

The silky smoothness of her cunt made my cock grow harder. The familiar ache that I'd been perpetually blessed with since meeting Suzy was almost too much to bear at times.

She rubbed her pussy against my palm. "Please, City. I

need to feel you." Her eyes fluttered, her breathing turning harsh.

Grabbing her by the waist, I spun her around to face the bed. "On your stomach, hands on the bed, sugar."

She smiled over her shoulder, her cheeks turning pink. "City, everyone's downstairs. They may hear or come looking for us." She placed her palms against the crisp white down comforter.

"Then you better bend over so we can be quick." I smacked her ass and watched her jump.

She bent over as she rubbed her ass, bringing her sundress up her legs, showing me a hint of thigh. She planted her elbows flat against the mattress and stilled as my hand caressed her ass.

My dick twitched, screaming to sink into her. I grabbed it, stroking the length as I hiked up her dress. Running my cock through her wetness, I sighed, knowing I wouldn't be walking around with a hard-on for the rest of the night.

I pulled her hips up, lifting her slightly off the bed, my dick touching her opening.

"Wait." Her body stiffened as she planted her face in the mattress.

"What?" I asked, with my cock in my hand, ready to push inside.

"Condom?" Her voice muffled by the blankets.

"Sugar, you're on the pill. We're about to be man and wife. We've done it without before. Right now, I want to feel you with nothing between us. I want to feel your silky wetness as I fuck the shit out of you."

She sighed, relaxing her body. "Okay, but—"

"Enough talking. The only words I wanna hear out of you are 'yes' and 'give me more.'" I leaned over her, kissing her shoulder as I jammed my cock into her.

Her body jerked, accepting all I had to give as she

melted into the mattress. The blankets were bunched in her hands as I stood, looking down at her.

I slid my hand up her back, tangling my fingers in her hair. Wrapping it around my palm, I grabbed it and pulled. She gasped, her eyes sealing shut as I thrust myself inside her. The flesh of her hip felt cool underneath my forceful grip.

Every time my dick slammed into her, my balls slapped her clit, causing her body to twitch and moans to escape her lips. I thrust harder, needing the release as I watched her body bounce off my shaft.

"You want me to stop?" I bit out, swiveling my hips to touch every inch of the inside of her pussy.

"No," she moaned.

"You love my cock?"

"Yes," she said as she bucked.

I pulled her down forcefully against my body. "This is my pussy." Pulling her hair harder, I wrapped it around my fist, holding it more securely. "I take it when I want, not when you want to give it."

"Yes, yes. Oh God, yes!" she yelled, her pussy convulsing against my dick. She drew her legs in closer together, almost crossing them, making her hold on my cock viselike.

I slid my finger from her hip to her abdomen and down to her clit. It was swollen, and she shuddered as I pinched it, rolling it between my fingertips.

Her face fell forward and she bore down, pulling the blanket between her teeth. She grunted, pounding herself against me as I worked her clit, bringing her to the brink of release.

"Say what I wanna hear." I stilled my hands as I pummeled her.

"It's your pussy," she moaned without hesitation.

I chuckled, biting my lip. Suzy went from saying "heck" to using the word "pussy" without hesitation since she met me. Hearing her say such dirty shit made my spine tingle. "Always, sugar. Come on my cock. Shows me who owns you."

Using two fingers, I covered her clit entirely, making small circles with the soft pads of my tips. Her grunts grew louder, her pussy milking me, as she tensed and stilled. My touch became more demanding, my thrusts rougher as I used my cock as my own personal battering ram. I wanted her to walk funny when she went back downstairs.

"Give it to me, sugar." I tweaked her clit, needing her to come before I did.

She sucked in a breath, not moving, as she came on my cock. As her body relaxed and she grew limp, I used it as an invitation to fuck her senseless. Her body bounced like a bowl of Jell-O underneath me.

The orgasm ripped through me, sending me collapsing on top of her, gasping for air. "Fuck," I moaned as I caught my breath, my knees feeling weak.

"Mm," she hummed as she lay underneath me, smiling.

Planting my palms on the bed, I trailed kisses across her exposed skin as I pushed myself up. Her ass was a light shade of pink from the relentless pounding I gave her. She lay there with her dress hiked up around her waist, her ass still in the air and her body bent over the bed. She looked how I felt: sated and happy.

I tucked my dick back in my pants, leaving the remnants of our mingled orgasm on my flesh. "Come on, let's get back downstairs before people come looking." I ran my fingers down her arm, stopping in her palm to make tiny circles.

"I don't want to," she whispered, her skin breaking out in goose bumps.

"No choice now, princess. Let's go." I grabbed her by the hips and pulled her upright.

She gasped as her eyes widened into saucers.

"What's wrong?" I searched her eyes, watching her face flush an even darker shade of pink.

"Everything just gushed out of me. Oh my God, it's running down my leg." She looked down. "I can't go down there like this." She glared at me.

My body shook from the laugh I couldn't hold in. "Sugar, go get cleaned up. I'll wait for you and we can go down together." I smiled, watching her move from one foot to the other.

"Ugh, this is so not sexy," she whispered, turning toward the bathroom. Her walk reminded me of the marshmallow man from Ghostbusters—her arms far from her side as she took large steps on spread legs. She stalked to the bathroom in the most ungraceful way, but that was my girl. I wouldn't change a thing about her.

As the bathroom door closed, I collapsed on the bed, placing my hands behind my head. She'd be feeling me in more ways than one for the rest of the night. She'd be my wife soon. *My wife.* It still felt foreign to think, let alone say, but there had been no other person in the world that had me the way Suzy did. I was hers completely, maybe more than she was mine.

I closed my eyes. I never knew life could be this fucking fantastic.

CHAPTER 5
SUZY

"IZZY, what did I tell you about tonight?" I looked at her as we entered the hotel suite. I couldn't pin it on her alone. She had help planning my bachelorette party. The girls in the wedding party plotted together to send me out of singledom in style. I knew that Izzy and Sophia would be a wicked combination.

The hotel suite was stunning. I'd never seen anything like it. It was larger than my first home and overlooked the ocean. The exterior walls were glass from floor to ceiling. The sunset made it look like an ever-changing picture hanging in a gallery. The red, purple, and orange shades reflected off the water as the sun kissed the horizon.

Izzy stepped in front of me, breaking me from my sunset trance. "I heard you, Suzy. We were good. Sophia helped me and you know that she always has your best interests at heart," Izzy said with a laugh.

Sophia was my best friend. She was my opposite, though, living life a little more carefree, taking chances, and was a little too much like Izzy for my liking. She may be a librarian, but the girl partied like a rock star. Fuck.

"What's wrong, Suzy?" Sophia asked, touching my arm.

"You two," I said, shaking my head.

Sophia's lips parted as she laid her hand against her chest. "What did we do?" Her innocent act wasn't convincing. Motherhood had softened her a little. She had more weight on her body and looked healthy. The happiness that had now filled her life was clearly evident when looking at her.

"I don't trust you and Izzy individually, and I sure as hell don't trust you together." I glared at her, watching a small smile creep across her face. My stomach filled with knots. The two of them didn't follow any of the normal rules, let alone mine.

"Suzy, would I do anything to upset you?" Her brown eyes twinkled as a large smile spread across her face. Crossing her arms, she tilted her head and waited.

I studied the look on her face. "Yes, yes you would. Just the girls tonight, right?" I asked, watching her reaction very closely.

She nodded, her brown hair bobbing against her breasts that peeked out from her V-neck dress. "I only invited the girls. I swear."

The knot in my stomach loosened a bit with her statement. "I just don't want there to be any trouble tonight."

"Oh, there won't be." She shook her head and wrapped her arms around me, drawing me against her body. "I'm so happy for you, Suzy. Do you think I would do anything bad and have to deal with Kayden's bullshit?"

"No," I whispered as I hugged her.

Kayden was her man and the father of her son, Jett. Their love was complicated. The road they traveled to happiness had been filled with bumps, but they made it through and never looked back. Kayden was a man I could rely on, a friend that would lay down his life for me. Sophia had told me that he could be "wicked jealous." Her words for him, not mine.

"Okay then, let's grab a drink. The girls are all about to arrive." She held me at arm's length, smiling and squeezing my hands. "We're here to celebrate before you become Mrs. Joseph Gallo."

"I don't want to drink too much, Sophia," I mumbled as we walked toward the already prepped bar area.

Izzy was pouring herself a hefty glass of Jack Daniel's as we approached. "What'll it be, ladies?" she asked as she set the bottle on the counter.

"Just a glass of wine," I said, looking at the dozens of bottles on display.

"No wine tonight, Suzy. Pick your poison." Izzy smiled, waving her hands over the liquor.

"Bahama Mama." I winced, my stomach rolling at the thought of getting drunk. "Light on the liquor, though."

"Honey, it's your bachelorette party and if you don't get shit-faced drunk and party your ass off then I haven't done my job as a bridesmaid." She smiled as she started pouring the rum in the glass.

I watched, my eyes growing wide as she poured and poured. "That's enough, Izzy," I said, placing my hand on her arm. "I want to make it until at least ten."

She burst into laughter as she set the rum down. "We'll get ya there. We have the whole night planned out. It's going to be one for the record books. When we're old and pissing our pants with dentures in our mouths, we'll be telling stories about tonight." She smiled, pouring the juices and rum in the cup before handing it to me.

I shook my head and grabbed the Bahama Mama from her hand. "That's what I'm afraid of," I muttered as I brought the glass to my lips. The rum didn't smell overpowering; maybe I'd misjudged the amount of alcohol she poured.

The fruity concoction of pineapple and orange danced across my tongue as the liquid slid down my throat, causing a slow burn. I closed my eyes, enjoying the taste, although it was a bit stronger than I wanted.

Izzy tipped my cup. "Drink up, girl. We have a big night ahead of us."

I batted her hand away, pulling the cup from my lips. "Last time I drank too much I ended up in your brother's bed." I smiled, my body warming at the memory.

If I hadn't been tipsy that night, I would've been a total mess the first time I saw him naked. The man had a kickass body, and don't even get me started on his piercing. If I had been stone-cold sober, I probably would've run out of the room screaming once that caught my eye. Even to this day, I get a thrill looking at him naked.

"You're a dirty whore and we all know it." Sophia nudged me, cackling like a loon.

"Am not," I said, my cheeks heating as I glared at her.

"Suzy," Izzy interrupted, "you're with us, your girls. You can drop the good-girl bullshit. We know you're a closet freak. If you weren't, you wouldn't be with my brother." She laughed.

A knock on the door saved me from the conversation. One by one, Izzy and Sophia's friends and mine from work poured into the door. My sister wouldn't be here tonight. She said that she couldn't get off work to be here in time for the bachelorette party. She'd make it for the rehearsal dinner. The girls in this room were more like family to me than my own flesh and blood anyway.

I stood at the window, watching the sun kiss the horizon as I sipped my drink. I felt blessed, surrounded by loving women, marrying the man of my dreams, and officially becoming a member of the Gallo family. The ladies chatted and drank, their laughter filling the room.

"Hey, you okay?" Sophia asked, standing at my side.

"I'm just so happy, Soph. I never thought I could be this happy." I turned to her, a sad smile on my face.

"What's the sad face for?" Her eyebrows drew together as she looked at me.

"I'm not sad. I'm just thinking about what City and I have been through. I almost shut him out of my life by judging him. I would've never known the love I do now. Then the accident happened and he was almost ripped from my life forever." I shook my head, trying to force the sad memories from my mind. "I'm so happy right now… happier than I've ever been before. Is this as good as it gets?" I asked, grabbing her hand and squeezing.

"Nah, there's more good things to come." She smiled, squeezing my hand. "Wait until you hold your firstborn in your arms. There's nothing like it." She smiled, releasing my hand. "I'm proud of you."

My eyebrows shot up at her words. "For what?"

She giggled, covering her mouth. "For staying with City. I know he scared the hell out of you. I know how OCD you are with your lists—even that fucking list of your husband requirements. You threw them out the window and took a chance for once. You listened to your heart and not your head. When I met him, I knew he was right for you." She wrapped her arms around me. "Now, let's stop talking sad shit and party our asses off. I have a night without Jett and Kayden. I want to get drunk and enjoy a night without baby food on my clothes."

I chuckled and squeezed her. "I love you, Sophia. For you, I'll party like it's 1999."

"God, you're such a dork," she said as she laughed,

holding me by the arms, shaking her head. "But I love you. I don't know why, but I do."

"Bitches, I better see you two drinking a little quicker," Izzy said as she grabbed my glass and looked inside. "Let me refill this. Sophia, want more?"

Sophia held her cup out, shaking it. "Feels a bit light to me. Another Jack and Coke, please." She handed the cup to Izzy.

"And I'll—" I started to say as Izzy started to walk away.

"Got it, light on the alcohol," Izzy yelled over her shoulder.

"Gifts! Let's do gifts," Sophia said, pulling on my arm.

I loved presents. It's not that I was materialistic; I just never had the type of family where the gifts were piled higher than me. I always received a couple of small gifts for my birthday or Christmas. My family decided to draw names for Christmas that year. Just when I thought it couldn't be more depressing, bam, wrong again.

"Okay," I said, nodding, trying to hide my excitement.

Sophia clapped, drawing everyone's attention. "It's time for presents!" she yelled, pulling me toward the couch.

I sat down on the large U-shaped sectional in the middle of the living room that faced the windows. Everyone fit snugly on the couch as I opened each gift. I felt slightly uncomfortable being the center of attention. I liked to blend in to the background, but I knew the entire weekend would be filled with uncomfortable moments. I was the bride, and as such, I'd definitely be the center of attention.

"Open mine next," Sophia said, holding out a pretty pink box with a giant white bow. I'd opened six presents so far and they'd all been lingerie and nighties to wear for

City. He'd love them, but I knew most likely one or two would get ripped. The man was a brute.

Pulling it from her grasp, I smiled nervously, unsure of what was inside. With Sophia, it could be romantic or downright dirty. "I don't trust you," I said, placing the box on my lap and pulling on the ribbon.

She chuckled, covering her mouth. "I wouldn't either."

I stilled my hand, looking up at her with a glare. "Do I want to open this in public?"

She nodded, her smile growing larger. "You do. Don't be a baby and open it already," she said, putting her hands on her hips.

I pulled the ribbon, letting the white material fall away from the present before tearing into the shiny pink paper. When I opened the box, I gasped and put the lid back on. "Sophia," I said, trying not to laugh.

"You have to show us," Izzy said as she stood. She grabbed her phone from her pocket and held it up to take a picture. "Come on, Suzy. We're all girls here. Don't be a pussy."

I sighed, realizing I wouldn't win the battle. "Fine," I said, opening the lid and grabbing the first object. Fuckin' Sophia. I held it up and listened to the whistles and giggles.

"What the fuck is that?" Mia asked.

"That, my dear," Izzy said, snapping a photo, "when assembled, is a spreader bar." Izzy giggled and snapped another picture.

My face grew flushed, but I couldn't help but laugh. "I've never had a problem keeping them open for City." I winked at Sophia. She and I always swapped stories about sex. Before City came into my life, sex had always been bland and boring. I'd lived vicariously through her and always went to her for advice.

"Oh, I know. You've turned into quite the little sex

kitten since meeting City. This gift may seem like it's for you, but it's really for him." Sophia smiled and looked very pleased with herself. "Next."

"Whore," I mumbled as I pulled out a pair of nipple clamps.

"I don't want to think of you using any of this shit with my brother. I can never look at you two in the eye again. I know too much. Too much, I tell you." Izzy snapped another photo before taking a seat at the end of the couch.

I quickly pulled out the other objects, crotchless panties and a crop, and held them up before dropping them back in the box. The crop was the one I'd always wanted and admired. It had a heart made of leather on the end. I just loved the look of it, but it had to sting like a mother when hit with it.

Knock. Knock.

"Oh," Izzy said, jumping from the couch. "There's my gift. I had to have it delivered."

I looked at Sophia and she shrugged. Motherfuckers. I knew they wouldn't listen when I said no strippers. I hung my head, rubbing my face, as I heard the door open.

"Why, hello there, officer," Izzy said. She giggled and backed away from the door.

For the love of God—I wanted to kill her right then.

"I heard there's a disturbance up here. I'm here to investigate," the man, who obviously wasn't a cop, said as he looked around the room.

I thought for a moment that I was in a movie. Cop stripper comes to the door and then the real party starts. The last thing I wanted in the world was someone other than my fiancé touching me.

"She's right over there—the blonde in the middle. She's a real handful." Izzy looked at me with a smile, and winked.

I blushed, all eyes turning on me as he started the little CD player he had in his hand. The girls started to scream, scrambling from the couch.

I sat alone, leaning back, and crossed my arms over my chest. He handed the CD player to Sophia as he approached me. He stalked toward me, untucking his shirt and shaking his hips. Izzy held her phone in our direction.

"Don't you fucking dare take a photo of this," I warned. The last thing I needed was this getting into City's hands. He wasn't a jealous man, he knew I was his, but still, there would be a sting.

"You're such a killjoy," Izzy said as she shoved the phone in her pocket.

"Bad Ass" by Kid Ink played as the stripper tried his best to seduce me. He wasn't bad looking—blond hair, thin but muscular, and beautiful brown eyes. He ripped his shirt open, exposing a hairless chest. He turned, shaking his ass in my face as he ripped off his pants. Was he twerking?

I wanted to laugh, but I didn't want to be rude. He was trying hard to impress me, but he wasn't my City. I uncrossed my arms, letting them fall into my lap, as I watched him shake his ass. He turned and I came face to face with his cock, thankful it was tucked neatly in a G-string. Wouldn't work for City and his well-endowed package.

"Smile, for shit's sake. At least pretend to have a good time," Sophia whispered in my ear. "As soon as he's done with you, the rest of the girls will get their shot at him."

I turned to her and glared, but did as she said. I smiled and pretended to enjoy myself. My stomach flipped when he sat on my lap and started rubbing against my chest. He nuzzled his face in my hair as he scooted forward, and all I could think about was City, and how he loved being wrapped in my gold locks.

His small, semi-erect dick touched my stomach, and I cringed. I closed my eyes, thinking about something other than what was happening.

"Hey," he whispered in my ear. "Don't worry, the song is almost over."

I opened my eyes and blew out a breath. I couldn't be the only ambushed bride in this uncomfortable situation.

"Thanks," I whispered, and smiled. His words put me at ease and helped settle my nerves, knowing the torture was almost done.

When the song ended, he grabbed my chin, kissing me on the cheek. My eyes grew wide as I pulled my head back, letting his fingers fall from my chin. He smiled sweetly and turned his attention to Mia sitting next to me. I sighed, happy that it was over and I could relax.

I stood on wobbly legs and approached Izzy. She couldn't stop laughing. "Happy with yourself?" I asked, my hands on my hips.

"Very." She laughed louder. "You're done now, Suzy Q. Drink up. Let the other girls enjoy him for a while. We'll head down to the party around the pool in a bit."

"I need the entire bottle of rum to forget the feel of him against my body." My body shook as I remembered foreign skin against mine.

"Well, good thing for you I brought extra. Help yourself," she said with a grin, motioning toward the temporary bar with her head and wiggling her eyebrows.

"I'm still pissed at you," I said as I pointed at her and glared.

"You love me, don't bullshit yourself." She kissed my cheek and walked toward the gaggle of girls stuffing ones in the strippers G-string.

Grabbing my phone off the table, I checked my messages. Nothing. City and I hadn't spent much time apart since the motorcycle accident, and I missed him. I didn't want to be the clingy, annoying fiancée, but I couldn't help myself, I sent him a text.

Me: Having fun?

I set my phone down and grabbed the bottle of rum and poured half a glass. I didn't know how much to put in a Bahama Mama, but it looked like the same amount Izzy poured earlier. I added the juices and watched the color change to a salmon pink after the grenadine splash. It was as pretty as it was tasty. I sipped it, sat down at the dining room table, and waited for his reply.

City: Miss you, sugar.

That was a vague and cagey reply. He didn't say if he was or was not having fun. I didn't want to know what the boys had planned for him tonight. No one would tell me anyway, or any of the girls, for that matter. I sent him a quick message as I watched the bump-and-grind show taking place on the sectional.

Me: Miss you too.

Sophia sat down next to me and frowned. "Why are you over here and not over there with the rest of the party?" She tilted her head and chewed on her bottom lip.

"Just rather watch that hot mess than participate. I could ask you the same thing. Why aren't you copping a feel?" I raised my eyebrow and challenged her. I didn't need an answer. She felt the same way I did.

"Hell no. I don't need someone pawing at me. I'm here to have a girls' night, not stare at his tiny junk."

I choked on my drink, and wiped the liquid off my chin. "You noticed that too, huh?" I asked.

She laughed, throwing her head back and relaxing in the chair. "Gotta be blind not to. You ready to be Mrs. Joseph Gallo?"

"Yeah, I'm excited, but you know I don't like too much attention."

"Well, you're going to be the center of attention here and there this weekend. Might as well get used to it." She grabbed her Solo cup, downing the last remnants of her drink.

"At least City will be by my side." I checked my phone, but there wasn't a new message.

Izzy ripped the phone from my hand. "Oh, no. This is a man-free night. This is all about us celebrating and partying our asses off. No phones, no Joe. Got it?"

"You're a bitch," I said as she shoved my phone in her back pocket. "If this is your idea of celebration then you're not who I thought you were, Izzy." I stuck my tongue out.

"This is the pre-party. The real fun starts downstairs. The nightclub opened an hour ago. No good club starts until eleven. Keep your granny panties on. We'll be going shortly. Keep drinking." She gave me a cocky grin and walked away.

"I love her," Sophia said, getting up to refill her cup.

"You would," I mumbled before downing the last of my Bahama Mama, a slow burn sliding down my throat and spreading throughout my body.

Mia sat in the chair Sophia had been in. "It's nice to finally get a night away from the guys, isn't it?" she asked, smiling before she took a sip of her drink.

"I guess so. I love City, but I love my girls too."

"There's nothing wrong with that, Suzy. It's good to have some time apart. I've spent as much time with anyone as I do with Michael. I mean, I love him—fuck, most days I can't get enough of him—but I needed tonight," Mia said as she leaned back in the chair, resting her head against the high chair back.

"Are things okay with you two?" I asked, concerned

about them. I loved Mike and adored Mia. I wanted them around and loved any time we were all able to hang out. With all of our work schedules, it wasn't easy.

"Yeah, things are great. Sometimes we get in arguments, but that's when he wants to pull his man bullshit, and I eventually put him in his place." She laughed, bringing the cup to her lips. "Gallo men are a breed of their own."

"Yeah, no truer words have ever been spoken."

"Are you ready for the wedding?" she asked me, tilting her head and twirling the cup in her hand.

"Ready as I'll ever be."

"You have that need for control, like Mike. It'll go off without a hitch, Suzy. Every Gallo will make sure it does. I'll help too. I'll do anything you need that day."

"Thanks so much, Mia. I just want it to be perfect."

"Perfection is overrated," she said, smiling at me.

"On my wedding day, I don't think it is," I said, my stomach turning at the thought of anything going wrong.

"Suzy, it's life's imperfections that stand out and make memories. They're what great stories are made of, and we'll tell them over and over again. Imperfections make the world more interesting. Think about your relationship with City, how you began. Was it perfect?"

I shook my head, the power of her words calming my rumbling stomach. "Hardly. We hit some bumps along the road."

"Does it make your love story less worthy or the journey less sweet?" Mia asked.

"No, it makes me hold on tighter, thinking of what I could've lost."

"Perfection isn't all it's cracked up to be. Just enjoy the day. All that matters is that you're husband and wife at the end of it all. Not if the cake was perfect or if the seating chart was right. Just Joe and you becoming one."

I leaned forward, wrapping my arms around her. "You're right, Mia. Everything else is trivial. Thank you for your kind words. I couldn't have picked a more perfect person for Mike."

"There's that 'perfect' word again. I'm far from it, but we're a good fit," she said, hugging me back. "Now, I'm ready to party my ass off with the girls and worry about the men and wedding later. You in?" she asked, releasing me.

"All in. Let's do it," I said, standing to find Izzy and Sophia. I was ready to dance. Clearly, I'd had too much to drink.

CHAPTER 6
CITY

"I CAN'T BELIEVE that shit can even be done," Anthony said, holding his stomach as he laughed.

"She has mad skills." Mike shook his head, all of us still stunned.

"When she shot that thing out of her pussy, I almost shit a brick." Anthony scrubbed his hand across his face, shaking his head.

"A ping-pong ball. Jesus Christ, I'll never be able to see anyone play that fucking game again." Mike grabbed the beer from the cup holder and downed it.

We were safely on the limo bus after a rather interesting trip to some shit-ass dive strip club in Tampa. It wasn't my idea of a good time, but since Mike and Anthony planned the entire night, I sat back and tried to enjoy the ride. I felt guilty watching strippers, knowing that Suzy was off enjoying a peaceful night with the girls. Izzy promised me that they were just going for drinks and maybe dancing and that they'd be staying in a hotel room so they wouldn't drink and drive.

"Why the fuck aren't you talking?" Bear said as he nudged Tank.

I shook my head, laughing at the mix of guys on this bus. For some unknown reason, Mike and Anthony decided to invite Bear, Tank, and a few other guys from the Neon Cowboy. They knew each other from Inked since they were not only friends but also clients.

"I'm talking. Just listening about the pussy show." I glared at Bear and then looked at Tank, tilting my head while I studied his face. "What the fuck is that smirk for?"

"You're so pussy whipped." Tank tipped his glass, his smirk turning into a smile. The corners of his eyes wrinkled as he chuckled and took a swig of beer.

"Fuck off," I growled. "I'm not pussy whipped. Why look at ground meat when I have grade-A platinum pussy at home? I know you boys don't know the difference." I smirked, looking to Mike. "Not you, brother, you get the good shit too. You know what I mean."

He smiled, nodding. "I do, but I am still in disbelief. Mia better never shoot anything out of that pussy. Shit's too good to ruin with a ping-pong ball or anything other than my dick, fingers, and tongue," Michael said, making a V with his fingers and tonguing the void.

"Clearly you've had too much to drink," I said, looking at him, unable to contain my laughter.

"Two fuckin' pussy-whipped bastards. You sure you two still have your balls attached?" Bear slapped his knee.

"Why don't you suck my dick and find out, motherfucker?" I smirked as Bear stilled and gagged. "You're just jealous, plain and simple."

He mumbled, bringing the bottle to his lips. "You know I've always been fond of Sunshine. Couldn't be pussy whipped over a better girl."

"We're here," the driver called out as the limo-bus stopped in front of a beachside hotel.

"What the fuck are we doing here?" I looked out the tinted windows, confused by the destination. I didn't think we'd end the evening at a hotel. We'd already seen the strippers, so I didn't think that awaited us inside.

"Shepard's has the best fuckin' nightclub in the St. Pete. Get your old grumpy ass up and let's dance." Anthony stood, taking the glass from my hand.

"One, I don't fuckin' dance without my woman. Two, don't ever touch my beer. Three, this wasn't supposed to be a night for you to find a piece of ass," I said as I climbed off the limo bus.

"Fine, you drink and stew in your moodiness while the rest of us enjoy the ladies, right, men?" Anthony pumped his fist, his body shaking with excitement. "Right?"

Michael cleared his throat, looking away from Anthony. "I'm with Joe. I'd rather drink and bullshit than look at any other women. Mia would have my balls in a sling if I even thought about looking at another woman. I'll hang with my brother while you bastards find your next victims." He laughed as he walked by, and slapped me on the shoulder. "I got your back," he said softly so only I could hear.

"More for us," Tank said, heading toward the door.

"Yeah, this looks like your type of place, Tank." I shook my head. "The girls are going to run away screaming from your ass." The warm air of the Florida night felt good against my skin. The salty smell of the air and the gentle breeze of the ocean were soothing.

"I'll show them what a real man looks like," Tank said. "They're too used to these pansy-ass boys that pluck their eyebrows and wax their body hair. They need a little Tank in their life. What the fuck are those douchebags called again?"

I rolled my eyes. The man was clearly full of himself. "Yeah, I'm sure they do. How the fuck am I supposed to know what they're called?"

"Metrosexuals," Bear said, giving a weak smile.

"What the fuck?" I said, totally in shock. I never ever in a million years though Bear would know that fucking term. A big, burly biker like him should not know that term. "You reading *Vogue* magazine or some shit?" I raised an eyebrow, studying his face.

His cheeks turned pink as he looked at the ground. "I have sisters, asshole. Their boyfriends are metrosexuals. Beats the fuck outta me. They throw the term around like it's the most glorious thing. Someday they'll figure out what they're missing being with such a pussy."

I laughed along with the rest of the guys. "Had us worried there for a second," Tank said, smacking Bear in the back of the head. "I was about to do a dick check."

"I know you've always wanted to get your hands on my cock, Tank. I don't swing that way. Sorry, buddy."

I smiled as we walked through the lobby. I had the best friends and brothers in the whole fucking world. Before Anthony pushed open the doors to the pool, the glass panes started to shake from the bass of the music on the other side.

"Ready, boys?" Anthony asked, looking like he was about to enter a little piece of heaven.

"Just open the fuckin' doors already," I growled.

He nodded, pushing open both doors at once. We took two steps and stopped dead to take in the sight before us. Girls in bikinis, skimpy dresses, and various other kinds of tiny, barely there clothing writhed and danced to the beat of the techno music.

"Wow, I've been missing out at that hick bar," Tank said, his voice filled with disbelief.

"Neon Cowboy women do not look like that." Bear held his hand out, moving it up and down, motioning toward the crowd, and licked his lips.

"There is sure as fuck is something to be said for city girls." Tank headed toward the crowd, winding his way through the ladies.

At least Tank and Bear didn't come in their camo or some other redneck attire. They wore clean denim jeans, black t-shirts, and boots. We looked like the redneck biker version of the Rat Pack. Our tats were clearly visible on our arms—metrosexuals we most definitely were not.

"Bar," I growled, pulling Tank off the back of some chick. He had her by the hips and she was pushing back against him with a big smile on her face.

"What the fuck, man? I was enjoying myself."

"She had a ring on her finger, dumbass," I yelled over the loud music.

"Who cares? I was looking to hit it and quit it." He laughed, making a smacking motion while thrusting his hips.

"Shots. We need them in mass quantities." Bear threw a fifty on the bar.

"That won't get you far here, Bear." Michael threw an extra fifty on top. "This isn't the Podunk bar you're used to. This is the city, and everything is three times as much."

We leaned against the bar, studying the dance floor like a scene from *Saturday Night Fever* as we waited for our tequila shots and beers. I reached in my pocket for my phone as panic started to set in. Fuck.

"What's wrong, Joe?" Michael asked, resting his hand on my shoulder.

"I don't have my phone. Suzy's going to be pissed if I don't text her back."

"I got it in my pocket. You'll get it back tomorrow. Tonight it's all about us and not our ladies. She'll be fine. It's her party night too. Trust me, those girls have her too busy to even bother looking at their phones. So chill the fuck out and drink." Mike shoved the tequila shot under my nose as a smile crept across his face.

"You're right." I grabbed the drink from his hand and turned toward the guys. "What are we drinking to?" I asked, raising the glass.

"Platinum pussy and unlimited blowjobs." Anthony clinked his glass to mine as all the guys joined in with a laugh.

I grimaced as I downed the liquid. Tequila and I were never friends. We slammed the shot glasses on the bar, grabbing our beers to wash it down.

"Another," Tank said, motioning to the bartender. "Same," he yelled as the man approached.

"Gonna be one of those nights, huh?" I said, sipping my beer as I looked around.

The setting was amazing. Suzy would love it here. She didn't like to dance when I met her, but when we were on the dance floor together, our bodies moved as if they'd known each other a lifetime. She knew how to move, but being with me gave her the confidence to feel uninhibited in the sack and in a club.

"Earth to Joe." Bear tapped me in the head, annoying the shit out of me.

I swatted his hand, ready to tear his finger off, and turned toward him. "You wanna lose that finger?" I smirked, moving into his personal space.

"Shut the fuck up and drink, shithead." Bear pushed my chest, knocking me back a step.

Grabbing the drink off the bar, I slammed it back, enjoying the warmth. "Ahh, another," I said as I put the glass down, turning to see everyone's mouths agape. "What?"

"Jesus, you're going to be shitfaced. Pace yourself, brother." Michael threw back his drink, calling the bartender over.

We spent the next hour laughing and drinking. We talked about women. Michael and I spoke of our girls while Tank, Bear, and Anthony talked about their plethora of pussy. The stark contrast of the caliber of pussy the three of them enjoyed was astounding. I knew the club bitches Tank and Bear spent their nights with, and I wasn't too impressed. They could do better, and hell, they deserved more. They may be rough around the edges, but they were good, honest men.

Anthony was just Anthony. He was a manwhore to the nth degree, enjoying life a little too loosely. I couldn't blame the guy, but at some point, you have to give up the chase and enter the adult world.

"Here," Anthony said, nudging me. "You look a little lost in thought, or you're already shitfaced." He laughed, pushing the glass of amber liquid in front of me.

"I'm not even close to being shitfaced."

"I want to do a special toast," Michael said, holding up his glass, waiting for us to follow suit. As we raised our glasses, holding them together, he spoke. "To Thomas. He couldn't be here again, but this one's for him." He frowned, his eyes glistening a little in the club light. "To the best goddamn brother out there. May he stay safe and come back to us in one piece." A weak smile formed on his face as he brought the glass to his lips.

My chest felt tight as I thought about Thomas. I wanted him to be here to celebrate this weekend with us, but he had gone too far under at this point. We were on a no-contact basis the last few months. We could check in with his superior, but beyond that, we hadn't heard from him. "Way to bring a party down," I said, shaking my head. "To Thomas." I downed the tequila before wiping my mouth with the back of my hand.

I looked at Anthony, and his eyes were the size of saucers. He wasn't moving, the shot in front of his lips, frozen in place. "What the fuck, man?" I asked, turning to see what caught his attention.

What the fuck? My heart started to hammer, my mind racing as I fisted my hands at my side. *There's no fucking way.* I shook my head, trying to get rid of the image, hoping it was an optical illusion. Fuck, it wasn't.

Across the pool danced *my* bride-to-be with some motherfucker doing the bump-n-grind. I moved forward, but a hand stopped me, clamping down on my arm.

"Don't cause a scene, City," Bear said, gripping me tightly.

I looked down at his hand, a growl starting deep in my throat. "That's my woman. No one, and I mean no one, puts their hands on her." Pulling my arm from his grip, I stalked across the pool, cracking my neck and preparing for the shitstorm that was about to happen.

Sophia stopped dancing, her mouth hanging open as she nudged Izzy, motioning to me with her head.

"Fuck," Izzy mouthed, shaking her head, her eyes growing wide.

With Suzy's back to me, I grabbed the asshole groping Suzy's collar, removing him from my fiancée. Suzy turned slowly, all the color draining from her face as her eyes found mine.

"Fuck off," I growled, pushing him away as I tried to restrain myself.

"You fuck off, asshole. I'm dancing with the beautiful blonde. She ain't yours." He moved forward, standing toe to toe with me.

I snarled, moving closer to his face. "She's my motherfucking fiancée. You had your shitty-ass hands all over her."

"City," Suzy said, grabbing my arm. "Baby."

I pushed her away, not looking in her direction. "You need to back the fuck off and go find some other pussy. This one is *mine*," I roared, grabbing his shirt and pulling him closer to my face.

"I didn't hear her say no when I started dancing with her, motherfucker." His words were slightly slurred as tiny droplets of his spit hit my face when he spoke. "Her ass felt so good in my hands."

"City," Bear said, touching my shoulder. "Not here, man."

"What did you just say?" I asked, tightening my grip.

"Her ass…you can bounce a quarter off that shit." His mouth slowly turned up into a cocky-ass grin.

As I released him, I pushed him back and swung. I connected with his jaw, the bones crunching under my knuckles. His arms flailed as he fell to the ground and I grasped his face.

"Keep your fucking hands to yourself, dickhead." I spat on the ground next to him. "Worthless piece of shit."

He dragged his hand across his lips, wiping the blood that had trickled out of his mouth. I fisted my hands at my side, waiting to see if he'd retaliate, but he stood slowly and walked away. Pussy.

Bear patted me on the back. "Can't say the asshole didn't deserve it."

"He deserved more. If we were at the Neon Cowboy I

would have beat him unconscious, but here it's like a damn show."

I looked around the crowd that had gathered. People were smiling and laughing and looked impressed. Such is city life at a club. They just wanted to see someone get their ass kicked. I closed my eyes, trying to calm my breath before turning to see Suzy.

Her arms were crossed and her head cocked as she glared at me. "You're such a caveman. Does everything require violence?" She snarled.

I'd never seen Suzy so pissed off. She had no fucking right to be pissed. I was defending her honor, *my* soon-to-be bride. "You're pissed at me?" I asked. "Why the fuck are you pissed off at me? You're the one letting him manhandle you."

Her glare turned ice cold as she walked toward me. Her hands dropped to her side as she stopped in front of me. "You knock a guy on his ass and you want to know why I'm pissed off?" She poked me in the chest, her nail digging into my skin. "It's my bachelorette party and I was having some harmless fun. What the fuck is wrong with you?" She smacked me in the chest, trying to push me backward.

I grabbed her wrist, pulling her closer. "Some asswad has his hands on my woman and I'm just supposed to, what? Tap him on the fucking shoulder and say may I cut in? No, I'm going to confront that shithead and do what I have to do. I'm the one that's pissed, and rightfully so. You *let* him touch you. What the fuck happened to faithfulness?" I released her arm as her eyes flickered to the ground.

Her eyes returned to mine filled with anger and hurt. "I was being faithful, you big, dumb oaf. It's a bachelorette party and I'm here with your sister. I wasn't doing anything wrong. You're just being your difficult, overprotective self." She shook her head. "You always want to solve things with your fists. We're not twelve anymore, City."

"Sugar, I'll protect you until my last breath. I don't share, not now and not ever. You're mine and only mine. No one is allowed to put their hands on you, no matter the situation." I grabbed her by the waist, drawing her to my body. "Maybe I'm being harsh, but the thought of someone else touching you just pisses me off. I tried to control myself, but the prick had to keep running his mouth." I touched her cheek, holding her face in my hand.

Her face softened as she leaned into my touch. "He did. I'm sorry. I'm drunk and we're just having some harmless fun."

I leaned in, hovering just above her lips. Her eyes fluttered closed as I inhaled the smell of Suzy. The scent wasn't right. "What the fuck?" I sniffed her cheek and neck. She had a sweaty, musky scent on her skin. "Why do you smell like a man?"

Her eyes flew open and grew wide. "What are you talking about?" she whispered.

"You smell like another man's been pawing you. That jagoff didn't touch your face. Why the hell does your face and neck smell like someone else?" My heart started to pound sporadically; my chest felt hollow except for the flutter of my heart.

"I don't know what you're talking about. I haven't touched anyone." She grabbed my shirt, holding me to her.

"Like fuck you haven't. I can smell him." Nausea overcame me as the realization that Suzy had been that close to another man. Maybe she wasn't the woman I always thought she was.

"City, I haven't touched anyone. You're making shit up."

I backed away, dropping my hand from her cheek. "I find you with some guy with his hands all over you and now I can smell someone all over your skin. Don't you have anything to say for yourself, or are you just going to deny it?"

She looked to the sky and back to me, her eyes glistening in the light. "I didn't do anything wrong," she yelled, her hands fisted at her side.

I shook my head, feeling my heart shattering into a million tiny pieces. The thought of her cheating on me made me feel like death would be preferable. I didn't want to look at her anymore. I couldn't take the lies or the dull ache in my chest. "I don't believe you," I whispered, looking over her. I couldn't stomach looking in her eyes anymore.

"City," she pleaded, reaching for my arm.

I recoiled, moving my body out of reach. "No, not this time, sugar. I need some time to myself," I said as I turned my back to her.

I didn't want to see the hurt on her face. I didn't have to look at her to know it was there, but I was too pissed off to stick around and talk about it. I needed to get away and cool off.

"Bro, where ya going?" Michael said, stepping in front of me.

"I need to be alone, brother. I'm taking a cab home," I said, trying to control my breathing. I closed my eyes and breathed out through my mouth before looking him in the eyes.

"Come on. We have the party bus. We can go somewhere else." Michael gave me a fake smile.

"Fuck that. I'm going home. Take the party bus and

enjoy the night. Tell Suzy to stay here with the girls. I need to be alone tonight."

I walked around him, leaving them behind. I found a cab and headed home. I tried to process how the night went so terribly wrong. Did I overreact? Probably. Did someone touch my fiancée? Most definitely. Could we be fixed? Only time would tell.

I closed my eyes; the blur of palm trees made my head hurt more than it already did. I thought about everything we'd been through in the last year. Suzy lost her good-girl image and stole my heart. I wrecked on my bike and almost died. The woman nursed me back to health and waited on me hand and foot.

It may have been a bachelorette party, but the shit still stung. My overactive imagination and the words the cocksucker spoke were like a punch to the gut. I knew my Suzy. She wouldn't cheat, but the thought of someone else touching her made my stomach hurt and my heart ache. I literally pushed Suzy away and turned my back on her. I let my anger rule instead of using my head. I reacted without thinking and would have to deal with it tomorrow.

I rubbed my face, wishing I could wash it all away and go back in time. I'd been a total dumb fuck, and there would be a heavy price to pay and most likely groveling. I wasn't one to grovel and beg, but this was my sugar. I'd do anything for her, to keep her, and make her mine. The closer I got to the house, our house, the more I knew I fucked up.

After paying the cab driver and walking up the driveway, I pulled out my phone and checked my messages. Not a message since I'd left her.

Me: I'm sorry. I love you.

The house was eerily quiet. It had been quiet before, but tonight it was deafening. Suzy was missing. Her joy and laughter usually filled the space. The girl was a damn chatterbox at times, and as I walked to the bedroom I realized how much I missed it—how much I missed her. The stillness of our house made me feel uneasy. I wanted my woman in our bed with me. I wanted to hear her giggle as I whispered in her ear before she fell asleep. She was the sunshine in my day; she softened me and filled my life with happiness.

I emptied my pockets, placing my wallet and keys on my nightstand. I removed my clothes, the stench of the clubs clinging to the fabric as I tossed them to the floor. No reply from Suzy as I crawled in bed, laying the cell phone next to me. I didn't want to miss her message. I stared at the ceiling, watching the fan create moving shadows in the darkness. For the first time in months, I felt completely alone.

Fuck, maybe I *was* pussy whipped.

CHAPTER 7
SUZY

FUMING. It's the only word I could use to describe what I felt. City had always been a little on the impulsive side, but tonight put the fucking icing on the cake. How could he think I had been unfaithful? I told Izzy no strippers, but did she listen? Of course not, when does she ever listen to anyone?

I'd had too much to drink, but I was still in control. I wasn't sloppy drunk, just at that point where everything was wonderful and nothing got me down. Well, nothing until Mr. "She's Mine" Caveman killed the party. When the guy that City laid out tried to dance with me, I said no and pushed him away. Izzy intervened. Fucking Izzy, said it was my last night and every girl had the right to dance with whomever they wanted before they're officially off the market.

I didn't see any harm in it. It was just a dance and nothing more. My girls surrounded me and they would never let anything happen to me. Furthermore, I don't cheat. It's not in my nature. I'm madly in love with City. I don't mean just that type of comfortable love. I'm talking that "take my breath away, make my stomach flip" type of love that I couldn't imagine being without. But, and this is a huge but, could I deal with his testosterone-laced, fist-throwing macho bullshit for the rest of my life?

If I answered the questions based solely on the amount and way I loved him, the answer would be yes. If I used my brain and really thought about City and his quickness to stake his claim and scare anyone with a cock away from me, the answer would be, "I honestly don't know." He said that's his way of protecting me, and it's how he's built.

The night I was attacked at the Neon Cowboy, his level of protection increased and became almost stifling at times. Somehow I managed to survive the first twenty-something years of my life without his watchful eye and brute fists. The trauma we endured during our relationship didn't help matters. My assault and then almost losing him in the motorcycle accident—they were events that put a strain on our emotions but brought us closer together.

The night we sat in the hospital waiting to hear if he would survive was the longest night of my life. I couldn't form a coherent thought until Mia told us that he'd survive. I felt like my world was ending. I didn't have control and I hated it. Control was something I strived to maintain. I made my lists and planned everything out. Having City's life hanging in the balance and relying on someone else to make him better was maddening.

I didn't think I could ever get mad at him again, but here we were. City walked off and left without talking to me. He didn't want to believe anything I had to say. He jumped to his crazy-ass conclusions and stalked off.

My mind was hazy as I sat on the barstool and watched the club moving to music that was muffled in my ears. I couldn't process anything but my thoughts of City and what the fuck just happened.

"Suzy, let's go upstairs, babe." Sophia grabbed my elbow, trying to get me to stand.

"No," I whispered, not ready to move.

"Come on, I'll go with you. Let's get out of here so we can talk," she said as she brushed my hair off my shoulder.

I looked at her with blurred vision; a line of tears sitting in my eyes hadn't yet fallen. "What's there to talk about? He walked out on me."

"Now listen to me, woman. He loves you and you love him. You both have been drinking and the scene went south quick. You know that isn't how City is, babe."

I blinked, letting the tears cascade down my cheeks. "That's exactly how he is, Sophia. I don't know if I can deal with that forever." My voice cracked as I wiped my cheeks.

"Up ya go, sugarplum, upstairs for you. You've obviously had more to drink than I thought if you're questioning your future with this man." She grabbed me around the waist, helping me stand on steady feet.

"Fine, Soph, but only because I could use a little peace and quiet. There's no one else I can talk to about him and get an honest opinion but you. They're all related or partial to the Gallo family." My legs felt rubbery as we walked past the dance floor and made our way to the outside elevators. "Thanks, Sophia." I smiled at her. She was my best friend, the only person in the world that knew everything about me. We'd been through too much together to not be able to read each other like an open book.

She smiled back at me but didn't say a word as we entered the elevator. I sagged against the wall, trying to keep my balance as it was ascending to the top floor. As soon as we walked into the suite, I kicked off my shoes and threw myself on the couch. Wrapping paper, boxes, sex toys, and lingerie were strewn around the room. Partially empty glasses, bottles of liquor, and champagne sat on the coffee table. The night had started with so much promise.

"All right, beautiful. Spill your guts," Sophia said as she sat down next to me and put my feet in her lap. God, I missed times like these. Sophia and I used to stay up late at night having talks about men and our problems. Life had changed so dramatically for both of us over the last two years. Being here with her, like this, made my broken heart long for the olden days.

"Did you hear what he said to me?" I asked, nestling my head into the soft throw pillow.

"I did. He was drunker than I've ever seen him."

"So what, are you saying I should give him a pass?"

Shaking her head, she rested her hand on my chin. "Never. Fuck that. I've learned you can never give someone a free pass, but don't throw it all away. Look, I fell in love with Kayden, and Lord help me, that man has been a whole heap of trouble. I should've been tougher on him and called him on his bullshit more. I paid the price, but I've learned and now we're in a better place. You need to talk to City and tell him how you feel."

"He hurt me tonight, Sophia." I closed my eyes, remembering how my stomach fell when he pushed me away.

"Physically?" Her eyebrows turned downward as her eyes snapped to my face.

"No, he hurt my feelings. He basically said I cheated on him. The accusations stung." The tears started to flow easier. His words finally sank in, and I processed the entire scene as if watching a bad movie. "He's never been mean to me. Tonight he was just a plain asshole."

Sophia chuckled, covering her mouth with her hand.

"What's so funny?" I squinted at her, not understanding the humor of the situation. "I'm sitting here pouring out my soul and crying, and you're laughing. What the hell, Sophia?"

"You said asshole like it was a word you used every day. Not so long ago you were using terms like 'get the heck out of here' and 'you big b.' The shit just rolls off your lips like it's been part of your vernacular for years." She rubbed my leg, running her nails over my skin. "He's a man, Suzy. They do not like to see their woman near other men. That guy said some nasty shit too. I'm surprised City didn't beat the fuck out of him until he was unconscious."

I sighed, putting my arm over my eyes. "City changed me. I can't deny it. He made it sound like I was a piece of property. I mean, why doesn't he just piss on me like a dog marking his territory?" My eyes were heavy and burning. The tears and alcohol made it hard to keep them open.

"Now you're just being overdramatic. Let's get you tucked into bed and see how you feel in the morning." Sophia moved my legs to the couch and pulled me up by my arms. "A little help would be nice," she said, as she tried to hold me in a sitting position.

"I'm just so tired. Just leave me here." I opened my eyes to look at her, and quickly closed them after seeing she wasn't amused.

"Get your ass in that bed. All the drunk bitches will be back and they'll wake you up."

I stood, using Sophia for leverage, and wobbled. "Yes, Mom. You're so damn bossy." I smiled, leaning forward to kiss her on the cheek. "I've missed you, Soph. I don't know what I'd do without you."

She wrapped her arms around me, embracing me in a tender hug. "You'd be at home making lists about lists." She chuckled, releasing me and helping me toward the main bedroom.

"You're probably right. I was such a boring human

being." My voice had become quiet, almost mouse-like as sleep started to overcome me.

"In you go, princess," Sophia said as she pulled back the covers.

I didn't bother to get undressed. I just wanted to sleep. I wanted tonight to be over and to deal with everything tomorrow. Grabbing an extra pillow, I turned on my side, tucking it into my body. I'd grown used to snuggling against City. I needed something to fill the void, and the pillow was my only option.

The lights turned off before I heard the click of the door as I drifted off into a restful sleep. All thoughts and worries disappeared as I dreamed about my City. His deep voice, ice-blue eyes, and the feel of his arms wrapped around me. I could feel the love he had for me even in my dreams. He invaded every part of my life, became ingrained in my entire being.

I loved him even subconsciously.

CHAPTER 8
CITY

I ROLLED OVER, feeling for my phone, but didn't find it where I left it. Somehow, during the night, I had pushed it under Suzy's pillow. I tossed and turned, waking up feeling like I hadn't slept a fucking wink. There were no new messages or calls on my phone, and no word from Suzy or any of the girls.

Bits and pieces started coming back to me as I lay in bed staring at the ceiling. I'd fucked up, and managed to do it royally. I left Suzy behind without so much as an "I love you," just an accusation and shitty words. I had to fix it. I fucked up and I had to man up and say I was sorry.

I grabbed my head, the throbbing almost blinding as I climbed out of bed. The quiet from the night before that felt deafening now became overwhelming. I couldn't sit around the house today and idly wait for Suzy to come home so that I could ask for her forgiveness. I had to go to her, find her, and mend the shattered pieces of our relationship.

Leaning over the sink, I stared at myself in the mirror, and was disgusted by the person looking back. I was better than this. The man that acted out last night wasn't me. He was a jealous asshole and I'm a lovesick fool. I quickly showered and brushed my teeth before throwing on my jeans and t-shirt. I didn't give a fuck what I looked like; I just had to get to Suzy.

I barreled down the highway, making my way to the hotel. Izzy hadn't replied to a text I sent her before I left. I kept the phone in my pocket on vibrate, but it remained still. I weaved in and out of traffic, needing to not waste another minute away from Suzy.

The closer I came to the hotel, the more butterflies filled my stomach. What if she didn't forgive me? I knew I'd hurt her, and I prayed that our love for each other could overcome the words of the previous night. As I shut off the bike, sitting in the parking lot of the Shepard's Hotel, I texted the only person that may be awake at this hour — Sophia. It was only eight a.m., but I was banking on her above anyone else.

Me: Sophia, it's City. I'm at the hotel and need to see Suzy.

I walked toward the door, waiting for a reply, with the phone gripped tightly in my hand. A lump formed in my throat, worry hanging in the air so thick I could almost taste it.

Sophia: Room 1215. She's still passed out but I'll let you in. You have a lot of sucking up to do.

Sophia wasn't a bullshitter, and she was Suzy's best friend. I knew no truer words were ever spoken.

Me: I plan to do a lot of sucking up. I'll do anything.

Sophia: Anything?

Me: Just open the damn door, woman.

Sophia: You better make it good. I'm waiting.

The elevator ride seemed to take forever, stopping on

every other floor to let off guests. Everyone had been downstairs enjoying the complimentary breakfast. When the bell chimed and the twelfth floor was illuminated, I thought my heart literally stopped in my chest.

Fisting my hands at my sides, I squeezed them, trying to release some tension. I lightly knocked, waiting for Sophia to answer, and swallowed hard. My mouth felt dry, my stomach ready to expel the last ounce of alcohol, and my heart was ready to burst from the rapid pounding in my chest.

"Quiet," Sophia said after she opened the door. "Follow me." She motioned and led me through the suite.

Izzy lay on the couch, passed out and oblivious to my presence. Someone else I didn't recognize, mostly because they were facedown, lay on the floor next to her. The hotel suite was a mess. Wrapping paper, boxes, clothes, and glasses were everywhere. The girls had partied harder than I would've thought, but then again, this was Izzy's doing, and she didn't do anything half-assed.

Sophia stopped in front of the door to a bedroom and crossed her arms over her chest. "Now listen here, mister," she said, poking me in the chest.

I looked down at her bony finger digging into my flesh, and smiled. The girl had balls, and big ones at that. I loved Sophia for the simple fact that she was Suzy's friend, but she and I could've been friends if we had met first. She had the piss and vinegar that reminded me of my sister. She was fierce, loyal, and cared deeply.

"She's crushed, and I haven't seen her since I put her to bed last night. She loves you, City, and you better get down on your knees and beg for her forgiveness. Do whatever it takes."

"Yes, ma'am." I nodded. She hadn't told me anything I didn't already know.

"Don't be a smartass," she said, slapping me on the shoulder. "You made her feel trashy and like shit. You need to make her feel like the princess she deserves to be treated as. You've always done that for her. Made her feel good about herself. I was always your cheerleader, even when she wasn't sure about you. So don't fuck this shit up."

"I got this." Fuck, I really hoped I did.

"You better, but I want to tell you a few things first. The guy she was dancing with, she didn't want to dance with him. Not at all, but your sister told her it would be her last dance as a single girl and she couldn't turn him down. She said some bullshit about bachelorette etiquette. Your sister can be very persuasive." She paused, tapping her lip with her finger.

"Fuck, she's a pain in the ass." I sighed, looking toward my sister passed out and dead to the world.

"Second, the smell on her last night was the weirdo stripper your sister hired. Suzy told her more than once that she did not want a stripper under any circumstances. The guy came in and did a quick dance, but Suzy was totally uncomfortable. As soon as he realized that, he broke contact and gave her a sweet kiss on the cheek when he was finished. She didn't touch him at all and he didn't do anything inappropriate." She straightened her back, looking me straight in the eyes. "City, if you would've seen him you would've laughed. You're like an Adonis compared to this man. You're the only thing that has Suzy's eyes and heart. Grovel, my friend, grovel." She leaned over, kissing my cheek before she left me to enter the room.

I stood there staring at the door, and closed my eyes. I'd been a complete tool. How in the fuck did I even think Suzy would allow someone to touch her or that she'd been unfaithful? I knew Suzy inside and out, but I let my territorial bullshit get in the way. My heart ached at the thought that maybe I made our relationship fubar. Was it fucked up beyond repair? Had I crossed the line that she wouldn't forgive? I'd listen to Sophia's advice and beg for her forgiveness. Not as a sign of weakness, but because of the love I had for her. It was the only way I could fight for what I wanted most—Suzy.

I opened the door slowly, trying not to startle Suzy. Sunlight streamed through the sheer drapes along the wall behind her bed. The rays cascaded across the floor, framing the bed and my bride-to-be. I stood at the foot of the bed, staring at her. Her long blonde hair was fanned out across the pillow, making a halo and giving her an angelic look. My heart ached at the thought that I could possibly lose her. Maybe I fucked up so badly that she wouldn't forgive me. Sometimes words are more painful than any physical harm inflicted by another person. Pain evaporates, but words last a lifetime, replaying in our memories and feeding on our insecurities.

Her soft snores and heavy breathing mingled with the sound of the waves crashing on the shore below. She clung to a pillow, holding it against her chest, her arms tightly wound around it.

Sitting on the bed, I tried to keep my movement to a minimum, not wanting to wake her just yet. She was mine, and had been the only person I'd ever used that term with. No one else had a chance to capture my heart, but Suzy and all her sweetness bored into my heart like a cavity from too much sugar.

I kicked off my shoes, needing to touch her, to hold her in my arms. My body ached for her. I didn't feel comfortable in my skin without contact from her. I couldn't explain it, and I'd never voice it in front of the guys. They already thought I was a pussy-whipped asshole.

Grabbing the pillow, I pulled it from her arms, making sure she remained asleep. She didn't move or twitch as her arms fell against her body. I threw the pillow on the floor, crawling under the covers next to her, and pulled her against my chest. Her breathing changed as she snuggled against me, burying her face against my shirt. I closed my eyes, enjoying the quiet moment and the feel of her in my arms. As soon as she realized I was here, there'd be hell to pay.

I peppered kisses against her temple, brushing back the hair on her forehead as I inhaled the smell of the woman that had stolen my heart over a year ago. It wasn't a pure scent; the alcohol she'd consumed the night before permeated her skin. If we had both been sober, last night wouldn't have happened. Really, if I hadn't consumed a few too many shots and seen someone touching what was mine, then it wouldn't have happened.

Her body stiffened in my arms, and I closed my eyes, knowing the moment had been broken. "Suzy," I whispered, trying to hide the fear in my voice.

"What are you doing?" she asked, her voice laced with anger as she pushed against my chest.

"Sugar, don't push me away. I'm sorry." I tightened my grip, holding her head against my chest.

"I don't want to talk to you." She didn't touch me or return my embrace.

"Don't talk, then. Just let me talk while I hold you." I held her tighter, resting my chin on top of her head as I wrapped my legs around hers. I caged her in; there was no escape and I had a captive audience. "I'm sorry I was an asshole last night." I sighed, knowing my words weren't enough to make up for my behavior.

"More like a giant dickhead," she interrupted, not sagging into my embrace like she normally did.

"Call me what you want. All the terms fit. I'm sorry I didn't listen to you last night. I had too much to drink, but I'm in no way blaming the alcohol. I'm solely responsible for my actions. I fucked up, sugar. I didn't mean to imply that you had been unfaithful to me. Seeing you with that guy and then smelling someone on you pushed me over the edge." I inhaled, winded from the words that I had said without stopping. I was too worried to break in the middle of my speech.

"I would never do anything to risk our relationship, City," she said, digging her fingernails into my bicep.

"I know, sugar, I know." I kissed the top of her head and rested my cheek against her silky, golden hair. "Please forgive me. I have no other excuse except for the love I have for you. You've scrambled my brains. I've never felt as territorial or protective over someone like I do with you. When I see someone touching you, I want to rip their hands off and shove them down their throat. I control it most times."

"No you don't." Her laughter broke the tension, making *me* laugh.

"Trust me, sugar, I do. I wasn't going to hit the guy last night but he wouldn't shut his fucking mouth. He kept talking shit and I couldn't hold back anymore. I couldn't stop myself from knocking him on his ass."

"City," she said as she adjusted her body, looking into my eyes. Her lip trembled as she spoke. "I'm not upset about you hitting him. He deserved it. You hurt me by questioning my faithfulness. You made me feel dirty." A single tear formed in the corner of her eye and slid along the bridge of her nose.

I wiped the tear with the pad of my thumb, cradling her face in my palm. "I never want to make you feel that way. You're the most pure and honest person I know,

Suzette. I know you're faithful and I never meant for it to sound otherwise. I'm sorry. You consume me and became a part of me. Your love is as vital to me as the air I breathe. The thought of losing you terrifies me." To admit the last sentence scared the shit out of me. I'd never felt so vulnerable in my life. My heart and happiness lay in her hands.

"Promise me you'll never make me feel that way again, City." She blinked, causing more tears to trickle down her cheek. The redness in her eyes made the blue even more breathtaking. "You're the one person in the world that I thought would always have my back. I never expected you to treat me that way, and I won't stand for it. I refuse to be married to a man that treats me like that. If you do it again, I may not be so easy to find."

"I promise, Suzy. I will never act like that again. I love you more than anything in the world. I'd kill for you and give my life to save yours." I enveloped her in my arms, squeezing her tightly against my body. "You're everything to me and I will do everything in my power to show you how much you mean to me. I will spend every day showing you all the love I have for you and profess my love to you on my deathbed."

"Jesus, you're so morbid. 'I promise' and 'I'm sorry' would've been enough." She laughed, wrapping her arms around my body.

"It takes more than two words to explain the amount of love I have for you, but right now, I'd rather show you." I smirked, grabbing her chin and bringing her lips to mine.

"Oh, how are you going to do that?" she asked with garbled words as she spoke against my lips.

Breaking the kiss, I looked in her eyes. "I'm going to make love to my fiancée the day before our wedding." Her breath hitched as her eyes searched mine. "Tomorrow you officially become Mrs. Joseph Gallo."

"Why can't you become Mr. Suzy McCarthy?" She giggled, rubbing her nose against my cheek.

"Not how it works, sugar. I'm the man and you're the woman, but you can call me whatever the hell you want when we're in private." I smirked, nipping her nose with my teeth.

"Mmm, I like the sound of that." A warm smile spread across her lips as her body melted into mine.

I kissed her lips, gently prodding, trying to find her tongue. I wanted to taste her. "Suzy, why won't you kiss me back?" Maybe her heart hadn't caught up to her words. I prayed to fuck that was the case. When someone won't kiss you and show you the love you want to convey, it's like a stake to the heart.

She covered her mouth with her hand. "I didn't brush my teeth yet. I think a small furry animal died inside my mouth last night." The corners of her mouth peeked out the sides of her hand, the smile touching her eyes.

Laughter bubbled out of me, slow at first, until my entire body was shaking as her words hit me. "Baby, I don't care if you have bad breath. I won't breathe through my nose." I leaned my forehead against hers.

She shook her head, moving her face farther away from mine with her hand still covering her mouth. "Not happening. Either I get up and brush my teeth or you don't get a kiss until after."

"You feel this?" I asked, pushing my erection into her stomach. "I'm not waiting until you find your toothbrush and get lost in the bathroom. I need to feel you from the inside. I don't give a fuck about your breath."

"I'm not going to kiss you," she said firmly, her mouth set in a firm line.

"Didn't say anything about kissing you, sugar. I want to fuck you, and I only care about your pussy right now." I was done discussing the topic. I needed to be inside her and I needed it now. My body craved her and my heart needed her; I wasn't in the mood to be patient.

CHAPTER 9
SUZY

"I LOVE when you talk dirty to me. You just want to mark your territory." I smirked, watching him hop off the bed and unbutton his jeans.

"You bet that sweet ass I'm marking it. I'm going to crawl so far up that pretty little pussy that I'll ruin you for life." He shucked his pants, kicking them to the side as he pulled his t-shirt over his head.

What the man didn't understand is that he had already ruined me. I was destroyed, damaged goods, and no one would ever compare to him. As hard and sexy as he was, the soft and loving side of City was what ultimately stole my heart. The man loved me so fiercely that no one could ever come close. The small looks he stole when he thought I wasn't looking, the loving touches as I fell asleep, and the sweet nothings he whispered in my ear when he thought I was dreaming—those were the things I loved most about him.

I yawned, pretending to be unimpressed by his words and sexy-as-hell naked body. "Well, you can try anyway. I'll let you know if your words ring true."

He grabbed the comforter, yanking it off my body before pulling me down the bed by my feet. I squealed; the quickness of his movements caught me off guard. Pulling me off the bed in a standing position, he quickly stripped me of my clothes.

"So far, a C for effort. You can do better." I smiled, watching the corner of his lip twitch.

He placed his hands under my arms, firmly gripping my waist before throwing me on the bed. He pounced on me, not giving me a moment to catch my breath before smothering me with a perfect closed-mouth kiss. My stomach fluttered like it did the first time he kissed me. The nerves and emotion of the last twelve hours poured out through our lips.

I dug my fingers into his dark locks, fisting the hair in between my fingers as I held his mouth to mine. I wished I had brushed my damn teeth. I wanted to taste him. He pulled away, breaking the connection we had, and looked down at me. The heat of his chest seared my skin and the thump of his heart matched mine. He was just as nervous as me, both of us on edge from last night.

"This will be the last time I'll make love to you before you become my wife." He smiled; his teeth sparkled in the sunlight.

"What about tonight?" I asked, totally confused.

"Sugar, I can't see the bride the night before the wedding. We've talked about this before. I'm going to stay at my parents'."

"I don't like that idea. That's two nights not sleeping in your arms." I sighed, rubbing my thumb across his unshaven cheek. The roughness matched the man more perfectly than the silky skin I felt some days.

"Me either, but it's only for one night. We can't break tradition."

"Make it good, then, handsome. Make me still feel you when I walk down the aisle tomorrow." I always felt him for hours afterward. The days when he was insatiable, I could feel him for days, often sore the next time he wanted to fool around. Knowing that this was the last time before we were married warmed me and turned me into a puddle of goo.

Growling, he brought his mouth down on mine. I moaned, the regret about brushing my teeth growing. His tongue darted out, sliding across my lips before traveling down my jaw to the sweet spot on my neck. Goose bumps and shivers racked my body as the warmth of his mouth and coolness from his breath skidded across my skin.

When he captured my nipple in his mouth, nibbling on it with his teeth, my entire body convulsed. The rough stubble of his face, the sharp pinch from his hold, and the silky smoothness of his tongue flicking the hardened tip had me seeing stars and moaning his name. I held him to me, fingers wound in his hair as he sucked and flicked until I begged.

"Please, City. I want to feel you," I said.

Grunting as he held my nipple between his lips, he lifted his hips and fisted his cock. The cool metal rubbing against my clit made me twitch before he rubbed the tip through my wetness. As I thrust my hips forward, trying to force him to put his dick inside me, I could feel the deep, low laugh in his chest.

"So ready, sugar. You're always ready for my cock," he whispered against my breast.

"Yes! Yes," I chanted, growing impatient with his lack of thrust.

Swiping it through my wetness again, he placed the piercing against my clit and made tiny circles, capturing my clit with the motion. The combination of the hard metal and smooth tip drove me closer to the edge, but I didn't want to come like this. I closed my eyes, sealing them tightly, trying to stave off the orgasm that was about to rip through me.

"No," I whispered, "not like this."

"You want to come on my cock? You want to feel me thrusting in and out of you as your pussy squeezes me like a vise?" he asked, his voice low and husky.

"Don't make me beg," I said, keeping my eyes closed, moving my hips, trying to escape his cock circling my clit.

Without warning, he rammed his cock inside me in one quick thrust. My eyes sprang open; I felt completely filled as a tiny spark of pain shot throughout my body. He pulled out slightly and stilled, staring down at me with a cocky grin on his face.

"Is that how you want it, sugar?"

"Don't stop. I'm so close." I pulled back and pushed myself forward, fucking him. I couldn't take the lack of motion.

Slipping his arms under my back, he held my shoulders, as he began to rock into me. Each lash of his cock against my G-spot sent tiny shock waves through my system, making my toes curl. I grabbed his hips, relishing the feel of his muscles constricting as he moved inside of me. Our bodies worked in unison, driving me toward an orgasm I knew would leave me breathless and with blurred vision.

His hips started to rotate as he pulled out and rammed back into me straight. The movement intensified the pressure building inside of me. His breathing became ragged as he maintained the momentum, driving into me without mercy.

Colors dotted my vision, the light almost blinding, as everything in my body coiled and released at once. I felt like a slingshot pulled to the max and then let go, flying forward with no escape or ability to control the outcome.

I screamed, "City," as my body became rigid and my breathing halted. My head flew off the pillow, my body grounded by his hold on my shoulders as my curled toes started to cramp.

My core convulsed around him, the hardness of his cock giving nothing as he continued in the pursuit of his orgasm. His moans turned to growls as he stiffened above me, emptying himself inside me. Gulping for air, he collapsed on top of me, his body twitching with aftershocks.

I closed my eyes, listening to our mingled breaths as I enjoyed the afterglow. The feel of his weight crushing me made me feel encapsulated, as my body grew limp underneath him.

His breathing slowed as his breath skidded across my ear; the low growls of pleasure bringing a smile to my face. As he pulled out, everything he'd just worked to achieve slid down my body, forming a pool on the bed. I still hadn't gotten used to the feel of a man coming inside of me. I felt like I wet myself and couldn't stop it.

"Let me grab a washcloth," he said as he pushed off the bed.

I grabbed his arm, stopping him. "Let me. I'm dying to brush my teeth. I want a proper kiss." I smiled at him, trying not to run my tongue across my dirty teeth.

He collapsed against the mattress, staring up at the ceiling as he rested his hand on his chest. "I'll be waiting." He grabbed my arm with his free hand, sliding his palm down my arm. "Make it quick," he said with a crooked, happy smile.

I groaned as my feet touched the floor. The aftereffects of an evening of overindulgence and wicked high heels hit me. I swayed, grabbing the mattress to steady myself.

"You okay, sugar?" City asked as he sat up and touched my hand.

"Fine, baby. Just not as young as I used to be. Can't party all night and bounce right back."

"I doubt you partied all night too much even in your college years." He laughed, covering his mouth with his hand.

"I didn't sit in my dorm room and study all the time," I said sarcastically. It was all bullshit. I rarely partied. The number of times I had been drunk in college I could count on one hand, but sometimes I didn't like to be reminded of just how much of a good girl I had been.

"Uh, huh," he said, resting his head on his hand as he watched me walk away.

I flipped him off, a small chuckle escaping my lips. He knew me too well. Knew I could never escape my good-girl qualities even though I liked to pretend I had a badass side. I knew I was a cream puff, and I accepted it, though I did so begrudgingly.

My mascara was smeared down my cheeks, the result of my crying last night over City. I looked as bad as I felt. My hair was a tangled mess, makeup half on but not in the right places, and my eyes were swollen. Thank God the wedding wasn't today. I'd have to live with horrible wedding pictures for the rest of my life.

Grabbing the tube of toothpaste out of my toiletry bag, I stood on my tiptoes and leaned into the mirror. Shit, I looked horrible. I quickly backed up, not needing the up-close reminder of last night. After washing him from my body, I covered my toothbrush with paste. I needed to clear the funk out of my mouth. My mouth felt drier than the Mojave Desert on a blistering summer day. Just as I stuck the toothbrush in my mouth and started scrubbing, I heard my phone chirp.

"Suzy, your mother sent you a text," City yelled from the bedroom.

Fucking great. I loved my mom, but she added an extra bit of pressure and stress to an already nerve-racking situation. Weddings are supposed to be blissful, but no one seems to tell you about all the turmoil and decisions that need to be made. My mother could be judgmental at times, and I often felt like my decisions weren't good enough.

I pulled the toothbrush out of my mouth, balancing the paste remnants on my tongue as I yelled, "What's it say?"

I scrubbed my teeth, my motions more feverish at the thought of my parents being in town. She always watched City with a suspicious eye when she didn't know I was looking. She was happy that he had money, although it wasn't the reason I fell in love with the man. I would've been with him even if he were only a tattoo artist. It's a good job, and he's talented. She couldn't get beyond his looks. He had a roughness about him, and the tattoos didn't exactly win him any points in her mind. She'd bust a cork if she knew about the piercing that decorated his lower extremity, or if she ever found out that I had my nipple pierced.

"She just wants to know if she should be at the rehearsal dinner early to help."

I spat the toothpaste into the sink, cupping water in my hand and swishing. The last thing I wanted was my mother there for her type of help. Everything was ready and all we needed to do was show up, including her and my father.

I washed my face quickly, erasing the nightmarish mess

from the smudged makeup before returning to the bedroom.

"She's become such a pain the last few months," I said as I crawled in bed.

"She's still your mom and she loves you," he said, grabbing my hand and planting soft kisses across the top.

"You grew up with a different type of mother, City. Your mom has made me feel more like a daughter than my mother ever did. Don't get me wrong, I love her, but she doesn't know how to make me feel loved." I closed my eyes when they watered as I thought about what it would've been like to grow up calling Mrs. Gallo Mom. I always felt like my parents had to fit me into their schedule, and often there wasn't a slot for me unless I had called in advance.

"Let's just get through the next thirty-six hours and everything will go back to normal. You have the Gallo family now, and they're not letting you go."

I'd felt like a member of the family since that first Sunday dinner so long ago. They made me feel like I belonged and had always been there. My sister and I had never even really been close. I didn't ask her to be a part of my wedding party. Izzy had become more of a sister to me than she ever had. We don't get to choose our family, but we do choose those people we let into our life, and with whom we spend time with going forward. For me, the people I wanted nearest were the Gallos. They were a loving and diehard-loyal group. Above all else, they had each other's backs and no one could tear them apart. They accepted each other for their flaws, embraced the bad with the good, and loved unconditionally.

"We should go soon. I have a ton to do before the rehearsal dinner tonight." I snuggled into his side, enjoying the last moment of peace.

He pulled me tighter against his chest, rubbing the

tender skin on my upper arm as he kissed my hair. "It'll all work out. Somehow it will all fall into place."

"I'm sure you're right." That statement was a total lie. I couldn't give up my incessant need to be in control and plan every last detail.

"You can't control everything in life, but I know you try like hell. It's one of the things I love about you."

"Tell me five other things you love, City." I swiped my fingers across his chest, stopping on his nipple to tug on his piercing.

"Where do I start?" he said before rattling off a list that left me feeling more loved than I had ever felt before. The list wasn't filled with vain things like my beauty, which would fade over time, but the things that made me as a person. My success, education, kind heart, and silliness were just a few things he listed without much thought.

"I love you, City," I said, moving my body to plant a wet, sloppy kiss on his lips.

Breaking our connection slightly, he whispered, "I love you too, sugar." He kissed me with as much fervor and passion as he did the first night we met.

We made love one more time before dragging ourselves from the hotel room and heading home to prep for the chaos that awaited us. Wedding weekend was in full swing and there was no turning back.

CHAPTER 10
CITY

NEVER IN A MILLION fucking years did I think I'd be standing in a church dressed in a tuxedo—not as a groom, at least. I wasn't a cynic. I'd just never found anyone worthy of my time or commitment until Suzy walked into my life. Sometimes when we least expect it and stop looking, fate has a way of playing its hand. Mine came in the form of a drop-dead gorgeous girl broken down on a deserted street. I thanked my lucky stars each goddamn day that her car was a piece of shit.

"You look a little nervous, son," Pop said, slapping me on the back, pulling me from my thoughts.

I rubbed my hands together; they slid easy from the sheen of sweat that had formed over my entire body. I wiped my brow, feeling more nervous than I had ever felt in my life. "I am, Pop. Just never thought I'd be standing here."

"Amazing the place hasn't burst into flames," Anthony said, and laughed. "We surely aren't the churchgoing crowd, and Lord knows we've broken more than one commandment." He fidgeted with his bowtie, pulling it away from his neck.

I laughed. His words were true, but that wasn't why I was nervous. I turned to my Pop, who had a smile on his face. "Did you feel this way when you married Ma?"

He nodded, his smile growing larger. "I was scared as hell, son. It's a big step to take in one's life. It's a serious commitment, but times are different now. I didn't live with your mother before we got married like you've lived with Suzy. It was a leap of faith." He grabbed my shoulder, squeezing it gently. "Do you love her, son? The type of love you can't be without for even a day?"

"I do, Pop. I know she's the one. She makes me a better person, and I want to be surrounded by her and make a family. I want to be in your shoes one day. Suzy is more than I deserve."

"She isn't more than you deserve. You two were made for each other. Just like your mother and me. She brings peace and tranquility to my life, and gave me an amazing family. My life would've been meaningless without her."

I didn't doubt that marrying Suzy was the right decision. The events of Friday night scared the shit out of me. The thought of losing her drove me half insane. I'd never wanted to need someone in that way, but I did with her. I needed her in my life, needed her to be mine, and wanted to spend the rest of my days on Earth with her.

The door creaked open as Ma poked her head inside. "Where's my baby boy?" she asked, opening the door with tears in her eyes.

"Why ya crying, Ma?" I asked, as she wiped the tears.

"Damn, I'm going to mess up my makeup." She pulled a tissue from her bra and blotted the skin under her eyes. "I just saw Suzy and she looks stunning. I'm the happiest woman in the world today. They're tears of joy."

"How is she, Ma? Is she okay?" My heart pounded, my throat feeling constricted by the button-up shirt.

"She's better than okay; she's glowing and ready for the ceremony to start." Ma wrapped her arms around me, holding me against her as she spoke. "You've made me a happy woman, Joseph. I couldn't love Suzy any more than I do if I had given birth to her myself." She rubbed my back as she kissed my cheek.

"You just have baby Gallos in your mind, Ma," Michael said as he kicked back in a chair against the wall. He looked so put together and calm.

"So what?" she asked as she placed her hands on her hips and turned toward Michael. "I'm old, boy and all I want is a baby…just one damn baby. Is that too much to ask?"

"Not really, Ma, but it'll happen when it happens. We're still young and enjoying our life," Michael said, leaning forward, resting his elbows on his knees.

"By the time I was your age, I had four children. I enjoyed every bit of my life, and maybe more so since it was filled with such love. Children don't end your life, Michael, they add to it."

"Bullshit," Anthony muttered, covering his mouth and coughing.

Ma narrowed her eyes at him. "Anthony, you better stop acting like a playboy and living your hollow existence. You have to settle down sometime, and when you do, you'll regret all the years you spent alone."

"I'm rarely alone, Ma." He smiled, his hair flopping over his forehead.

"I mean emotionally alone." She stared at him, waiting for him to respond, but he didn't. "Okay, I want a picture with my son on his wedding day. Where's that damn photographer?"

Pop walked toward the door, pausing as he opened it. "I'll go get him."

As the door clicked shut, my ma turned to me. "Nerves are normal, son. Once you see how breathtaking Suzy is in her dress, everything else will fade away." She rested her head on my chest as she held my hand.

"I know, Ma. I'm just ready to get this started. I hate waiting; I've never been a patient man." I kissed the top of her head, getting lost in the strawberry scent from my childhood.

"You don't say." She laughed, squeezing my hand. "Just like your father." She sighed, drawing her body closer to mine. "I wish Thomas could've been here. I'm more worried about him than I've ever been, Joseph."

"I know, Ma. I haven't spoken to him in a while. He's too deep undercover now. I don't like it, not one fucking bit."

"Y'all are going to burst into flames with the language in this room. We are in a church," Izzy said as she entered the room with Pop and the photographer.

"If you haven't, then no one will, Izzy," Anthony said with a laugh.

"Enough. Let's take some photos. We have five minutes until you boys need to be at the altar."

Five minutes felt like an eternity as we took more pictures than I wanted to count. My line of sight would have a perpetual dot from the camera flash. By the end of the night, I'd have dozens of tiny blobs in my eyes and possibly be partially blind. We took photos as a group, the Gallo family minus Thomas. We took turns taking pictures with our parents; it wasn't often that we were all dressed up and in one place together.

I was thankful when there was a knock on the door and a voice said, "It's time."

Cracking my neck, I straightened my back and headed for the door. Ma grabbed my arm, stopping me. "I'm proud of you, baby." She smiled and released me.

I nodded, leaving the tiny room and heading toward the church. Anthony and Michael filed in behind me as we stood in our designated spot at the top of the altar in front of the crowd. The church was packed with people, many faces I didn't know. Ma and Suzy went overboard on the invites, but my mother insisted that her friends be invited, besides our gigantic family that had flown in from all parts of the world. The Gallos didn't know how to do anything small.

As the music started, the doors in the back of the church swung open and the entire church stood and turned. The attention no longer on me, I squinted down the aisle, catching a glimpse of Suzy. She looked like an angel dressed in off white.

The tulle straps created a V, encasing her breasts. The fact that I knew the word tulle disturbed me slightly, but Suzy had educated me about bridal fashion…whether I wanted to know it or not. The bodice was form fitting; a wide ribbon around her waist held a large fabric flower just below her left breast. The bottom of the dress was loose with layers of tulle that flowed and shifted as she walked. It wasn't over the top of puffy shit, it was perfect and totally Suzy—classy and sweet. I couldn't wait to rip the fucking thing off her. A veil covered her face, more traditional than I thought she'd be. I desperately wanted to see her.

She walked arm in arm with her father, slowly moving down the aisle, facing forward. I rubbed my hands together, the last bit of nerves leaving my body, replaced by excitement and a calm that I hadn't expected. When she stopped in front of the first step, our eyes connected.

Through the thin veil, I could see the smile on her face as the priest approached her and her father.

The priest stepped down and said, "Who gives this bride away today?"

"I do," her father said, releasing her hand and lifting her veil. He placed a chaste kiss on her cheek before stepping back.

Suzy ascended the stairs, stopping in front of me with teary eyes.

"I love you," I whispered, trying not to become misty-eyed myself.

With a smile on her face, she tilted her head and said, "I love you too."

Sophia reached around and grabbed the flowers from her. Suzy held her hands out to me, and I grasped them with both of mine and squeezed. With one last smile, we turned toward the priest and waited.

We stole glances at each other as he spoke; his words were lost on us. With our hands in each other's, we faced forward and tried to pay attention, but it was impossible. I leaned over, close enough for only her to hear. "You look beautiful, sugar."

She blushed, squeezing my hand. The priest cleared his throat; clearly, we had missed something, as we were so lost in each other.

"The rings," the priest repeated.

I turned to Michael, my best man and brother, and held out my hand. He placed the two platinum bands in my palm and I closed my fingers around them. I had hers engraved with *You're mine, sugar.* A simple statement, and she was from the moment she walked into my life. I handed him the rings and we watched him bless the metal, saying a prayer over them before returning his attention to us.

"Suzette, repeat after me," he stated, turning toward her.

"I, Suzette McCarthy, take you, Joseph Gallo…" She repeated his words, never breaking eye contact with me. She slid the ring on my finger, a smile on her face, as we both felt the power in the moment. Her voice never wavered as she finished with "Until death do us part." She wiped a tear from her eye as she finished. I had to fight every urge I had to wrap my arms around her and kiss her.

"Joseph, repeat after me," the priest said, holding her ring in his hand.

I repeated the words, without missing a single one, letting the power behind the statement seep into my veins. We were connected, a single soul in front of the eyes of God, joined in holy matrimony. We never broke eye contact, keeping each other grounded in the moment.

As I slipped the ring on her finger, I held her hand in mine, running my fingertips against her dampened flesh. We stood there for a few more minutes after I finished my part of the vows and stared at each other. He could've said the church was on fire and we wouldn't have known. I always looked at Suzy, usually watched her sleep, but to stand here and just look into each other's eyes was some heady shit. I loved this woman, more than I loved anyone or anything in my life, including myself.

"I give you Mr. and Mrs. Joseph Gallo," the priest said as we both turned to him. "You may now kiss the bride."

Without needing another word, I grabbed her by the waist and pulled her to my body. Stopping briefly above her lips, I searched her eyes and could see only joy. I crushed my lips to hers as the crowd began to whistle and holler in the background. Their voices faded away as I kissed her, my wife and bride.

When we backed away from each other, we both had

watery eyes. As we turned toward the people, now on their feet, I grabbed her around the waist and held her to my side. Our friends and family clapped and cheered as we made our way down the aisle and out of the church doors to the small bridal suite.

As soon as I closed the door, I pulled her into a kiss. Not the small kiss I gave her in front of the family, but one that left us both breathless and needing more.

"We did it, sugar. You're mine forever," I said, as I swiped my fingers against her cheek.

"No, baby, you're mine." She smirked, a devilish expression on her face as she leaned in and captured my lips.

CHAPTER 11
SUZY

AFTER WE GREETED the guests at the door, my feet were on fire. The shoes I had picked were beautiful and made me feel almost the same height as City, but the damn things were like torture devices. I loved how the satin ribbon of the high heels intertwined and laced up my feet, stopping around my ankle with a bow. It was too bad the dress was so long that no one could see them. I grabbed City's arm, leaning over to rub my ankles.

"You want to go change your shoes?" City asked, watching me with a concerned look.

"You think we can sneak away for a minute upstairs? I'll never be able to dance in these."

"It's our wedding, sugar. We can do anything we want." He smiled and winked at me. He turned toward his mother and said, "Hey, Ma, we're going to run upstairs and get different shoes for Suzy."

She smirked, not believing the reason for our hasty exit. "Sure, just don't be too long, son. We have a wedding to celebrate."

City nodded, holding my hand and pulling me from

the line. As we walked out into the hotel hallway, he grabbed me by the waist and scooped me up into his muscular arms. I squealed from the sudden movement and sighed as I rested my head on his chest. The intense pain in my feet turned into a dull throb as he carried me to the elevator.

"It's great that we had the reception in a hotel. Makes life so much easier," he said.

Reaching up, I touched his cheek, still not believing we were married. "We really did it, huh?" I asked.

"We did, sugar. Now comes the fun part," he said as the doors to the elevator opened.

"Dancing?"

"Fucking my wife," he said, a deep growl low in his chest.

He quickly adjusted me as the doors to the elevator closed. Pushing my back against the wall, he pressed the STOP button on the elevator as soon as it moved. Holding me against the wall, with one arm supporting my weight, he quickly undid his zipper and reached under my dress.

His eyes twinkled as a naughty grin decorated his face. "No panties again. It must be my lucky day."

"I wanted to give you a surprise when you put your head under my gown for the garter."

"Don't give a shit about that right now. I want to fuck my wife, right here, right now."

I didn't speak, just threw my head back as he thrust inside of me. I wrapped my legs around his waist, holding him to me as he moved. He nibbled on my neck and kissed my lips as he pulled out and slammed back into me. The building tension from the day quickly drove me to the edge as his body slammed into my clit.

I panted, so close to the edge as he rocked his cock into my core. Within minutes, our bodies shook and we both came on bated breath. Our bodies were dotted with perspiration, and our breathing was ragged as he rested his forehead against mine. He must have pressed the STOP button, because the elevator began to move again as he pulled out and zipped back up.

As he cradled me in his arms, I felt utterly loved, completely content, and totally sated. He carried me to our suite, placing me on the couch as we entered. He knelt down and undid the cloth straps on my heels. Grasping my feet in his large hands, he massaged the ache out of them.

I moaned, throwing my head back against the couch cushions. "That feels so gooood."

"I should feel insulted that you're moaning more now than when you were in the elevator." He laughed, pushing harder on the tender flesh.

I giggled, kicking my feet out of his hands. "I'm okay now. Let me grab my shoes before they send out the search party." He backed away, grabbing my hand and helping me stand. "Fuck," I said as his come dripped down my leg.

"What?"

"I feel like I just peed myself, damn it." I sighed. "I can't go down there like this." I lifted up my dress, touching the wetness with my fingers.

"You grab your shoes," he said as he stood, "and I'll grab a washcloth."

"Okay, but you get to do the honors," I said as I walked to the bedroom with my legs as bowed out as possible. I didn't want it to get on my dress any more than it already had.

City entered the bedroom behind me, disappearing into the bathroom for a moment. I grabbed the pair of white tennis shoes I had brought just in case I needed some relief, and waited for him.

"Just stand there and let me do it all, sugar," he said as

he knelt down and disappeared under my dress. He wiped my legs gently before taking great care, and probably joy, in wiping his come from between my legs.

"Don't get any ideas," I said, feeling a tingling from the warm washcloth.

"I can control myself only for so long." He laughed as his head popped out from under the layers of lace. "Give me your shoes."

I handed him my shoes and stood still looking down at the man I loved. I held his shoulder, trying to maintain my balance as he placed each shoe carefully on my feet and laced them up tight. They felt like tiny pillows, relieving the pressure in the muscles of my feet.

"Better?" he asked, running his hands up my legs.

"So much better. Thank you, City."

"It's my job to take care of you," he said as he stood and grabbed my chin. "I plan to spend my lifetime doing just that, sugar."

"Mmm," I mumbled as he leaned forward and kissed me.

I could've collapsed in his arms and fallen into a peaceful slumber, but there was a party going on downstairs and we were the main event. We couldn't miss it even if we were exhausted. As we entered the ballroom, the party was in full swing. The DJ was playing instrumental music before dinner, and many of the party guests surrounded the bar in conversation.

"Hey, sister," Izzy said as she walked toward me. "I'm so excited to be able to say that and it be true. I've always wanted a sister." She wrapped her arms around me, squeezing me a little too tight.

"Can't breathe," I whispered.

"Man up," she said as she released me.

"I'll be back, ladies; I'm going to grab a drink at the

bar with my boys," City said as he kissed my cheek and left us alone.

"Where's your sister?" Izzy asked, looking around the crowd.

"Don't know, and don't give a shit either."

"You know you've turned into a badass with a potty mouth, Suz." She smiled, shaking her head.

"City. It's all his fault."

"I'd like to think I played a part in it too." She laughed.

"You're always getting me in trouble, Izzy."

"Me?" she asked, holding her hand to her chest.

"Always."

A man cleared his throat next to us and we both turned in his direction. "Excuse me, ladies, I don't mean to interrupt."

"Well then don't," Izzy said, looking the stranger up and down.

He was big and handsome as hell. He reminded me of an Italian version of the Rock. Muscles bulged from his suit, and he had close-shaven black hair, shimmering green eyes, and knockout lips. They were the puffy kind that fit his strong jaw line perfectly and called the name of countless women.

"Don't be rude, Izzy," I said, turning to face him. "How can I help you?"

"I'm a friend of Thomas' and he asked me to drop off a gift on his behalf." The man held out an envelope and waited for me to take it.

"Is he okay?" Izzy asked before I could thank the gentleman.

"He is, and he's very sorry he couldn't make it," he said, looking down at Izzy as if he was not sure of how to take her change in attitude.

"Don't mind her," I said to him, my eyes flickering

between the two. "Thomas is her brother."

"Ah, you're *that* Izzy," he said, his lips turning up into a smile. "I've heard a lot about you."

She snarled, not entirely liking the shitty grin on his face. "And you are?" she said, holding out her hand for him to take.

"James." He grabbed her hand and stilled. "James Caldo."

"Never heard of you, Jimmy," she said with a twinkle in her eye.

"Perfect," he said as he brought her hand to his lips and placed a kiss just below her knuckles.

I could feel the electricity between the two of them. Izzy basically eye-fucked him as he kissed her hand. As soon as he looked up, her face went back to a pissed-off sneer. The girl could play a good game, but as an observer, I could see the lust.

I coughed, breaking the moment of awkwardness for myself. "Thanks, James. I'll give this to Joseph for you. Why don't you stay and enjoy the wedding?" I said, smiling at the man. He'd taken the time to get dressed up and I wanted to see Izzy squirm, in all honesty.

"What?" Izzy asked, turning toward me.

"We have plenty of food and I'm sure the Gallos would love to talk with you about their Thomas." Izzy gave me the death glare. "You can keep James company tonight, Izzy. You didn't bring a date." I smiled, and I could almost see the venom dripping from her fangs.

"I'd love to stay. Thank you. Izzy, would you like a drink?" he asked, still holding her hand in his.

"Only because Suzy would want me to be a gracious host," she said, looking at me out of the corner of her eye.

"I don't want to put you out or anything. I'm a *big* boy and can handle myself. I just thought you could use a drink to unwind a bit. You feel a little tense, and that mouth of yours could get you into trouble."

"I don't need a babysitter, Jimmy, but I'll take the drink."

"It's James," he said, squeezing her hand.

I'd been around Izzy enough to see when she was attracted to someone, and she was to James. She may not want to admit it—Izzy often picked guys that she could push around—but I had a feeling James could give her a run for her money.

"You two kids play nice," I said as I waved and walked toward my husband. I curled my arms around his waist, leaning my head on his back as he stood talking to Michael. "Hey, baby. Someone dropped this off for us."

"What is it?" he asked as he grabbed the envelope from my fingers.

"A card from Thomas."

I could feel his chest tighten before he tore the envelope open. His eyes scanned the card, his eyebrows drawing together as he read the message from Thomas.

"What does it say?" I asked, dying to know what Thomas wrote.

City sighed, pinching the bridge of his nose before handing the card to me. "Read it for yourself, sugar."

"Are you sure?" I asked as I opened the card. He nodded and closed his eyes. Inside was a brief message from Thomas.

Joe,

Sorry I couldn't be there for your wedding. I'm in deep…too deep to get away, even for your wedding.

I'm safe, my cover still intact. Shit's worse than we thought and I'm trying to bring them down as soon as possible. I couldn't take the chance of blowing my cover and risking the lives of our family. This is the path I've chosen, and I refuse to risk anyone's life but my own.

Please know I love you and can't wait to meet Suzy. Give my love to everyone.

Love Always,
Thomas

I closed the card and handed it back to City.

He shoved it in the inside pocket of his suit. "Who gave it to you?"

"The man over there." I pointed down the bar where James and Izzy stood with shots in their hands. "The one with your sister."

"Who is he and why is he having a drink with my sister?"

"He's Thomas' friend and I invited him to stay and enjoy himself. Izzy will take care of him."

He rubbed his face. "That's what I'm afraid of," he said, his chest expanding before he exhaled.

"Don't worry, City. They're like oil and water," I lied. "You don't have to worry about him. He knows all about your sister from Thomas."

"That may not be a good thing either. I'm going to go introduce myself," he said, trying to break free of my grip.

"Oh no you don't. Give them some time to talk."

"I want to talk to him about Thomas," he said, turning to face me with no smile on his face.

"Come on, kids," Mrs. Gallo interrupted. "It's time to be seated for dinner."

I smiled at him, happy that he couldn't barge into the conversation his sister was having with James. It looked heated and made me giddy inside.

"I would say you're both in cahoots if I didn't know any better," he said before kissing my lips.

"You're going to need some fuel for our wedding night." I laughed, burying my face in his chest.

"Sugar, I could live off you alone."

"Pffft," I said, pulling him toward the table at the front of the dance floor. "I wasn't born yesterday, City. You do need to eat."

He leaned down, his hot breath against my ear. "The only thing I need to eat is your pussy."

My core convulsed; the sated feeling I felt before evaporated and was replaced with lust and an ache between my legs. "Don't you start," I said as I took my seat.

"I've only just begun," he whispered in my ear as he pushed in my chair.

I smiled, looking at the crowd, wishing I could run out of here and back to the suite with him. It would be hours before we could escape this place. I figured I'd use the time to torture him as much as he tortured me.

Our guests started clinking their glasses as the rest of the wedding party was seated. I leaned over, placing my lips on his and inhaling the scent that was distinctly him—musky and male and pure sex. I ran my hand up his leg, resting it against his cock and squeezing. His body twitched as he sucked in a breath. He broke the kiss, looking at me with a mischievous grin.

"Do it again and I'll take you in the bathroom and fuck you. I don't care who's in there."

I bit my lip, trying to hide my laughter. He wouldn't dare. I loved this man, caveman attitude and all.

I played nicely as we tried to eat our food, constantly interrupted by the clinking of the wine glasses. It was cute at first, but then it just became annoying. I was starving, and eating had become impossible. After ten minutes of trying to choke down the steak, we both gave up and headed into the crowd to greet the guests we missed earlier.

The rest of the evening was fantastic. It was amazing being surrounded by so much love. Everyone I cared for was there. Sophia and Kayden, minus the little bundle of boy. My friends from work, the boys from the Neon Cowboy, and everyone else that played a role in our life. My parents and sister were there too, but they mainly stayed with my side of the family and stuck to themselves. Pity, really. The two sides would probably never mingle, but then again, I could choose whom I spent my time with.

The most memorable part of the evening was our first dance as husband and wife. We picked "All of Me" by John Legend as our song. It was City's choice; I loved it and couldn't deny him his request. It was perfect. It was our story tied up in one song. It was written for us, or at least it felt like it had been.

City sang it in my ear as he held me against his body and we danced. Tears formed in my eyes. The man could be romantic, and I believed every word of the song. Hearing his deep voice in my ear professing his love through lyrics made me melt. I buried my face in his chest, wiping my tears against his jacket as the song came to a close.

He grabbed my face, looking into my eyes before he kissed me. The love I felt in this moment was almost overwhelming. Sometimes his touch made me feel weak in the knees, like a teenage girl that was lovesick.

I was blessed to spend an eternity with this man.

CHAPTER 12
CITY

WE SPENT two weeks in Italy, touring my homeland, and I showed her the vineyard my family owned. It had been her first time outside of the US and I wanted her to experience the beauty that Italy had to offer. Suzy fell in love with the people of Italy. The culture is so different than in America. Life was slower; people enjoyed the simple things and didn't move through their day at breakneck speed.

Although neither of us wanted to say goodbye to Italy and head back to reality, the moment we walked into our home, everything felt right. I carried her over the threshold, not wanting to break tradition and also being told by Suzy that it was a requirement. I laughed when she refused to walk into the house until I picked her up and carried her inside.

Waking up in our bed made me feel more rested than I had in over a month. Suzy slept peacefully at my side with the sheet covering half her body. Her breasts were exposed, her hair flowing around her head, as she softly snored.

I kissed her neck, feeling her pulse under my lips. She stirred, a small moan coming from her lips.

"Morning, sugar," I said against her skin.

"Morning, husband." She stretched, the sheet cascading down, exposing her entire body.

"I love the sound of that," I said as I partially covered her body with mine.

I slid my hand up her side, stopping on her breast, feeling the fullness in my hand. I rubbed my palm against her nipple, feeling her twitch. I grabbed it with my fingers, giving it a slight tug.

"Ouch," she said, her face contorting.

"Sensitive today. Is it time for your period?" Typically that was the only time she complained that my touch was too tough or abrasive.

"I haven't been keeping track. It must be," she said with a yawn as I cupped her tit in my palm.

"They feel fuller than usual," I said, squeezing them lightly.

"I probably gained ten pounds in Italy. The food was so amazing."

I looked down at her. I knew her body like I knew my own. I'd spent hours worshiping it. "Suzy, are you...?" I sucked in a breath. Suzy's body hadn't changed in the year since we met. No amount of pasta or Gallo family meals had added a curve to her hourglass perfection. Missing her period and her overly sensitive nipples had my mind spinning.

"Oh no," she said, sitting up quickly, grabbing her breasts. "I can't be."

"I'm greedy and want you all to myself, but when it happens I'll be the happiest man alive, sugar." I touched her stomach, resting my hand against her skin and smiling.

"I'm on the pill, but I missed a couple days with

traveling. I can't be," she said, blowing out a puff of air, resting her hand against mine. "I'm sorry I forgot my pill, baby."

"I fucked you so much there should be quadruplets in there." I laughed, moving to rest my head against her abdomen. She snaked her fingers in my hair, massaging my scalp. "There's no greater honor than for a woman to carry a man's child. Don't ever say you're sorry. When it happens it happens, but let's try to not have it happen so soon." I kissed her stomach, making a ring around her belly button.

"Your mom would be so damn excited," she said, pulling my face up.

"You'll make her the happiest woman in the world someday, Suzy." I kissed her lips, enjoying the feel of her against me. "But would you be happy, sugar?" I asked, looking into her eyes.

"I'm not ready to give *us* up yet," she whispered. Suzy swallowed hard and rubbed her forehead. "City, what if I am?"

"If you are," I said, rubbing her cheek with my thumb, "I won't be pissed off. You'll be carrying a part of us and we'd still have nine months to ourselves before our world would be rocked."

"I'm not ready," she whispered, her eyes closing as she frowned.

"Sugar," I said, touching her chin and forced her to look into my eyes. "You can handle anything. You're stronger than you think, and I'll be here with you when it happens. Let's not worry about something that we can't control. We'll find out soon enough if you or aren't. You worry too much. I'm sure it's just the stress of the travel. Let me help you forget." I smiled as I watched her gnaw on her lip.

"You're right. I'm sure it's from the stress of the wedding and travel. How are you going to make me forget?" she asked, and wiggled her eyebrows.

I crushed my lips to her mouth, devouring her lips. She melted into my touch, her mind occupied by the feel of my rough hands gliding across her soft skin. I made love to Suzy in our bed for the first time as husband and wife. Life couldn't get any better.

CHAPTER 13
CITY

CHRISTMAS

SUZY and I decided that we'd wait until Christmas day to share the news with the Gallo family. My parents had everything they could ever want, and buying a gift for them was a bitch. The one thing we could give them that they couldn't get anywhere else was the news of their first grandchild.

"You ready for this?" I whispered to Suzy as we sat down on the couch.

"Who's going first this year?" Anthony asked, sitting next to Izzy on the floor.

"I'll go last," Izzy said, leaning back, looking uninterested.

"That's total bullshit, Izzy. You always want to be first," Michael said, sitting down next to Mia on the love seat.

She placed her hands on her chest as she spoke. "Being the baby earns me the right to always go first. I was left out of everything growing up. Christmas day was mine, all mine."

"Please, you were so far up our asses, you were never

left out of anything," Michael said, laughing and wrapping his arm around Mia.

Suzy leaned over, whispering in my ear. "I'm kind of nervous. Everything is about to change." Suzy turned her attention back toward the family.

I nodded, leaning over so only she could hear. The shit was about to hit the fan, but for once, it would be a great thing. "Just be ready to have your eardrums shattered." I laughed. God, the Gallos could be loud, but I imagined my mother's happy screams would be near window-cracking volume.

"Why don't we start oldest to youngest," Anthony said.

"That's not necessary; your father and I don't need presents," Ma said, sitting in her chair next to the Christmas tree.

My parents had outdone themselves this year. The Christmas tree almost touched the ceiling. They never went with an artificial tree. My pop had to cut down a tree each year. My parents spent days finding just the right one on their property before cutting and hauling it inside. Thank God they had boys, because it took all of us to help him carry it inside and set it up. Ma spent days decorating it, adding ornaments that dated back to our childhood. The woman kept every decoration we ever made, and they lined the tree.

"Ma, stop. You and Pop deserve presents. You've always spoiled us and now it's our turn to give back," Izzy said, turning toward Ma. "Not really happy about the oldest-to-youngest thing, but I can wait."

"You're a sweet dear," Ma said, leaning forward, stroking Izzy's cheek.

I rolled my eyes. The sugarplum fairy must've invaded my sister's body.

"Open my present first, Ma," Izzy said, reaching under

the tree and pulling out a small box wrapped in red glitter paper and a silver bow, which she handed to Ma.

Ma shook it, putting it next to her ear. "Hmm, I wonder what it is."

"Just open it," Izzy said, bouncing on her knees.

"Patience, Isabella. It's a virtue," Ma said, pulling the ribbon and removing the bow.

"Virtues and me don't get along," Izzy said, her laughter growing loud.

"You're a Gallo, none of us do," Pop said as he smiled at Izzy and chuckled.

Ma opened the box, a giant smile spreading across her face. "Oh, Isabella, it's beautiful." She pulled a bracelet lined with rubies and diamonds from the box.

"It's our birthstones together, Ma," Izzy said, crawling closer to her. "Can I put it on you?"

"Yes, I'd love that." Ma handed the bracelet to Izzy. "It's beautiful. I love you, baby girl." Ma leaned forward, kissing Izzy on the head as she snapped the bracelet around Ma's wrist.

"Love you too, Mama." Izzy moved the bracelet so the stones sat on top and were visible, before crawling back to her spot next to Anthony.

"City, why don't you go next," Michael said, winking at me.

"Did you tell him?" Suzy mouthed at me with wide eyes.

I shook my head, because I hadn't said a word to anyone. "No, brother, you go ahead," I said, trying not to spoil their gifts by going before them.

"I can't follow up Izzy's gift. You always give strange things to Ma, so I'd rather go after you," Michael said as he slapped his knee.

Everyone laughed, and Mia elbowed him. I always

bought Ma something special and meaningful. The woman didn't care about price; she only wanted something that was heartfelt and meaningful.

"I hadn't planned on giving Ma our gift so soon, but we'll go now just to make you happy," I said with a smirk. He'd shit a brick in a moment…it served his ass right for his shitty comment.

"I want to give it to her," Suzy said, placing her hand on mine before pushing off the couch.

We'd spent hours talking about the best way to break the news. Suzy decided to have a shirt made that said "World's Greatest Nana," along with the first ultrasound photo tucked underneath. Damn kid looked like a jellybean, but I knew it was enough to make my ma squeal.

"Izzy, can you give me the big box with the snowman paper, please," Suzy said as she approached the tree.

Izzy grabbed the box, shaking it as she handed it to Suzy. "Is it an ugly Christmas sweater? You know a girl can never have too many of those." Izzy smiled as Suzy ripped it from her hands.

"Shush it, you. I'm still mad at you," Suzy said, sticking out her tongue at Izzy. She turned toward my parents, sitting in their favorite chairs next to the tree, side by side. "We had something made for you this year, Mom." Suzy handed her the box and came back to sit at my side.

"That's so sweet of you, dear," Ma said, tearing the paper slowly.

"It's for both of you," I said, grabbing Suzy's hand, giving it a squeeze.

"Thanks, son," Pop said, watching Ma open the box.

As she pulled the shirt from the box, Izzy said, "I knew it. Ugly Christmas clothes. Nice, brother."

"Izzy," I warned.

My ma's eyes grew wide, her lip trembling as my pop

grabbed her arm. Her mouth dropped open as she read the shirt. "Really?" she whispered.

Pop reached in the box, pulling out the ultrasound photo and bringing it close to his eyes.

"What the hell is it?" Michael asked.

Ma turned the shirt around, a giant smile on her face. "Promise me you two aren't joking?" she asked, holding the shirt in the air.

"We would never joke about that, Ma," Suzy said, squeezing my hand and leaning into my side.

The shrill scream from my ma had me covering my ears. She hopped from her seat, coming at us quickly.

"Fuck," Michael said, clearly understanding the error of his previous statement.

My ma was so lost in her baby haze that she didn't even flinch at his statement. She stopped in front of us, tears just starting to stream down her cheeks. "When?" she asked, clutching the shirt in her hand.

Suzy laughed, hopping to her feet. "August," she said, wrapping her arms around my ma.

"Oh my God, August is so far away, but there's so much to do," Ma said, grabbing Suzy and squeezing her tightly.

I stood, walking toward my pop, holding out my hand. "Congrats, Grandpa," I said, waiting for his response.

He placed his hand in mine, pulling me toward him, embracing me. "I'm proud of you, son. Damn proud. There will finally be someone to carry on the family name…about damn time." He laughed, patting me on the back.

"Only if it's a boy, Pop," I said, sighing and feeling completely content.

"Look around; boys are genetic. Girls are an anomaly in this family."

Ma grabbed me, pulling me from his arms. "And you, how could you keep this from me?"

"We wanted to be sure, Ma. Don't be mad," I said, kissing her cheek.

"I'm not mad. I don't know if I've ever been as happy as I am right now," she said, resting her head on my chest. "A baby, finally a baby," she whispered, her tears soaking through my shirt.

Over my shoulder, I could see everyone surrounding Suzy. She beamed, a giant smile on her face and her cheeks slightly pink. She didn't like attention, but she'd better get used to it. She'd be the center of attention until the baby arrived.

Anthony touched her stomach. "Wow, it's going to be like the movie *Alien*. That's some scary shit, Suzy." He smiled, patting it before moving like the creature that busted out of John Hurt.

Mike batted his hands away from Suzy. "Stop it, you dumbass. You're scaring her. Congrats, doll. I'm so excited to finally be an uncle." He smiled at her, wrapping her into his arms, but holding her like she was breakable.

"Maybe someday Mia can be an aunt?" she asked as she pulled away to see his face.

Mike laughed, nervously looking at Mia. "We'll see. I'm still trying to figure out if she's 'the one,'" he said, and laughed.

Mia smacked his ass, causing a loud crack to fill the air. "You could only be so lucky," Mia said. "Come here, Suzy, give me a hug, Mama. Are you ready for this?"

I watched my family as they showered her with love. We weren't the main attraction anymore; the world would now revolve around the baby.

Suzy huffed out a breath. "Ready as I'll ever be." She shrugged before hugging Mia.

"Congrats, Suzy," Izzy said, pulling Mia off Suzy. "Remember, that baby better have a vagina." Izzy poked her in the stomach and bent down next to her belly. "Hey, little girl, Auntie Izzy will teach you everything you need to know about life," Izzy said, rubbing her hand over Suzy's stomach.

The color drained from Suzy's face, as her eyes grew wide. "Izzy, we don't know the sex yet, but boy or girl, they'll be lucky to have you as an aunt." Suzy looked at me with her eyes bulging like she was scared to death of Izzy getting her hands on our baby. There were worse things than having Izzy teaching a girl how to be strong. Izzy could be a pain in the ass, but she was a tough cookie. The man that could tame her would have to be a beast, if it was possible at all.

Thank you for reading Hook Me & Throttled. The family saga continues in **RESIST ME!**

Izzy Gallo has never been described as a member of the weaker sex. She's a woman who doesn't take shit from anyone. Growing up with four older overprotective brothers has hardened her, making her a force to be reckoned with.

Against the wishes of her two brothers, Joe and Mike, Izzy takes a weekend trip to Bike Week in Daytona, turning her world upside down.

Over her head, in a world she doesn't understand, there's only one man who can save her.

James Caldo has dedicated his life to protect and serve as a member of the DEA. He's cocky, overbearing, and doesn't take no for an answer – the Gallo men have nothing on him.

When their paths cross, James makes Izzy question everything she believes about completely surrendering to the opposite sex.

Does James have what it takes to overpower the headstrong Izzy, capturing her heart forever?

Turn the page to read a SNEAK PEEK of Resist Me or tap here to download your copy and read now.

Get ready for the fierce and feminine side of the Gallo family with another smokin' hot romance in RESIST ME.

My heart stammered in my chest as the sound of police sirens filled the air. I opened my eyes, the red and blue lighting bouncing off of Tommy's jacket. I gave him a squeeze as he slowed the bike and waved off the rest of the guys.

We pulled off to the side of the road as the police cruiser stopped behind us. The lights continued to flash, but the screeching siren noise turned off before I heard a car door slam.

"Sir," the familiar voice said as he approached us.

The sound of his voice alone had my pussy clenching. Fucking cunt had always been a problem. I didn't like James. It needed to cool its fucking jets and not think about his cock. James wasn't the man I wanted…I couldn't top him.

Thomas sat still, peering in his side mirror until James came to a stop at our side. The others were far enough away, leaving us behind to deal with the cop issue.

"Get her the fuck out of here. Blow is in her left jacket pocket."

"Hey, Iz," James slithered out as he slowly looked me up and down.

I lifted my chin, staring him in the eye without a smile. "Jimmy," I replied, the corner of my lip twitching.

God, he looked fucking good. No, good wasn't the right word. He looked fucking amazing dressed in the law enforcement uniform. The brown dress shirt hugged his muscles, looking like a second skin against his tan flesh. The shitty polyester pants the force handed out clung to his muscular thighs, showing off every dip and crevice in his body. The gun sitting around his waist reminded me that he wasn't a man to be crossed, though I liked to push his buttons. He could easily overpower me, and for some reason, the thought turned me on.

His jaw ticked as I spoke his name. He hated when I called him Jimmy, said it reminded him of a child. I'd used it to only piss him off, crawl under his skin like he had mine.

Tommy handed over his license and registration, shoving it in James's hand as he openly gawked at me.

James turned his attention to Thomas and cleared his throat. "What the hell are you going to tell them?" he asked, motioning toward the red taillights off in the distance.

"I'll figure some shit out. She's just another pussy to them. She's not a club whore or an old lady. She's inconsequential."

"Men are such fucking pigs," I bit out. "How can you even be around those douchebags? You don't think that way, do you?" I asked, looking at Tommy.

"Fuck no. I'm just playing the part. Ma did not raise me to think that way."

James laughed, drawing my attention in his direction. Why did he have to be so damn handsome? I mean, Jesus. Why couldn't he be plain and not fantasy inspiring?

"And you?" I asked him, wishing I could wipe that shitty smile off his face.

"Oh no, doll. I love women. Not all of them are just a piece of ass. Not even the ones who slink out of my hotel room before the sun rises." He grinned.

My eyes grew wide as a lump formed in my throat. He wouldn't dare tell my brother. Would he? I mean, the man had cockiness down pat, but he wouldn't be dumb enough to clue my brother the fuck in on our sex Olympics.

Tommy shook his head and turned to look at me. "Can I trust you to listen to him?" he asked, squinting as he peered at me.

"I'll listen," I said, as James began to chuckle. I moved my eyes from Thomas to glare at James. "I can't promise I'll do as he asks, but I'll listen and do what I feel is right."

"Izzy, for fuck's sake. Just fucking listen for once in your life. I know you bow down to no man, but this is your life we're talking about. I have enough shit to worry about and don't need to worry about you getting home safely," Tommy snarled, keeping his eyes focused on me.

"I'll be good to her," James promised as he stopped laughing and cleared his throat. "I won't let her out of my sight and I'll keep her safe. You couldn't put her into more capable hands." James smiled, giving me a quick wink.

I turned to Tommy, unable to take the smug smile on James's face any longer, and spoke the words he wanted to hear: "Yes, I promise to do whatever is necessary to get home safely."

"Off the bike, ma'am. I need to search you. You too, Blue," James barked out, stepping away from the bike.

We climbed off, me with the assistance of my brother, and turned our backs to James. He frisked Tommy first. I straightened my back and watched him as he touched my brother, moving quickly and thoroughly and finding nothing. It was all for show. I knew I wouldn't be so lucky.

As he turned his attention to me, I closed my eyes and waited.

I knew he wouldn't be so quick when touching my body. He wouldn't make it obvious to my brother or the eye of an outsider, but I remembered what his hands had felt like on my body. The amount of pleasure the strong hands had given me. The feel of them on me and in me was like nothing else I had ever experienced.

"Back on the bike, sir," he ordered. "Ma'am, hands behind your head and do it now!" he roared, as I was lost in my memories.

As Tommy took his place on the bike, keeping a lookout for any stragglers from the club, I sighed and tangled my fingers together behind my head. Thankfully my back was to him. In this position, my breasts were pushed out farther, leaving myself exposed. He started at my wrists, brushing against my skin with the tip of his rough fingers. Tiny sparks shot down my arms, a direct line to my nipples. I opened my eyes, sucking in a breath before closing them again.

I didn't have to see his face to know that he had a grin dancing across his lips. His giant hands swept down my arms and stopped just above my ribcage. The tips of his fingers grazed my breasts as his hands slipped down the front of my torso before he searched my waistband.

No matter how hard I tried to control a reaction or think of anything other than his hands on me, my body responded. I twitched and silently swore. I rolled my eyes at the feeling of being defeated. He knew in that moment that he had an effect on me. I was fucking doomed.

I could feel his breath against my ear. My body shuddered as my heart skipped a beat, before it was gone and his hands slid down my legs.

Please don't…

Fucker.

His thumbs touched the holy land as his hands glided up my legs. As he reached the V of my legs, I swear to shit my heart stopped dead in my chest. I sucked in a breath, trying to calm my insides as my head dropped.

I was happy when his hands left my legs until he caressed my ass, all in the name of a search, but I knew he was enjoying it too much when he gave it a quick, hard squeeze.

"Must you?" I whispered as he moved closer, reaching into my pockets.

"Yes," he whispered back, his mouth coming close to my ear. "Think of all the *fun* we're going to have as I give you a *ride*."

"You're an asshole," I hissed, turning my face to look at his profile.

"That's one part of you I haven't *yet* explored," he whispered in my ear, low and close enough that Tommy couldn't hear.

I gulped, closing my eyes and using all of my self-control not to turn around and give him a piece of my mind. I couldn't react in front of my brother or the other eyes that could possibly be on us.

"What do we have here, ma'am?" James asked, pulling his hand from my pocket and dangling the small bag in front of my face.

"It's not mine, officer," I pleaded, shaking my head and playing the part.

"Place your hands behind your back. I'm placing you under arrest," he said, grabbing my arm, gingerly moving it away from my head and down to the small of my back.

"Must we do this?" I asked, looking toward Tommy.

Tommy winked, not giving any other physical indication that everything was okay.

"We must, doll. Give me your other hand."

I wrinkled my nose and ground my teeth as I felt the cold steel of the handcuffs slap against my wrist. Great. Not only was I being placed in his custody, I was starting off bound and in his possession without a means of escape. Being with the men of the MC had felt less scary than what I felt about being a captive for James.

"I'll leave them loose so they won't pinch, but you can't get out. Not yet at least," he said as a low, slow laugh tickled my ear.

I glared at Tommy, not looking at James as he marched me toward the back of the police cruiser. He placed his hand on my head as he helped me into the back seat.

"Stay put," he ordered as I moved my legs inside.

"Where the fuck am I going, genius?" I blurted out, the anger dripping from my voice. My hands were restrained behind my back and I was about to be locked in the police car.

"You better watch that smart mouth of yours, doll." He grinned, leaning against the frame of the car.

"Or what? Are you going to rough me up, Jimmy?" I snuggled back into the seat, adjusting my body and trying to find a comfortable position.

"I'd hate to add resisting arrest to your charges." His grin turned into a smirk as he wiggled his eyebrows and licked his lips.

"Just get this shit over with so we can get the fuck out of here," I hissed, not finding him charming at all.

"As you wish." He slammed the car door, leaving me with my thoughts as he approached Tommy and spoke with him.

I watched through the windshield as they exchanged

some heated words—or at least they made it seem like they were. A dull ache settled in my chest as I watched them speak. This would be the last time I'd see my brother for some time. The not knowing was the worst part. Tommy looked over at me a couple of times as they finished their conversation. My nose began to tickle as tears threatened to fall.

When James slid into the front seat, he didn't speak. He turned on the car and started to pull away after Thomas had sped down the road.

"When are you going to let me out of these fucking cuffs?" I asked. My wrists already felt the bite from the metal digging into my skin.

"Tomorrow," he answered calmly, looking at me in the rearview mirror. His eyes changed from the smile I couldn't see but knew was there.

"You can't keep me like this until tomorrow." Anger built inside me. My body was almost vibrating as I stared at him in the mirror.

I knew I was now a pawn in his game. I'd have to play by his rules. I was pissed at Thomas for leaving me with James, and at asshole Flash for being an idiot and not realizing the amount of shit he was bringing me around this weekend.

James looked at the road, the corner of his eye crinkling as he spoke. "Harder for you to run away like that. Plus, you look fucking sexy when you're pissed off, Izzy."

"Jimmy, look, I didn't mean—"

"James." His eyes momentarily flashed in the rearview mirror before leaving me again.

"James," I hissed, holding the end, letting the letter stick between my teeth. "I'm sorry about what happened." I looked down at my knees, chewing the inside of my lip.

"I'm not," he said flatly.

"It wasn't nice of me to leave without saying goodbye. I was a jerk. Can you forgive me?" I wasn't really sorry for anything, but I wanted the damn cuffs off my wrists.

One-click RESIST ME and read now!

ABOUT THE AUTHOR

Chelle's a full-time writer, time-waster extraordinaire, social media addict, coffee fiend, and ex-history teacher.

To learn more about Chelle's books, please visit menofinked.com.

Join my newsletter by visiting
menofinked.com/news

Join my **Private Facebook Reader Group** at
facebook.com/groups/blisshangout

Want to drop me a line?
menofinked.com/contact

Where to Follow Me:

facebook.com/authorchellebliss1
bookbub.com/authors/chelle-bliss
instagram.com/authorchellebliss
twitter.com/ChelleBliss1
goodreads.com/chellebliss
amazon.com/author/chellebliss
pinterest.com/chellebliss10

MEN OF INKED SERIES

"One of the sexiest series of all-time" -Bookbub Reviewers Download book 1 for FREE!

- Book 1 - Throttle Me (Joe aka City)
- Book 2 - Hook Me (Mike)
- Book 3 - Resist Me (Izzy)
- Book 4 - Uncover Me (Thomas)
- Book 5 - Without Me (Anthony)
- Book 6 - Honor Me (City)
- Book 7 - Worship Me (Izzy)

MEN OF INKED: SOUTHSIDE SERIES

Join the Chicago Gallo Family with their strong alphas, sassy women, and tons of fun.

- Book 1 - Maneuver (Lucio)
- Book 2 - Flow (Daphne)
- Book 3 - Hook (Angelo)
- Book 4 - Hustle (Vinnie)
- Book 5 - Love (Angelo)

MEN OF INKED: HEATWAVE SERIES

Same Family. New Generation.

- Book 1 - Flame (Gigi)

- Book 2 - Burn (Gigi)
- Book 3 - Wildfire (Tamara)
- Book 4 - Blaze (Lily)
- Book 5 - Ignite (Tamara)
- Book 6 - Spark (Nick)
- Book 7 - Ember (Rocco)
- Book 8 - Singe - (Carmello)
- Book 9 - Ashes - (Rosie)
- Book 10 - Scorch - (Luna)
- Book 11 - Torch (Trace)

ALFA INVESTIGATIONS SERIES

Wickedly hot alphas with tons of heart pounding suspense!

- Book 1 - Sinful Intent (Morgan)
- Book 2 - Unlawful Desire (Frisco)
- Book 3 - Wicked Impulse (Bear)
- Book 4 - Guilty Sin (Ret)

SINGLE READS

- Mend
- Enshrine
- Misadventures of a City Girl
- Misadventures with a Speed Demon
- Rebound (Flash aka Sam)
- Top Bottom Switch (Ret)
- Santa Baby
- Fearless

NAILED DOWN SERIES

- Nailed Down
- Tied Down

- Kneel Down
- Stripped Down

TAKEOVER DUET

What happens when you sleep with your biggest enemy?

- Book 1 - Acquisition
- Book 2 - Merger

FILTHY SERIES

- Dirty Work
- Dirty Secret
- Dirty Defiance

LOVE AT LAST SERIES

- Book 1 - Untangle Me
- Book 2 - Kayden

View Chelle's entire collection of books at menofinked.com/books

To learn more about Chelle's books visit *menofinked.com* or *chellebliss.com*

MORE BOOKS BY CHELLE BLISS

View Chelle's entire collection of books at **menofinked.com/books**

Original Men of Inked Series

Join the Gallo siblings as their lives are turned upside down by irresistible chemistry and unexpected love. A sizzling USA Today bestselling series!

Throttle Me - Book 1 (Free Download)

Ambitious Suzy has her life planned out, but everything changes when she meets tattooed bad boy **Joseph Gallo**. Could their one-night stand ever turn into the real thing?

Hook Me - Book 2

Michael Gallo has been working toward his dream of winning a MMA championship, but when he meets a sexy doctor who loathes violence, his plans may get derailed.

Resist Me - Book 3

After growing up with four older brothers, **Izzy Gallo** refuses to be ordered around by anyone. So when hot, bossy James Caldo saves her from trouble, will she be able to give up control?

Uncover Me - Book 4

Roxanne has been part of the dangerous Sun Devils motorcycle club all of her life, while **Thomas Gallo** has been deep undercover for so long, he's forgotten who he truly is. Can they find redemption and save each other?

Without Me - Book 5

Anthony Gallo never thought he'd fall in love, but when he meets the only woman who doesn't fall to her knees in front of him, he's instantly smitten.

Honor Me - Book 6

Joe and Suzy Gallo have everything they ever wanted and are living the American dream. Just when life has evened out, a familiar enemy comes back to haunt them.

Worship Me - Book 7

James Caldo needs to control everything in his life, even his wife. But **Izzy Gallo**'s stubborn and is constantly testing her husband's limits as much as he pushes hers.

MEN OF INKED: HEATWAVE SERIES

The Gallo's Next Generation

Flame - Book 1

Gigi Gallo's childhood was filled with the roar of a motorcycle and the hum of a tattoo gun. Fresh out of college, she never expected to run into someone tall, dark, and totally sexy from her not-so-innocent past.

Burn - Book 2

Gigi Gallo thought she'd never fall in love, but then he rode into her world covered in ink and wrapped in chaos. Pike Moore never expected his past to follow him into his future, but nothing stays hidden for long.

Wildfire - Book 3

Tamara Gallo knew she was missing something in life. Looking for adventure, she takes off, searching for a hot biker who can deliver more than a good time. But once inside the Disciples, she may get more than she bargained for.

Blaze - Book 4

Lily Gallo has never been a wild child, but when she reconnects with an old friend, someone she's always had a crush on, she's about to change.

More Men of Inked Heatwave books to come. Visit menofinked.com/heatwave to learn more.

Men of Inked: Southside Series

The Chicago side of the Gallo Family

Maneuver - Book 1

Poor single mother Delilah is suspicious when sexy **Lucio Gallo** offers her and her baby a place to live. But soon the muscular bar owner is working his way into her heart — and into her bed...

Flow - Book 2

The moment **Daphne Gallo** looked into his eyes, she knew she was in trouble. Their fathers were enemies--Chicago crime bosses from rival families. But that didn't stop Leo Conti from pursuing her.

Hook - Book 3

Nothing prepared **Angelo Gallo** for losing his wife. He promised her that he'd love again. Find someone to mend his broken heart. And that seemed impossible, until the day that he walked into Tilly Carter's cupcake shop.

Hustle - Book 4

Vinnie Gallo's the hottest rookie in professional football. He's a smooth-talker, good with his hands, and knows how to score. Nothing will stop Vinnie from getting the girl—not a crazy stalker or the fear he's falling in love.

Love - Book 5

Finding love once is hard, but twice is almost impossible. **Angelo Gallo** had almost given up, but then Tilly Carter walked into his life and the sweet talkin' Southern girl stole his heart forever.

ALFA Investigations Series

A sexy, suspenseful Men of Inked Spin-off series…

Sinful Intent - Book 1

Out of the army and back to civilian life, **Morgan DeLuca** takes a job with a private investigation firm. When he meets his first client, one night of passion blurs the line between business and pleasure...

Unlawful Desire - Book 2

Frisco Jones was never lucky in love and had finally given up, diving into his new job at ALFA Investigations. But when a dirty-mouthed temptress crossed his path, he questioned everything.

Wicked Impulse - Book 3

Bear North, ALFA's resident bad boy, had always lived by the friend's code of honor—Never sleep with a buddy's sister, and family was totally off-limits. But that was before **Fran DeLuca**, his best friend's mom, seduced him.

Guilty Sin - Book 5

When a mission puts a woman under **Ret North**'s protection, he and his longtime girlfriend Alese welcome her into their home. What starts out as a friendship rooted in trust ignites into a romance far bigger than any of them expect.

Single Novels

Enshrine

When Callie's life crumbles around her, can she trust her attraction to ruthless Bruno?

Mend

Before senior year, I was forced to move away, leaving behind the only man I ever loved. He promised he'd love me forever. He vowed nothing would tear us apart. He swore he'd wait for me, but Jack lied.

Rebound

After having his heart broken, **Flash** heads to New Orleans to lose himself, but ends up finding so much more!

Acquisition - Takeover 1

Rival CEO Antonio Forte is arrogant, controlling, and sexy as hell. He'll stop at nothing to get control of Lauren's company. The only problem? He's also the one-night stand she can't forget. And Antonio not only wants her company, he wants her as part of the acquisition.

Merger - Takeover 2

Antonio Forte has always put business before pleasure, but ever since he met the gorgeous CEO of Interstellar Corp, he finds himself wanting both. And he's hoping she won't be able to refuse his latest offer.

Top Bottom Switch

Ret North knows exactly who he is—a Dominant male with an insatiable sexual appetite. He's always been a top, searching for his bottom…until a notorious switch catches his eye.

Love at Last Series

Untangle Me - Book 1

Kayden is a bad boy that never played by the rules. **Sophia** has always been the quintessential good girl, living a life filled with disappointment. Everything changes when their lives become intertwined through a chance encounter online.

Kayden the Past - Book 2

Kayden Michaels has a past filled with sex, addiction, and heartache. Needing to get his addictions in check and gain control of his life for the sake of his family, Kayden is forced to confront his past and make amends for the path he's walked.

Do you LOVE audiobooks?

To check out my entire audio library, please visit menofinked.com/audio for more information.

Want the latest audiobook news and special giveaways! Join here: menofinked.com/audionews

HOOK ME ACKNOWLEDGEMENTS

I would like to thank my readers, fans, and supporters. You've made the last nine months the most amazing experience of my life. I'm blessed to have such amazing friends. You've cheered me on when I was too tired to write, and your amazing reviews drove me forward, trying to bring you *Hook Me* as quickly as possible.

Thank you to Melissa Gill for helping me design an amazing cover once again. It's hard to top the *Throttle Me* cover, but I love the *Hook Me* cover almost as much. I can't wait to work on the rest of the Gallo family. I know I drive you crazy with my need for perfection, and I love that you're willing to be patient with me.

To Tee Tate, a.k.a. Eden Butler, thank you for reading *Hook Me* over and over again making it ready for the world. Your comments helped keep me calm during the two short months between releases. You're an amazing editor and an even better writer. I want to write like you when I grow up, babe.

Brenda Wright, you rock! Even after surgery you were willing to drop everything and format *Hook Me* for release. You've been a constant in my life since my very first release. I love you, B.

Kaylee Lovering, thank you for keeping all my shit straight the last couple of months. I could never have finished *Hook Me* so quickly without your help. You're always willing to do whatever to help keep me writing. I'm happy to have you as part of my team.

Renita McKinney, I can't thank you enough for reading *Hook Me*. You always believe in me and are ready with kind words to help inspire me. Thank you for proofreading *Hook Me* quickly even after your root canal. I love you, R.

To my beta group, you are large and you know who you are. You girls rocked my socks off. Your funny posts and comments in the beta group helped keep me laughing during the writing of this book. I couldn't have completed it without you.

To all the bloggers out there have supported me through the journey, I am thankful for each and every one of you. You've been amazing with the Men of Inked series and I hope you'll continue reading the rest of the series. Every time I see my books mentioned on your sites, I still sit there in shock. You're the best.

I'm sure I forgot a million people at this point, and I'm sorry. My mind is a muddled mess from trying to get this book out for everyone to read. I hope you enjoy Michael as much as Joey.

Printed in Great Britain
by Amazon